W

THE OLD ROSES GROW

Eureka Springs Second Chance Romance Complete Series

GRACIE GABLE

PINK ROSEBUD PRESS

Published by Pink Rosebud Press

Published by Pink Rosebud Press.

Cover design: Sarah Hansen
Cover art: Jesus Leguizamo
Interior formatting: David Provolo

www.graciegable.com

ISBN: 978-1-955028-09-7 (paperback)
ISBN: 978-1-955028-20-2 (hardback)
ISBN: 978-1-955028-12-7 (ebook box set)

Names: Gable, Gracie, author.
Title: Where the old roses grow: Eureka Springs second chance romance complete series / Gracie Gable.
Description: Santa Cruz, CA: Pink Rosebud Press, 2024.
Identifiers: LCCN: 2024903387 | ISBN: 978-1-955028-20-2 (hardcover) | 978-1-955028-09-7 (paperback) | 978-1-955028-12-7 (ebook)
Subjects: LCSH Eureka Springs (Ark.) | Ozark Mountains--Fiction. | Love stories. | Romance fiction. | BISAC FICTION / Romance / Contemporary | FICTION / Romance / Firefighters | FICTION / Romance / Later in Life | FICTION / Small Town & Rural | FICTION / Southern | FICTION / Romance / Clean & Wholesome
Classification: LCC PS2607 .A35 W44 2024 | DDC 813.6--dc23

PART 1

CHAPTER ONE

ROSE

I never thought I'd miss freeways or the din of LA. What was I thinking? Mom tells me you can find love in unexpected places, and that it's just as easy to find a good man in a small town in Arkansas as it is in LA. I don't know, I've been looking around and I'm not seeing much—but Mom says if you wish for the life of your dreams, it's not enough to just want your dreams. You must live your dreams.

A shriek.

The high-pitched voice startles me, interrupting my thoughts, and my yogurt pours all over my pink sweater. I manage to miss the graded homework on my desk.

I search the classroom to figure out the cause of the commotion, because you can never really know with first graders. Nelisa's meltdown intensifies.

"You can't marry me! You're married to Susie. That's pigamy," Nelisa fusses with Tom.

"Bigamy," I correct her as I walk to her, my game face on and trying very hard not to laugh.

"Nelisa," I start gingerly. The snaggle-toothed little girl stands there gripping a broken crayon in her pudgy hand. I pull her closer to me.

"Tell me what happened."

"It's Tom!" Nelisa points accusingly at a freckle-faced boy who looks sheepish and stares at me with unblinking eyes. I call them both to my table.

"No more fussing," I insist, wagging my finger.

I make them apologize, face the class, and promise to be on their best behavior the rest of the day. Of course, I don't believe that for a minute. I estimate it won't even be ten minutes before Nelisa and Tom argue again, but their apology will maintain the peace for a little while. It occurs to me that relationships are hard, no matter how old you are.

I return to my desk and grade homework while the children go about finishing their classwork. As I grade, I notice an anomaly—Lily Adams. A sweet, thin-limbed girl with big brown eyes like Bambi. Her shoulder-length chestnut hair is done up in mismatched pigtails. I often fix them for her in class. Lily didn't do her homework... again.

I sigh. The weekend awaits. I want to curl up on my couch and watch *Friends* reruns with cheap grocery store wine. I don't even wish for much, but I can't get one calm night with this job. I facepalm. The kids look at me and I coo them back to their work.

After school, when everybody's parents pick them up, Lily Adams stays with the principal, Jolene McCarthy. Jolene is a tall, wiry forty-year-old woman with long, straight, jet-black hair who looks like a schoolmarm. She's prim and brisk and all business. Some of the other teachers call Jolene mean and grumpy, but I sense a hidden tenderness underneath all that gruffness, and I like her.

I must relay my concerns to Jolene. I find her reading a book with a steamy romance cover, and I stifle a giggle. Lily Adams sits beside her quietly looking at a picture book, appearing so tiny and vulnerable. My irritation towards her parents returns.

Why wouldn't the parents care about their daughter's schoolwork? Jolene looks up and raises a brow. Oh, Jolene doesn't speak much. Her look tells me I need to state my business. Ok, fine.

"Jolene, there's a problem with Lily," I say. Jolene gives Lily a once-over.

"I don't see it." Jolene places her book on the table, cover side down.

"It's with her schoolwork. Lily never does her homework or anything, really."

"Oh, that's bad."

I nod. Jolene waits for me to say more. "I want to see her parents and tell them about this problem of hers."

"I support that. You should see her dad, then. He won't be here to pick her up until four o'clock." Jolene resumes reading her book, dismissing me.

I check my watch and make a plan. I know what I'm going to do. I walk home and take a bath, happy to pull off the yogurt-stained sweater. It was cute in the morning, but it doesn't look good now with yogurt stains. I throw the slightly damp sweater in the laundry basket, amazed at the humidity of Eureka Springs, Arkansas compared to the desert climate of Los Angeles. Mildew lurks everywhere. My shoulders slump thinking of everything I left behind in LA.

It's for the best, I think.

I'll wait till five o'clock, I tell myself. Before I settle down to watch a movie, I look up Lily Adams' address on my phone and notice it's only three streets away from my bungalow.

I fall asleep watching a movie and don't wake up until five-thirty p.m. Annoyed at myself for letting my nap last that long, I grab my purse and walk to Lily's home, arriving at her front door a few minutes later. I didn't know who I expected to see opening the door, but definitely not the man who opened it.

I wonder if he tends the rose bushes in the front yard. The exquisite, expertly pruned roses look like specimens belonging in an arboretum, full of fat buds. He doesn't seem exactly the type to fuss over rose bushes. After all, his daughter brings unkempt hair and undone homework to school every day, and no one ever mentions the mother.

He stands there—absurdly tall, around six foot four, with his sexy three-day-old stubble, a chiseled jawline, and oddly expressive dark, deep-set almond eyes, like black cherries floating in milk. He's lean and muscular, with a velvety, olive complexion that sets off his luxurious raven hair. I feel the urge to run my hands through his mane. He looks like he's in his early forties, a few years older than me. When he speaks, his voice sounds gruff.

I didn't expect this. *Who is this gorgeous man?*

His eyes narrow. "And who are you?"

I clear my throat.

"My name is Rose Aberdeen," I blurt out as my voice cracks mid-sentence, sounding vulnerable. It surprises me. I don't want to come across as weak.

He stares at me blankly, waiting for me to expand on that one sentence. I'm not sure why he doesn't introduce himself.

"I am Lily's teacher. Please, let me in. I really need to speak with you." My resolve returns.

And then his eyes widen and gloss over. He pauses. My eyes hold steady as I focus on him, waiting for his response. I can almost hear his thoughts spilling forth beyond his silence.

"Sorry—I lost my train of thought. . . Your name, Rose—that's such a lovely name."

He falls silent. A soft look passes over his face. It looks bittersweet.

I stand there, stunned by the tenderness of his face. I sense something deeper going on, something having to do with my name, but I don't know what it could be.

Then his face returns to an impassive look as if nothing happened in the last few minutes.

I expect his expression to soften again, but it doesn't. He

just opens the door a little bit further. I assume this means I can come in.

When I enter the house, I see Lily eating popcorn and watching TV. Another bowl of untouched popcorn catches my eye, and I know it must belong to this man—Lily's dad. Lily looks like his double. Engrossed in the show, she doesn't notice my presence until her father announces it.

"Miss Aberdeen." Lily's face lights up.

"Hello, Lily." I smile. I always smile at my students whenever possible because I feel like they're one of my own, though I'm childless.

"I'll be speaking to your teacher in the dining room, Lily." Mr. Adams' tone is serious. "Stay here."

"Yes, Daddy." Lily turns back to the TV and her popcorn as he walks me to the dining room.

"Why exactly are you here?" he asks.

"Mr. Adams, I'm here because of Lily."

"Okay." His voice sounds bland as he draws out the word, not quite following yet.

"I'm here because Lily doesn't do her homework, ever. It's bad for her..."

Lily's dad glowers at me. "You're here to tell me how to raise my daughter?"

Oh my goodness. Why is this man making it so hard for me? I notice a slight flush on his cheeks as his irritation surfaces. I can't deny how sexy that makes him look.

"No, Mr. Adams, I'm just telling you that I think your daughter needs a bit more attention."

He gestures back to the couch, where I suspect the two spend a lot of time together.

"You think I'm not giving her enough attention?"

I square my shoulders. "I don't think. I *know*."

"You *know,* because you spend hours of undivided attention with her five days a week?"

I bristle. *How dare he refer to my large class size.*

"Because my daughter didn't do a little homework doesn't mean I'm not a good father."

I rub my temples. Not even ten minutes in this man's presence and I already feel a headache coming on.

"None. Lily has done *none* of her homework."

"She's a first grader. What value does homework have for someone her age? It's not SATs or ACTs. This isn't college prep."

"Mr. Adams..."

"Miss Aberdeen, you come here to tell me I suck at parenting. I wonder, does Jolene know you're here? Did she give you her approval for this?"

My anger flares. This strange man is threatening me. I flip my strawberry blonde hair over my shoulder.

"I said nothing about you sucking at parenting, just that Lily isn't getting any attention at home regarding her schoolwork."

"Well, you are her teacher at school. Shouldn't you handle that?"

"I'm handling it by telling her father that his daughter needs attention for *homework.*"

"So, I'm right."

"There's no right or wrong." I raise my voice a bit, hoping to get my point across. "We have a common interest—your daughter. She's a brilliant child. She's a wonderful girl, but Lily needs a little help and attention, and I need you to give her that."

This time, Lily's dad doesn't glower. He just stares at the dining table for a long time and taps on the wooden surface with his fingertips.

"I'm usually so tired that I barely have time for homework." He scratches the back of his neck. I notice he doesn't mention

Lily's mother. I know not to ask.

"I get it, Mr. Adams, and I can help. Let me tutor her twice during the week for free. Lily can eventually learn how to do her own homework, and she'll improve as my student. It's a win-win."

Her father looks at me skeptically. "How is it a win for you? I'm not paying you."

"Nah, but I'm helping a student, and that's the joy of being a teacher. And Mr. Adams?"

"Huh?"

"You don't fix her hair properly. It's a shame because she's got beautiful hair. YouTube is a great help," I say.

He watches me, his mouth open.

I march into the living room and tell Lily goodbye. Her eyes stay glued to the TV.

"Thank you," Mr. Adams says as I approach the door to leave.

"Anytime," I say, feeling fulfilled.

When I get home, I crack open a bottle of cheap wine and watch reruns of *Friends* to celebrate. *How do those six characters get along so well? I guess anything's possible in Hollywood sitcoms.*

I once thought anything was possible in LA. How wrong I was.

CHAPTER TWO

JAHI

I wear headphones at work, but I don't listen to songs. My best friend and colleague, Matthew Youngblood, comes into the fire station and sits beside me. I call him Matt. He's in his late thirties, a few years younger than me, and he's the quintessential southern California surfer dude with a mop of blonde hair. He's an inch taller than me at six foot five, and he's ripped with a six-pack, the envy of the squadron.

Matt's blackened uniform smells of grease and dirt. He looks at me. "I know you're not listening to any darn thing."

I grin. People call me the fire station's grump, and I'm aware of my reputation. I usually only speak with Matt. I heard he once bragged to the other firefighters about it. I find Matt likable if you overlook his incessant talking.

"I'm definitely not," I admit.

Matt laughs loudly. "Well, will you not ask me what happened today?"

"Heard about a kitchen fire." I might be quiet at work, but that doesn't mean I don't hear gossip. I hear it well.

"Yes. A six-year-old turned on the stove," he informs me.

"That's too bad. Parents not home?" Unsupervised kids cause many of the fire accidents in town.

"A sixteen-year-old babysitter, not watching the kid. Playing video games. Talking to her boyfriend."

I shake my head. As a firefighter and paramedic, I know our fire station would go out of business without fires and medical emergencies to tend to, but I hate knowing people can get hurt before we arrive.

"Well, did you call the parents to inform them about what happened?"

"I did."

"Good." I look at Matt. "You should change out of your uniform so we can get lunch, or what do you think?"

"I like that idea. We think alike."

We walk into the cozy, six-tabled Nibbles Eatery. I order Eggs Benedict and Matt orders the Blue Crab quiche, having barely gotten in under the eleven o'clock wire, when breakfast stops being served. Matt shows me the drawing his daughter gave him yesterday—a drawing of his family of four figures in a dreamlike setting with a house, pond, orchard, horses, and a barn. The only drawing Lily ever gave me revealed a train set she wanted for her birthday. I worry about raising her up to be a tomboy.

"Spill," Matt says, giving me a look that says he doesn't want me to lie about the fact that something bothers me.

"It's Lily," I say.

"What's wrong with Lily? Did you do something? Is it because of how grumpy you are? There's only so much a little girl can take, you know. Father or not," Matt teases.

"I didn't *think* about problems. Now, I'm not so sure."

"What's wrong, Jahi?"

I run my hand through my hair in frustration. "Lily's teacher came to see me at home on Friday."

"Children at this age usually get into problems with other kids. It's no biggie, but then again, Lily is a sweet child. I imagine the other kid is at fault." Matt shrugs as if he's diagnosed the problem and fixed it all at once. It's lucky for him and his daughter to be able to lean on his wife when troubles arise.

I furrow my brow. "That's not the problem."

"What is it, then?" Matt takes a huge bite of his quiche and waits for me to talk.

"It's her homework. She's lagging. Her teacher is complaining that I don't help her enough… at all, really."

"Do you not help her with her schoolwork?" He looks genuinely surprised.

"No, and now I feel guilty about it. I don't even think about schoolwork. It doesn't cross my mind. Whenever I'm with her, all I remember is that she's my daughter and I want to spend time with her."

"That's normal."

"Mm-hm." I take a bite of my Eggs Benedict.

"Now that the teacher told you about the problem, it's easier. You've just gotta pay more attention to her schoolwork."

"I don't have to."

"Why? Jahi, look…" Matt leans forward, ready to give me a lecture. It makes me smile as I see what a decent and good friend he is.

"The teacher offered to teach her at home for free. Twice a week," I say.

"You must have made a good impression. The teacher wants to help. That's great!" Matt winks. "This teacher must have seen how helpless you are."

"Good impression? I fought with her." I almost laugh at myself. I can't believe my defensiveness towards Lily's teacher. She merely tried to help her student, and I put up major resistance.

"What the hell, Adams? What did the teacher do wrong?"

"I just thought the woman was implying I'm not good at parenting."

"Why in the world would you think that?"

I stare at my only friend. "I don't know."

"You're such a child sometimes. But heck, it all worked out

in the end. You've got a free teacher for Lily. Your daughter's school work will improve. You don't have to change a thing."

"Yeah, a win," I comment dryly.

Matt touches my shoulder. "I have a feeling I said the wrong thing."

"Kind of," I say.

"What's the problem?"

"I feel guilty," I admit.

"Of course you feel guilty. You fought with someone who tried to help you, but then again, who doesn't? Look, it's not that hard."

I shift in my seat. "Tell me."

"You said she'll be coming over to teach Lily twice a week. Get something for her. Chocolates? Wine? Flowers? I don't know. Just apologize. You'll feel a lot better."

"Is that how you feel better when you apologize to your wife?"

"Jane? I just apologize to her, so she won't kill me in my sleep."

I laugh. "That's not true. Jane is the sweetest woman I know."

"She's pretty good at hiding who she really is."

"You're badmouthing Jane. I'll tell her." I laugh.

Matt gives me a look. "If you want me alive, you better not."

"Fine," I say as if it's a burden.

We eat the rest of our food in silence.

"She mentioned something about Lily's hair, too. Something about it being messy. Asked me to watch YouTube."

"Jane commented on it, too, before."

"Not to my face." My eyes narrow. Does everyone notice that my daughter's hair isn't always properly done except me?

"I told her there's no need. You're a great father. Who cares if you can't make a braid? Besides, Jane fixes it for her whenever she comes over."

I shake my head. "Tell Jane thanks for me."

"I'll be sure to." When we finish, we walk back to the fire station. Four hours later, I gruffly say goodbye to Matt.

I go straight to Lily's school. Sometimes, she complains about being bored hanging out with Jolene, who is a bit too serious for my taste. Most times when I arrive, I see Lily poring over some new picture book about animals that I'm sure Jolene handed to her.

When I arrive at Jolene's office, I don't see Lily waiting for me. I assume she must be in the bathroom. Jolene plays light jazz on her phone as she reorganizes her desk drawers.

"Hi, Jolene. Where's Lily? Is she in the bathroom?"

Jolene looks at me, confused. "Why are you here? She's already home."

"Home?" I look at Jolene, aghast. Did she let my little daughter walk home alone?

"Why are you here in my business looking confused? Rose took her home, said you both agreed she'll be giving her homework help. Don't worry, Rose is there with her."

My shoulders relax. The panic over my daughter's safety is resolved. "The thing is, I forgot. I forgot about that. I got so used to coming here to pick her up."

Jolene gives me a blank look. "Sure."

I resist the urge to hit myself upside the head at my forgetfulness. I rush home. When I get there, I see Lily and Rose together on the couch. Rose's bulging canvas bag is resting on the floor, but I can't see what it contains. She reads out questions from a textbook and Lily answers with excitement.

I watch Lily happily responding to Rose. Lily might be a child, but I've noticed she doesn't respond well to strangers. She's a tad bit wary, something I'm certain she inherited from me. Rose isn't a stranger, though. She's her teacher, but I didn't expect my daughter to warm up to her so fast. Rose notices me.

"Mr. Adams." Rose's eyes lock onto mine. She comes across

as demure, but I imagine something smoldering behind her innocent facade.

I manage a smile. "Call me Jahi. I didn't know you would bring Lily home today."

"Yeah, me neither, but I freed up my schedule, and I thought, what better day? Besides, she always looks so bored at Jolene's, so I swooped in to rescue her." Rose flips her strawberry blonde hair nonchalantly. Blind as I am to social cues, it's something I've seen women do when they're attracted to a man.

My face flushes. "Thanks." I look at Lily. "Do you want a snack?" She nods. "Why don't you get one, baby doll?" Lily heads for the kitchen and I shift my focus to Rose. "Look, we should talk."

Rose looks at me quizzically. I recognize that look from our first meeting. She follows me to the dining room.

"Feels like *déjà vu*, huh?" she comments. "Same place, same time, but on a different Friday. Are we about to argue again?"

Her eyes twinkle with silent laughter. I smile a little.

"No, I'm just surprised you came today. I planned to buy you a bar of chocolate before your first tutoring session so I could apologize. I feel bad about the way I spoke to you on Friday."

She regards me for a moment. *Can she read my face and see how bad I feel about it? Will she use it against me?*

She looks at me with a quirked eyebrow. "A bar of chocolate? You must think my forgiveness is cheap."

"Nothing of the sort. I just thought..."

Her lips part in a smile. "That's a joke. Besides, I sort of understand your reaction to me on Friday. As a parent—not that I'm a parent—I would hate a teacher marching into my house and telling me how to raise my kids."

"My behavior excuses nothing. I'm sorry."

"I'm sorry, too. I guess I didn't give you much choice about the tutoring thing. I just get overzealous sometimes."

"I can tell." I laugh a little.

"So, are we good now?"

"As far as I know."

"Good, because we need to put aside our differences for Lily's sake." Rose stands to leave. She goes to the living room and kisses Lily atop her head.

"See you next time, huh?" Rose lets herself out and waves at us both.

"By the way, I love chocolate," she calls out before shutting the door behind her.

CHAPTER THREE

ROSE

It's Friday and while I want to rush to my house as fast as I can to watch *Judge Judy*, I remember I haven't taught Lily anything after school since Monday and I agreed to do it twice a week.

Suppressing a grumble as the school day ends and wanting to relax, I go instead to pick up Lily from Jolene's. Seeing me, her face lights up and she bubbles with laughter—the only silver lining of giving up my Friday night to do more teaching.

"Miss Aberdeen," she says before throwing her tiny arms around my waist.

Laughing, all the feeling of reluctance leaves me. She embodies perfection. Taking her hands in mine, we walk to her home. Glancing back before we round the block, Jolene stands there watching us, nodding her approval.

When we get to Lily's house, we work on her homework first. I explain to her it means she can play all weekend if we get this done. She works with earnestness. I work through some of the schoolwork too—grading papers, planning next week's lessons.

After two hours, I decide enough is enough. She looks hungry. Not wanting to poke around in Jahi's home, I suggest we go out to Red's Pizzeria, and she likes that idea.

After dinner, we come back and watch *Teenage Mutant Ninja Turtles*. She points out Blue as her favorite character. Wanting to appease her, I point out Blue as my favorite, too. We laugh about her dad preferring Red. After a while, I feel a heaviness pushing on my shoulder and realize Lily is asleep.

Her father should be back by now. I love doing things for Lily already, but a nanny, I am not. I prop her against a pillow and look for her bedroom. I feel guilty poking around their house, but what else can I do? Lily needs to sleep, so I carry her and lay her on her bed.

I can't leave her alone. So instead of going home to watch *Judge Judy*, I watch it at Lily's. Two hours later, Jahi arrives, his face and clothes blackened with soot.

"Mr. Adams." I rub my eyes, weary from the long evening.

"Jahi." He corrects me. I nod. It still doesn't sit right to call a parent by their first name.

"Hope you didn't go to Jolene's again."

"Yeah. I almost did, but then I remembered I haven't seen you since Monday. Where's Lily?"

"Asleep."

"Already? I need to wake her up. She must be famished." His mind seems flustered. I guess firefighting and dealing with medical emergencies will do that to a man.

I laugh at his look of panic. "There's no need. I fed her already."

He looks around. "What did you make?"

"Make? I took her to Red's Pizzeria. We enjoyed a lovely dinner. By the way, you're very late today." I almost bite my lip from saying that. Why am I talking to him like we're friends? We're not friends, I remind myself.

He walks into the kitchen and grabs a bottle of water.

"Got an emergency call."

I don't want to seem nosy. So, I stare at him until he notices, waiting for him to continue. When he says nothing, I bite the bullet. "What sort of emergency?"

He looks pained. "A man's shop burnt down. We went to save him. There were several people in the building."

"No way. I hope everybody is okay," I gasp.

"Yeah, I know. Me too. Sometimes, though, I go to the hospital and check on people we've saved."

I shake my head in pity. *What horrors must he have witnessed in his job?*

"Not everybody is fine. Some people have serious injuries and one person might end up disabled." He looks depleted.

"No, that's terrible." No wonder he looks like he's been through hell and back.

"It is."

"And you have to go through it every day."

"Not every day. At least I hope not." He laughs sardonically. "Sometimes, I don't go with them. Some of us need to stay back at the station."

"Okay."

He gets up and goes to the foyer, and I see a gift basket of chocolates near his work bag and jacket.

"Here." He sets it on the kitchen counter—a small wicker basket with a pink ribbon spilling over with all varieties of chocolates. I look at him.

"Well, I got this gift basket since I didn't know your preferences for chocolate."

"Thank you." Yes, I don't know him well, but I can see his stubborn streak of not letting me drop the idea of the chocolates. "Apology accepted."

He laughs happily. "You know, I worried it might be too much. Matt says gifts can scare women away."

"Doesn't scare me. I love chocolate. It'll be good for when I'm binge-watching TV."

"Something it looks like you're already doing right now." He says, motioning to the television.

I grin. "You caught me red-handed, but that's not a crime."

We sit together in silence for about five minutes, but I can't take it anymore, so I speak up. "Can you show me how to connect my phone to the TV screen?"

"Sure," he says, walking with me to the living room. After he shows me how to connect it, I pull up YouTube and find a video on how to braid a child's hair. I feel his eyes on me as I search for the simplest video. My eyes land on a four-minute tutorial.

A woman shows how to braid hair with a girl around Lily's age and teaches three simple styles. Jahi watches. His eyes track the video like a crouched cat tracking a bird, Sphinx-like, while his hands enact the braiding movements, twitching like a cat's tail.

I show him two more videos and then tell him I must leave. He nods as he escorts me to the door.

"Nothing like watching *Judge Judy* with no pants on, a bottle of wine, and…" I hold up the chocolates. "Chocolate!" I throw him a playful look.

He smiles. He seems to like my goofy ways.

"Goodbye, Miss Aberdeen. Next week, then."

"Rose," I correct him.

His eyes drop to the rose bushes lining the walkway to his front door. A ghost of a smile crosses his lips. His brown eyes raise to meet mine.

"Rose," he says.

CHAPTER FOUR

JAHI

I fall into a routine with Rose and Lily. Every Monday and Friday, Rose is a constant presence in our house. She walks Lily home from school, tutors and feeds her, and stays until I get back from work.

Sometimes, Lily is asleep by the time I get home, the work of her competent teacher. Other times, Rose stays and we talk about work.

On Monday morning, I'm called to a kitchen fire. When we get there, we find an unconscious woman in the house and pull her out.

But I feel a nagging uneasiness—a gnawing feeling that I'm missing something. When I was last in the house, I remember squinting through the smoke and noticing an odd shape in the kitchen corner. That shape bothers me—it doesn't add up. *What can it be? Does the mom have a baby?* Horrified, my heart in my throat, I rush back into the inferno, and crawl on my hands and knees, searching and feeling my way in the darkness. That's when I hear a baby's cries. I bump into a burning cot by the kitchen sink and find her. Knowing that seconds matter, I hold her to my chest and run as fast as I can.

I hand her over to the paramedic in the ambulance. The baby's mother awakens from her stupor, terrified and confused.

"We have to get you to the hospital," Jerry Joe, one of the firefighters, tells her.

"No!" she screams. "Where is my baby? Did you get my baby?"

Jerry Joe points at me. "He got your baby out."

The mother beckons me to come closer. She reaches out weakly and mutters a thank you in my ear. I feel like I don't deserve it. I can't get the baby's burnt skin out of my head, something she'll live with for the rest of her life if she survives. That fact throws me into turmoil. I'll never forgive myself if the baby dies. I'm so upset that even Matt can't get three words out of me.

Dejected, I go home to find Rose and Lily poring over picture books.

"Jahi," Rose says softly, comfortable enough to say my name. She looks at me and her face falls—she must notice the haunted look I can't hide. "Are you okay? Rough day at work?"

It would be stupid to lie. I know my face reveals my inner turmoil.

"Yes," I say. Lily looks up at me.

"Well, before you arrived, your neighbor called."

"Elaine?" I ask.

"Yes," she answers. "She wants to know if Lily can come over and play with her daughter." Too tired to say no, I nod, grateful to talk to Rose about today. Lily jumps up, excited to play with her friend.

Rose takes her next door. I don't know what she says to Lily when she bends down to speak to her at the door, but I imagine she tells her to behave. In my mind, I thank her for that. It's the same thing I tell Lily before letting her visit someone else's home.

Rose returns. "So, what made your day so rough? Another fire incident? One of the teachers said you all handled it quickly, and it didn't sound too serious."

"Sometimes, gossip in this small town is true," I tell Rose. "We've dealt with bigger and worse fires."

"So, what's the problem? I imagine that means less work." She speaks in a soft, coaxing voice. What a gifted teacher she must be—it's simply the best way to talk to kids.

"I... I found a baby."

Rose gasps. She watches my expression and slowly shakes her head in horror.

"No," she says, then stops herself. "I'm so sorry."

"I saved the baby. At least I hope I did."

Rose sighs. "That's a relief then, isn't it?"

I want to agree with her, but an image of the baby's charred skin flashes in my mind. A third-degree burn. It seemed to be limited to her arm, but how much smoke did she inhale? Could she breathe? Will she end up in the ICU on a respirator? Will she get a secondary infection? Most importantly, will she survive? And if she survives, she'll have months of painful treatments in the burn unit of the hospital ahead of her.

"When we got the call about the fire, we didn't know how many people needed rescue. I crawled on my hands and knees to stay under the toxic smoke that billowed all around me. A wall of five-hundred degree, super-heated fumes hit me when I entered the structure. Sweat streamed down my back and soaked my uniform. The fire was well underway by the time we got there. We had little time to think or plan."

"Oh dear." Rose lifts her hands to cover her mouth like she's praying.

"Yeah. Wearing forty-seven pounds of protective gear and dragging a hundred pounds of hose burns an unbelievable amount of adrenaline."

"Whoa, I didn't realize the heaviness of the equipment," Rose says.

"The smoke blinded me, but I could hear myself breathing like a scuba diver with a respirator. I tried to keep a rhythm to my breath to stay calm. I heard lightbulbs popping, glass breaking, bookshelves falling. Everything crackled like the loudest campfire

I ever heard. The sound exploded all around me. I wondered if the roof might collapse."

"Oh my goodness, that must've been terrifying." Rose shakes her head.

"Honestly, I've never been so scared. I pulled out my thermal imaging camera to search for victims but only saw a woman. We didn't know about the baby. I found the woman in the kitchen, unconscious. We figured her husband worked, and she stayed home alone during the day. None of us thought about a baby. We carried her out. While we attended to her, I remembered a blurry image in the room's corner, and something about it bothered me.

"The situation was right on the edge of the point of no return, but I knew I must go back in to look, to be sure no one else remained in the house. As soon as I went in, I heard crying. That's when I saw a baby's cot on fire. I moved towards it, felt a soft form, scooped it up, and ran outside—a baby girl, about six-months-old, the skin on her arm blackened. She must have inhaled a lot of smoke."

Recalling this, I can't bear to say what I'm thinking. *What if she doesn't survive when she gets to the hospital?*

Rose looks at me kindly. "I see why you're sad, but you need to give yourself some credit."

"A baby almost died and she may still."

"A baby almost burned alive by the fire her mother probably caused. Do you know you didn't just save the baby? You saved the entire family. Do you think the mother will be able to live with herself? You listened to your intuition and ran back into the fire. You saved that baby's life. You're a hero."

"I..."

"I'm sure the fire station agrees."

I don't agree entirely, but the weight on my chest lightens, and

I breathe easier. "Thank you, Rose. You should be a therapist."

She smiles. "I am."

"What?"

She laughs at the shock on my face. "I worked as a therapist in LA before I divorced my husband and moved here to be closer to my mom and sister. At the time, I saw few opportunities for being a teacher there and no compelling opportunities to be a therapist here, so I became a first-grade teacher in Eureka Springs. There was an opening when Lily's teacher got sick and they were desperate."

"Right. I can see that, given the circumstances," I agree with her.

"I'm glad you do." She grins.

I look at her and remember what I wanted to ask her before the fire happened. "I think it'd be good if we exchanged phone numbers. We can speak sometimes if there's some scheduling or… other things." I wait to see if she agrees.

"Sure." We exchange numbers and she leaves. I wonder if she has a bit of extra bounce in her stop, but I attribute this feeling to my smoke inhalation and push it aside.

CHAPTER FIVE

ROSE

I break two eggs into the flour mixture as Maria Callas's voice soars despite the tinny sound of my phone's speaker. I sing along to Puccini's *Vissi d'arte* from *Tosca*—one of my favorite arias. The opening lyrics translate to *I lived for art, I lived for love.* Those words mirror my life.

In high school, I took operatic voice lessons. I imagined myself singing on stage at La Scala in Milan or at least the Dorothy Chandler Pavilion in LA. Dad saw himself as an opera aficionado and held season tickets at the Pavilion. Mom hated opera. She didn't understand it, nor did she attempt to, but went along to appease him—just one more sign of how little my parents shared in common.

I think pursuing opera in high school, and later in college, reflected my attempt to connect with Dad in case he ever returned. One of his un-lived dreams was to be an opera singer.

My ex-husband Lee Hawthorne hated it when I sang arias and criticized me so viciously that it shut me down for years. It's hard to live with your heart in your throat all the time. But now, I can sing with abandon all alone in my little bungalow. Besides, I'm making brownies, a source of joy and something that makes me feel close to my mother.

After putting the brownies in the oven and setting the timer to twenty-two minutes, I go to my room and tear everything apart just to rearrange it. It seems like the logical choice after finishing the laundry on a sunny Saturday morning. This was one of the habits that bothered Lee when we lived together.

Lee complained bitterly about my house cleaning. He said I rearranged and misplaced his stuff, and he never knew where to find it. Another one of his lies. His disorganization was rabid and indiscriminate with his things strewn haphazardly like the aftermath of a tornado hitting a Patagonia store, but he took it out on me. It didn't seem to affect his work as a surgeon. As far as I know, he never mistook the heart for the spleen.

This seemed to be a pattern of his. He collected insults with a disciplined studiousness in the same way that other people collect stamps or coins or Birkin bags. I called him an insult collector behind his back. He was prickly and constantly searching for evidence that others devalued or disrespected him in some way. And where did this come from? From his rotten relationship with his mother—a cold fish, like one of those strange prehistoric species from the bottom of the ocean, all bulging eyes and razor-sharp teeth, a nightmare lurking in the dark. To say we did not get along would be an understatement.

His mother ignored and rejected him repeatedly. She kicked him out of the house after high school graduation when he refused a four-year football scholarship to Colorado, leaving all his belongings on the front porch. No big surprise, then, that he reenacted that primary relationship and inflicted sadism on me. I believe he had a deep-seated hatred of women because of his horrible relationship with his mother. Yeah, so I knew all this, but I remained in love with him. I thought my love could heal him, and I convinced myself only I could do it. You could say I had a savior complex—determined to repair his narcissistic injuries once and for all. He would be unconditionally loved. But that's not how it turned out.

At parties, Lee recited to our families and friends the story of my habit of moving his things around when I cleaned, as if it were an endearing trait, a quirk of mine he found adorable and not something he lashed out about in private. I was tempted to call him Dr. Jekyll, but fear of his retribution made me hide that impulse.

Later, he tried convincing me to stay home rather than go out with him. He showed faux concern and said he knew I must be too tired to go anywhere after listening to clients complaining all day, but I dismissed it. I knew what I wanted. I wanted to be with him. Meanwhile, he slipped away any chance he got and went to parties without me.

The last miscarriage—I almost lost track of how many occurred—marked the final straw that broke our marriage. I promised to stop thinking about it, but found it hard not to. Riddled with anxiety, I became obsessed with the idea that something was terribly wrong with me. Why was I not able to carry a pregnancy to full-term? Lee blamed it on me, saying I was too anxious, but I had a terrible feeling it was something more ominous. I just didn't know what it was and none of my doctors did, either.

We lived together for ten years. That was the huge bulk of my early adulthood because we got married when I turned twenty-seven and was still in grad school.

My sister railed against our union, advising me it'd be better to experience my twenties unmarried, but being love-struck at the time and my ears deafened by the conviction I had found my one great love, I rejected her pleas. Besides, Mom and my sister felt wary about him, convinced that something in his eyes looked wrong. They said they couldn't pinpoint exactly why, but asserted that he seemed mentally ill. Now, I regret not listening to them.

Being young and unworldly when we got married, I think Lee resented me for stealing his youth, but in my defense, he asked *me* to marry *him*. What a man-boy. I was smitten by his boyishness, a kind of Peter Pan, and what my Jungian analyst called a *puer aeternus,* an eternal youth. I worshiped his exquisite athletic physique and brilliant mind. A sculpted, six-foot tall, blonde surgeon who looked like a Greek god. A perfect specimen and my dream come true. So, of course, I said yes.

Sorting out my underwear by colors, I remember how Lee initially found this adorable. But after living together our first year and seeing how fixated I could be on it, it irritated him. At first, I thought, *This phase will pass.* I made endless excuses for him whenever he mistreated me. It was just another bad day at work arguing with the head of the department. People can have bad days. I must have annoyed him. He's under a lot of stress as a surgeon.

When his contract didn't renew at the hospital, I thought it must be because the chief of surgery envied him. Lee told me his colleagues felt threatened by his brilliance. As valedictorian of his medical school class, many of his classmates hated him, especially the men. But soon enough, I ran out of excuses, and saw clearly his self-destructiveness, inability to hold a job, and continual mistreatment of me. Even after I saw it, I wanted to unsee it, to undo it, to fix it. I felt like an orca carrying her dead calf, refusing to release it. I demanded we go to couple's therapy.

The oven beeps, intruding on my thoughts. *I wanted our marriage to work so badly.* I remove the brownies from the oven. The rippled and crinkled crust looks like hardened volcanic lava. Instead of releasing poisonous gasses, a most heavenly fragrance of chocolate billows through the kitchen, transporting me momentarily to the warmth of childhood.

Not wanting to keep all the brownies to myself, I cut a huge slice, packaging it in wax paper. I throw on jeans and a blouse, a gift Lee gave me for our last anniversary. I didn't get him anything because I assumed our marriage was over, but he surprised me and we made love passionately that night. It was our last day married.

I walk briskly to Lily's home. I wonder if Jahi will find it weird that I'm showing up at his house unannounced. If we turned the tables, I might find it weird too. I knock on the door before I can talk myself out of it.

Jahi opens the door in his pajama pants. He looks surprised as he stands there in his blue-stained t-shirt.

"Hello, Jahi. Where's Lily?"

"Helping me cook."

I laugh. That explains what looks like blueberry sauce on his chest. I've always loved cooking, and it's the thing Lee almost stopped me from doing. Cooking is great, but I love feeding people even more.

Jahi smiles. I kiss Lily on her forehead after she runs to the door to greet me. Jahi looks on.

"Daddy's trying to cook," she tells me.

I nod. "I can see that."

"He doesn't know how to," she asserts.

"Hey! You say you like my sandwiches," Jahi teases his daughter. Lily giggles and looks at me like we share an inside joke.

Jahi shoots us a look of being betrayed. "Really?" Lily and I laugh together.

"Great Saturday, huh?"

"Indeed. Not that this isn't a pleasant surprise and all, Rose, but why are you here?"

I give him a little smile and hand him the bag. "Well, I made some brownies. I thought it'd be good to bring some."

Jahi looks at me like I've grown a second head.

"You brought us brownies?"

"Mostly for Lily. But for you and Lily, yes."

Jahi grins. "Since you're here, stay. I'm making pancakes with huckleberry sauce, but I'm having trouble getting the batter right."

"You couldn't make the batter," Lily says in a sing-song voice.

"And you made a mess in your kitchen." I laugh at Jahi.

"It used to make my wife so angry. I cleaned up after, though, but she still got mad that I dirtied the kitchen in the first place."

I look at him softly. He has an ex-spouse too. "Lily's mom?"

"Lily's mom," he confirms.

I look at Lily. "I'll stay for pancakes, then. And huckleberry sauce, wow. Are those like blueberries?"

"They're related—just smaller and darker. Huckleberries grow like weeds around here," Lily chirps.

"Oh, you're a clever one," I say and Lily beams.

"She sure is. After we eat, you can watch me teach Lily chess."

I look at him. "You play chess?"

"Only in the last thirty years. I've been playing since fourth grade."

My mouth flies open. "Really?"

"Yes."

"You sound like you're bragging. I'll school you in it."

"What? That's not possible."

"It is." After we make pancakes and eat, I help Jahi wash the dishes and then he brings out the chess board.

"You must be in the mood to lose," Jahi tells me.

"No, you must be in the mood to lose," I echo, egging him on. I watch *Judge Judy* or read books on my couch every weekend. What a refreshing change to shake things up.

The first game lasts for a whole fifteen minutes.

"Checkmate!" Jahi announces with authority.

I growl playfully. "No! No way!"

"Yes, way!"

I grumble. "Let's play another game."

We rearrange our pieces on the board. Lily watches. She roots for her dad. I can tell because she lets out a scream when her father checkmates me.

Jahi beats me in the second game, too. I groan.

"Fine, I give up. You're the best. Ugh."

Jahi laughs. "I'm teaching Lily. I could teach you, too, if you wish."

I smile. "Sure."

After that, I watch him teach Lily. He tells her to name the chess pieces and how each piece can move. Anytime she makes a mistake, he makes them start over and patiently explains it to her again.

Later, Lily and I watch cartoons. I spend the entire day with Jahi and Lily without realizing it.

"I've got to go home now. Stephen King's novel is waiting for me," I tell Jahi and Lily.

"Who is Stephen King?" Lily asks.

"Only the best author in the world," I tell Lily.

"You like him?"

"I love him," I say.

"Wait, really?" Jahi asks.

"Yes, really." I kiss Lily on her forehead and then leave Jahi and Lily alone. I feel almost sad to go.

CHAPTER SIX

JAHI

I pack Lily's lunch and give her a little piece of Rose's brownies. I take a bit more for myself. What a thoughtful gesture for Rose to bring us goodies. I want to do something nice for her in return, but I don't know what.

I head to work. Matt is already there playing a mindless game on his phone, blasting aliens or some such. He smiles when he sees me.

"You're late today, buddy."

"Yeah, Lily didn't want to go to school."

"Maybe you should have brought her along to work with you," Matt says.

"She went after I told her it meant she wouldn't get to see Rose."

"It's so great that your daughter loves her teacher."

"I think so too."

"It might be that she's not the only one who likes the teacher." Matt fixes me with a look.

"What?"

"You told me we would spend Saturday together."

"I didn't know she planned to ply me with brownies. What the heck could I say? Don't come to me bearing gifts of heavenly brownies because my adult friend might get mad that I'm not spending time with him."

"Oh, don't make it sound that way. I'm not mad. If anything, I'm quite happy. So, what did y'all do?"

"We cooked breakfast, and we played a little chess."

Matt smiles. "I imagine that went great."

"It did. I won twice."

Matt shakes his head like he can't believe me. "You didn't let her win?"

"Why would I do that? I mean, she's a good enough player, even better than I expected, but I couldn't just let her win. She's not good enough to beat me."

"I don't know what to tell you," Matt says.

I bring out the tiny brownie and pop it in my mouth, relishing the yummy taste.

"The brownie?" Matt asks me.

"Yeah."

He smiles. I glower. "You've been smiling so much, and it's really creepy. Stop it."

"I can't be happy around my own friend?" Matt taunts. I pin him with a stare.

"Fine. Okay. I'll stop."

I put on my headphones without music. We hear someone yelling and glance at each other before running outside to investigate the ruckus.

Two of our firefighters are exchanging blows, punching each other bloody, like Ali and Foreman in The Rumble in the Jungle—fighting to prove who reigns. Nobody intervenes. Everyone appears frozen from the shock of it, but soon my mind snaps in place and I realize this could turn deadly.

Not able to stand it any longer, I rush in to separate them. I don't want to see either of them get knocked out or die of a brain bleed from an epidural hematoma. Matt joins me and the rest of the firefighters pile in.

We pull them apart. Both men sustain busted lips, one nurses a cut above his eyebrow that looks like it will require sutures, and the other thinks his ankle might be twisted.

Matt and I take Larry away. We clean out his cut, put butterfly strips on it, and tell him he needs to get it sewn up. He sits quietly, only wincing sometimes. We don't ask what caused the fight. We figure if Larry wants to tell us, he will.

"We fought because of my wife," he confesses. I sigh. I don't know why I didn't see that one coming.

"Why? Why are you fighting for your wife?" Matt asks.

Like she's some chew toy. I complete the sentence in my head.

"You can't tell?" Larry asks.

"No, we can't," I say. Matt throws me a look—a look I don't really understand.

"Tina's been cheating on me for a while."

After he says this, it feels like an arrow thrown directly into my heart, as if I'm reliving my life with my estranged wife, Susanne.

"Did you just find out recently?" Matt asks.

"No," Larry says simply. "She cheated with Christopher, a man from church. I didn't find out on my own. She confessed. She bent down on her knees and pleaded with me to forgive her, saying it will never happen again. I believed her. I love my wife so much."

"We know."

"I thought she made a mistake, so I let it go. We've got three children and we love them. It'd be stupid to separate. I don't want to do that to my kids."

"I understand," I say gravely.

"The second time she messed around with our mailman. I came home early and caught him in our bed. We spoke about it, and our pastor encouraged us to try couple's counseling. My wife told the counselor I caused our troubles. Somehow, I let her blame me and I believed what she said."

"Oh, she's gaslighting you," I say matter-of-factly.

"Now, it's my co-worker," he continues, ignoring my comment.

"Larry—" Matt starts.

"I know what you're going to say. Why am I fighting with my co-worker instead of with my wife? Because I'm outraged. Even though I'm not thinking straight, I've got to make the right decision, and I've got to make it soon."

I watch the muscles of Larry's jaws twitching. His brow furrows, and he clenches his fists so tightly his knuckles blanch. But I know underneath his angry facade, he carries a huge load of sadness and hurt. The third betrayal is pushing him to the brink as his marriage dissolves in front of his eyes.

A divorce awaits, and it will be messy. Their kids will choose sides, and there might be a fight for custody. There will be attorneys and therapists. Vast amounts of money will go up in smoke. It takes its toll on people.

I never went through the divorce process because my wife, Susanne, didn't care enough to ask for a divorce or fight for Lily. She never wanted a child, anyway, even though she pretended she did.

She just left and didn't look back as if we never existed as a couple. For months, I dug myself deep into a hole of depression. I hated myself. Every day I spent questioning my existence and asking the world if I didn't deserve to be loved. Or have closure? Or any explanation from the woman I married and took to the altar. Matt talked me out of my sadness at the time. I'm forever grateful to him for not letting me push him away when I needed him most.

Larry sits quietly.

"You know what you need to do, right?" I ask Larry.

"I know." Larry's voice cracks. "I know."

"I'm so sorry," I tell him.

"It will be messy and all. The fight for the kids? Going to

court? Having to explain to people—I know it's terrible, but we'll be here for you," Matt says.

I glare at Matt. *We?*

He glares back at me. "Won't we, Jahi?"

"We will."

"Thank you," Larry says. "I should go." He gives us a mock salute and leaves.

Matt stares at me. "That's sad."

"Some people are just unlucky with this stuff," I sigh.

Matt's eyes soften. "On another topic, should we eat something and then I tease you about Rose some more?"

I frown at my friend. "What the heck is wrong with you?" I laugh. Matt can always make me laugh.

"Since y'all are paying each other visits now, go to her house, too. With Lily, of course. Get her another gift," Matt says.

"No, she is Lily's teacher."

"Who said she isn't?"

"I know what you're trying to do, and I won't fall for it."

"You know, I have been asking you to play chess with me for a long time." Matt laughs at me.

"We never really have the time, and you know it."

"What do I know? I know nothing. You made time to spend with Rose."

"You're behaving like you're in high school."

"I'm not that far from eighteen," Matt says jokingly. "You barely have any hair on your head that isn't gray."

"Are you shaming me? For being old?" I eye my friend.

"Maybe," Matt says.

"You're a fake friend."

We break into laughter, but the thought of Larry still bothers me. That night, while Lily sleeps, I wonder if it'd be weird to call and ask about him and see if he needs any help. We've never really spoken before, so I decide against it. Despite everything, something in me says guys don't do this. There's no law against it, but there might as well be.

CHAPTER SEVEN

ROSE

The bell rings, signaling the end of the school day.

"Wait here. We'll head over to your house in a moment." Just as I say this, my phone rings. I see an unknown number, but answer it anyway. Silence.

Then, I hear heavy breathing and the call goes dead. Perhaps a prank caller found my number.

"Okay, let's walk to your house," I tell Lily. We start making our way out of the school's front doors when the phone rings again. I sigh, expecting a repeat performance, but this time the person speaks. My heart almost stops. *I'd know that voice anywhere.*

The voice is Lee Hawthorne's, my ex-husband. *How did he get hold of my new number?* Out of anger for Lee's egregious treatment of me during the later years of our marriage, I blocked and deleted his phone number when we divorced. Neither name nor phone number came up when he called, so I foolishly answered it, expecting at worst a sales pitch or political fundraising. Now, he's sucking me into his sick vortex.

"Hello?" I answer.

Lily mouths at me to hurry.

"Wait here," I mouth back, gesturing for her to sit down. She obediently nods and sits in a chair by the front office, as if realizing the seriousness of the situation.

"What do you want? We agreed never to contact each other again," I say stiffly, my voice sounding oddly mechanical. I hear giggling in the background, and almost hang up, but stop short.

"Look, just tell me what you want. I've got things to do. If you have nothing to say, I'm hanging up."

I hear Lee laugh. An iconic laugh I used to love hearing early in our relationship. During the later years of our marriage, I made sacrifices just to hear my husband laugh. Now, he's back and laughing so easily. What did he say in court? Rose is the problem—isn't that what he said? I never hated my own existence in my entire life as much as I did at that moment. I cried right there on the court stand while my lawyer tried yet failed to console me. The judge asked us to take an hour-long break, and I wept inconsolably.

"You're still as serious as always. So straight and narrow, and ready for business."

"Lee," I warn. "I didn't pick up your call so we can get nostalgic. State your business or I hang up." I scowl. I mouth another apology to Lily.

"Fine, I just... I wanted to tell you I'm getting married in August. Yes, you mentioned we shouldn't speak to each other again, but I thought it might be good to tell you."

"How's it good to tell me?" Hot tears burn my eyes and spill down my cheeks. I've moved on from the mess of our marriage, but it still stings.

"I want you to be there, Rose. Please be there. My fiancée, Iris, would like to meet you."

Without warning, I hang up, surprised by the power of my impulse. My eyes land on Lily, who watches me intently, and I give her a plastered smile.

I take her straight back to Jolene.

"Jolene, I won't be able to take Lily home today." Jolene adjusts her glasses and observes me for a moment. "Tell Jahi so he can pick her up. I need to be alone."

"Is everything okay, dear?"

Tears well in my eyes with a salty sting as I try to blink them back. A futile effort, like a picket fence against the tide. My knees tremble, but I don't collapse.

"No," I tell her honestly. "Lee just called to inform me he's getting married."

Jolene lurches so quickly, I almost get whiplash.

"That monster!" Jolene mutters. "That little piece of..."

"Shhh... There's a child here, Jolene."

Jolene looks at Lily, whose hand I'm still holding. She takes Lily's other hand and Lily lets go of mine. "I understand. Go home. Draw yourself a bath and take a nap. You can choose not to come to school tomorrow. Heck, take the week off. I'll step in and teach your class."

"Thank you." My voice breaks as I hug her.

"I will come over next time," I promise Lily. She nods and waves and looks at me with the most tender eyes I think I've ever seen. *She's an old soul, something I loved about her from the moment I met her.*

When I get home, I collapse on my bed, shaking uncontrollably. Everything seems surreal, the sky appears harsh and overexposed, burning my retinas in a kaleidoscope of lurid chromatic colors, creating a reality that can't possibly exist. It's like the moment Lee served me with divorce papers the day after our anniversary, the day I thought our marriage got back on track. Oh, boy, was I wrong.

On that infamous day of destruction, he started out by looking at me with pitying eyes, the corners of his mouth weighted down as if attached to little lead fishing sinkers. But a mood of impatience came over him, and he shoved the papers across the kitchen table.

Then he switched to a forlorn look, trying to flip the narrative and make me feel sorry for him. But I saw something phony in his expression, something mask-like. His words said one thing—how sorry he felt about needing to end our marriage, but his face said something else. It looked contrived. I noticed something strange. His eyes betrayed a look of glee, a sort of "I gotcha, I win" look.

Deep down, I knew this was a steaming load of crap, another version of his "it's you, not me." But part of me believed it at the time, despite my anger towards him.

But the truth is, Lee fell out of love early on and never fully committed to giving our marriage a chance. Now he wants to marry another woman.

Lee called me a "quotidian" therapist. He was a wordsmith and loved intimidating me with his vocabulary. When I looked up the word, I realized he was disparaging me with fancy language, slaying me with syllables. I remember thinking, *What? I'm a mundane, everyday therapist in his eyes?*

As if that weren't enough, he continued inflicting insults. He said, smiling, "You're just a class below a big shot therapist." Like a narcissist demanding centrality of the narrative, he expected me to mirror and admire him even as he criticized me. Most of the time, I complied. With a narcissist, if you don't comply, they attack. It sickens me to think about how I abandoned myself. To Lee, I was just one more source of narcissistic supply.

Why did I allow his terrible treatment of me? Now, he's replacing me with a new woman and he's euphoric.

I'm a psychologist, and I don't know how to heal myself.

Still clutching my red leather crossbody handbag and wearing red and white striped espadrilles, I hate myself as I sob into a pillow. Here I am flopped on the bed like a beached whale, letting a man get the best of me. I get up, pull off my school clothes, and draw a bath. Afterwards, I find my favorite pajamas and plod into the living room to watch *Love Island.*

I watch as couples cuddle, and my heart swells. The doorbell rings and I jump. I'm not expecting anyone. It must be Jolene coming to check up on me.

I open the door.

It's Jahi.

"Hi." I stand there, mouth agape.

CHAPTER EIGHT

JAHI

The moment Rose opens the door, I know Jolene nailed it. Rose looks at me with bloodshot, puffy eyes. She sniffles and wipes her nose on her pajama sleeve. I don't see any wine on the table. She probably doesn't indulge in day drinking, or maybe any drinking at all.

"Hi," she says and lets me in. "Why are you here?" She doesn't sit, so I just follow her lead in case she wants me to leave.

"Jolene called and told me to pick up Lily myself because you're having some kind of personal crisis. I was worried about you."

"And where's Lily?" she asks.

"Still with Jolene."

"That little girl must be bored to death," she says and sits down. I take that as my invitation.

"Are you okay?" I ask. I give her a look and then want to punch myself. "Sorry, stupid question. Of course you're not."

"I'm not."

"Can I help?"

"Drink with me," she says.

I nod. "Absolutely."

She goes to her kitchen and returns with two wine glasses and a bottle of wine.

"Here. It's a cheap grocery wine. I love what James Thurber said about wine like this, 'It's a naïve, domestic Burgundy without any breeding, but I think you'll be amused by its presumption.'"

"The best kind," I assure her, and laugh. She unscrews the bottle and unceremoniously splashes a yeoman's share into each glass. She's brainy and funny even when she's devastated.

She smiles, but her eyes are sad. "Thanks for this. I hope it's not inconvenient for you."

"What? No way. I wanted to check up on you."

"You're sure Jolene didn't tell you to come here? You know, giving you a little nudge?" She makes air quotes.

I laugh. Jolene can be pushy at times. "I wish to give her credit, but sadly, she didn't."

Rose hands me a glass of wine.

"Cheers," she says flatly. She downs the wine in two reckless gulps and pours another while I watch. She finishes and pours a third glass.

"Why are you not drinking?"

I watch her. "You need it more."

She nods. "You're right, Jahi. I need it. I need surging high tides of wine, great sloshing oceans of wine to fix this. I need all the wine in the world, so my ex won't have any at his wedding. What is a wedding without wine? I hope it flops. I wish them everything bad," Rose spits out the words. She finishes another glass.

"That's why you're sad? Your ex-husband is getting remarried?" I ask.

"Yes. That man told me marriage wasn't for him. Something must be wrong with me. Men always leave me. I'm too broken, and I can't see it. My ex-husband saw it and thought the best thing was to leave me alone with it." Rose cries, and my chest tightens.

"How could I have let him deceive me? I let him treat me so badly and degrade me at every turn. My mom and sister thought he was terrible. They despised him. They believed he was ill, but I repeatedly made excuses for this idiot. I hate myself for being so stupid."

I listen as she rages and wallows and finishes the entire bottle of wine.

"Did you mistreat your wife, too? Lily's mother?" Her words sound slow and thick, the alcohol erasing her usually crisp articulation.

"Not that I know of," I say carefully. She's becoming illogical.

"What happened, then? Did she cheat?" She gives me a once-over. "I don't see why she would, though."

I suppress a laugh. She swallows. She must be drunker than I think.

"I'm not aware of her cheating on me."

"So, why did you get a divorce? Huh? You're saying you're innocent?" Rose squints at me with eyes red-rimmed and glossed over from too much wine.

"I didn't get a divorce. But I genuinely don't know, Rose," I say softly. "Maybe I just didn't deserve to be loved or who knows, maybe I got cheated on. I don't know any of this because my wife just got up and left."

Rose looks at me pathetically. I almost laugh again. What a pitiful pair we are.

"That's sad. So you're estranged from your wife? Explains why Lily's hair is messy most of the time."

"I'm trying. I watched more videos after that day."

"I'm sure," she says sarcastically. "This is my last bottle. You think you can go to the grocery store and get me one more?"

"I think you need to sleep."

"What? No. I don't feel sleepy one bit." Despite her protests, I hold her around her waist and help her stumble to her bedroom. As soon as her head touches the pillow, her eyes close, and she falls asleep. I place a glass of water beside her bed and by this time I hear her snoring, though it sounds more like purring.

I pick up Lily from school and bring her home. She watches

me as I silently warm up the pizza for our dinner.

"What's wrong with Miss Aberdeen?" Lily asks.

How can I explain the term to her? She won't understand. Not something I want her to understand, either.

"A part of her broke." *Her heart,* I add in my head.

"Is she sick?"

I nod.

My daughter looks worried. "Did you take her to the hospital?"

"No, your teacher will be fine."

"Did the doctor kiss all her owies better?"

I laugh at my daughter's naïve questions. "Yes, baby."

"I want to be a doctor, too."

"You will be." I kiss her head and smile down at her.

CHAPTER NINE

ROSE

On the way to the fire station with Lily in tow, I figure it might be a stupid decision, but Lily bubbles over with excitement over the possibility of seeing her father.

Yesterday, when I informed Jolene about my plan to visit Jahi at work, she gave me the widest grin and then shooed me away, embarrassed perhaps to reveal her interest in my personal life.

When we get to the station, a firefighter Lily calls Matthew stands there, towering over us with his six-foot-five frame. This man looks like a Greek statue with his tousled blond mane and ripped physique. He could have been the model for Michelangelo's *David*, but the timing is off by a few centuries. There's a playful air about him with his boyish grin and twinkling, electric blue eyes and he looks like he belongs on a surfboard at Zuma Beach in Malibu.

Lily throws her arms wide and gives him a hug, and he snatches her up and juggles her around.

"Hello," he says quietly, acknowledging me. I smile, not wanting to be rude.

"We're looking for Jahi. Jahi Adams. He works here."

"That's my best buddy."

My eyes narrow. I don't imagine Jahi having a best buddy. He doesn't talk much and mentions no friends. I wonder if Jahi thinks the same.

Matthew leads us to Jahi. We see him hunched over the table watching videos on his phone. As we move closer, we see the braiding videos. I smile. He didn't lie when he said he continued to study how to braid Lily's hair.

"Hi Daddy," Lily giggles, excited to surprise him.

Jahi turns, shocked, and then opens his arms wide as Lily leaps into his embrace.

The tender looks between father and daughter mesmerize me. I've dreamt of this kind of moment for years, imagining it coming alive in some distant future, in some possible life. And yet, it's here in front of me, in this moment, this fleeting, precious moment, and I know I will cherish it forever.

"Hi Rose." Jahi says softly.

Matthew notices the looks between us and scoops up Lily, saying, "Baby doll, let's go look at the fireman's pole." Lily nods and off they go.

Jahi invites me to sit.

"I wanted to see you," I say. I expect him to say we could have seen each other at home, but I know he wouldn't say that. Jahi is too kind for that.

"I wanted to see you, too. See how you're doing."

"Thank you. Lee kept calling. He probably expected me to break down after that stupid call, and I proved him right."

Jahi smiles sympathetically. "You're upset because you understandably broke down when your ex-husband told you he's getting remarried?"

"Understandably? I made a fool of myself in front of a parent."

Jahi swallows. "I'm not just a parent. We're friends."

My mouth opens. "Do you really think that?"

"You think I go to the other teachers' houses?"

"I don't know what to think."

He laughs. "You're funny."

"Thank you for what you did. I spiraled. I can't believe I lost control. I promised myself he wouldn't have that much effect on me anymore."

"Y'all stayed married for so long. That's understandable. You think you've gotten over them, but I don't think you ever do."

"That's genuinely sad. Oh yeah, before I forget, Jolene sends her greetings."

"She pushed you to come?" Jahi asks.

"No," I say. "Sorry, I dragged Lily with me. I figured she might be glad to see you."

"She is. I'm her favorite person."

I raise a brow, pretending like I didn't know this. "I don't know. I might be her favorite person."

Jahi gives me a mock glower. "You know, I'm going to leave work early today. Get Lily ice cream." He stops. "And you. Would you like to join us?"

"Yes, of course. I haven't eaten ice cream in a long time."

"No way. I bet your freezer is filled with ice cream." I can tell he likes to joke.

"It used to be," I admit. "I'm out."

"Too bad. Matt will be mad I'm taking Lily away from him. It's almost like he's her second father."

"The man that brought us here?"

"That's him," Jahi clarifies.

"He said something about being your best buddy. I don't see it," I say, hoping I'm not offending him.

"Why not?"

"I just." I pause, hoping to not fall into a trap. Maybe I shouldn't mention it. "I just don't see it."

"I understand," Jahi says gently. "I don't see it either, but he truly is my friend. He didn't leave me to myself when I started working here. He made sure I didn't isolate myself. He showed me the ropes. I'm grateful to him."

"As I am. That's sweet of him."

"I think so too," Jahi says. "Now, let's go get ice cream and annoy the heck out of my best buddy."

"I'm sure he hates you sometimes."

"Ain't that the truth!"

He's loosening up around me. It must result from my dramatic breakdown, the only advantage of what Lee did to me.

We find Matthew and Lily playing a game. Matthew shows Lily pictures on his phone and she names the pictures, giggling all the while.

"Sometimes, I feel like my friend is taking my own daughter away."

I grin. People in his daughter's life love her so much.

"Matthew, I'm sorry, but I'm here to take Lily away from you," Jahi says.

"On what grounds? If it's for her homework help, I'm sure her teacher won't mind teaching her here."

"Not teaching," Jahi says. Lily pouts and Matthew looks disappointed.

"I'm leaving Uncle Matt?" she asks.

"To go get ice cream!"

A grin spreads over her face. "Let's go!" Lily says.

Matthew mockingly protests. "Aw, kids. So fickle. Can't believe I put my trust in you, Lily."

"I'm sorry, Uncle Matt. I'll bring you a cone."

Matthew bends down to hug her. "Don't apologize. You're too cute to get mad at." He picks her up and tickles her, then sets her down on her feet.

"Fine, go get both of us ice cream." Matt throws his friend a look I don't understand. Jahi seems to understand and gives a mock salute.

Jahi takes us to Ice Cream Delights, noted for their Blue Bell ice cream. We place our orders and find a table. Lily tells her father about the fight between two of her classmates. Jahi listens intently and smiles as she animatedly tells him about her day.

"So how do you handle this?" Jahi asks. I can't tell if he is asking out of concern for me or his daughter. Lily never fights. I've never quite seen any child like her.

"I call them to my table and we talk, and then I make them apologize to the class. An hour later, you'll hear another uproar, and I have to repeat the entire process. It keeps the peace for a while."

"That sounds tough, but you're a strong woman," Jahi says.

I blush under his gaze. I'm glad I didn't let our first interaction determine our relationship because I'm realizing what a gem this man is—one of the best people I've ever met. I admire and respect him. As a firefighter and paramedic, he risks his life every day for others. He's deeply kind and thoughtful and adores his daughter on top of it all.

"Thanks. And you. A literal hero," I say.

His face flushes. "I wouldn't call it that."

"Trying to be humble?"

He looks at me playfully. "Is it working?"

"I don't know. I can't tell. Do you think it is?"

"Daddy, I want another one," Lily interrupts us.

"Lily..."

"Daddy." Her eyes widen in the cutest expression. Jahi sighs. How could he say no to his charming daughter? He follows her to order the Chocolate Peanut Butter Overload ice cream cone.

"Last one," Jahi says gruffly, but Lily is giggling. She must know she's her father's weakness. I smile as she offers her father her ice cream, telling him to take a lick.

CHAPTER TEN

JAHI

I don't know what my mother is saying to Lily, because I can't hear her. Rose and I text back and forth, discussing the merits of Stephen King novels and arguing about the best ones. When I learn she deems his works better than any other author's, I devour his novels. I hope to add something interesting to our conversations and connect with Rose on a deeper level.

When I got her number, I thought Lily would be the only thing we spoke about, but we had far-ranging discussions about everything from thoroughbred horse racing to the best decor for a farmhouse living room.

My sister, Chrissy, walks over and puts her head on my shoulder. I wonder if this is her barely disguised attempt to peek at my screen. I hope not.

"What are you doing texting so much? We know you're a caveman. Why are you living on your phone? What the heck? What's going on, brother? I know something is up and don't you dare tell me there's nothing."

With great effort, I look up from my phone. Chrissy's sartorial interests amuse me. She outdid herself this time. She's decked out in her Sunday best pink frilly dress, white cashmere sweater, and vertiginous Louboutin stilettos, even though it's just our traditional monthly family dinner. I like to joke about Chrissy's fancy shoe collection, an anomaly for someone from the boondocks—the Gianvito Rossi's, Jimmy Choo's, and Manolo Blahnik's. She studiously crosses her legs and flashes the iconic red soles, even though most of us in these parts don't appreciate the significance of it, or think maybe she walked in a pool of red paint. Wobbling on spindly toothpick legs, her heels click erratically on the kitchen floor, breaking my concentration. She's definitely not used to walking in them.

These days, whenever my family sees Lily, they get angry at my estranged wife all over again. I ignore most of their trash talk and just eat Mom's delicious beef brisket, roasted Brussels sprouts, and baked cheesy mashed potatoes finished off with maple pecan pie for dessert. We're all in too much of a food coma to be angry after that.

Sometimes, we play chess afterwards. But it feels bittersweet. I imagine how my father would have adored Lily, but he never got the chance to meet her. I have recurring dreams where Dad is still alive and playing chess with his one and only grandchild, and both are laughing uproariously, as if the rest of us don't exist.

The more boisterous and celebratory our family dinners, the more I miss Dad. It's as if our moments of joy tap a well of grief and bring up the sting of forever losing my father. My mind replays in slow motion the horrible moment when Dad collapsed that terrible day when I was only fifteen. It can take days after these dinners to recover some sort of equilibrium. Sometimes, I can't stand to go to the dinners, but I can't stand to not go, either.

"You're taking a long time to answer, brother."

"What question do you want me to answer, Chrissy?"

"Everything!" she cries. "Mom, can't you see Jahi glued to his phone? It's unlike him. He's lost in thought."

"You hardly look away from your phone, even when eating. Jahi, baby, is there something you want to tell us?" Mom asks.

I shake my head firmly. My family means well, but they're nosy. No way will I mention Rose.

"I know he's texting a woman. I know that much," Chrissy asserts.

Lily focuses on the cookie my mother gives her, unbothered by the bantering of the surrounding adults. I almost wish I could go back to her age again, but I had a terrible buzz cut. I don't relish the humiliation of showing up at school and being made fun of for my hair.

"What your sister said, is it true? Are you texting a woman?"

"Maybe," I say. "It could be my eighty-year-old neighbor. Did you think of that, Chrissy?"

"No, because that's impossible. We're not dumb, Jahi. We can read your face. You better spill so I can help."

"I don't need your help."

"You know you need me."

I shake my head. Chrissy's delusions can be funny sometimes. "I don't."

"And stop lying about your old neighbor. I know she can't really use a smartphone. She confessed that much to me."

Lily stops eating her cookie and stares at us.

"Chrissy, stop it. I'm not texting anybody."

"We know that's a lie, baby," Mom says.

I try to change the subject. Chrissy and Mom become unstoppable anytime they decide to gang up on me. Sometimes, thinking about those times makes me uneasy.

"Mom, it doesn't really matter. Besides, why don't you ask Chrissy why her husband isn't here?"

Chrissy shoots me a dirty look. "Stop trying to change the subject, you little..."

I laugh. "Little? I'm your older brother, and I'm bigger than you."

"Why's your husband not here?" Mom asks Chrissy. She must have wanted to ask, but didn't know how.

"We're not talking about that. We're talking about Jahi and his sudden obsession with texting."

"We can talk about both of you. You're *both* my children."

"We had a fight," Chrissy concedes.

I feel bad. I admire my sister's marriage. It always seems perfect. Every time I watch Chrissy and Lucas bicker, I feel a stab of envy because I know it's temporary and they'll make up. At least she's in a stable marriage. Is this still true?

"Oh, I didn't know. I thought work got in the way," I say.

"He has work stress, but he meant to make time for dinner. He's mad at me."

"Why?" I ask. I understand how she feels about me texting now.

"Well, we never really talked about it, but recently he started mentioning having kids. Kids. I've never really thought of that. He says he wants kids. I don't mind kids, so I've gone off the pill. I've seen a doctor and whatnot."

"So, what's the problem? You don't mind kids."

"Yeah, I love Lily so much. I would like to have a child, but the doctor says I can't. At least, not on my own. IVF."

"Okay and..." Mother persists and I wonder how Chrissy feels. My sister detests being put on the spot.

"Mother, I'm scared. IVF destroys a lot of marriages and I don't want my marriage ruined, but what I'm trying to avoid is exactly what is happening right now. I didn't realize he wanted a child this much, and I'm disgusted at myself for being oblivious and just finding out now."

"It's not your fault he didn't tell you," I tell my sister. "Y'all should have talked about this before."

"We did, just not deeply, and we both said we didn't mind having children later. His nonchalant comment made me question his interest in having kids. I thought it was an afterthought.

Today, I expected him to come along, but he said he couldn't. He claimed work problems. Or something."

"Chrissy, I'm sorry. It's concerning that this topic of having children erupted out of nowhere and now communication with Lucas is fraught," I say to my sister, but I'm privately worried they're teetering on the perilous edge of avoidance or, God forbid, the death spiral of blame.

"I'm sorry too," Mom agrees, but I can tell she wants to say more.

"I'll tell you this, sister. If you don't want to do IVF, forget about it. I don't want you doing something just to please a man, especially something so huge as having kids."

"Thank you, Jahi. You're so nice sometimes."

"Sometimes?"

My sister smiles. Her mood seems lighter after sharing with us. "You know what I mean. Stop acting like you're so surprised and you don't know just how mean and aloof you are sometimes."

"I am not aloof. You're lying and I don't like it," I say. We laugh together as our mother watches.

"I didn't realize the effectiveness of Jahi's subject change. You're smart, Jahi, but I haven't forgotten," Mom says.

"I haven't either," Chrissy chimes in.

I'll never get out of this if I don't give my sister and mother an answer. They'll nag me to the bitter end, and it will prove exhausting.

"I've been talking to a woman."

"Not that I would mind if it were a man," Chrissy says.

This forcing of information annoys me, but I know it comes from a place of love. They'll support me no matter what.

I smile at my sister. "It's Lily's teacher. Her name is Rose Aberdeen. We've become friends over the past few weeks."

"How old is she?" my mother inquires in her usual nosy fashion. I resist the urge to laugh.

"How old do you think she is, Mom?"

"I don't know, Jahi. You tell me. I'm not playing the guessing game with you."

"Sorry. She's thirty-seven. Jolene didn't know for sure when I asked."

"Jolene?"

"The principal."

"So, you've been sniffing around." Chrissy looks impressed.

I roll my eyes. My family weirds me out sometimes. "A little."

"So, you're dating your daughter's teacher?" Mom asks, eyebrows raised.

I don't correct my mother. No need to give her any surface area to glom onto. "Mom, this sounds like an interrogation, and I don't like it."

"And when have you liked anything, Jahi? Except my cooking, of course."

"No, she came to my house to tell me I need to give Lily more attention with her homework and then she offered to teach Lily."

"Oh, she's so kind. I don't think you deserve her. You put me on the spot literally some minutes ago," Chrissy says.

"Yeah, she's a sweetheart, and I didn't know you two were having problems in your marriage, Chrissy. I'm sorry."

"Can we meet this Rose person?" Mom asks.

"Call me anytime and I'll be here to meet her too," Chrissy says.

"Only because you're so doggone nosy," I tell my sister. She laughs.

"No, you can't. She's just a friend, okay? You can't meet her. It'd be awkward," I say, but deep down, I wish she could meet my family and we could get closer. Every time I learn something new about Rose, I like her a little more. When she showed up in my life, it felt like an emerging rose bud in my garden of old roses—tender and full of promise.

When my mother and sister discovered my rose garden, they wept. It reminded them of Dad and his dad, Big Daddy, who grew old roses in Eureka Springs for as long as anyone can remember. My mother thinks it goes back further than Big Daddy, a lineage passing from father to son, cultivated over generations like the roses themselves.

When Rose showed up on my doorstep that auspicious day, it riveted me. I never imagined a woman like her knocking on my door. Her face was unforgettable—radiant, like the beauty in Botticelli's *The Birth of Venus*, a painting in one of Dad's art history books I stared at as a child. Her face was otherworldly, as if from another time and place, and I couldn't get her out of my mind. She was like one of those *forever paintings* Dad always talked about, a painting once seen you never forget.

And when she revealed her name to be Rose, it felt like a dream, a sort of reverie. Or maybe some kind of *déjà vu*. I fell silent. She didn't know how much her name meant to me.

It brought up so many memories of Dad and Big Daddy. Everyone knew about their old roses—their quiet interest transmitted from generation to generation, father to son, a kind of lore or glue that held us together in the face of life's vicissitudes that felt more like a prayer than anything I ever experienced in church. I'm not sure how far back the lineage goes, but it may be many generations. Dad kept a section in our garden preserved for his beloved roses and I promised him I would keep the tradition alive. I've already talked to Lily about the importance of this family tradition, and I look forward to passing along my knowledge to her, so the lineage will continue unbroken.

My sister breaks my reverie and blurts out that she thinks it would be cool for me to mention my rose garden on social media. I ignore her.

"Yeah, this 'friend' you talk about, wouldn't you like to ask her first? Know what she thinks?" Mother presses me.

"I don't know, Mom."

"Jahi," she says warningly.

"I'll think about it."

"You're a good kid."

"I'm forty, Mom."

My mother squints at me. As if on cue, the bird of the old cuckoo clock pops out of its little door and chirps eight times and then four rotating figurines finish with a little ditty. I scoop up Lily, the sleeping beauty, and drive us home.

CHAPTER ELEVEN

ROSE

I study the email a bit too long. Enid Armstrong. My best friend. A sweet Black woman I worked with as a therapist in Los Angeles.

She sent me an email around three a.m. telling me of the new job she got with a hospital looking for therapists. She said there's one vacancy left, and she thought of me as perfect for the position.

I call her when I wake up, and she picks up on the second ring.

"Hello?"

"Enid, it's me," I tell her in a rush. "I got your email."

"When did I see you last, Rosie? Oh, my goodness. How's small town life treating you? Do you love it way more than hanging out with me?" Enid's voice teases.

I laugh. My eyes water. "I've missed you so much. How are you?"

"Wonderful, and would be even more terrific if you answered positively to my email. I've already informed my boss about you and the company might contact you, too, but I wanted you to hear it from me first."

"Oh, Enid."

"Are you still able to therapize people over there?"

I laugh. "Not really, no. I'm an elementary school teacher here."

"That's reasonable. You minored in education and got a teaching credential. It's only right you're using it to help kids,"

Enid says. "Do you remember that time when a patient asked you to marry him just because he loved the fact that you helped him get over his ex?"

I remember it clearly. While Lee thought I wasn't a big shot therapist, people sought me out at my job. Of course, I remember. Daniel Walter. I liked him, too. Not the way he wanted, though. He got a divorce after his wife almost ruined him by cheating on him repeatedly. I helped Daniel as much as I could. He thought I was Jesus reincarnated… with two X chromosomes this time. The next thing I knew, he proposed marriage.

I wondered if I had even done a good job with him at all—he had this positive transference to me where I was his savior. He believed marrying me would redeem him, bring him a sense of trust in life, and deliver him from the terrible troubles he lived through with his cheating wife. But that's Daniel, and I still have a soft spot for him.

"Of course, I remember. Lee hated that."

Enid scoffs. "Oh, forget about Lee. He's impossible."

I smile. I love Enid's protectiveness. She never liked Lee and made sure I knew it. Whenever we met at gatherings, she made a point of glaring at him or avoiding him completely. She acted like he didn't exist. He hated it because he couldn't stand to be ignored. It bothered me for a while but then I dropped it, reasoning that my best friend didn't have to like my husband and vice versa.

"I'm a Scorpio. I can walk into a room and size up people, Rose. He's a pathological liar. You're better off without him."

"Yeah, he never liked much of anything, but he's found something he fancies," I start sadly.

Enid listens quietly. "And what does that mean?"

"Lee is getting married again. He invited me to the wedding. He said he thought it'd be impolite if he didn't. I think he did it on purpose to rub it in my face that he moved on before I did."

"I'm sorry, babe. He's sick. You know this, right? Besides, it's not a competition on who moves on first. I'm sorry you endured him for so long."

I fled LA right after our divorce and came to Eureka Springs, Arkansas. I needed to start over in a small, safe place—a place I could afford near my mom and sister. Lee showed his corrupt side and drained our bank account before I left, which added to my desperation to find a job. At the moment, I just wanted out of there, away from Lee's orbit and anything that reminded me of him. Later, I was able to recover my share of the assets with help from an attorney friend whom I had met when we were both in grad school.

I looked for clinical positions as a therapist, but I didn't see any in this small town, but there was a first grade teacher position available and I took it. Pretty soon, I found that teaching children gave me purpose. Connecting with six- and seven-year-olds made me happy. There's something special about the day-to-day, nitty gritty, down in the sand experience of working with first graders. I love the immediacy of it, the feeling of possibility, the innocence and sense of hope, and the unfettered self-expression of the children. It also took my mind off my heartbreak.

"I'm sorry, too, Enid."

"So, will you go?"

The question stops me. Lee's revelation upset me so much that I haven't thought about what I want. *Do I want to grace his wedding with my presence or not?*

In fact, I want to find his fiancée and warn her to run away as fast as possible. I remember counseling patients to flee when they found themselves ensnared in the spider's web of an abusive, narcissistic partner. *I wish I had left Lee when I saw the signs of his personality disorder.*

She is prey. He is a predator. She will never win. He will devour her and spit her out when she's no longer of use, no longer reflecting his glory. He sees her, and everyone else, as a narcissistic supply to bolster his fragile sense of self. *Run, baby, run.* This is the only thing I can imagine saying to her.

"I don't know, Enid. I haven't thought about it. What do you think?"

Enid stays silent for a bit. "You've been so upset that you haven't even given yourself time to think about it, is that it?"

Ever perceptive—and while those traits can get on my nerves half the time, I miss them now.

"Yeah, and that's not a crime," I defend myself.

"Oh, never said that, babe. Besides, I don't think it's wise for you to seek advice from me."

"Why not? You're a therapist. I'm sure you will give me wonderful advice."

"Yeah, but I don't do therapy for a good friend. I'll give you the advice a friend would give, but I won't tell you what to do. If it were me, I would arrive at the wedding wearing the most scandalous dress and causing a ruckus. Probably even put something in his drink he's deathly allergic to."

"No, I can't do that," I say.

"I told you that you wouldn't like my advice. So, what do you think about my email?"

"Thanks for thinking of me, Enid. It looks like a beautiful opportunity, and I'll most likely accept it, but I need time to think about it first. Okay?"

"Sure, love. And of course, I thought of you. A psychologist who got a marriage proposal is an amazing therapist."

I laugh. "You're never going to let me live that down, are you?"

"No." Enid's airy voice and attitude lift my mood. "Bye, Rose."

"Bye, Enid." I hang up and take a shower before making my way to Jolene's.

Jolene stirs the concoction in the professional grade stainless steel pot. The kitchen smells of something savory—black noodle soup. Obsessed with Korean food, you can predict that her daily menu includes some sort of Korean dish—whether a side or the main entrée. If you know anything about the cuisine, you might imagine an immensity of possibilities. Unfortunately, I know nothing about it.

"Hi, Jolene."

"I don't know if I should call this a delightful surprise," she remarks at my unannounced visit.

"Sometimes, you're a bit too honest," I say, appreciating her consistency. She's so consistent, that I can predict her words before she says them, sometimes.

Jolene looks at me. "You're here because you need advice," she says.

I laugh nervously. "Who's the therapist between us, again? It looks like the career might fit you more."

"Oh, quit it and just ask for what you need."

I swallow. She may not be as friendly as Enid, but she shows up as a friend in her own way. She dishes out the noodles on our plates.

"I bought too many noodles, anyway. Glad you're here, so my food won't go to waste."

"So, you're saying you're using me as a garbage disposal?" I joke.

"Maybe." She shrugs her shoulders and then directs me to eat. "So, what do you want to tell me, girl?"

I take a forkful. "This is yummy."

"Don't let the food distract you from the real problem you came here for."

"Fine, I got a job offer that requires me to move. Go back to LA, you know, the works. I'm here to ask for your advice."

"Wait. You're asking me for that type of advice? You know I can't help you, right?"

"Why not?"

"That's your decision. I can't make it for you. You'll have to live with the consequences of it. You're the one to decide."

"I don't know what to do."

"When you first came into this town, you didn't like it so much. What's changed? Why is there any reason for you to turn down the opportunity? Does this have anything to do with Jahi?"

The one thought I've been avoiding since I heard the news comes back to haunt me full force.

"I… I don't think my connection to him is serious enough for me to turn down this opportunity."

"You don't sound very sure, my dear."

"I… I'm not," I stammer. "I don't know."

"Dear, you must decide."

I'm here at Jolene's for clarity, but I don't receive any. Instead, I'm confused. I eat the rest of my black noodles with a side of uneasiness.

CHAPTER TWELVE

JAHI

Ask her out! Another one of Chrissy's texts appears. *You know you like her!*

I sigh. Chrissy's been harassing me with barrages of texts ever since the family dinner. Matthew doesn't let up on disturbing me, either. He texts and reminds me day and night, whether at work or at home.

As I fight off Chrissy's texts, Matthew approaches me.

"Hey, Jahi," he says, his voice playful.

I slam my hand to my face. I can predict his next words, and I already plan to do the thing people harass me about. Matthew and Jane think being single doesn't suit me and that I need a push, so every time I drop Lily off with them, Jane "gently" reminds me to ask Rose out.

I've mentally planned it all out. Rose will come as usual to teach Lily. After finishing their lessons, I'll take Rose outside to talk and bring up the topic smoothly. Hopefully, her answer will be yes.

"Don't facepalm," Matthew says.

I feel like putting him in a full nelson. "I already know what you're going to say, and God help us all."

"Oh, don't be so dramatic. I'm just trying to be a good friend and give you a nudge, that's all."

"You called me at two o'clock this morning."

He laughs. "Friendly nudging," he reiterates.

I'm on the brink of punching him in the arm. "Well, you

don't have to do that anymore. I plan to ask her out today. Does that make you happy? I hope it does because if it doesn't, I don't know what will."

"It definitely makes me happy, and another advantage is Lily already knows her and kinda likes her, so it'll all be good. No need for an introduction."

"I don't need you to read the advantages and disadvantages. I already thought about it myself."

"Oh. Please. You need me."

I laugh at his delusion. "Leave me alone, okay?"

"Sure, Jahi. But hey, I've told Jane everything, and she's as excited as I am for you two lovebirds."

I shake my head. "You're a parrot."

"One last thing, Jahi. My surfer buddy told me that women are like cars—some are designed for comfort, while others are designed for speed. I know this sounds callous, and it's probably why my surfer buddy is still single. But you've tried speed with Susanne and maybe it's time you try comfort, because it's staring you in the face with Rose."

All day, I pray for quiet with no fire or medical emergencies so I can get home to Lily and Rose. I can't wait to talk to Rose and hold her in my arms and kiss her like I've been wanting to.

When the shift ends, I race out of there as fast as I can, before anyone can call me back. Officially off duty, I make my way home. When I open the door, I see Rose and Lily immersed in a storybook. I pause, watching their radiant faces and listening to their bubbling laughter. Time stretches into slow motion. *This is one of those forever moments I'll never forget.*

"Hey, you look like you're lost in thought. You're back sort of early," Rose comments and breaks me out of my trance. She's wearing a light pink cashmere sweater and black slacks.

"You look pretty," I blurt out. I see the shock on her face. I wish I'd told her all this time how lovely she is.

"Thanks, Jahi. My new sweater is working wonders."

Lily looks up, surprised. "Hi, Daddy!" she says in a treble voice.

"Baby, I'm going to take you to our neighbor's now. I need to talk to your teacher."

Lily grumbles. "I said I would stop playing the game."

I laugh. She thinks I plan to report her to Rose. "I won't tell your teacher you've not been listening to me, don't worry."

She looks at Rose and smiles sheepishly.

I take Lily to our neighbor's house. When I return, I see Rose watching TV.

She knits her brow. "Jahi, are you having problems with Lily? Is it something I can help with?"

"No, I have to tell you something."

"Go on." Her phone beeps. She glances at the screen and smiles. I wonder who is calling. *Another suitor?* My heart sinks.

I should have thought about the fact that other men would be interested in her, even here in Eureka Springs.

"That's my friend, Enid. We worked together as psychologists in Los Angeles."

"Yeah, you've mentioned her," I say. I smile with relief.

"She emailed me out of the blue at three o'clock this morning. I meant to mention it to you when we texted, but I thought I should tell you in person because it's big news."

"Oh." I wonder about the big news.

"Well, a new hospital opened in Los Angeles, and she got employed." She grins and I smile, but I don't know why she thinks it's significant for me to know about Enid getting a job.

"So, Enid..." I nudge her so she'll tell me why I should care about her friend.

"We worked together as therapists at a hospital. She and my ex-husband hated each other. I moved here because of the split, but we promised we would live together in the same city again."

"Oh?" My eyes widen in horror as I realize what she's about to reveal.

"Yeah, so there's a vacancy at the hospital where she works, and she told her boss about me. She thinks I'm perfect for the position."

"Oh, and what did her boss say?"

She laughs. "Well, I don't know the type of persuasion she wields over her boss, but he called and left a message saying the job is mine if I want it. The only issue is I must move back to LA. That's the sad part. I've connected to Lily and my students here so much. Even Jolene."

She waxes on about the things she'll miss about Eureka Springs. I'm not sure how much I hear after that. She vaguely mentions me, but quickly waves it off and says we can text whenever we want.

She falls silent and gazes at me. "Did you hear what I said? Were you listening?" she asks. She looks puzzled. "Oh!" she says after a long silence. "I can't believe my lack of manners. You were about to say something and I just kept going on about this job offer. I couldn't keep it to myself. I apologize."

"No. Don't worry." Sadness and shock washes over me.

"So, what did you want to say?"

"Nothing. Nothing at all."

She frowns in confusion. An awkward silence sets in and I feel as if I'm in a time warp—a sort of anti-gravity pushing me away from her rather than pulling me in.

"I must say goodbye to Lily. I've gotta catch up on *Judge Judy*."

I bid her goodbye, sitting on my couch, staring into the distance.

PART 2

CHAPTER ONE

ROSE

Beatrice.

My sister. I've been so wrapped up in telling Jahi my big news about the LA job offer, it didn't occur to me to mention it to Beatrice. How could I forget her?

She's three years older than me, and we've always been close, except for the years I was married to Lee. Growing up, it surprised people to find out we were sisters. We look nothing alike. Beatrice takes after the Fergusons on Mom's side, with her black eyes, luxurious, shoulder-length auburn hair, olive skin, and five foot seven, athletic build. I look like Dad's mother, Emeline Tate, with my long, silky, strawberry blonde hair, emerald eyes, pale, freckled skin, and slight five foot five frame.

My sister and Mom live together in Fayetteville near the University of Arkansas campus. They wanted me to move in with them when my marriage to Lee fell apart, but the teaching position in Eureka Springs was too good to pass up. It's only an hour away and besides, I loved the idea of hiding out in this small town, a hippie haven in the Ozark Mountains.

I want to tell them about the job offer, and that I'm planning to move back to Los Angeles for a clinical opportunity. More than anything, I want to see them, and now that school is out for the summer, I can have a nice long visit.

Seeing them will make things clearer, I'm sure.

After telling Jahi the news, I expected to feel lighter, like I've gotten something out of the way, but I don't. Instead, I feel like

I'm leaving behind something unfinished. Rather than calling Enid to tell her I'm ready to uproot my life once again, I decide to see my family and talk it over with them.

I'll show up unannounced. I'm sure if I give them a heads up they'll make a fuss about nothing, and I'm not ready for that. Talking to Jolene didn't give me perspective, and deep down I'm a little scared that even seeing my family won't help.

Jolene applauded my decision to visit Mom and Beatrice and wished me luck with her barely there smile. I packed enough clothes for three weeks and set out on Highway 45 South, the winding road to Fayetteville.

It's a town of around 95,000 people—larger and more sophisticated than Eureka Springs, with its population of 2,500 residents. I've only been there a few times. I know the address, though, because even while I was with Lee in LA, my mother constantly bugged me to visit in her extremely long emails. She typed her address in bold, all cap letters at the end of every email, not realizing she was screaming at me.

When I arrive at Mom's house earlier than expected. I sit in my car for a full five minutes. It's a Craftsman bungalow and looks like it's at least 2,000 square feet, much bigger than anything I could afford in LA. My mother splurged when she bought it. It's old but not shabby, with a lemony yellow front door in the middle of a sprawling veranda. My father would hate it for being too cutesy and just-so, but he doesn't get a say. He's long gone.

I was little when he left, only seven-years-old. There's an image that replays in my mind—Daddy's scratchy beard tickled my neck when he hugged me that morning. His eyes had a far-away look, a look I'd never seen before, and he smelled funny. I still can't identify the scent, but it was almost like a combination of almonds and burnt rubber.

"Rosebud," Dad whispered, his eyes watery like a puddle shimmering in the dappled morning light.

It surprised me because it was his nickname for me, a name he hadn't used since I was in nursery school. Getting into his classic white MG, he fixed his inscrutable gaze on me for what seemed like an eternity. Time stretched out as if in slow motion. And then, the world snapped into place like a jig-saw puzzle, and he drove off. Dad always waved when he rounded the corner of our street, but this time he didn't.

I never saw him again.

Finally, I get out of the car. There's a white-cushioned Sunday porch swing with lime green pillows on the broad porch. It's elegant, something Mom would never have given herself in the past. It occurs to me they might not be home.

It was silly to drive here unannounced. I might have to find a hotel. *Did I expect their lives to stand still while I caromed through my life?*

I knock gingerly. No answer. Exhaling, I knock again, louder, but feeling hesitant. Hearing shuffling behind the door, I debate knocking again. The door swings open.

"What the heck…" Beatrice's voice causes a wave of nostalgia to wash over me. My eyes meet my sister's. She pauses before pulling me in for a hug.

"What? I can't… Rose! Holy… Mom is going to lose her mind." She sounds so excited to see me I forget my problems for a moment.

"Great to see you, Beatrice," I say finally. She gives me a look that takes me back to earlier times—that iconic *"Wait… what?"* look that pervaded our teenage years. Most people called her B, like the letter in the alphabet, but I always thought it was weird, so I stuck to Beatrice, or occasionally Bea, which sounds like "Bay." When we were in high school, we quarreled so much over her name because she thought B was much cooler.

"Can't say the same," she teases.

"Where's my mom?" I ask excitedly. Bea is right. Mom is going to lose her mind. We spoke recently, and I didn't know I was coming to Fayetteville, so I didn't mention it to her.

"You just arrived and you're saying, 'my mom'? She's *our* mom." Beatrice's grin is still visible. "We've both missed you, and you look good."

I wink at her. I like how fast we fall into playful banter—like old friends.

"So, where is she?"

Beatrice doesn't need to answer because I know Mom is in the kitchen. She's cooking something savory—the house smells like home. I recognize the fragrance of garlic, onions, cumin, and oregano and know it has to be chili verde, an aroma from childhood.

Beatrice catches me sniffing and laughs. "It's for Mom's book club."

I raise an eyebrow. "Book club? There's a lot I need to catch up on."

Beatrice leads me through the house. In the kitchen, Mom is wearing Beatrice's floral maxi dress with flowing sleeves and mouthing the lyrics to a song playing on her phone. I soak up the image of my mother for a full minute before announcing my presence.

"Mother?" Only one person calls Mom that and it's me. It's a throwback to times when we watched historical dramas before I left for college. She turns so fast I'm scared she'll get whiplash. Her eyes widen when she sees me.

"Rose?" Her voice rises to a high soprano. Her face is ashen, like she's seen a ghost. I want to smile but can't. My throat catches, and my vision blurs as tears fill my eyes. I've missed my mother. I wish I had visited her more often and regret neglecting her over the years.

"In the flesh."

Mother laughs and throws her fleshy arms around me. She squeezes me while I rest my head on her shoulder. She still smells the same—of licorice root, warm bread, and a tiny whiff of rose petal soap she says reminds her of me as a baby. Breathing in her essence floods me with memories.

We hold each other until Mother cries. Tears spill down my cheeks, too. Beatrice joins us when the tears dry. She's stoic and avoids emotional displays. Whenever bad things happen, she sucks it up and moves on. I guess this is what you do when you're the oldest child of a broken home.

We embrace in a group hug. I smile at Mother as she holds my face in her palms like I'm a child and pinches my cheeks, giving me a once over.

"Are you even eating, Rose? You look skinny." And just like that, Mother is back to her normal self. She is past the surprise of my arrival. Now, she's ready to light into me about not eating enough.

"Mom!" Beatrice warns. "She hasn't even brought her stuff inside yet. Give her an hour or two."

My mother raises her hands in mock surrender before going back to cooking. She assures me she has plenty of food.

"What are you making?"

"Chili verde."

"I thought so." I raise two thumbs and Mom smiles. "I need to get my suitcase and unpack. I'm tired from driving the winding road." I emphasize the drive because, knowing my mother, she'll think I'm lazy and trying to avoid work.

"Hey, the drive is only an hour," my mother ribs me.

Beatrice shows me to the guest bedroom. "Is something

wrong?" she asks as soon as she closes the door.

Eventually, Mother is going to come asking, too, and I wonder what I'll tell her. She doesn't leave any stone unturned when interrogating people, especially daughter-type people. I'm going to have to tell them the truth, anyway, because I need a fresh perspective.

"What do you mean by that?" I play dumb, hoping she'll realize what I'm trying to do, be considerate, and leave me alone—but I should know Beatrice better than that.

"Stop playing dumb." There's no malice behind her words, just concern. I love my family, but they know I rely on myself. Even while growing up, I rarely went to Bea or Mother until something was dire and I couldn't handle it on my own. Of course, she figures out something is wrong this time.

"It's a long story." I'm not dismissing her, just trying to get her to understand, and she does. She flashes a smile but tells me I should remember I can't evade her or Mom forever, like I don't know that already. I smile anyway and tell her I love her.

I'm waiting for my chili verde. That dish reminds me of a trip through New Mexico, where we stopped for spicy chile verde wrapped in warm, supple homemade tortillas on our way to Arkansas. Nostalgia overtakes me and I feel sad about staying away for such a long time.

CHAPTER TWO

JAHI

As I climb into the fire truck, I try to push Matt's words out of my mind. I don't want to think about Rose. I miss her terribly.

It's the worst timing imaginable. Just when I realize I've started developing feelings for her, she leaves her job and takes off to see her family. She says she's planning to move to Los Angeles after the trip, and I don't know if I'll ever see her again. I regret not telling her how I felt about her when I had the chance.

I slam the truck's door, trying to clear my mind. I need to focus on the task at hand—dealing with my daily duties at work and being ready to respond to emergencies.

One guy at the station whose dad is a surgeon said being a firefighter is like being an anesthesiologist with hours of boredom punctuated by moments of terror. And sometimes people die despite your best efforts. Cleaning, checking equipment, and recharging batteries can have a soothing effect. The training sessions, cardio workouts, and weightlifting are a side benefit to the job with the added benefit of generating a prodigious appetite.

I'm not fond of the paperwork and business inspections, but it's all part of the territory of being a firefighter. Eighty percent of the work is monotonous, but boy, this gives us a respite from the sheer horror of accident scenes, fires, and swift water rescues.

A call comes in from the dispatcher, about a fifty-five-year-old man with sudden severe chest and upper back pain. Most likely it's a heart attack. As we drive to the location of the emergency, my mind wanders. I think about Lily and how much she suffered when her mom Susanne disappeared. How could she have abandoned her daughter?

I think about Rose. She's a devoted teacher, and Lily loves her. Is she going to leave us? The waterfall of their laughter when they're together at the house fills my heart, but now feels bittersweet. It's hard to imagine our life without Rose. I feel the emptiness already, like the void I felt when Dad died. Lily's life will be affected by another loss of a mother figure. It's not just Lily's life that will be affected. I realize just how much Rose's presence means to me, too.

Matt interrupts my thoughts. "You know, I think I can hear your heart thumping."

I give Matt a stern look. "I said I don't want to talk about it, Matt."

"Okay, okay," he says, raising his monster-sized hands in surrender. "I'm just saying it's okay to admit that you miss her. It's normal, man."

I sigh. "I know it's normal. Of course, I miss her. She's a significant part of our lives. But I don't want to think about it."

"Alright," Matt shrugs his shoulders. "I get it. But you know, sometimes it helps to talk about things."

I nod, not wanting to argue any further. We arrive at the location of the emergency and jump into action. When I eyeball the man, I know he's in trouble. He's prostrate on his bed, short of breath, sweating profusely, and moaning in pain. His pulse is weak on the left wrist but stronger on the right.

"My back… ripping pain," he gasps in a barely audible voice and moans.

"We've got you," I say, trying to comfort him as I quickly start an IV. Every second counts, so I've got to act fast. I listen to his heart and lungs and examine his abdomen.

While pressing his abdomen and checking his aorta, I'm surprised to discover a throbbing mass measuring about eight centimeters across. In disbelief, I check again and sure enough, his aorta is too wide. This is an ominous sign. It must be an aortic aneurysm, and it might be dissecting. It's a deadly situation where blood creates a new channel, and the aorta could rupture. If this happens, there's not much to be done. I use the portable ultrasound to check and sure enough, it confirms my suspicions.

"Matt, call Washington Regional ER and tell them we've got an eight-centimeter aortic aneurysm in an unstable patient and it might be an aortic dissection. We need a helicopter. Get a hold of the vascular surgeon on call," I say, my voice shaking. Matt is on the phone in seconds.

"They're prepping the OR, calling in the team. The helicopter is already on its way," he says a few moments later.

We stabilize the man with fluids and pray his situation is salvageable… that we've gotten to him in time. My heart pounds as we wait. The patient looks younger than his age, with a tall, athletic build and broad shoulders like a swimmer's, maybe someone who swims the butterfly. He's a strapping man, sort of like how Dad looked when he died. These cardiac cases shake me up for days. I dread having a patient die on me.

The helicopter arrives in a wash of dust. Paramedics lift him onto a gurney, and they disappear into the sky. When the man arrives at Washington Regional in Fayetteville, they rush him to the OR. If all goes well, he'll have a second chance at life. We clean up the scene and sit in the truck for a bit, silent, dehydrated, gulping water, and processing what just happened. As we drive back to the fire station, drained from the drama and the adrenaline rush, I'm lost in thought, missing Rose, and regretting my decisions even more.

Matt senses my mood. "Hey man, you did a great job of

diagnosing him. They've got him in the OR repairing it. He's likely to survive."

I force a smile. "Thanks, Matt. I appreciate it."

He pauses and then continues, "You know, you can always tell me whatever's on your mind. I'm here for you."

I hesitate before finally giving in. "It's just… Rose. I miss her so much, and I regret not telling her how I feel. I don't know if I'll ever get the chance to see her again."

Matt nods in understanding. "I get it. But you never know what the future holds. Maybe one day you'll have the chance to tell her how you feel. And if not, at least you'll have closure that you tried."

I nod, feeling a slight sense of relief. "Thanks, Matt. I really appreciate it."

We arrive back at the station, and I go straight to my locker to change out of my uniform. I check my phone and see a missed call from Lily's school. I call them back, and I'm told Lily has fallen and injured her wrist. What rotten luck only three days before summer vacation!

I rush to Lily's school and find her in the nurse's office, crying. I kneel beside her and hug her tightly. "It's okay, baby. Daddy's here. Let's get you to the hospital."

As we drive to Eureka Springs Hospital, guilt washes over me. Lily needs me, while thoughts of Rose have preoccupied my mind. I promise myself to focus on Lily and her needs from now on.

At the hospital, we see an orthopedic surgeon who confirms that Lily has fractured her wrist. "It's a torus. That's a buckle fracture of the distal radius," he says.

I nod. He talks to me like a colleague because he knows I'm a paramedic. I've seen a lot of wrist fractures in kids, but I don't know all the terminology, one more reminder of my regret over not going to medical school.

"It's one of the most common fractures we see in children. It's when a child falls and tries to catch herself and ends up breaking her wrist," he continues. He puts a short plaster cast on Lily's wrist, and turns to her with fatherly concern. "You'll have the cast on for six weeks, and we'll get an X-ray in two weeks. Take it easy, young lady." He pats Lily's shoulder as she nods.

"What about physical therapy?" I ask.

"Yes, she'll need six weeks of PT to strengthen her wrist, but it shouldn't be too arduous. I wouldn't recommend lots of running or ball sports this summer, but something like swimming is ok after the cast is off."

Lily remains upbeat despite the dent in her summer plans of playing with neighborhood kids. She's excited about the prospect of learning to swim properly instead of just paddling around. As we leave the hospital, I think of how Rose would have handled the situation. She's always been good with Lily and knows how to calm her down. I want to call and ask for her advice, but I know it's too late. She's gone.

The rest of the day is a blur. I take care of Lily and try my best to keep my thoughts under control. Matt checks on me a few times, but I don't want to talk about my feelings. I just want to go home and sleep.

As I get into bed that night, my day feels incomplete and I wonder why. I saved a man's life and got Lily's wrist fracture taken care of in the ER. It's been a full day, so why do I feel empty? As I close my eyes, I think of Lily and how much she needs me. I promise myself to focus on her and try my best to be the parent Rose would be proud of.

The next morning, I wake up to Lily's giggles. She sits right on my chest in bed. For someone with a cast, she's pretty active. I smile, feeling grateful for her love. She reminds me of all the good things in life.

As we sit down to eat, I notice the empty seat at the table. It's so quiet without the bursts of laughter and animated banter between Lily and Rose—a joyous, jazzy rhythm like popcorn popping.

I finish my pancakes and hug Lily. "I love you so much."

She smiles. "I love you too, Daddy. Are you feeling better now?"

I nod, feeling content. "Yes, I am. And you know what? Daddy's going to make sure we have the best life possible. We're going to make the most of every day and enjoy every moment."

Lily beams. Perhaps she doesn't know why I'm going on like this. She's just a little kid and here I am being over the top, all philosophical and existential, when all Lily really needs is a hug. Rose's absence is making me lose my mind. I've only known her a short while, and we even got off on the wrong foot, but now it seems she holds the key to my heart.

I hug Lily tightly and feel determination swirl through my mind. I know it won't be easy letting Rose go, but I'm ready to face the challenges of raising my daughter without her help... and love.

As I head to work, I feel a newfound purpose. I'm a father, a firefighter, and a friend. I'm also someone who misses Rose. But I know I must move forward and create a life she would be proud of.

I arrive at the station and see Matt doing pull-ups. He's constantly working out, something I need to do before I get terminal dad bod with sad love handles, worse without someone to love them or handle them. Or, as my dad called them, "flying buttresses." Dad said they looked good on medieval cathedrals, less so on middle-aged men. Matt doesn't say a word about Rose, but I know he understands.

I inventory and re-supply the medical bags and truck. Matt

has already checked the fluid levels of the motors. I test batteries, making sure the thermal imaging cameras which help us detect heat, see through smoke, and look for victims are ready to go. Then I start the daily mopping and disinfecting bathrooms. Call me strange, but sometimes this mindless stuff is therapeutic. At this moment, the Zen monks have nothing on me.

We head to the grocery store to get provisions for the shift. Today it's my turn to cook an early dinner for the squadron. I'm going to make my famous Firehouse Chili with buttermilk biscuits and a mixed green salad. Maybe even brownies for dessert, the dark chocolate ones with the crinkly tops and luscious middles and a hint of orange… the kind Rose gave to Lily and me. I sigh.

As we drive off, I think of Rose again. But this time, I feel lighter. I know no matter what happens in the future, I will always cherish my memories of her. I'm ready to face the challenges that come my way and embrace life's predicaments.

By the end of the day, I'm emotionally exhausted. Yesterday's emergency with the guy with the aortic dissection wiped me out. He reminded me of Dad. I can't get the memory of that terrible moment when Dad collapsed out of my head. It haunts me and makes me hold my breath when I deal with cardiac patients.

Dad suffered a massive pulmonary embolism, a saddle embolus which is the worst kind. He didn't stand a chance. That clot hung like a saddle over the intersection of his main pulmonary arteries. It slid to one side and closed off one of those arteries. The thing that killed him wasn't his lungs, it was his heart, the failure of his right ventricle, a low-pressure system suddenly faced with a high-pressure, clotted-off lung. When I see heart patients, I worry. *Will they die on me like Dad?*

Near the end of the shift, Matt and I complete our paperwork and debrief. A call comes in and Matt hands it to me.

"Hey Jahi, it's Dr. Hanson. I just want to let you know our man survived."

"Whoa. Thank goodness."

"Yeah, it was dissecting as we went in. In a few more minutes, it would have ruptured, and he would have been dead. We got it just in time. Opened him up. Clamped it and grafted it and we closed. Got him stabilized. He's in the Cardiac ICU. He's gonna be fine."

"Whew. That's such a relief. Thank you for letting me know."

"Hey, thank *you* for saving this man's life. He'd be dead if it were any other paramedic who showed up. It's impressive you knew to evaluate for an aortic aneurysm. It's notoriously missed in the ER. So, thanks again. By the way, his wife asked who saved him, and I told her about you. She wants you to know how grateful she is. Who knows? Maybe they'll visit you in groovy Eureka Springs sometime," he laughs.

"Yeah, that would be great. Thanks Dr. Hanson. I appreciate your kind words. Means the world to me."

After I hang up, I see Matt watching me. He pats me on the back. "Good job, Jahi. You're one hell of a paramedic. You could have been a doctor. I'm still thinking about yesterday and how you figured out what was wrong with that man."

"Thanks, Matt. I appreciate it," I say with a tight smile, regretting failing organic chemistry and never becoming a doctor.

Driving home, I think of Lily and how much she needs me. I text Jolene to make sure she's waiting with Lily at the doorstep. Jolene shoots back a text showing her grumpy nature, but I don't fault her for it. She's one of the few trustworthy people I've ever met, and for that, grumpiness is a small price to pay.

CHAPTER THREE

ROSE

I can't avoid Mom and Beatrice for long.

On the third day, Mom looks at my bare feet and says, "Your toenails look awful. Let me paint them."

"What are you talking about? They look fine," I say in an irritated voice. I know it's not about my toenails. They're coated in white varnish with no chips, but my mother won't stop until she gets what she wants and neither will Beatrice, so I humor them.

Mom selects a hot pink nail color which would have thrilled the six-year-old me but is definitely not my style at thirty-seven—but Mom insists. Beatrice follows us around like a fly stalking a horse.

At the dining table, my sister watches. "Look, if Mom won't talk, I will. I'm tired of you moping around."

My eyes narrow in confusion. I want to argue and insist that it's not true, but I don't want to prolong the matter. It's true that I'm glued to my phone half the time, hoping Jahi will text first, because I don't know what to say to him.

Staring at Mom and Beatrice, I inhale a deep breath, trying to find the right words to explain why I'm in Fayetteville.

"Okay," I start slowly, "I came here to get a fresh perspective on things." I watch as their expressions change from confusion to interest. "See, I got a big offer in Los Angeles in a hospital-based clinical psych practice, and I figured I could use this time to reflect on my future. I loved being a therapist, and I miss it. It's been a dream for me to help people psychologically."

My mother leans forward, her eyes narrowing. "Rose, that's wonderful news and I love having you here, but why on earth would you need to come to Fayetteville to reflect on your career?"

I swallow hard, feeling nervous as I realize the real reason I need to be in Fayetteville.

"Mother," I say. "There's more to it than a job offer. I met someone. A man in Eureka Springs. He's the father of Lily, one of the first graders I taught. His name is Jahi, and he's struggled and gone through a lot. He's a single dad because his wife ran off, and he's doing his best to provide for his daughter, but he's clearly overwhelmed."

Beatrice nudges me, her eyes looking worried. "Rose, what are you saying? You came to Fayetteville because of a man?"

I shake my head, trying to clear my thoughts. "No, no, it's not like that. I came here to get distance from my life and reflect on my future. But meeting Jahi and Lily makes me realize I care about helping others."

My mother sighs heavily, as if trying to understand what I'm saying. "Rose, I love seeing you, but I still don't understand why you couldn't have just taken a break in Eureka Springs."

I need to share my reasons for coming to Fayetteville, even though I haven't fully processed them. "Something just felt off about my life in Eureka Springs, and I needed to get away to figure it out. Jahi and Lily are an unexpected part of that journey. And besides, being with both of you gives me peace."

Beatrice smiles and nudges me playfully. "I get it, sis. Sometimes we need a new place, new people, and new experiences to help us see things clearly. We just want to know more about Jahi and Lily."

I nod, relieved my sister understands. "Well, Jahi is a single father, and he's struggling to balance work and taking care of Lily. He's a firefighter and paramedic and he's trying to give his daughter a good life, even though her mother disappeared without a word when she was a toddler. He's also dealing with some other personal issues he hasn't shared with me yet, but it's clear he's going through a tough time."

Mom and Beatrice exchange looks. I know this is brittle territory mentioning a parent who disappears. Mom's voice wavers. "That sounds like a lot to handle. I hope he has someone to turn to for support."

"He does, but he also needs professional help. That's why I'm staying for a while, to see if there is anything I can do to help him and Lily."

Beatrice furrows her brow. "But Rose, don't forget about your own life and goals. It's okay to help others, but you can't forget about yourself."

I smile at her, grateful for her concern. "Thanks, Bea. You've always had my back. I haven't forgotten about myself, but I believe helping others is a big part of who I am."

My mother gets up from her chair. "Rose, we support you no matter what you decide to do. You're smart and strong and beautiful, and we're proud of you."

A lump forms in my throat. "Thank you, Mom."

We sit in silence for a few minutes. The crick in my neck releases and my shoulders drop. It feels good to share my thoughts with my family, even though I'm still confused about my future.

As we sit together, I think about Jahi and Lily, wondering what they're doing. I realize that while I came to Fayetteville to reflect on my life, meeting them gives me a feeling of possibility. But as much as I want to help them, I know I need to figure out my path first. I can't ignore my dreams and goals for the sake of others, no matter how much I care about them. I've made that mistake before, with Lee.

"Thanks, Mom and Bea," I say as I stand. "I'm going to head

out now and clear my head. I'll be back soon."

Bea hugs me tightly. "Take care, Rose. We love you."

Walking out into the cool evening air, I feel hopeful. I still have a long way to go, but I've got the support of my family, and I'm confident I'll find my way. Wandering along Dickson Street near the university, I climb the stairs towards Old Main, the original stone building on the campus from the 1880s.

I see alumni names stamped into one of a network of sidewalks radiating from the iconic building, covered with more than a century of names. After many decades of rain, snow, and scuffling feet, some of them have eroded and are hardly legible. Decay has not yet blurred or erased the names of recent alumni. It makes me think about life's brevity and how quickly one's youth disappears. The other day, I was a freshman at UCLA, almost twenty years ago now, and I don't think they have my name stamped anywhere for posterity, maybe just a few zeroes and ones in a computer somewhere.

Where did those years go? They dissipated like morning fog. I wasted them on a self-absorbed man-boy and now what do I have to show for it? A whole lotta nothing. I know Papa, my mother's father Aaron Ferguson, said that when you're reckoning the pluses and minuses of your life, you also have to count the train wrecks avoided, but that provides precious little comfort right now. It feels more like the train of conjugal bliss has left the station.

One day I'll be sixty-two and looking back, remembering that beautiful man and his beautiful child in Eureka Springs. But he'll be sixty-five and married to someone else and Lily will be thirty-two, almost my age now.

Will she be happy? Will I miss seeing her grow up and call me Mom, or Stepmom?

My buzzing phone jolts me out of my reverie.

It's Jahi texting, "Hey, how are you doing?"

My heart throbs in my chest.

"Just hanging out at the university."

We text back and forth a few times, but I feel a little let down. Our messages are cryptic and awkward. I don't want them to be that way, but I can't break out of it, like some weird jinx where everything comes out wrong.

I end the string of texts with, "I'll visit you and Lily soon." *But will I?* What if I get the position in LA and need to hurry there? Will I have to leave without saying goodbye?

That night, sipping hot chamomile tea on Mom's porch, I look up at the constellations. As a child, I studied the night sky and asked the universe to find Dad. I wondered if he was looking up at the same stars. Here I am, decades later, still searching for answers. I don't know where Dad is and I don't know what to do about Jahi. But at this moment, I'm at peace. I don't feel like a failure who can't decide what to do with her life. Headphones in place, I listen to my favorite opera playlist. Beatrice joins me with a cup of her own.

We sit in silence. I love how we don't need to say a word, and it feels totally natural. No self-consciousness.

"Did I ever tell you about Mom and the plumber?" Beatrice breaks the silence.

"No. What did I miss out on when I was in LA?"

"A few years ago, we called a plumber to fix the leaking shower. He stayed a few hours, bantering and flirting with Mom."

"Did Mom like him?"

"Yes, she did. He was cute. Mom went out on a few dates with him. She told me he took her out to dinner at The Venesian Inn in Tontitown."

"Whoa. Tontitown is miles away. That sounds suspicious."

"You're good, Sis. My thoughts exactly. Mom seemed oblivious, so I pointed it out."

"What happened?"

"It went downhill. Mom asked around and discovered from her hair stylist that he had a wife and two kids! After that, she called him an old fool and decided men weren't worth the trouble."

"Poor Mom. She's had bad luck with men. But then, so have I. Maybe it's in our blood." I shake my head and decide to focus on the present. "Let's talk about you. Tell me about your life in Fayetteville."

"I work at Cheers at the Old Post Office on the Square, waiting tables. I like it… especially because of a cute guy my age, Andrew, who comes in regularly." Beatrice's face turns scarlet at the mention of Andrew. She looks radiant, and it delights me to see her excited about someone after years of being single.

"That's great! I bet he's in love with you," I tease, as my sister looks sheepish. "How long have you had the job?"

"Two years already. It's gone by fast."

"I'm happy for you. I love you, B."

She grins at me. She loves it when I call her B. "I love you, too. What do you think? Spa day next?"

"There's a spa in town?" I joke.

My sister shakes her head and nudges me playfully. "You're silly."

We laugh like we did when we were in elementary school.

CHAPTER FOUR

JAHI

It's been a long week at the station, and I need to blow off steam. So, when Matt asks me to join him for a drink, I say yes. I drop Lily off at Jolene's, who meets us with a slight smile. Lily bounds out of the car, clutching her bag of toys and crayons and who knows what else and waving goodbye. Jolene assures me she and Lily will have tons of fun. Jolene is likely to entertain Lily by reading a book on botany or watching educational programs while eating steamed broccoli and sitting up straight.

Matt and I head to one of our haunts—Missy's White Rabbit Lounge, a local bar minutes from the fire station. We sit on the outdoor patio overlooking the town and order drinks. Matt has a gin and tonic and I order a pint of German lager, crisp and cold and malty.

As we nurse our drinks, Matt's forehead wrinkles.

"What's up, Matt? You look worried."

Matt exhales as he runs his hands through his blonde mop of hair. "It's Jane. She nags me constantly. She won't leave me alone or let me do anything by myself. It's getting to me," he confides.

I consider his words. Matt's a surfer dude. He's spent years as a single man surfing waves in southern California. He's rather boyish. Maybe he isn't that great at being a husband. I listen sympathetically but can't help thinking maybe Jane has a point and is just looking out for him.

"Maybe she just needs attention," I offer.

"Yeah. I'm gone a lot, that's for sure, with work and then

fishing any chance I get."

"I know you need to fish to decompress from the stress of being a firefighter, but you need to think about your wife, too. She's the best fish you'll ever catch."

"You're right, Jahi." Matt laughs, but then looks pensive and turns to me. "That's enough about me. What about you?"

"I've definitely got troubles of my own. When I texted Rose to check in, it was awkward. The texts were short, and I couldn't decipher her tone. She acts like she's doing just fine, which bothers me. It makes me think I'm trapped in the friend zone."

Matt listens with a sympathetic ear and offers advice. "Maybe there's a reason for this, some grand design in the universe. Maybe it's just meant to be this way. Who knows?"

"Yeah," I say, downcast.

"Focus on spending time with Lily. After all, she's the most important person in your life," he suggests.

I nod. As darkness envelops us, we turn to lighter topics, reminiscing about old times and sharing funny stories. Being with Matt lifts my mood, but there's a chill in the air and I know it's time to head home. I've got to pick up Lily and get her ready for bed.

I say goodbye to Matt and head to my car. As I drive to Jolene's, I can't shake the feeling of missing Rose. But Matt's words ring true, and my focus turns back to Lily. She's the most important person in my life, and I need to make sure she is happy and taken care of. When I arrive, Jolene greets me with a smile and leads me to her living room where Lily is laying on the floor coloring in a book about dinosaurs. She looks up, her eyes sparkling with excitement.

"Daddy!" she exclaims, bounding into me with a big hug.

I lift her up and we chat about her school day, what she learned, and all the details of the activities and squabbles. As we drive home, Lily chattering away, I realize Matt is right. Lily is more important to me than anyone or anything.

We get home and I help Lily prepare for bed. Since Rose left, she's been clingy at night and having trouble falling asleep. Some nights she awakens from nightmares about monsters, tiptoes into my room, and lays down on the twin bed in the corner. In the morning, I wake up to find her there. I don't say a word about it. It's like the times when she wets her bed, which increased after her mother left and still lingers. I strip the sheets and remake the bed as if nothing happened.

Lately, she's been requesting I read her old favorite, *Goodnight Moon,* night after night. It's a book from babyhood, the same book I read to her when Susanne left.

As I tuck her in, she asks, "Daddy, can we get ice cream tomorrow?"

I nod. I'll do anything to take away her heartbreak, both when her mother left and now that Rose is gone—anything to make her happy.

"Of course, Lily," I say, kissing her forehead. "Anything for my little girl."

As I head to my bedroom after Lily dozes off, I think about Rose. But this time, I don't feel as sad or desperate to reach out to her. I realize I have something more important right in front of me—my daughter. As I fall asleep, I'm grateful for Matt's words. I need to focus on the present and not dwell on the past or worry about the future. I've got my daughter, my job, and my health. This is enough.

Over the next few weeks, Lily and I go on expeditions, splashing around at Lake Leatherwood with her wrist cast wrapped in a plastic bag, exploring Onyx Cave Park, and watching big cats at Turpentine Creek Wildlife Refuge. We even indulge in the Crescent Hotel's Ghost Tour, a slightly hokey tourist attraction most Eureka Springs natives never experience. It's a balm for my soul to build memories with my daughter. And with each passing day, Rose's memory fades a little more.

One morning at the station, I get a call from an unknown number.

"Hello?"

"Hi Jahi. It's me. Rose." Rose's voice sounds strange, not like her at all, sort of hollowed out, as if in an echo chamber.

My heart pounds so loudly I wonder if she hears it. I want to keep her on the call, but I don't know what to say. We talk for a bit, catching up on each other's lives, but it feels like chit chat, superficial and stilted. On the one hand, I'm relieved to hear her voice and know she's okay, but things aren't the same. I feel distant, not as attached as before. I wonder if she notices.

After we hang up, I feel lighter. Sometimes people come into our lives for what seems like a moment and then they're gone. It's essential to appreciate them while they're here. But the most important relationships are constant.

In the end, the night out with Matt helps me realize what matters. It's not about chasing after people who have moved on or worrying about the future. It's about finding joy in the present and appreciating the people who are here for us. And that's exactly what I plan to do—be here for Lily and make the most of every moment with her. I want to savor these fleeting moments of her childhood.

When Lily goes on a playdate with Matt's kids a few days later, I feel a stab of envy. I yearn for a family like his. *Should I text Rose again?* I want to, but I worry it might disturb her. Instead, I go home and tend my roses, and it makes me miss her even more.

She's just as beautiful and tender as my flowers. Whenever I look at my roses, I see her radiant face. She's the real deal and I regret not telling her how I felt about her that last day we were together.

Maybe she wouldn't have responded the way I wanted. There's an eighty-percent chance she wouldn't. Maybe everything she was doing was simply because she was nice and not because she liked me. And really, what's there to like? Lily's mother decided I wasn't lovable and seemed surprised she put up with me so many years.

I try to stop myself from thinking about it, but I can't. I accept the fact that Rose affected me that much, not just me, but Lily, too. She's simply like that… a whirlwind, an energy so warm, so embracing and beautiful that her absence stings my heart. Does she feel my absence, too? It's doubtful. Maybe she thought I was boring and was ready to move on. Besides, I couldn't compete with her ex, the doctor.

I tap my phone screen, prepared to text her, but I freeze. *What if she doesn't want me texting her?* I keep thinking about it, riddled with doubt. *Does she miss Lily as much as Lily misses her?*

Sometimes, during dinner, Lily mentions how much she misses Rose being her teacher. When I help Lily with her summer school assignments, she stiffens as hard as an oak plank. She frowns, sticks out her lower lip, stamps her feet, and demands to see Rose. I don't know what to say when she asks about her and why she left.

Sometimes, I say, "I think Rose has family business to tend to."

Nothing I say appeases my daughter.

Like a playlist on endless repeat, Lily insists, "I want Rose. Why isn't she here?"

If I didn't already like Rose, I swear I would be jealous of this woman who engenders so much love and admiration from my daughter. Rose has a gift of entering your life and taking her place in it. I admire and respect her. We settled into each other's lives so fast with a kind of ease and flow when she'd only just started teaching Lily.

Lily and I absorbed Rose into our little family like cream to coffee. She was part of us, and we looked forward to seeing her. I liked her fresh perspective on things and the way her eyes sparkled when she talked about her students. I respected her opinions on books and got goosebumps whenever I saw her name pop up on my screen.

If I wasn't a grown man, I'd say I'm nursing a crush—but that's so seventh grade. I'm a forty-year-old father to a seven-year-old daughter. I can't call it a crush, but it feels tender like first love, like my heart quickening for the first time, and I feel vulnerable. She holds so much power over me, and I don't like how that makes me feel.

Why can't I just text her and tell her I miss her and see what happens? How did I become such an emotional wimp?

I compose a message, but stop and fling my phone to the side. What the hell am I doing? I don't want to appear clingy. When I was with Susanne, I called or texted whenever I felt worried, even though she expressed displeasure about this countless times. I was trying to make sure she and Lily were safe. Susanne ignored me. Sometimes, when I recount the incidents, I can't believe how oblivious I was. I could whack myself upside the head to change what happened, but it's too late. No matter what I did, it always ended in the one thing I had no power over—Lily being motherless.

What will I do when my daughter gets her period? I suppose I have my mother and sister for that. For a while after Susanne left, I considered sending Lily to live with Mom so she'd have a mother figure while I lived out the rest of my life in solitude.

When Matt heard about my idea of living alone, I remember him saying, "Stop acting stupid and pathetic, Jahi."

Now that I think about it, he was right. Thankfully, my family and friends didn't give up on me despite how weirdly I acted during that time. It shook me terribly, but I got back on my feet.

CHAPTER FIVE

ROSE

I inhale the delicate lavender scent with its soft, powdery notes. The hot water in the hydrotherapy tub at The Bodhi Tree Spa envelops me. My mother and sister are the two most important women in my life, and I need a day to slow down and spend time with them.

As we relax in our lounge chairs and enjoy fruit-infused water, Beatrice expresses her excitement about her new relationship with Andrew Marshall. My mother, meanwhile, shares stories from her youth I've never heard before.

I simply listen, content to bask in the warmth of their company. Being together like this—just the three of us—is a rare treat.

We head to the sauna, and my mind drifts back to a pivotal, heartbreaking moment in childhood. Our father left when I was only seven and Beatrice was ten. It was tough for my mother to raise two young daughters on her own, but she did it with grace and resilience. I was young, but blamed myself for my father's absence. I must have done something wrong. My little mind convinced me it was my fault. I thought my father was a hero, not the lunatic who left his family, disappearing without a word. I had faith in my father then—faith that he would return. At least, way more faith than I have now.

I look at Mom and feel grateful for her sacrifices to keep us going. Our childhood was challenging, but Mom was our rock, creating a stable home no matter what. And now, as we unwind at the spa, I realize just how much we flourished under her care.

She would have been a great therapist—a natural.

Steam billows out as we open the door of the sauna. We step into the eucalyptus-infused space, and I cough reflexively from the pungent oils as hot air hits my unprepared lungs. My chest tightens, and it takes a while to breathe easily. It's like being in a cloud. Indistinct human forms mysteriously emerge and disappear.

"Wow, that caught me by surprise. Let's go to the infrared sauna next—the salt cave sauna. Hot and dry is easier for me than steam."

"Ok," Beatrice leans over and whispers.

Who knew there would be a time when we'd have access to this kind of luxury?

My father left us in abject poverty, at least compared to before. Coloring every scrap piece of paper, I was a kid who wanted a box of sixty-four crayons, not just eight. I yearned for the Barbie Pink Collection with the dazzling hot pink ball gown, long white gloves, dangling rhinestone earrings, and glittery high heels. I wanted what other kids had, but Mom could only afford second-hand toys and clothing, crumbled crayons, and dolls from Goodwill or garage sales. I shiver, remembering my childhood after Dad left. It was terrible, but Mother made it survivable.

"So, Beatrice," I start in a singsong manner. Beatrice doesn't like my new tone of voice and throws me a suspicious glare.

"I don't like where this is going," Beatrice snorts.

Mother is already leaning into me with a conspiratory look in her eyes. She always wants to be in on the fun when we gang up on the other person. She lives for it, and these are some precious memories.

"Andrew, oh Andrew," I whisper dramatically, placing the back of my hand on my brow like a Victorian era fainting figure and my mother giggles. She gets it instantly. She's the best person to conspire with.

Bea glares. "Mom!" Beatrice warns, her brows knitting together in frustration. "Even if this girl is choosing to be childish, does that mean you have to do it too?"

My mother and I cackle like witches. Beatrice makes a phony freaked out face while we gently nudge her to tell us more about Andrew.

"We actually have a date later this week," she concedes.

"What the heck?" I whack my sister playfully on the shoulder. "We spoke two days ago about him and you're just telling me this now?"

"What else I gotta tell you about? My bowel movements?"

This is what I miss about my sister—the banter. I adjust the towel on my head and give her a cheeky smile. "Just admit you're excited about this, or are you not?" My sister's lips pull up into one of her quirky smiles. The one I love. "Keep smiling like this at Andrew, and I guarantee the date will never end."

Beatrice blushes. My mother shakes her head and grins.

"I don't need to hear this," she starts to say, but I'm in bliss, enjoying the infrared sauna and humming to myself. "Stop that." My sister scolds, but I enjoy annoying her, so she changes tactics. "Maybe when we get our massage, the masseuse will be cute. Flirt with him, Rose." Beatrice raises her eyebrows as she turns the focus on me.

The thought of flirting stops me cold. It's strange. I feel oddly loyal to Jahi even though we're only friends. If I tell Beatrice of my loyalty to someone when we haven't yet defined our relationship, she's going to wag her finger. I laugh to myself. I won't say anything about it. I don't want to face her scorn.

"I've got an idea. Let's go to Hugo's for dinner," Beatrice suggests.

Mom kicks up a fuss. "Why should we go out to eat when we can eat at home?"

My mother never likes the idea of eating out at restaurants. Growing up, money was in short supply and she took us out to eat only if there was no other option. Mom would rather toil away in the kitchen cooking a meal from scratch with just a few ingredients. I suppose her upbringing in the South shaped her this way. But Bea and I have been fantasizing about a Hugo's hamburger for days now, and we will not be put off. And it's not like this is a French-server-and-starched-white-tablecloth kind of place. It's a college town neon-lit basement dive, full of exuberant students and gales of laughter, punctuated by high fives.

Beatrice and I don't question it. We know Mom's issues with spending money. She was in over her head raising two girls on a shoestring budget, but as we get older, we eat out as much as possible when Mom's not around. Subconsciously, my sister and I are making up for lost time and all the things it deprived us of growing up. *How much of human behavior is making up for stuff you feel you missed out on?*

"It's been a relaxing spa day, Mom. I don't want you cooking in the hot kitchen, getting your neck worked up into knots," Beatrice says and flashes a look, signaling me to back her up.

Winking obnoxiously at my sister, I say, "Mom, listen to B. She knows what she's saying. We won't spend much if that's what you're worried about. We won't order any drinks, appetizers, or desserts—just the main dish, no sides." My mother glares at me and whacks Beatrice upside the head, meaning to be playful in her annoyance.

"Ouch. Why don't you do that to Rose, too? Why only me? Is it because she's the baby of the family? Are you trying to show us you have a favorite? Just for that, we're going to order fries."

My mother raises a brow at my sister, and they exchange a look I can't decipher, but Mom then throws a stern look at me.

"I don't have a favorite, you know that," Mom insists.

"Mom, we're grown-ups and we're going out to dinner," I say to distract Mom, uncomfortable with favoritism.

I want to explain the situation to my family, but fear they'll shut me down the moment they realize I'm psychologizing them. They hate it when I do that, but I know the reason in my head.

When Dad left and we had to manage our financial situation alone, eating out was a luxury. Now, we're okay financially, but Mom still feels the need to manage everything because she's used to living like the sky is falling.

It's like our grandparents suffering through the Great Depression as children. For the rest of their lives, they feared ruin. It didn't matter that their lives turned around and they had plenty of money in later years. They collected scratch pads, gift wrap, foil, and twist ties from bread loaf bags. They repurposed gunny sacks into dresses, curtains, underwear, and quilts. In case history repeated itself, they kept everything and threw nothing away. They'd known poverty on a visceral level and lived with empty stomachs and shattered dreams of attending college. Scrimping and saving money, they denied themselves the simplest luxuries—weekend getaways, a singular splurge at Christmastime, an occasional fine meal at a restaurant.

Mom comes around. We convince her we should celebrate our reunion by eating out. I wonder how she feels about our spa day. We blew a lot of money on it.

When Mom is out of earshot, I ask Beatrice, "What does Mom know about how much money we spent today?"

"She thinks we used a gift card," Bea raises her eyebrows, shaking her head.

I erupt in laughter, so much so that my belly aches for ten minutes.

Bless her heart, Mother will never change.

CHAPTER SIX

JAHI

As I pull into the driveway of my childhood home, I'm overcome with nostalgia. It's been a month since our last family dinner, and I'm looking forward to catching up with my sister Chrissy and her husband Lucas Sanders. But more than anything, I'm excited to see my mom and watch her bond with Lily.

Walking in the door, I hear uproarious laughter echoing from the kitchen. Chrissy and Lucas are chatting with Mom and preparing dinner. Lily runs to them, her eyes lit up with excitement.

"Uncle Luke! Aunt Chrissy!" she exclaims, throwing her arms around their legs.

They greet her with smiles and hugs, and my heart swells.

During dinner, my sister and Lucas talk about their trip to Scotland. I admire their long-term relationship and hope they have resolved their tension about having kids.

Chrissy hasn't mentioned the conflict about getting pregnant, so I don't bring it up. They look happy as they tell stories of staying at the Balmoral Hotel in Edinburgh and taking the train to St Andrews, a medieval college town on the North Sea favored by the British royals. My sister spent her junior year abroad at St Andrews as an art history major and has yearned to return ever since.

"We had Champagne at Rusacks St Andrews," Chrissy gushes, "And we ate haggis at The Criterion."

"What's haggis?"

"It sounds disgusting, but it's tasty. It's spiced meat and oats inside a sheep's stomach."

"What? I think I'd find that hard to stomach," I joke.

"Ha ha, you're funny, Jahi." Chrissy rolls her eyes.

"How did you like Scotland, Lucas?"

"I loved it. I got in a round of golf at the Old Course." Lucas beams.

"Wow. That's an achievement. I've heard it's hard to get privileges there."

"It sure is." Chrissy nods. "He had to get an attestation from our local club to play there."

"Did you visit your old haunts?"

"Sure did. Walked on West Sands Beach, went to St Salvator's Chapel and listened to the choir on Sunday, ate Arbroath smokie haddock at Tailend, drank frosé at The Adamson, and ate ice cream at Janetta's. It was great fun, and I felt sad to leave." Chrissy falls silent and her lower lip trembles. She has a soft spot for Scotland. I remember how depressed she was when she returned home from her year abroad.

Lucas jumps in to fill the silence. "Hey, what about you, Jahi?"

"Well, I've been taking care of my baby doll." Lily smiles. She likes it when I call her that. "And I had a bunch of emergencies. I diagnosed a man with a dissecting aortic aneurysm." They're riveted when I tell them the story, but my mind keeps drifting back to Rose.

As we finish dessert, my mother interjects with a mischievous glint in her eyes. "So, Jahi, tell us more about this Rose lady," she says, prompting a round of laughter from Chrissy and Lucas.

A flush of heat spreads in my chest and cheeks. I've been thinking about Rose a lot, but I'm not ready to talk about her with my family just yet. It's private, and I don't want to bring it up in front of everyone at the dinner table.

But my mother, being a persistent woman and slightly untethered by several glasses of wine, isn't about to let it go. "Come on, Jahi. We want to know more. Is she someone you're interested in? Does Lily like her?"

I sigh, realizing there's no getting out of it. "Well, she was Lily's teacher before she moved away. We had a bit of a texting session a while back, but nothing really came of it."

My mother looks puzzled. "And? Why didn't anything come of it? Did you like her?"

I hesitate, not wanting to divulge too much. "She was a brilliant teacher and someone who had a positive impact on Lily's life. But things didn't work out between us, and that's okay. We've both moved on."

Of course, we haven't both moved on. I plan to pull Chrissy aside afterwards and tell her Rose is moving away, and I regret not telling her how I feel about her. And also, how I don't want to be one of those guys who stands in the way of an exceptional woman chasing her dreams.

My mother looks disappointed. Fortunately, my sister comes to the rescue by telling us about the dinner she made for Lucas after their trip to Scotland. It was *boeuf Bourguignon*, a recipe she found in a Julia Child cookbook. Another favorite of hers is *coq au vin*. I avoid telling her I'm content with *un hamburger*, because she scoffs at me when I speak French. I have to admit, my accent is terrible. French people could identify me as an American in a crowd at one hundred yards.

My sister loves cooking anything French. I think because it gives her a chance to show off her fluency in French. She's fancy like that. But I also think it might be her way of keeping her husband happy. I'm not sure. I've been worried about them since she confided to us about their conflict around having children.

After dinner, Lily and Mom cuddle on the couch, bonding over their shared affinity for silly jokes. I love watching them together, knowing my daughter has a special, unbreakable bond with her granny. I gesture to Chrissy to follow me into her childhood bedroom.

"I missed my chance with Rose. I was about to ask her out, but she told me she has a job offer in LA and will probably take it," I whisper.

"Oh no. I'm so sorry. It's sad that you missed the chance to tell her how you feel. I understand how devastating this is. Keep me updated. I'm your sister and deserve to know what's going on in your life," she asserts in a serious tone.

I laugh her off, but underneath my laughter, I'm glad she knows what I'm going through.

The last time I spoke to Jolene, she said she didn't know if Rose would move to LA or stay in Eureka Springs. It feels like she's gone. The bottom has dropped out, as if I'll never see her again. No matter the encouraging words I say to myself, whenever I'm alone and yearning for her, the words are empty.

My sister and Lucas go home shortly after, leaving me alone with Mom.

"Jahi," my mother says, her voice soft. "I want to tell you something. Watching you with Lily tonight, I feel so proud of you. You're an amazing father, and I'm grateful you're my son. You're a natural born father."

Touched by my mother's words, my eyes grow misty. "Thank you, Mom. That means everything to me."

"I'm surprised you have the energy for anyone else, seeing the way you treat Lily." My mother smiles at me playfully.

"Is there anything you want to tell me? Like you're jealous or something, Mom? Are you not getting enough attention from me?"

My mother raises her eyebrows playfully and then guides Lily and me to sit on the couch and watch a wildlife documentary. We don't hear most of it because Lily comments incessantly. She finds something to say about everything. Whether it's the lions or the elephants, she loves them all.

"You're the sweetest, smartest, and most beautiful granddaughter in the world," my mother gushes.

Lily beams when her granny boasts about her.

"Mom, she's your *only* granddaughter. Heck, she's your only grandchild." I laugh, and Mom and Lily join me.

People say Lily looks exactly like me. Mom says it's a blessing she hasn't taken many physical attributes from Susanne, and I agree. It's hard to imagine being reminded of my estranged wife whenever I look at my daughter. I know I would love her, though, no matter what. Lily is the light of my life and without her, I would barely live. I would merely exist.

I watch her point her dimpled index finger at the enormous screen. I love those little dimples in her hands. A momentary wistfulness washes over me. One day, knuckles will take their place and those precious dimples will disappear forever.

I love my daughter more than life itself.

CHAPTER SEVEN

ROSE

I wake to the sound of soft summer raindrops tapping against the window of my attic bedroom. It's a soothing sound that makes me want to snuggle deeper into my down comforter and drift back to sleep. But I know I have to get up and start my day. Today is the day I'll follow Beatrice to her job and explore Fayetteville.

Beatrice loves waiting tables at Cheers, the fanciest restaurant on the square. She works long hours most days, serving Southern American cuisine to discriminating clients. But she enjoys her job, and always comes home with interesting stories, smelling like smoke from the mesquite wood fired grill.

I dress quickly, throwing on a cute summer skirt and top and a cashmere sweater in case I get cold. Running a brush through my strawberry blonde hair, I look in the mirror and am alarmed to see bloodshot green eyes staring back at me. I must have stayed up too late reading last night. I apply pale pink lipstick and a bit of blush to my cheeks, and grab my notebook and pen to take notes.

When I get to Cheers, Beatrice is already there, setting up tables and filling salt and pepper shakers. She smiles and gives me a quick hug.

"Are you ready to see the sights of Fayetteville?" she asks, grinning.

I nod eagerly. "I can hardly wait."

We set off into the morning mist, Beatrice leading the way. I follow closely, taking in the town's ambience. The streets are quiet, with only a few cars and pedestrians. The shops and restaurants are just opening, with owners cleaning windows and putting up signs to advertise their products. We walk down Dickson Street and she points to her favorite boutiques and restaurants. Finally, we arrive at the Walton Arts Center, a program supported by the largesse of the Walmart fortune, marking the entrance of the University of Arkansas campus.

"Do you know Fayetteville is called the 'Athens of the Ozarks'? Isn't that cool?" Bea asks.

"No, I didn't know. That's an illustrious name. Why is it called that?"

"It's the academic center in these parts and there's a lot of innovation going on because of the university."

"Well, it sure is beautiful up here in the hills," I say.

"Ah, yes. The hills. It's known for having seven hills, just like Rome or Boston or San Francisco."

"Wow. I love that. Seven is my lucky number."

"I know. It always has been… that and the number two," Bea adds.

We continue walking, and Bea introduces me to some locals. Everyone seems to know my sister. It's like two degrees of separation from everyone in the entire city.

We circle back to Cheers, and Beatrice goes inside to begin her shift. I stay outside, watching people as they go about their day, wondering about their lives. Families and couples walk together. Teenagers saunter, relishing the golden days before graduation. They seem blissfully unaware of the impending currents of life that will carry them in divergent directions. *It's always later than you think.*

As I sit there, a thought occurs to me. Maybe I can work here, too. A new company establishing psychotherapy practices nationwide employed Enid. Despite my streak of bad luck in the relationship department, maybe my good luck in my career will hold, and I can still rely on it. I might open a branch in Fayetteville. It's a hotspot, gaining recognition as one of the best places to live and has the backing of the Walton family. Maybe there's a way for me to have it all.

I escaped LA because I thought I couldn't handle the big city life without Lee. Now, Fayetteville reminds me of Eureka Springs, but with more people, and it gives me a sense of possibility.

I realize Fayetteville is technically a small city of around 95,000 residents, with its own rhythms and pace. But it has a sense of community that is hard to find in larger cities. Everyone seems connected, and it's easy to see why Beatrice loves it. I make a mental note to keep my eyes open, to see if I can find a sense of belonging here.

In the early afternoon, Beatrice takes her break and invites me to join her. She pours me a cup of coffee and I steal a few of her fries as she eats lunch, remembering the rule that food has no calories if I take it from somebody else's plate.

"Great place," I say, scanning the restaurant. "It has such a cozy, small-town vibe. Being used to LA, Fayetteville is a small town."

"I love it here," Beatrice replies, taking a bite of her French Dip sandwich. "The customers are mostly regulars and have their own quirks and stories. And the owner, Mr. Johnson, is like a second father to me. He's the father we didn't have."

I know she's bubbling over about Fayetteville because she's infatuated with Andrew, but this reference to our father unnerves me. She rarely ever mentions Dad, but here it is. Our dad haunts us in seen and unseen ways. He's always here like a ghost, lurking in the background, pervading every waking moment. *Is my sister aware of his poisonous effects?* Dad shows up like a weeping wound whenever we have a relationship with a man. It's like a wound that can't be surgically closed because it's contaminated, and must heal by *secondary intention*, from the inside out. Healing like that takes time and has setbacks, both physical and psychological.

I wonder how much of life is determined by the negative instead of the positive. Are our crucial choices ruled by leaving behind the bad rather than moving towards the good? Is it "anywhere but here" instead of "I want to go there?"

The analogy for psychological healing is clear. It's ironic I learned about wound care from Lee, who, despite his flaws, is a top-notch surgeon who treats patients with a tenderness he never showed me.

Has our father, who inflicted pain on all of us, undermined her life as much as he's undermined mine?

I smile, my face tight. "That's nice. Having people like that in your life is important."

We talk a while longer, and I watch as Beatrice chats with customers, pouring coffee and making small talk.

The rest of the afternoon I explore the campus, reflecting on my college years, startled by how young the students look. They're as close to kindergarten in age as I am to them. When I return to Cheers, Beatrice is clearing tables and washing dishes, her face looking weary. I offer my help, and she accepts. From my perspective, Beatrice fulfills and lives up to her potential, even if others don't see it. It doesn't matter if she uses her college degree in sociology or not. She loves her job, and she doesn't fancy the idea of marriage, something my mother and I accept. Mom and I both know her issue with marriage is obviously because of our father, because you don't have to be a meteorologist to know which way the wind is blowing.

Together, we're a blur of activity as we clean tables and her colleagues nod in appreciation. When we finish, Beatrice turns to me. "You know, Rose, I think you'd be great working here.

You're good with people, and you have a keen attention to detail."

We head outside. Fayetteville looks different in twilight, as the lights from shop windows and restaurants cast a warm glow on the sidewalks.

"Do you want to explore a bit more?" Beatrice asks.

I agree, and we walk around the Square. It's a peaceful moment, and I'm content being here with my sister. As we walk, my thoughts return to my plan of reaching out to the company in Los Angeles. Beatrice gives me a lot to think about. I simply want to have it all.

I feel an urge to message Jahi and mention the possibility of staying in Eureka Springs or working in Fayetteville, but I want to be cautious. I'll do nothing that risks breaking my heart. But then I think about Lily. I adore that little girl.

While talking to Bea, a text comes in. It's Enid. I'm ashamed. It's been three weeks since she told me about the offer, and I haven't given her a response.

She writes a simple "Hey." Pressure builds in my temples as a tension headache brews. It reminds me of being a kid. I had lots of headaches and missed a great deal of school. I was silly enough to believe my mother wouldn't want me around if I got poor grades or something equally ridiculous.

Why in the world would I imagine my mother abandoning me? It must be because my father hated me and that colors everything.

After Dad left, I knew how hard my mother worked to make sure we had the things we needed. It would break her heart if I failed in school. One day, I finally opened up to Mom, and she told me she was heartbroken that I would think she'd turn on me. She said she was proud of me, no matter what. That day, Beatrice saw me crying in Mom's arms. It was like all the pressure I'd been holding for so long melted away. I collapsed from the relief but then suffered a massive migraine. It was like the release of a pressure valve after taking final exams. Indeed, I got terrible migraines after every major test in high school and college.

I pick up my phone and text Enid. I need to know if I can get back to my calling as a psychologist and still stay in Arkansas.

When I taught in Eureka Springs, I had a strong bond with the kids. In fact, they were my happy place—their chattering and bickering kept me entertained, but I missed my patients. I didn't fix them, no one can do that, but I enjoyed helping them feel better about themselves. I taught them they could not only live with their demons, but move beyond them. The connection I felt with some of my patients was beyond words. It was something potent and in-articulable, something sacred.

I want that back, the feeling of working in a new environment and continuing to develop as a psychologist, but I also want Jahi. I can admit that to myself, at least. I want Jahi so much. His devotion and tenderness with his daughter touches something deep inside me.

There are different layers to him. He isn't two-dimensional, like some men I've known. On the surface, he might look like a handsome, brooding firefighter, but I love the fact that he grows old roses in his yard.

He adores his daughter and dedicates his life to her, and that says it all. He's everything I wish my father had been. Lily loves him. It's the deep love and trust of knowing your parents will give their life for you in a heartbeat. I love seeing this, and I respect him for being this kind of father. It's everything.

And here he is, the man of my dreams, the man I wish my father could have been to my mother and our family. This big, beautiful, soft-spoken man—a man of contrasts—a man who fights fires, saves lives, reads and discusses Stephen King, and grows old roses. A man whose daughter trusts and adores him, and a man I adore, too.

There are so many memories already—the gentle way he taught his seven-year-old daughter how to play chess, his kind and respectful gaze, his humor. There are just too many things to list that I appreciate about him. He was so gentle with me when Lee broke my heart again. I thank everything holy in the universe for Jahi—that he came to my house that day to look after me.

So why did I leave him when there was so much possibility?

I'm wondering about that now.

CHAPTER EIGHT

JAHI

I wake up early with a nagging sense of unease lingering in the back of my mind, like a terrible memory.

When I get to the fire station, I notice Matthew isn't around. Maybe he's stuck in traffic or just running late. I tick off my checklist of daily duties, beginning with mopping the bathroom. Several hours pass and still no sign of him.

That's when my phone buzzes, and I see a message from my estranged wife, Susanne. I stand there frozen, barely believing the words on the screen. It reads, "Hey Jahi, I think we need to talk."

Ugh. What in the world? Why is she texting me now, after all these years?

The last time we spoke, things ended on bad terms. We never officially divorced, but Susanne just left me and Lily without a second thought. It was as if we never existed.

I resume scrubbing the toilets, hoping to flush bad thoughts from my mind. But my mind wanders. Flashbacks of our troubled marriage and the burden of raising our daughter alone floods my emotions.

Susanne often lashed out, accusing me of not doing enough or being enough for her. She claimed I was a slacker, that I didn't have high aspirations. She wanted me to be a doctor, not just a paramedic, and certainly not a firefighter. I don't know why she had such contempt for me. She was only ambitious in her conniving. I felt like I was in a glass bubble. I never knew when I'd blunder into it, shatter the glass, tick her off, and cut myself.

But the biggest betrayal was when she left us without warning. She went away on a girl's weekend to Las Vegas and never returned. There was frantic calling and texting for days, with no reply. I had to tell Lily, after her incessant questions, that I didn't know where Mommy was. That still haunts me, the forlorn look on Lily's face, like those faces I've seen on TV documentaries of children abandoned in Romanian orphanages. Susanne left me to pick up the pieces and raise our daughter alone. It wasn't easy, but I had to make it work, for Lily's sake.

With a heavy sigh, I finish mopping the bathroom floor and try to focus on the present. I check my phone, and there's another message from Susanne. It reads, "I know we had our issues, but I'd like to talk things through. Can we meet up later today?"

I hesitate, wondering if I should reply or just ignore her. But then, the image of Lily flashes in my mind, and I realize I have to try for her sake.

I text back, "Okay, let's meet at Basin Spring Park at three p.m."

My apprehension grows as the day progresses. I can't stop thinking about it.

What does she want to talk about? Is she trying to weasel her way back into my life? Is she going to ask for money? I never know what to expect with Susanne.

When three o'clock arrives, I head to the park. My heart flutters when I see Susanne getting out of her car. She looks different. Her hair is shoulder-length and dyed blonde in a pageboy with bangs and a blunt cut. She's lost about twenty pounds and is lean, bordering on gaunt, like a hungry tigress. I almost don't recognize her. Despite the changes, I still feel physically attracted to her, to my chagrin.

She's the first to speak, which is no surprise, given she is always the dominant one in our relationship.

"I'm so sorry for the way I treated you during our marriage. I regret how I left you and Lily. That was wrong. I don't know if I'll ever be able to forgive myself," she says, looking contrite.

But as she keeps talking, I realize she's still the same woman I married. She's a self-absorbed phony, only ever thinking of herself and what she wants.

"I need your help, Jahi," she says, her voice trembling. "I've gotten myself into some trouble, and I need a place to stay. They've kicked me out of my apartment, and I have nowhere to go."

Without thinking, I say, "What kind of trouble?"

She hesitates. "I got into some financial problems. I took out a loan from a loan shark. I couldn't make the payments, and now they're after me."

Susanne has always been careless with money, but I never thought she'd get mixed up with something like this. She's gotten herself into a situation she can't handle. My mind races with ways of helping her. Maybe I can let her stay with me for a little while. But this could lead to trouble. Big Momma's words echo in my mind: "Don't go borrowing trouble."

"I'm sorry, Susanne, but I can't help you," I say, trying to steady my voice. "You made your decisions, and now you've gotta suffer the consequences. I'm done. I'm just done."

She stares at me, her upper lip curling in contempt in a look I've seen a thousand times. "I knew you'd say that. You're always so doggone self-righteous."

My jaw clenches. Gritting my teeth, I feel the urge to leave. But before I can, Susanne says something that makes me freeze.

"You know, Jahi," she starts, her tone sarcastic as a strange look crosses her eyes. "You never officially divorced me. You could be in trouble if someone finds out."

My heart sinks. She has a point. We never went through with the divorce. *How can you serve papers to someone who disappeared?*

She ensured I never found her. It's a trap. She always keeps her options open.

"Don't even think about using that against me," I warn, my voice low and gravelly, like a wolf preparing to bare his teeth.

Susanne holds up her hands, as if in surrender. "I'm not trying to blackmail you, Jahi. I just think you should know."

Yeah, right. She's bluffing. Methinks she doth protest too much with that phony, "I'm not trying to blackmail you, Jahi" business. Then why is she bringing it up? Unable to sit still any longer, I stand. "I think it's time we end this conversation. I must go."

Susanne says nothing as I walk away. I feel her eyes boring into me, imploring me back to her destructive ways. But unlike the Biblical story of Lot's wife, I refuse to look back, refuse to be consumed by the flaming sulfur of her moods, refuse to deny all that I value—determined not to look back at the fallout of my life and be turned into a pillar of salt.

As I walk to the fire station, my mind races. *Should I get a lawyer and complete the divorce? Is Susanne trying to use this as leverage to get me to help her?* I don't know for sure, but one thing is clear—I can't let her manipulate me.

Despite the nagging feeling in the back of my mind, I force myself to focus on work. I can't let this distract me from protecting and serving Eureka Springs. It isn't until later, when my shift ends, that I allow myself to think about what happened today. As I drive home, I know I have to decide how to handle Susanne's reappearance in our lives.

When I get to Jolene's, Lily is waiting for me, her face bright with excitement.

"Daddy, Daddy, look what I made at school!" she exclaims, holding up a folded paper model of a firetruck.

I smile at her enthusiasm. "Wow, it's so red, Lily! You must have worked hard on it."

We get home, eat dinner, and the events of the day slip to the back of my mind. I focus on Lily's stories from school and try to enjoy the moment, as I promised myself I would when Rose left.

After we finish eating, I give Lily a bath and tuck her into bed. I read her trusty babyhood favorite, *Goodnight Moon,* and then *Charlotte's Web.* She's asleep by the time the eight-year-old Fern feeds the baby pig milk from a bottle at the end of the first chapter. I tiptoe to the den and settle down on the couch with a glass of wine. But try as I might, I can't shake the shock I'm feeling about Susanne's reappearance.

I can't let this slide. In the morning, I'll call a lawyer and start the divorce proceedings. I won't let Susanne ruin my life or Lily's. As I drift off to sleep, my mind feels lighter.

The next morning, I contact a lawyer who worked with my dad after a firehose's worth of coffee and a hearty breakfast of eggs, bacon, and hash browns to steel my resolve. It's time to end it, once and for all. My buddy Matt has the day off. There's no pep talk when I need it most.

I regret dating Susanne Bryant from high school. She revealed herself to be untrustworthy, and I don't have drugs or alcohol to blame for my decision. It was a terrible, clear-headed choice in my rudderless youth—a youth riddled with grief after Dad died. I saw red flags early on, but like a bull in the ring, they made me charge instead of retreat.

Not smart. Not only that, I blamed myself for the mess of our marriage.

I had a child with a woman so narcissistic she didn't mind abandoning her baby daughter. *Who does that? Why the hell does she think I'm going to help her pay off a loan after everything she did to us? How could she think I'd be receptive to that?* She's full of herself and delusional, that's for sure.

The next day, Susanne tries contacting me multiple times. I

throw away my SIM card and make sure everyone knows my new number, though I don't divulge why I changed it.

I don't tell Mom about Susanne. She'll freak out because she despises her. She calls Susanne "coyote evil," meaning something so bad it's like coyotes chewing their own leg off to escape a trap.

When everything fell apart with Susanne, I realized mothers see through people who are not good for their sons and daughters. They have our backs and know what's best for their children, with a few spectacular exceptions like Susanne—a landmine in a peaceful pasture. Mom saw through her when I didn't. She knew Susanne would be a terrible mother. Even Chrissy missed it like I did... but Chrissy never liked people much, so she didn't waste her time thinking about them.

CHAPTER NINE

ROSE

The day I leave Fayetteville, Mother cries even though I told her the night before it's time for me to return to Eureka Springs.

"I intend to write a letter to Enid to see if there's any way I can take the job opportunity without leaving Arkansas," I say to appease Mom.

"Oh, I love that idea, Rose." Mom nods enthusiastically, but as I'm packing my bags to leave, she grabs my arm like a child holding onto a parent leaving for work.

I look at Beatrice to save me. I can't tell if it's because Beatrice is the oldest, but she usually has a better grip on how to handle Mom.

"Mom, c'mon, now. Stop acting like she's dying."

My mother glares at her, acting betrayed. "Why would you even say that? You're always saying things like that, and I don't like it—not one bit."

Beatrice throws me a look. Mom will lecture her later for sure.

"Baby, I think it might do you some good if you stay for a week more," Mom urges.

I laugh. Beatrice and I exchange a look.

"I'll come and visit you more, I promise."

"You won't," she insists, looking deflated.

I don't know what else to say to my mother, who is hell bent on making me feel guilty. Since we couldn't afford to travel much as children, Mom makes up for it by taking us on guilt trips.

"Promise. Cross my heart. Does me promising you mean nothing to you?" I ask.

"No!" My mother flashes a look that has Beatrice and me giggling.

I'm leaving Fayetteville and returning to Eureka Springs after weeks of agonizing over the decision. I've spent most of my time with Mom and Bea, reconnecting after years of physical distance.

When I went to UCLA at eighteen, they left for Arkansas, where Mom grew up and where we have extended family, going back at least three generations. I wasn't interested in moving there after college because I was starting grad school in psychology. Meeting and marrying Lee sealed the deal of me living in LA. Mom and Bea thought marrying Lee was a bad idea and I couldn't face their scorn. Lee couldn't care less about them, and it was hard for me to get away. Lee's attitude infected me. I saw Arkansas as provincial and unsophisticated, not like the scrambling, frenetic, brightly lit anthill of LA. I regret that now.

Being with Lee was like having a tantrum-throwing two-year-old. *Enfant terrible*, the terrifying child, I used to say under my breath whenever he'd blow up at me.

I think the chasm in my relationship with Mom and Bea widened the longer I stayed away. I wonder if they felt I abandoned them just like Dad did. They sometimes made snide comments about how similar Dad and I were in gestures and temperament. I didn't see the similarities, but who knows? It's true that I abandoned my patients in LA when I moved to Eureka Springs for a fresh start. Even though I explained it to them, and even though they said they understood—to me, it's still a relative abandonment. They must have had some feelings about that.

Just like the original abandonment by Dad, and later Lee, now here I am reenacting it at every turn—with my patients, with Mom and Bea, and now Jahi and Lily. It's called a repetition compulsion, where people relive painful events to gain control. Or, better yet, that old definition of experience being that which enables you to detect a mistake when you make it again.

People often play out and inflict these reenactments on others. I know this theoretically, but here I am doing it, anyway. So maybe they're right. Maybe I have more than a bit of my dad in me. I'll have to monitor this. I don't want to be like him, but do I have a choice?

Undoing the pain I caused my family is uncomfortable, but necessary for healing our relationship. But as much as I would like to stay in Fayetteville and try to fix things, I can't ignore the fact that I need to find a job. The hospital in Fayetteville doesn't have any openings for psychologists, and I haven't found suitable work anywhere else in town. So, I'm making the hard decision to leave my family behind and head back to Eureka Springs, where I hope to start anew one more time.

The drive isn't easy on the winding country road, even though it's only forty-five miles on 45 North. My mind spins. *What if I don't find a job?*

I left my teaching position in Lily's school at the end of the term because I realized I wasn't being true to myself. I've always been a psychologist. Maybe I was born on a couch. Teaching children was a godsend. It saved my devastated heart. But now, I'm ready to get back to my true love.

But what if I can't make ends meet? What if leaving my sister and mother again is a mistake?

I'm thinking about setting up a psychotherapy practice in town. I didn't do that when I first moved here. Everything was fraught, and I needed a job I could step into, not a job I needed to create. I realize my job doesn't have to be a clinical practice in LA.

The next few days are spent in a state of anxious waiting,

checking my phone every few minutes for Enid's response. Each time, I feel a pang of disappointment when I see there is still no message. I can't keep waiting forever, but I don't know what else to do.

In the meantime, I text Jolene and we make plans for dinner. As I drive to her house, I feel nostalgic. I've spent some of my happiest times in this town teaching and building relationships with the students and staff at the school. I miss that sense of connection and purpose.

I arrive at Jolene's and she embraces me in a big hug.

"Come in, my friend. You're looking skinny." Jolene eyes me like a hawk as I walk into her living room and plop onto her red velvet sofa.

"You sound like my mother." I laugh. Wafts of pungent spiciness fill my lungs. "By the way, what is that yummy smell?"

"Korean bibimbap."

"What's that?"

"Oh, just a delicious mixture of veggies, rice, and spicy gochujang paste."

"You always wow me with your cooking. You're like a secret chef."

"Well, you deserve it, Rose. You deserve the best." Jolene looks at me with a tenderness I've never seen from her before, and it makes my eyes well up in tears.

Between bites, I tell Jolene how anxious I am about finding a job. I know she'll take me back if I ask for a teaching position. She might be a grump to others, but she has a soft spot for me. At first, I was anxious about being favored by her because I thought the other teachers might hate me for it, but they were accepting.

The conversation turns to my mother's sadness when I left Fayetteville.

"You need to visit her on a regular schedule," Jolene advises, but I don't need her to lecture me.

"You're right. I need to make up for lost time." Sadness comes over me as I say this. I love being with my mother and Beatrice and I haven't realized how much I miss them until these last few weeks. "I'm sad I've missed so much of my sister's young adult life. It's almost like I didn't know her anymore. I have so much to catch up on," I confess.

"I can imagine that, but now you're only an hour away, so be sure and block out your calendar to visit frequently."

I nod and switch the subject. "You know, Jolene. I might not want to work as a teacher anymore."

"Really? You're so talented and the kids love you."

"Well, I love the children too. It's just that when Enid called about the job opening in LA, it made me realize how much I miss my work as a psychologist. So… I'm thinking of opening up a clinical practice here."

She gives me a knowing look. "You want to stay in Eureka Springs?" She doesn't mention Jahi or Lily, but I know she's thinking about them because I see it in her eyes. I respect how she doesn't say his name because it would be awkward.

"I love Fayetteville, but it's my second choice. Right now, I want to stay here," I say, frowning.

"What's wrong? You're frowning."

"I'm worried about Enid and hope I haven't offended her. I haven't heard from her in weeks. Loyal friends are hard to find."

"Don't worry," Jolene says. "Something good will happen no matter what."

Finally, it's time to go home, back to my bungalow. I've missed it.

As I make my way out, I say offhandedly, "I have plans to see Jahi."

She hesitates for a moment but says nothing.

CHAPTER TEN

JAHI

My lawyer and I become fast text buddies. I want to avoid Susanne and her ability to ruin people's lives as much as possible.

When I hear a knock at my door, I'm not expecting to see Susanne. After our park rendezvous, I don't want to see her again except in the courthouse to complete our divorce. She left Lily and me without so much as a goodbye, not counting our ill-fated meeting about loan sharks. But there she is, standing on my doorstep, looking apprehensive.

"Jahi, can we talk?" she asks, her voice hesitant.

I pause for a moment, unsure of what to say. I don't want to bring up past hurts, but I can see the pain and regret etched on her face. Against my better judgment, I let her in.

We sit in the living room, and I offer her a drink. As I pour her a glass of iced tea, I notice how much she's changed. She looks older, more worn down by life, sort of dried-up, something I didn't notice in the park. But there's still a hint of the vibrant, beautiful woman I once loved.

"Jahi, I'm sorry," she says, her voice barely audible.

I raise an eyebrow, surprised by her apology. She never apologizes for anything, that phony apology in the park notwithstanding. I don't trust it. "What are you sorry for?"

"For everything," she says, tears welling in her eyes. "For leaving you and Lily, for the way I treated you, for the loan shark mess. I'm going to therapy, and I want to make amends for the mistakes I've made."

I listen to her words, feeling a mixture of anger and sadness, but I know her history of saying one thing and doing another. Showing up at my home unannounced, she catches me off guard, and I'm not sure how to respond.

"I appreciate the apology, Susanne," I say finally, my voice measured. "But the damage is done. Lily and I have moved on, and I don't want to revisit the past."

Susanne's face falls, and for a moment, I think she might cry. Sure enough, she does. *But are those crocodile tears she's shedding?*

"I understand," she says softly. "But Jahi, I miss Lily and you. Can't I be part of your lives again?"

I hesitate, torn between my desire to protect my daughter and my pain and hurt feelings. Susanne left us without a second thought, and now she wants to waltz back into our lives.

Before I can respond, the doorbell rings. I excuse myself and answer it, shocked to see Rose standing there.

"Hey, Jahi," she says, looking slightly out of breath. "I came to drop off those books you lent me."

I can't believe she's back. When I gave her the books and she left without mentioning them, I thought, like her, they were gone for good. I cherished a sliver of hope that maybe when she saw the books, she'd remember me. It was a stupid thought, but I entertained it anyway.

Besides, I didn't plan to see her so soon. From our brief texting session, I gathered she met with her family, perhaps to see them because she plans to move to LA. The thought upset me. I don't want to think she would purposely leave me alone for a long time.

Rose's eyes widen when she sees Susanne sitting on my sofa. When I introduce them, Rose greets Susanne politely. "I'm sorry to interrupt," Rose says, her eyes meeting mine. "I'll leave these here and be on my way."

Before I can stop her, Rose turns to Susanne and says, "It's nice to meet you, Susanne. Jahi has spoken about you many times."

Susanne's face lights up, her eyes shining from her phony crying session. "Thank you, Rose," she says, her voice shaking slightly. "It's nice to meet you, too."

As Rose leaves, I feel a pang of unease. I don't want to talk to Susanne anymore, and I don't want to give her any ideas about coming back into our lives. I want to wind back the clock and undo what just happened.

But Susanne presses on, determined. "Jahi, please," she says, grasping my forearm. "I know I messed up, but I want to make things right. I want to be there for Lily, to be part of her life again."

I sigh, feeling the weight of her words. Part of me wants to believe her, to let her back into our lives, if only for Lily's sake.

Rose is gracious and seems to accept whatever the situation is, but I don't expect her to. Not just because I'm delusional enough to believe she would like to be with me, but because I never told her much about Susanne before—only that she'd abandoned Lily and me.

Rose must be feeling confused. She gave me a strange look, and I couldn't tell what it meant. Deciphering emotional Morse codes isn't my strong suit. Reading people is simply not my thing, but I could tell she wasn't happy with me. Heck, I wasn't happy with myself, either.

Susanne's actions left Lily without a mother figure, and me struggling with my mental health. My only offense was simply marrying Susanne.

Susanne's face appears drawn. It looks leathery and weather-beaten, like she's been through trauma. The uncharitable expression, "Ridden hard, and put away wet" comes to mind, though I feel guilty and rude even thinking about it.

Pesky subconscious, I chastise my brain.

Right after she abandoned us years ago, I felt like I was moving in molasses. It took great effort to leave the house, and even to attend to Lily.

In those first few years, Lily sometimes stayed by my bedside and cried. I couldn't handle it, so I relied on my family to look after my daughter while I stayed cooped up in the house, like some kind of cowering, burrowing rodent afraid of the light. The only time I went out was when I went to work. I found a kind of solace in helping others through their most difficult moments, as I realized there were others worse off than myself.

After a while, I figured I couldn't keep living like a hermit. My daughter was counting on me. It wasn't easy for Mom and Chrissy to step in, but neither of them complained. They didn't leave us hanging when it mattered most, so I couldn't leave Lily hanging either—just waiting for me to come around and toughen up.

And that was what I did. I went back to Mom's house and picked up Lily and brought her home. I reassured her how much I loved her and how sorry I was that I didn't pick her up sooner from Granny's. She must have felt a double abandonment. First her mother leaves and then her Daddy drops her off at Granny's. She was really little at the time and didn't understand, but I made a promise to myself to turn things around.

It sickens me to see how Susanne wreaks destruction at every turn—like Medusa with a head of venomous snakes whose stare turns people to stone, and if that doesn't kill you, the snake bites will. Now she's ruined my tender rapprochement with Rose.

When Rose met Susanne, she tried to mask her disappointment, but she wasn't fast enough. I saw the corners of her lips pulled down and her inner brow raised. I've never said much about Susanne, and now I'm paying for it. *Did I ruin our chances by being tight-lipped?*

Rose thought I wasn't taking adequate care of Lily and found out it was because her mother wasn't around. Surely, she thought little of Susanne, but, ever the gracious one, she didn't show it when they met. Looking at Susanne, one thing is for sure, she's wending her way back into my life. Slithering around like one of Medusa's snakes, and I don't like it one bit.

PART 3

CHAPTER ONE

JAHI

The light is unfamiliar as I swim to the surface of consciousness, following shimmering fragmented dream bubbles. It's late—way too late. Something is off. The sun feels harsh and bright behind my eyelids—too brazen and agitated for early morning. I jump from my bed, ready to prepare Lily for summer swim camp, but when I reach her room, someone has made the bed and Lily is nowhere to be found. The house smells of eggs and burnt toast.

Susanne stands at the stove in a fishnet swimsuit coverup and flip-flops, humming a tune, her hair wrapped in a silk scarf.

"Where's Lily?" I ask. I hesitate, realizing how suspicious my tone sounds. She's Lily's mother, even though not a good one. She abandoned us two and a half years after Lily was born.

"At the pool." She barely spares me a glance, as if her answer is obvious.

"Huh?" My heart constricts in my chest. Things are feeling out of control.

"I took her."

My brows knit together. "What the heck? Why didn't you wake me up?"

"Don't worry. I thought you needed to sleep," Susanne says.

I glare at her. *Who does she think she is, and why is she here?*

"Jahi, I'm trying. Want some breakfast?" she asks. She dishes an omelet onto my plate and pairs it with a tall glass of orange juice as I watch.

"What? Are you just going to stare at me while I eat?" I retort.

She shakes her head. "No, I'll eat, too."

Joining me, she picks at her food. I can barely eat. I can't stop thinking about this latest development of her returning to my life. It's surreal in the worst ways.

"So, Eureka Springs sure is changing. They've fixed it up… and your rose garden looks majestic."

I pause and fix her with a hard look. "Did you go near my roses?" I ask. She notices my anger and answers with caution.

"Well, I didn't touch anything. I just looked at it and boy, you're working hard in that garden. It's stunning."

I nod, deflecting her attempts to get into a conversation. It's not worth it. I don't like her and don't want to waste my time speaking to her. In fact, I want nothing to do with her. As Big Daddy used to say: *Don't let the door hit ya where God split ya.* I want to say that to her, but restrain myself. After pushing my food around and downing the freshly squeezed orange juice, I leave for work. Matt must be expecting me.

I'm not looking forward to working all day or sitting with Matt, waiting for emergency calls. I dread facing the potential of horrible traumas, but I want to speak to him. He doesn't know everything that's going on with me. I need to tell him, and fast.

I can't believe she's back. My estranged wife, Susanne, is making herself at home and sleeping in my extra bedroom. I'm uneasy, totally unsure of how to handle the situation. *What are the unintended consequences of letting her come back into our lives?*

After Susanne walked out of my life, without giving me the option to end the marriage, I assured myself I would have nothing to do with her again. I knew it was an excellent decision, but now I need to confide in someone, and Matthew is the only person I trust enough to share my personal life with. As we sit in the break room, I recount the events of the past few days.

"I can't believe it! Just like that, she's back? That must be rough." Matthew whistles slowly. "Have you seen any indications of her trying to use Lily as leverage?"

I know he expects me to say yes—that way he can go after Susanne himself. He loves Lily like she's his own daughter and never hesitates to show it. He'll do anything for her. After all, he's her godfather.

I nod. "She's trying to spoil Lily. It makes me paranoid. What's her hidden agenda?"

Matthew takes a long sip from his coffee and his eyebrows furrow. "It's a tricky situation," he says, his words measured. "But you need to keep a level head and not jump to conclusions."

Things are challenging when Matthew reminds me to keep a level head. I'm the levelheaded one in emergency situations, not him. I can't believe this switch in roles, and I don't like it.

I see his point of view but feel frustrated. "Matthew, it's not just that. Susanne's presence is ruining my chances with Rose."

"That's tough," Matthew affirms. "She's the perfect woman who came into your life out of nowhere, heaven-sent. Lily was lucky when Rose stepped in as her first grade teacher when the other teacher got sick. And Lily loves her."

"I know. I've liked Rose since the moment I first saw her when she marched into my house to give me the what-for about Lily's homework. I plan to ask her out on a date. But now, thanks to Susanne interrupting our lives, that seems impossible."

"What do you plan to do?"

"Not sure," I say, feeling deflated. "I'm just trying to consider my options. Honestly, I don't know what is best for my daughter, and that frustrates me."

Leaving the break room, I feel conflicted and powerless. I've got to be careful not to overreact, but find it hard not to because I'm so angry about Susanne impinging on our lives. I've got to take time off from work to clear my head and figure out what to do.

I ruminate about my relationship with Susanne. We struggled with a lot of difficulties in our marriage, but shared a bond with Lily. *Is it possible we can co-exist peacefully without resorting to drama and manipulation?*

When I get home from the station, I smell a savory aroma as I walk into the living room. Susanne is in the kitchen cooking spaghetti Bolognese, one of my favorites. A tossed Caesar salad sits on the kitchen island in a bamboo bowl with big wooden tongs sticking out. She set the table for three with our Italian flatware, linen napkins, and crystal wine glasses. I pause, raising my eyebrows. She never did this before. She was more likely to serve ready-made takeout food. *What's up with her?* I don't like this new Susanne. I don't trust her, and I don't know what to do with her. It's like she's wearing a mask—always smiling.

We haven't discussed sleeping and living arrangements. The tension sits there between us, unspoken. She's been here two nights already and unfortunately, she's seducing Lily by acting like a peer rather than a parent. She's buying her cheap trinkets, trying to win her affection one necklace at a time. Lily likes the attention but sees her as a friend rather than a mother. I wish my child held grudges so I could find a good reason to kick her out, but my Lily is so innocent and good-hearted.

Susanne looks up and keeps smiling. For a moment, I feel nostalgic. *We used to be happy like this. Maybe there's a way back, a way to work things out.*

"Hi Jahi," Susanne says. "I made dinner for us. Do you want some?"

I hesitate before agreeing. As the three of us sit down, we talk with Lily about her friends and her swim lessons. *This is supposed to happen in families, just like old times.*

After a dessert of strawberry ice cream and lemon sponge cake, Susanne offers to give Lily a bath and wash her hair, read her a bedtime story, and help her fall asleep.

I want to say no, to assert my authority as the father, but I'm conflicted. I don't want to cause trouble. So, I nod and watch Susanne take Lily's hand and off they go to the bathroom giggling like schoolmates. This happened last night, too. A pattern is forming, and it makes me uneasy.

It reminds me of the cautionary fable of the Arab and the camel. The camel—it's a fable, so camels can talk—asks permission from the master to put her nose inside the warm tent on a chilly night. The master agrees. Successive negotiations asking for the head, the neck, the front legs, and the body follow this. Finally, the whole camel is in the tent.

The interloper turns on the master and declares, "This tent isn't big enough for the both of us."

The moral of the story is how a sequence of small, good deeds can lead to unintended negative consequences. *I need to watch it with her.*

As I sit on the couch, I'm torn. Part of me wants to make co-parenting work with Susanne, but another part of me fears a trap.

Later that evening, Rose calls. She wants to talk about Lily's school for next year. As we speak, I feel a longing for her. I want to ask her out, but I know Susanne's presence will ruin it. In fact, it already has. After Rose's Fayetteville trip, she has never visited Lily and me since that disastrous day when she ran into Susanne at my house. She's avoiding me and I hate it.

I twist the sheets into a knot, trying to no avail to find a comfortable position. My mind searches, like a rat in a maze, frantic as I confront dead ends at every turn.

What options do I have? I must be careful and find a peace I can live with.

I can't keep acting this way. Will Rose ever come back and talk to me or give me the benefit of the doubt over how I'm handling the Susanne situation? I've never gotten the chance to tell her how much I like her, and I have no inkling how she feels about me.

Maybe Rose is disappointed I'm allowing Susanne back into Lily's life—a mother who abandoned her daughter. If that's the case, I understand her anger.

CHAPTER TWO

ROSE

When I tell Jolene I'm going over to Jahi's today, she says nothing. She just gives me a noncommittal grunt, but I can tell she approves. I plan to continue seeing Lily for her summer home tutorials, as if a seismic shift didn't happen the other day. After all, Jahi didn't warn me to stay away.

I need to gauge the situation since running into Jahi's estranged wife. I remind myself I don't have enough information about what's going on behind the scenes with the two of them. *Why let this woman stop me from helping Lily? I have a legitimate reason to show up.*

An idea forms in my mind of texting Jahi to inform him I'm showing up at his house soon, giving him just enough time to prepare, but not too much. I don't intend to cause problems, but I figure I can use the element of surprise to my advantage. Perhaps lady luck will smile at me. We'll laugh and hug and our lives will go back to before, pre-Susanne, when it was Jahi, Lily and me, the closest thing to a family I've experienced in my adult life.

I arrive at Jahi's house, unsure of what to expect. The return of Lily's long-absent mother leaves me feeling anxious, especially given my crush on Jahi. My heart races as I knock on his door. I hope it's all some kind of misunderstanding, that things will return to normal soon enough. It must happen. In fact, I pray in my heart Susanne is no longer here.

Jahi greets me warmly, as always, and I try to put my worries aside as we make our way to the living room. But as soon as I see Susanne sitting on the couch, my heart sinks.

She welcomes me cordially with a smile that makes me feel like an outsider. I can't help but compare myself to her—athletic, willowy, with perfectly coiffed pageboy hair. I feel frumpy and doughy in comparison, wearing jeans and a t-shirt, my hair in a messy bun. *She's just hanging out in his house! Why the heck does she even need to look so good?*

But the way Jahi looks at her breaks my heart. I bet they have a bunch of catching up to do. After all, they've got a daughter—Lily. They'll always have stuff to talk about.

Jahi glances at me. I wonder if he's hinting for me to leave his house, but I'm here for Lily. Jahi retrieves Lily from the backyard and when she sees my face, she jumps at me with excitement. My grin widens.

Just as quickly, though, my mood changes. I feel weights on the corners of my mouth when I see Jahi and Susanne chatting and laughing like old friends. He looks absorbed and happy to be with her. I feel invisible, six inches high and shrinking fast.

I try to focus on Lily, who sits at the kitchen table with her homework spread out in front of her. But my mind wanders—I feel like a failure. It makes me wonder how all my kids are going to do this school year. *Are they all going to do better without me?*

We work through her assignments as I steal surreptitious glances over my shoulder at Jahi and Susanne, unable to look away. I'm a spectator to their reunion, and it pains me to realize how alone and isolated I am. I wish she never came back. Without her around, Jahi and I talked for hours like the best of friends, but now that Susanne is here, we only exchange awkward glances.

When the lesson ends, Jahi thanks me and I make my way to the door as if in a daze—like a sleepwalking zombie, unable to process what just happened.

Susanne approaches me as I leave. Jahi stares at me, looking confused, as if to say he doesn't know why she's meeting me in the doorway. I don't even know if I want to hear why she's stopping me. I'm allergic to her. She's my competition. I hate her, and don't want to hear her phony voice.

"Rose." Susanne announces my name sarcastically, exposing a blinding flash of bleached white incisors. I try to return the smile like a mirror, but I imagine it looks like I'm baring my teeth like a wolf because that's what she's doing to me. Her barely veiled aggression is unmistakable. *What a nightmare.*

"Jahi tells me you tutor Lily just to help her. Is she lagging that badly?"

I regard her suspiciously. Her lips are drawn up and her face is frozen into a mask-like expression, making it hard for me to tell if she is accusing me of something.

"Well, she's a smart child. I just think she needs more attention for her homework and a good head start for next year to keep the momentum that we got going last year."

She throws me a look, suggesting she doesn't believe me one bit. Her frozen smile doesn't break. "That's great. Thank you. I know that. You were absent for a bit, weren't you?"

I don't know how to answer, so I just nod. After school ended, I spent six weeks in Fayetteville with my family, but it feels like I'm being accused of major crimes.

"Is there really a point to this? Does she need tutoring in the summer? Summer is supposed to be a time for fun. If there's a way to just ease you of the burden..." Her voice trails off.

"I'm not asking to be eased of the burden, Susanne. That's nice of you to think of me, though," I say through clenched teeth, getting out the door. I motion Jahi to follow me outside so I can tell him I'm staying in Eureka Springs, but Susanne stands squarely in the doorway, blocking my view.

Somehow, I'll stay in this small town, even though Susanne is back. I want to see if Eureka Springs has something for me, since it played a significant role in my healing after my divorce. This town is special, but now everything is different. I may never heal from seeing Jahi and Susanne being so chummy together. I fear this change may be irreversible—like how you can't unring a bell, or un-poison a well.

I walk back to my car and tears well up in my eyes. Jahi and Susanne have something I can never have, and it hurts more than I can articulate. I try convincing myself I'll get over him. But at this moment, my world is collapsing, like I'll never be happy again, the color leaching out of my spirit.

After leaving his house, I go straight to Jolene's. She'll probably make me eat some new Korean cuisine she's enthralled with and then she'll say men aren't worth it at all and she may be right. Jolene encouraged me to go to Jahi's house, though, even if with a minimal, non-committal grunt. I'm pretty sure she knows Susanne. It's a small town and Susanne, Jahi, and Jolene all grew up here.

I want to learn more about Susanne. When I get to Jolene's house, she's watching a sitcom. I'm not familiar with the show, but I sit beside her to watch it anyway, acting like I'm interested.

Jolene understands intuitively that something's wrong. She doesn't ask. I spill the entire story of what transpired between Susanne and me and the weird conversation we had just before I left the house. I almost left that last part out, but decided against it.

"Jahi must like you, and Susanne notices," Jolene says matter-of-factly after a long silence. I wait for her to talk more about the bombshell she just dropped on me. I can't understand how she could drop something that huge on me and then say nothing else.

"What does that even mean?"

"Hmm."

I glare at her lack of explanation. I can't believe her nerve. Afterwards, she opens a bottle of Syrah and serves leftover lasagna and a tossed salad. I'm surprised she's not serving Korean food, but I'm in a lasagna sort of mood because I need comfort food right now, so it's perfect. I leave, my heart shattering into fragments, and have the urge to hide under my blankets instead of sending the letter about clinical openings in Eureka Springs.

I want to fall into a hundred-year slumber, like the fair maiden in *Sleeping Beauty*, oblivious and anesthetized to my suffering—surrounded and protected by a tangle of brambles and a thicket of rose bushes and thorns. I'm cursed, as if from birth, to be unlucky in love. Like the old story, the curse unfolds when an evil fairy, Maleficent, causes the heroine to prick her finger on a spindle. Susanne is my Maleficent. Jahi is my prince, tending his roses but unaware of what they are guarding.

I want to be rescued by my one true love.

But until then, I must hide from the entire world.

CHAPTER THREE

JAHI

Today's my day off. Well, technically, I could get a call because I'm on backup duty, but it's unlikely. Lily's at swim camp and Susanne is visiting her mother, who lives in town. What a relief to have this delicious alone time on this rainy day without my estranged wife lurking around. She's invading my space and glomming onto me like an emotional vampire. She sucks the lifeblood out of my spirit, drains me with her neediness, and feeds off my energy, trying to gain power and control over me.

But I'm onto her. She sucked me in when I was distraught after Dad died. I was vulnerable then—a gangly teenager with an acne-riddled face, who witnessed his dad collapse and die right in front of him. I learned about mortality in a split second. Before that moment, I was immortal. Afterwards, I was immortal no more.

Thinking of Dad, I gaze out my rain-streaked kitchen window, my eyes scanning the dripping rose bushes dotting my backyard like specimens in an arboretum. Growing old roses goes back on my dad's side as far as anyone can remember. Big Daddy grew hundreds of roses, Dad too. Dad even named a rose after me, *Jahi Rose*. It's red and velvety with a scent of honey. Since Big Daddy and Dad are no longer here, I'm continuing the tradition.

The roses call me like the Sirens singing to Odysseus—as beautiful as Helen of Troy. They bewitch me and cast a spell. But in this case, they're not monsters and won't warble me to death and leave me in a field of bones, like in the old story. They're a benign, comforting presence, sharing their heavenly perfume as if they know I need it.

As I walk the sodden path of my rose garden, I look for the red velvet ones and find the *Jahi Rose.* My eyes fill with tears. I'm the age Dad was when he died—forty-years-old. My whole life, I've dreaded reaching the age when everything stopped for him. Before forty, I've mapped all my years onto his. At thirty-eight, I wondered, *What was Dad doing when he was this age?* Now and in the future, I'll surpass him, and I don't want to do that. I feel like a train running off the end of the track. He never got to be forty-one or any other age after that.

I see *Big Momma*, the rose Big Daddy named for his beloved wife, my grandmother. It's a voluptuous white rose with scents of honeysuckle. Walking along the wood chip path, there's a delicate pale pink rose tinged with white with scents of lilac and clove. An image of Rose flashes in my mind—it's the moment I first saw her—a picture of exquisite beauty with her subtle, almost fragile features, small bones, and radiant, otherworldly face, like a Botticelli beauty.

My reverie is broken by the loud beeping of my phone.

"Hey Jahi, it's me. There's a partially submerged vehicle in Mill Hollow Creek," Matt says breathlessly, urgency filling his voice. "The team from Fayetteville is on their way over with the heavy-duty tow truck and winch to make sure the truck doesn't sink any further. They've got to get the victims out fast, and need swift water rescue backup, just in case. Get over to the station STAT so we can help them out. We're all geared up. I've got the complete kit in the truck."

"I'll be there in two minutes," I say, grabbing my jacket, adrenaline coursing through my body. "It rained heavily yesterday. Is the creek swollen?"

"Yeah. They were crossing a low causeway that was underwater and slid into the creek. It's a full-size pickup truck with three passengers trapped inside. One of them is a little girl."

My heart drops when he mentions the child. "That water's cold."

I meet Matt within two minutes and we leap into the fire truck, the siren wailing as we round the curve from the station.

It's a thirty-five mile drive to Mill Hollow Creek, on the outer boundaries of our jurisdiction. I pray the victims are alive and not hypothermic and that the truck doesn't sink any further before the Fayetteville team gets there. There are so many variables. One slip on that muddy bottom before we get the victims out could spell catastrophe.

As Matt races the truck on the country road, I put on my dry suit, wet shoes, and life jacket so I'm ready to pounce when we get there. I stare at the floor of the truck, mentally rehearsing potential scenarios and remembering patterns I've seen in a dozen submerged vehicle accidents. Hopefully, it's on a stable riverbed. I worry because vehicles fill up with water within one to two minutes and I'm praying the truck isn't completely under water. When I look up, we're there. It's like we went through a time warp. There are moments I've experienced as a firefighter when it seems like the universe, or maybe it's our long-gone ancestors, watches over and guides us as we help others who are in peril.

I race out of the truck with my tools as Matt dons his uniform. My eyes zero in on the partially submerged, slightly tilted truck like a guided missile honing in on its target. The water level is at least halfway up the closed windows of the Ford F-150. It's a newer model, which means it has electric windows that won't open at this point because either the pressure won't allow it or the water has shorted out the electric circuits. Thankfully, the Fayetteville crew's tow truck got here first, winched it and stabilized the position of the truck.

One firefighter from Fayetteville tethers me with a line as I wade into the cold, moving water, feeling its resistance against my thighs. As I inch closer, the water rises to my chest. I see a man, woman, and child in the vehicle with water just below their necks. The blurry image of the three sharpens as I get closer. My mind registers their wide-eyed, panicked expressions before I realize who they are.

It's Clementine Crosby and her mom and stepdad! She's Lily's friend from first grade. I've hosted her for playdates at my house many times. I see a look of recognition in their eyes and pause for a second before my trained firefighter mind snaps into place like a jigsaw puzzle.

"Stay away from the window. I'm breaking it to get you out." Not sure they can hear me, I mouth the words and gesture as well. Whipping out my safety hammer, I smash the passenger side window. Glass crumbles as I knock it back to clear the way for their escape. Matt, tethered and standing in the water, is beside me.

They're shivering violently and have blue lips, but they're conscious, showing Stage I Hypothermia, the mildest form. This is good news because it's eminently treatable and they won't even need to go to the hospital. We've just got to get them out of the water, get them dry, and warm them up.

The stepfather, Roy, lifts Clementine into my arms, and I hold her firmly as she shivers. She looks terrified, but relieved to see me. I wade towards the shore and hear Matt behind me, carrying the mother, who is crying in gasps. A firefighter from the Fayetteville squadron retrieves the stepfather and helps him wade back to shore. We remove their wet clothes and dry their bodies with large towels as they shake uncontrollably. Our next step is to cover them with blankets and offer warm tea. Soon, they're able to talk without their teeth chattering.

"Thank you, Jahi and Matt," Roy says, his voice quivering. He recognizes Matt, too. Everyone knows Matt Youngblood in Eureka Springs. He's a fixture in town.

"You're welcome," I say.

"No problem," Matt replies.

"That was so scary when we slid into the creek and the windows locked up."

"I can only imagine the sheer terror of it. Thankfully, the truck stabilized in an area that's not too deep," I say, my mind flashing through images of Lily, Rose, and me in a similar situation. *What if something like this happened to us?*

I remember this blended family well. Roy treats Clementine like she's his own. The mother divorced the biological father when Clementine was two-years-old and no one is sure where he lives now. There's something about the three of them that mesmerizes me. When I first saw them in the submerged truck, with murky brown water swirling over the hood, their faces were etched with fear, which belied their understanding that they could die there. But the look on their faces also said if they were to perish, they wouldn't want to be with anyone else.

They've made it work. I think about my situation and imagine the possibility of creating my own happy little family like theirs with Lily and Rose. She would be a great stepmother and Lily loves her. *If they can make it work, why not me?*

CHAPTER FOUR

ROSE

Sometimes, I can be dramatic. I don't end up hiding under my blankets from the entire world like I fantasized. Instead, I spend three painful days staring at my laptop with bloodshot eyes, trying to write a letter to the group therapy organization Enid mentioned. I want to know if they'll consider opening a branch in Eureka Springs—a town in dire need of psychologists.

Unfortunately, my mind feels like it's moving in slow motion, as if through molasses and though I don't end up sleeping for a hundred years like Sleeping Beauty, my mind is ensnared in a thicket of thorns and roses as if no prince will come and rescue me. *Will I ever recover from the shock of losing Jahi and Lily?* Maybe this is what it feels like when you're dying on the inside, one heartbeat at a time.

The third day, I finally write the letter and the moment I send it, I feel a deep conviction to move on. If they say no to setting up a clinical practice in Eureka Springs, I'll see it as a sign from the universe that a higher power doesn't want me to be here. Well, that's technically a lie. I'm a spiritual person, not a religious one, and I believe in free will. I think God wants us to decide for ourselves what's best.

I shut my laptop, planning to get some wine to celebrate pushing through the torpor of heartbreak, but then I get a call from Beatrice. After my impromptu visit that led to a six-week stay in Fayetteville, Beatrice and I now call each other every day.

That visit worked magic on our relationship, making up for years of physical distance and silence. I couldn't hold anything back from her—she could read me like a psychic. I love that we're close again like when we were kids. We can talk and be silent together and it isn't awkward.

Expecting our usual banter, I'm not prepared for what comes next. I want her to say something fun, like she bought a sundress and strappy heels for a date with Andrew, or I should guess the new book Mom and her adorably dorky book club are reading. I answer the phone and what she says shakes me to my core.

"Rose, it's Mom," Beatrice says, her voice quivering. "She's sick, really sick."

Darkness envelops me like I'm in the Black Forest of fairy tales, full of mysterious and scary creatures. No light can penetrate it. My heart clenches. My mother was fine the last time I saw her a few weeks ago. But as Beatrice explains, she's deteriorated quickly, and now has a diagnosis of Stage II lung cancer.

"I need you to come here, Rose," Beatrice says, her voice raspy and breathless. "Mom needs you."

My mind races as I drive the winding country road to Fayetteville, an hour from Eureka Springs, enough time for my brain to imagine terrible scenarios. I can't believe it. Cancer doesn't happen to us—not to my mom.

When I get to the house, my mother is in bed, surrounded by pillows and blankets. A slight bluish cast covers her face like a mask. Her body looks drawn, her breathing labored, like she can't get enough air. When she coughs, her eyes widen in terror. *How can this be happening? She was fine when I saw her three weeks ago. What in the world is going on?*

I look at my sister to explain what went wrong with Mom. She's feeble, looking old and worn and precarious, like one of those leaning barns I see on the drive to Fayetteville. But I can't ask Beatrice anything because she looks like she might fall apart any second. I can't be the ill wind that scatters my sister's composure and makes her topple over.

"Rose, my dear, so good to see you," my mother whispers when I enter the room.

I can't believe my eyes. I was about to celebrate my resiliency over heartbreak with red wine at home while my mother withered away, dying in her bed. Maybe not dying, if the doctor let her return home. Oh, how I hate hospitals—the mind numbing bureaucracy, the wallet biopsies, and wondering whether you're going to emerge bankrupt or dead, or both. I've seen enough suffering of patients, being previously married to a surgeon, to last a lifetime. I pray Mom gets the excellent care she deserves.

I feel an unbearable emptiness and can hardly stand to see her like this. *Having lost Dad when I was seven, I can't lose Mom, too. I'm too young to lose her.* My mother has always been strong and vibrant, full of life. This frail, gaunt, sickly woman is unrecognizable, like a stranger. This isn't my mom. *How did it get to her so fast?*

She looked so healthy when I saw her last. I can't believe Beatrice called me every single day for the last month and we nattered on about mundane things like recipes and clothes while our mother lay on her deathbed. I want to spear my sister. *What was she thinking? Or was she in denial?*

But my mother still seems like herself in some ways. She asks about my life, my tutoring business, and my hopes and dreams. And then, as I prepare to leave, she drops a bombshell.

"Rose, I need you to do something for me," she says, her voice barely above a whisper. "The business opportunity you told me about—this is something that could be good for all of us, for our family. But I need you to promise me something. I need you to stay in Eureka Springs. You can't move, not now."

I'm taken aback. My mother has always supported my

dreams, but this is different—as if the fate of everything hinges on my staying in one place.

"I can't do that, Mom," I say finally, trying to keep my voice steady. "I need to figure out my job, my career."

"You really need to stay nearby," Mother insists. "This may be our last chance. We missed so many years together," she says, tears welling up in her eyes. My eyes mirror hers and fill with tears, too.

Mother's hands shake as she hands me the letter.

"Do you want me to read it now?" I ask quietly.

"Yes," Mom says, her voice barely audible.

My hands tremble and my vision blurs as I blink back tears and read the letter in silence. Mom watches me closely.

Dear Rose,

By the time you read this letter, you'll know about my diagnosis. It was such a shock when the doctor told me I have lung cancer that I couldn't believe his words. The child in me screamed in my head: Not me! I'm going to live forever.

Of course, I know we're all mortal and I guess the sand in my metaphorical hourglass is running out. I'm only sixty-eight, though. Surely I'll make it to seventy. I've always imagined living to one-hundred like my mother, who was blessed with longevity genes, but that blessing skipped me.

I've had a wonderful life and it's because of you and Beatrice. You are both the greatest joys of my life. You're everything to me.

There are some things I regret—one of the big ones is the deterioration of my marriage and how it negatively affected your life and the life of your sister. Yes, your dad disappeared and abandoned us, which was wrong, but I bear some responsibility for this, too. I'm a worrier, as you know, and I'm afraid I wasn't much fun for him to be around. I didn't understand his many interests, such as opera, evolutionary biology, economics, and politics, and just went along for the ride, sort of nodding and saying "yes, dear." Surely I was a terrible bore. It's no wonder he got in trouble for sexual harassment of his graduate student and maybe that's why he ran off in shame—or maybe he needed to avoid legal action from the university. I apologize for the broken family you and Beatrice endured. In my mind, this is likely a big reason you ended up with a man like Lee. He's a lot like your dad.

On that note, I regret rejecting Lee so vehemently that it drove you away. Even though I still detest the man to this day, I unwittingly put you in an untenable position of having to choose between your husband and your mother. I should have never done that. I was surly and derogatory towards him—no wonder you never visited. Who would? So, I want you to know I recognize it's because of me you couldn't visit all those years. Please, please, please do not for one minute blame yourself.

And one last regret—I'm so sad I never got you the St. Bernard puppy you desperately asked for throughout childhood after Dad disappeared. I hope one day you'll give yourself that little puppy.

You are the best daughter a mother could ever wish for. I want all your dreams to come true—I want you to meet your great love, to have children and a wonderful, loving family of your own and finally, to enjoy a deeply meaningful career as a psychologist or anything else you desire.

I love you dearest Rose, little "Rosebud," always and forever, ever, ever…

Love,
Mother

My mother knew about her diagnosis weeks earlier and wanted to protect me from another loss. I want to be raging mad at her. I want to swing my fists at things. I want to scream for hours on end, but I know life doesn't work that way.

But I also feel tenderness after reading her letter. *She partially blames herself for Dad's disappearance? She regrets her contemptuous behavior towards Lee?*

I need time to think about this, time to wrap my head around this letter and the fact that I may have to do something truly drastic. Even if I want to stay in Eureka Springs, I can't envision staying there just because my mother is terribly sick. I need to think about it first. Beatrice takes me in her arms, and we sob uncontrollably. Mother watches us both as we fall apart and try to pick the pieces up. It's beyond terrible. It's right up there as one of the most horrible experiences in my life.

Leaving the house that day, I feel a mixture of sadness and uncertainty. I don't know how to reconcile my own dreams and desires with my mother's urgent request. But I know that whatever lies ahead, it's going to be a rough, circuitous road. I don't know why I always get on the tough road. Maybe I have a lousy map or a crummy sense of direction. I finally want a relationship with a man after Lee and now his awful wife, who abandoned him and his daughter, returns, ruining everything. And then I get a nice job offer and suddenly my mother falls ill. I thought

I married a man who loved me, but it was a lie. I became a sad, lonely divorcée.

I can't keep doing this.

I can't keep living this life that is nothing but a string of disappointments. I promised my sister I would call her once I got home. It will take some days, but I already accept the fact that I need to take advantage of this moment and spend significantly more time with my family. I don't want to regret anything if Mom dies.

And as usual, I run to Jolene when I hear the news, even though I prefer to run to Jahi and tell him everything that's going wrong, but I can't. He has Susanne now. I tell Jolene the entire story and despite how emotionless Jolene is, she sets everything aside to accommodate me, insisting I sleep at her house so I won't be alone. She says someone needs to always be with me. *I suppose being there for Mom will force me to not think about myself so much, a backhanded blessing.*

At midnight, Jolene nudges me. "Hey, let's watch a movie."

Feeling numb, I oblige her. I end up bawling my eyes out at the end, even though the movie isn't sad at all.

Jolene watches as my tears fall on her favorite sofa. The red velvet one—her most treasured possession. Now it has salt stains.

"You don't need to cry, Rose," Jolene says softly. "We'll figure it out together."

I nod in silence. It's paradoxically one of the best moments of my life. It means the world to know she cherishes me. In the storm, the anchor holds.

CHAPTER FIVE

JAHI

I'm back home from the fire station exhausted but determined to talk with Susanne. Her presence irritates me. *How can she saunter into our lives, acting as if she can erase the hurt she inflicted on us years ago?*

She sleeps in the guest bedroom but keeps borrowing my bathroom even though there are two others in the house. She's invading my space and I don't like it. Why can't she accept that we can't live together? We never got along. So, why is she showing up now?

When I get home, Susanne is preparing dinner—shrimp and zucchini with spicy couscous, arugula salad, and sweet iced tea.

"Hey, why don't you two join me for dinner?" Susanne's voice is airy and lighthearted, as if she hasn't a care in the world.

I shrug. Too exhausted to cook, I grunt, "Sure."

She acts like a culinary expert, as if she has a passion for cooking. She's never been like that, at least not in all the years I've known her. Her new persona confuses me. Now she's channeling Martha Stewart.

Anytime I tell Matt about her antics, Matt's face turns scarlet with subdued anger, and he calls her devilish. According to him, Susanne is trying to lure me into a trap and ruin my life and while I don't completely agree, I don't entirely disagree, either.

I sit at the dinner table, staring at my plate as Susanne natters on about Rose.

"I don't understand why you keep inviting Rose here. Lily

doesn't need her anymore. She just gets in the way."

I ignore her snarky remarks because I know better. Ever since Susanne's return to our lives, Lily's been less confident, especially regarding her studies. Rose's continued presence is a godsend, helping her stay on track and prepare for second grade.

But Susanne doesn't see it that way. When Lily is out of earshot, she starts in, "You've got a crush on Rose. I see you flirting with her. You want her here all summer so you can ogle her," she accuses.

My blood boils at her accusations. *How dare she presume to know my intentions? It especially annoys me that her assessment is completely true in this case about my feelings for Rose. But besides that, she has no right to butt in.*

I became a single parent overnight, raising Lily on my own for years, while she abandoned us without looking back. I can't believe she feels entitled to have opinions about our lives. *Why does she presume she may step back into her daughter's life?* She lost her rights long ago.

"You have no right to butt in like this," I snap, my voice betraying the anger bubbling up inside me. "When Lily struggled in school, you were nowhere to be found. Don't think you get to decide what's best for her education. You don't know how much Lily suffered or how much I did. I wandered blindly in the darkness because my daughter's mother ran away to who knows where!"

Susanne flinches, her face pained. "Please, Jahi, don't be angry with me. I'm trying to make up for my mistakes."

And this gets under my skin—this meek voice—not the shouting, grating tone she used on me when we were together. I can handle the old Susanne, not this remorseful one that seems to regret everything she's done. *I can't stand it.*

"It's a little late for that, wouldn't you say? You left us, both of us, without a backward glance. And now you think you can walk back into our lives and start deciding for us? You didn't even let me decide whether I wanted a divorce. It was horrid. Do you get that? I was terrified and bereft. A full-grown man who had to figure out how to repair his broken heart and take care of a little girl in the meantime," I scoff.

Susanne stares at her plate, her hands folded in her lap. "I know I messed up. I know I'll never be able to fully make up for it. But I just want to do what's best for Lily."

I feel a twinge of guilt. The sadness in her voice undoes me. I know she's grappled with addiction and psychological issues, and I've been quick to judge her for it. But my anger is too raw, too deep, to let it go. *There's no excuse that can make up for what she's done. I've tried to forgive her because that's what I need to do to heal, but it's almost impossible.*

"You don't get to make that call," I state firmly. "Lily needs help, and Rose is doing a fantastic job. She's not just some crush of mine. She's helping our daughter, and that's all that should matter to you." *It's true. I have a crush on Rose, but that's none of Susanne's business.* Susanne's here because of her accommodation problem, but apart from that, I want nothing to do with her.

Susanne looks at me, her eyes apprehensive. "Do you really mean that, Jahi?"

I exhale heavily, the weight of years of hurt and disappointment bearing down on me. "Yes, I do Susanne. I want to believe you're trying to make amends, but it's hard to trust you after everything you've done. I'm wary of letting you back into Lily's life. It wasn't hard for you to leave our daughter the last time, so excuse me for being careful."

Susanne nods and stares at her food. "I understand. I'll try to respect your decisions."

I don't trust how agreeable she seems. I want her to scream

and shout in my face and tell me she wants nothing to do with me anymore, but she just stares at me as I reel off her flaws. She looks pathetic and apologetic, and it makes me cringe. *This is not the real Susanne. This is phoniness. I know her—I know her foibles, but I need to accept them, for now.* At this point in my life, I try to avoid problems as much as possible. Big Momma always said: *"Don't go borrowing trouble."* I try to remember her words. It keeps me sane.

My moods keep shifting, and I feel a bit of relief. *Maybe we can come to some kind of understanding, some kind of uneasy truce.* But the tense silence hanging over the rest of the meal tells me our road to reconciliation will be long and riddled with conflict.

As we clear the table, that nagging feeling of doubt returns. *Can Susanne ever make up for the years she missed, the hole she left in our lives? Can I ever forgive her?*

Only time will tell. But for now, we'll have to learn to coexist in this new, uncertain reality. For Lily's sake, if nothing else. Everything I ever did since Lily's birth, I did for her. Whenever I decided on something, no matter how small, I thought of Lily. She factored in as the most important consideration. *How will it affect her for Susanne to be in her life again?*

Lily sleeps in her bedroom after an evening of playing tag around the house with Susanne. Susanne is svelte and athletic and soon enough, I hear my daughter talking about running like it's her new passion. While I don't hate it, I don't like it either. Susanne's influence is taking hold quickly, and it worries me because she's wily and seductive. She's a fickle person with a mercurial temperament who might up and leave without warning. You can't predict what she'll do or say from moment to moment. I don't want my daughter becoming too attached to her.

I feel obligated to give Susanne the benefit of the doubt, though, because like my mother says, there's always good in people somewhere. You've just got to find it. My mother completely changed her philosophy in this case and now firmly believes Susanne has no redeeming qualities. Despite this, I must have seen something good in Susanne before we got married. Without her, there would be no Lily. The marriage deteriorated along the way and we need to find out what caused it and root out those problems. *We'll never know if I don't give her a chance to prove herself.*

A weight lifts off my shoulders as Susanne washes the dishes. We discuss Lily's needs and plans. A small step in the big scheme of things, but a start.

As bedtime arrives, Susanne hesitates at the door of her bedroom, her hand on the knob. "Jahi, I just want you to know that I'm truly sorry for everything I've done. I want to be part of Lily's life, and I'll do *anything* it takes to make things right."

I look at her, studying her eyes for any sign of sincerity. "I appreciate that, Susanne. But it's going to take more than words to make up for everything that happened."

She nods, a hint of sadness pulling at the corners of her eyes. "I understand. I'll keep trying, though. For Lily."

I watch as she closes the door, feeling a strange mixture of emotions. *Susanne has a long way to go before I can imagine fully trusting her again, but I also realize I want to give it one more try. For Lily's sake, if nothing else.*

As I head to bed, I think about the past and all the ways I could have done things differently. *Maybe if I had been more understanding, more patient, things would have been different.* But I can't change the past. All I can do is hope for a better future.

And maybe, just maybe, a future where Susanne will finally make amends for the mistakes of her past.

CHAPTER SIX

ROSE

Waiting to hear from Enid is making me anxious. So I do what I always do—I talk to Jolene.

"Hey, Jolene. I think I made a mistake by leaving my teaching role," I say hesitantly.

Jolene raises an eyebrow and says, "Rose, you're just restless because you're in between jobs. If it's money you need, you know I'll help you out."

My face flushes. *Is it obvious I'm worried about my money running out?*

"Besides, you can always draw unemployment. It's not a big deal," she says.

"Thanks, Jolene. I think I'm okay with my finances for now. It's just that I miss teaching. I miss the children."

"Well, you're a brilliant teacher, Rose, but in my heart, I believe your calling is to be a psychologist. I see that in you," she says confidently. "Besides… I could never live with myself if I steered you away from your life's work."

I'm touched by Jolene's tenderness and recognition of who I am. "Yeah, you're right, Jolene. I've always been a psychologist, even as a child. Growing up, I listened to my mother's woes and my friend's troubles. People said I was a natural therapist. Even my dental hygienist who has known me since childhood said she always saw me as a psychologist."

Jolene nods and then pulls out the Lee card in her pep talk. "I'm not being petty. Just loving the idea of you being the superstar psychologist "Dr. Rose," and Lee being threatened and jealous. He should figure out how wrong he was and regret leaving you."

"I understand the sentiment, Jolene," I say, laughing, as I wrestle to pull her closer for an embrace. "That's truly a vision."

Initially awkward with the somewhat forced embrace, Jolene's body softens. "Hey, you can visit the kids at school anytime. Maybe we could have you come give a talk about being a psychologist."

"Oh, I love that idea. It's good for kids to imagine possibilities."

Enid calls me after all these days. I waited so long for the call that I almost gave up.

"Hey, I'm sorry for going *incognito* for the last few weeks."

"No worries, Rose."

"What's up? Any news of a position?"

"Yes. Great news. There's a big possibility they might find a branch for you in Northwest Arkansas."

"Oh, I'm so relieved. But there's something I need to tell you." I inhale deeply, preparing myself to deliver the devastating news. "It's about Mom. She has cancer."

"Hey, let's switch to video," Enid says, her voice shaking. Her face appears, her brow wrinkled. "Rose, I'm so sorry. It's like I practically know your mom after all the things you've told me about her. Tell me how I can help. Just say the word and I'll be there."

"Thanks, Enid. I'm not sure what any of us can do. Cancer has a mind of its own. We all feel sort of powerless."

"Yeah, I understand."

"Besides, I don't need to be soothed. I'm not the one diagnosed with lung cancer. My mother is the one in terrible pain.

She can barely breathe and now she faces surgery, chemo, and immunotherapy. It all came on so suddenly, and she's never smoked a cigarette in her life, not even in the restroom in middle school. She could die even with treatment," I say, my voice quivering with emotion at the horrible reality my mother faces. *What I don't say is the odds are poor for non-small cell lung cancer—thirty-five percent for a five-year survival.* The more I think about it, the more my body shakes violently as tears spill down my face.

The conversation with Enid makes me realize I need to see Mom and Beatrice again, but first, I've got to go to Jahi's and tutor Lily. *The sessions with Lily are something I used to look forward to, but now I dread running into Susanne.* I'm missing the simpler days before she showed up. I just want to go back in time.

When Dad disappeared, I pretended a fairy would grant me my most treasured wish. My wish was for Dad to return. Now, that wish is undoing the last week when my world was upended. *I now hope to create a dual reality where my mother doesn't have cancer and Susanne disappears like someone lost on a hike. Then I can go back to the last fork and take the other branch.* I want to close my eyes and when I open them, make all the badness go away, but I guess life doesn't work like that. Or knowing my luck I'll get my wish, but there'll be some unfortunate side effect, like being turned into a newt.

In reality, Susanne wraps her suffocating tentacles around Jahi, rendering him defenseless. She devours him, leaving only picked over bones, bleaching in the summer sun. She's laying down the law that she wants me out of the picture. I don't present myself as a threat, yet she senses I am. She tells me to my face she doesn't want me to continue tutoring Lily, even though everyone can see clear as day that my tutoring helps her daughter immensely.

Perhaps I'm a reminder of all that she's not—a professional

woman and a consistent, loving presence in her daughter's life. Maybe I'm being biased, but I feel if I were Lily's mother, I'd definitely put her education first.

Of course, everyone is different and really, I classify Susanne into the category of cluster B personality disorder. It's not exactly the nicest thing to say, but it's the truth. Why do I think this? Well, she's definitely got a personality disorder. She has a maladaptive pattern of behavior that ruins her relationships and her life. She's a textbook case, and she's massively destructive.

When I was in grad school, we remembered personality disorders with the nifty mnemonic: "mad, bad, and sad". Mad is Cluster A, the Mad Hatter. They're not encountered too often. They're locked away, howling at the moon. Bad is Cluster B. They're normal enough to be in your life but cause trouble at every opportunity with their disruptiveness and entitlement. Sad is Cluster C, cautious and anxious. They're not encountered too often because they're avoidant.

So when I'm saying she's Cluster B, I'm saying this is code for the difficult patient. Susanne has a combination of issues—a bit of this and a bit of that—self-absorption, narcissism, borderline traits, and antisocial tendencies. One of her biggest problems is lacking empathy and being internally chaotic, dysregulated, and remorseless. She's manipulative, exploitative, and covers it up with crocodile tears. She leaves a trail of destruction wherever she goes. No wonder she's so flippant. I hope she has some iota of self-awareness even though she's disturbed. I like it when people do, but I doubt it with her.

Packing my bags for Fayetteville, I figure I'll stay a few days. I crave time with Mom any chance I get because I keep perseverating about her dying. Her odds for survival aren't great, but she's a fighter. The thing that eats at me is how fast her condition is deteriorating. It's like she's fallen off a cliff. *I'm scared.*

One last stop before seeing Mom. I approach Jahi's house and, sure enough, Susanne answers the door. Initially, she seems polite, but her unconscious micro expressions betray her. I notice her nostrils flaring and her lips forming a slight smile. An awkward silence hangs between us before she invites me in. I find Lily in the kitchen, who leaps up and throws her arms around my waist. I tutor her in math and end the session exactly one hour later, excusing myself and walking away feeling relief, yet sadness.

Driving with a heavy heart towards Fayetteville, images of my bedridden mother flash in my mind. I'm trying to stay optimistic, but it's almost impossible. As I drive on Highway 45, I try to distract myself from unsettling thoughts. But it's useless. I can't push away the ominous nightmares that riddle my sleep, causing me to wake up screaming and soaked in a cold sweat, my heart racing.

What if she doesn't make it? What will happen to me and Beatrice? Will I still have a family? Mom is the glue that holds our family together. She loves us both, but she's especially close to Beatrice.

My sister greets me at the door, her eyes inflamed from lack of sleep and worry. I hug her and she collapses in my arms.

"Rose, thank goodness you're here," she says with a relieved sigh. "Mom's been asking about you."

Embracing my sister, the weight of the situation presses down on me. "I'm here, Beatrice. I'll do whatever I can to help."

Over the next few days, I sit with Mom and hold her hand. I clean the house and cook for my sister. My mother can't eat much, so I make her bone broth or miso soup. I'm untethered from my life in Eureka Springs. Though only an hour away, it feels like a world apart, perhaps like how the "old country" feels to an emigrant, full of once-familiar and now odd customs, with strange clothes and hats.

I moved to Eureka Springs because of my lying husband, and I've felt happy there ever since. Well, at least since I met Jahi and Lily. But now, looking back, it feels surreal—sort of foreign and distant—as if I outgrew it or perhaps it outgrew me. I'm ashamed I've only come here to visit Mom and Beatrice when I have problems with my job or my love life. I almost hate myself for this now.

Beatrice notices my distant behavior and pulls me aside. "What's going on, Rose? You seem so far away."

I hesitate. "I don't really know, Bea. Being back here feels like a different world. I don't know if I'll ever be able to recover the way things were before."

Beatrice looks concerned. "What do you mean? I know it's hard, Rose. But remember, you have a life waiting for you in Eureka Springs. You've got your own dreams and aspirations to pursue."

I nod. *Indeed, I can't simply put my life on hold because of my mother's illness. I must keep going, even if it's scary and uncertain.*

The days are a blur of doctors' appointments with the surgeon and oncologist, medications, and emotional conversations. My heart aches to see my mother in so much pain, but I try to be there as a comfort for her.

After cleaning the dishes from lunch, my sister turns to me with a serious expression.

"Rose, I know it's hard to think about, but what are your plans after this? Will you stay in Fayetteville to take care of Mom?" I notice Beatrice's gaze leaves mine, and she fiddles with the dishcloth.

"Hmm. I'm not sure."

"Or will you go back to Eureka Springs?"

My heart goes out to my sister. She sees me as the worldly one, the one who takes chances… the one who left while she stayed. She waffles between thinking she needs my help and not wanting it. I take a deep breath and smile, doing my best to hide the weight of her questions. "I've been thinking about it a lot, Beatrice. Trust me. It's difficult. No matter what happens, I'm staying in Eureka Springs."

I thought seriously about moving to Fayetteville, but I don't fit in here. Mom and Bea are a solid team and always have been. *And I don't want to leave Eureka Springs. It holds such a huge part of me I just can't leave behind.* It came at a pivotal time when I needed a win. The failure of my marriage to Lee shattered and defeated me. This small town was a tonic for my soul, literally a spring of good feelings, freely gushing. I needed a job and a fresh start and the school was desperate for a first grade teacher. *What they didn't know is I needed them as much as they needed me.* I was desperate for meaning and redemption.

I'll never forget the children's ebullience and guileless ability to absorb new experiences like sponges. The children's sparkling eyes, especially Lily's, lit up my days and got me out of bed those first few tough weeks when I didn't know anyone.

At first, not knowing anyone was a benefit because I needed to keep to myself to heal. But later, when I needed human contact and nurturing, I found it in abundance in this small town. And of course, there's Jahi. My experiences in LA painted that city in a negative light. I'm sure for others it's a godsend, a place where dreams come true, full of opportunity and possibility, fame and bright lights. But for me, that special place is Eureka Springs.

Beatrice nods her head, looking contemplative. "I get it. I think I always knew what you had to do. You have your own life to live, and you can't put it on hold for us. We'll manage here without you. I promise." Her tone is sincere.

I throw my arms around her neck and pull her closer to me. I love her so much. Bea is the best. She's always been like that, ever the understanding older sister. She's found so much meaning here in this town. I'm happy for her.

"Thank you so much, B! You're the coolest." We tease each other even though the atmosphere is tense since our mother may be on her deathbed. *I'm forever grateful for Beatrice and everything she's done for me since childhood, and for once I decide to tell her.* After a while, she yells at me to stop thanking her because it's embarrassing, and then we just sit in silence.

"Just never move too far from Mom, though. You know that, right? I know she doesn't say it or show it, but I believe you're her favorite and always have been. You must visit all the time, okay?"

"Yes," I assure her, though I'm surprised by her assertion that I'm Mom's favorite. We tease each other a bit more, and my eyes water as I think about Beatrice and Mom alone together in my mother's last days.

I'm relieved she understands my predicament. It's so hard to make such a hard decision, but it's the right one. Besides, I wonder if it's actually relieving to Bea that I'm not moving to Fayetteville. It might disrupt the status quo. There's a long-standing equilibrium between Bea and Mom living together for two decades. Three is an awkward number. If I moved in with them, it might destabilize things.

Driving back to Eureka Springs, a feeling of peace settles over me like a down comforter. The road ahead is uncertain, and the journey will be difficult, but I know I'm making the right choice.

No matter what happens, I'll survive. I drive through the rolling hills and past the quaint farms of the Ozarks and tell myself I belong here. Eureka Springs may not be my hometown, but it's become my home in every sense of the word.

I feel a bit of elation as I arrive at my bungalow.

I'll continue to pursue my dreams. Perhaps I'll start a charity or volunteer at the local hospital. Maybe that's far-fetched and I'm getting ahead of myself, but I'm a dreamer—always have been. I don't know how Enid's job idea will pan out, but I can't wait to see how my life unfolds in the coming year.

CHAPTER SEVEN

JAHI

Loose lips and prying eyes are all around and sink me. My family finds out about Susanne. *Nothing stays a secret for long in Eureka Springs, and why would this be any different?* It's juicy material for the gossipy people in town. They've got nothing better to do than put their noses where they don't belong.

At our monthly Sunday dinner, it's clear Mom and Chrissy know about Susanne. I'm not sure how they found out. Lily said nothing.

Before we left the house, I told Lily not to say a word about her mom because I planned to tell everyone myself. Even though that wasn't the best excuse, my daughter agreed. I mean, she's only seven-years-old. It clearly wouldn't take much to deceive her, and while that's not my intention, I simply didn't know what to do. I didn't want to talk about it, but somehow my family got wind of the fact that Susanne was back.

The hounds of hell will break loose when I tell them.

My sister gives me a knowing look but says nothing. The unspoken tension hangs in the air like the smoke of a Cuban cigar—fusty, thick and persistent. I break the silence and watch my family pretend they haven't already heard the news. *Maybe I should leave now.* I could have stayed home and watched TV reruns, but if I did, my family would send out a search party for me.

It starts out okay. As we enter the house, Lily bounces with excitement beside me. Mom greets us with a big smile, and Chrissy gives me a quick hug. We sit down to eat, and the conversation flows. Lucas and I debate about the best universities in the South. I prefer Arkansas, the Athens of the Ozarks and he likes Ole Miss, the iconic university in Oxford, Mississippi. We take a well-worn detour into guy talk and bond over sports, discussing the merits of the football teams, coaches, and new quarterbacks, while playfully trash-talking the opposing team.

But then, the conversation takes an awkward turn when I mention Susanne's return and that she's staying with me. I know it sounds shocking to them, coming so calmly from me, and they have every right to be angry, given my family's fraught history with Susanne. Even Lucas stares at me in disbelief.

Chrissy erupts. "I can't believe you're doing this, Jahi," she says, her voice rising. "After everything she's done to you, you're going to let her back into your life? Into Lily's life? Are you a fool?"

Lucas tries to calm her down before she says something she can't take back, but fails woefully. My sister knows no bounds when she gets mad. Her anger spins out of control like a flaming tornado, devastating everything in its path. No one can withstand her tantrums.

I try explaining how Susanne has changed, and I'm giving her another chance. But my family is deaf to my pleas. They're concerned for my safety and Lily's. Secretly, I don't believe she has changed either, but I dig in deeper to defend my position, saying anything to get Chrissy and Mom off my back. I'm forty years old and they're still haranguing me.

"It's not safe, Jahi," my mom insists, her tone serious. "You need to think about Lily and what's best for her in the long run."

But I can't just cut Susanne out of my life. She's the mother of my child. Just this one time, I need to stick my neck out for her and give her another chance. I try explaining this to my family, but they don't want to hear it.

Chrissy takes it a step further, threatening to not speak to me if I continue allowing Susanne into my home. This hurts me deeply, but I stand resolute. Chrissy can be dramatic. There's fire in her eyes. *I think she's disappointed I took a long time to tell her about it.*

The discussion devolves from there, making it clear my family won't accept Susanne back into our lives. I leave dejected, reeling from their lack of support. Deep down, I know their skepticism is justified, but I don't want to admit it. *I feel it, too, but I want them to support me and soothe away my doubts.*

Susanne is different, and I want to give her one last chance. It won't be easy, but I'm willing to do whatever it takes to make it work. But I'm torn. There's still the issue with Rose. *I can't get her out of my mind.* I feel whipsawed choosing between two extremes—my problematic first love, Susanne, and the radiant, Botticelli-esque Rose. There's a momentum, a historical loyalty I have for Susanne. I've known her since childhood, and she was my high school sweetheart. *When I married her, I was all in.* As for Rose, she's a fascinating possibility, but it's all theoretical.

It gets down to the practical issue that Susanne is a known quantity, and Rose is not. *Does Rose like me as much as I like her? Could she be harboring unknown psychological landmines? Did Lee divorce her for a good reason?* By the time you're forty, you have enough emotional baggage for a tour group.

No matter what, I've got to give it one last try, for Lily's sake. I want Lily to have two parents at home. It doesn't matter how much she likes Rose. No one can replace her mother.

The mood at the dinner table sours. Lily picks at her food, her eyebrows raise and furrow. She cuts her eyes from person to person but doesn't say a word.

Mom's high-pitched Pollyanna voice punctuates the silence. "Oh, how pretty your braids are, Lily."

Chrissy rolls her eyes at Mom's attempt to diffuse the tension and exhales in scorn. To call it an awkward moment doesn't cover it. Mom always tries to salvage family arguments, but in this case, the damage is done.

The ghost of Susanne lingers like a dark cloud over the table, and the atmosphere is heavy and oppressive. Chrissy spits out Susanne's name with derision, calling her a sicko. She just can't hold her tongue even with Lily there. I hate when she's like this—a madwoman. How can Lucas tolerate her? Is he Saint Luke? Maybe there's more to their marital issues than whether to have a child or try IVF. She curses under her breath, and I shake my head. I need to get Lily out of here. I cannot sway Chrissy. You can't talk any sense into her at this point.

I'm sad when we say our goodbyes. I hate leaving on such an uneasy note. Their disapproval hurts. The thought of causing a schism makes my heart ache. I'll never lose their love, but it might feel distant and discordant if I go forward with my plans. But I can't give up on Susanne, not yet. I need to give her a chance to prove she's changed and can be a decent mother to Lily.

As we walk to the car, I hug Lily tightly, feeling a surge of protectiveness for her. *She's the light of my life and I won't put her in any danger—not for the sake of my personal feelings, not for anything.*

Driving home, I'm restless. I can't let the opinions of my family dictate my life. I need to do what's right for Lily and me, even if it means going against the people I love.

Susanne is waiting up for us, a slight smile on her lips.

I'm not alone in this. Together, we'll make things work, no matter what anyone else thinks.

It's the day after the showdown with my family, and I'm riddled with self-doubt. Things feel shaky, but I'm still compelled to give Susanne one more chance in our marriage, even though I'm torn up about it.

I want to make sure I'm not making the worst decision of my life. Will it end up ruinous if I take Susanne back? It's time to have a talk with her. *I can't blindly put my trust in someone I'm not sure of.* So, after she drops Lily off at school—something that's become routine in the last few days, a pattern I'm not sure I like—I call her.

My heart races as I wait for her to answer. So many years went by without a word from her and now she's here, living with us temporarily and we talk day and night. Something about this situation bothers me. I need to know if Susanne is serious about being here this time, or if she'll hurt us all over again.

When she finally answers, I take a deep breath, trying to keep my voice steady. "Susanne, I need to talk to you," I say, my heart pounding. "Can you meet me at the house, please?"

I wait anxiously as she drives across town. When she arrives, she looks stricken with fear and uncertainty. We both know this conversation is a watershed moment.

"Jahi," she says softly, taking a seat opposite me. "What's going on?"

I steel myself. "Susanne, we need to talk about why you're really here. I need to know you're not faking it this time, that you're committed to being here for Lily."

My family has solid reasons for rejecting her—reasons I agree with. She can be mercurial. You can't trust her. Everyone knows this about her, but if it's going to be good for Lily, I must reconcile my ambivalence.

Susanne's eyes flicker with hurt and disappointment, and I regret my words. But I can't back down. I must be strong. I need to know the truth, no matter how much it hurts. *Why am I feeling bad for her when she's the one who hurt us? It's like I'm making excuses for her.* I can't believe I'm doing this. When she showed up in my life out of nowhere, she wanted to use me to pay back a loan shark. But now, what's her reason for staying?

"I understand that, Jahi," she says, her voice trembling. "I know I hurt you and Lily before, and I'm so sorry. But I'm here now, and I want to make things right. I want to be the mother Lily deserves, and I want to be a good wife to you."

There's sincerity in her voice, and it gives me a glimmer of hope. But I can't forget the pain she caused in the past. *I need to be careful, to make sure I don't set myself and Lily up for more heartache.*

"Susanne, you need to understand. My family isn't happy about this," I say, my voice firm. "And frankly, I'm not sure where I stand, either. But I'm willing to give you one last chance if you're serious about repairing the relationship. If you're not, it's better for all of us if you leave now."

Susanne looks like I have slapped her. "Jahi, I swear. I'm serious this time," she says earnestly. "I will not hurt you or Lily again. I've made mistakes in the past, but I want to do better. Lily deserves a wonderful mother. I don't want to be the witch who left her family. It's a stretch for me to ask you to trust me, and perhaps I don't have the right to ask you for anything. I'm a totally horrible person, but I need you to trust me, Jahi. We can make this work."

I nod. I know I'm letting my family down—the ones who rescued Lily and me when Susanne kicked us in the teeth and left. And now, I'm suddenly back with the woman who caused such heartache. It's awful. *Does this even make sense?* I have to reassure myself every minute that I'm not making the greatest mistake of my life.

My resolve weakens as I search her eyes. *Is it possible she's really changed? Can we make it work and become a family again? Will Lily finally have a mother?*

I can't ignore the cautionary voice in my head. "I want to believe you, Susanne, but you must understand, it will not be easy. You have a lot of trust to earn back. And if you do anything to hurt Lily or me again, I won't hesitate to send you packing."

The threat hangs in the air, a warning I hope I never have to act on. Someone overhearing our conversation might believe I'm the one with the upper hand, but I'm not. That's an illusion. *I don't know if I'll survive if she walks out again. It would be like damage below the waterline and I feel I would sink.*

Susanne appears on the verge of tears, but nods resolutely. "I understand, Jahi. Earning back your trust is something I'm determined to do. I'm willing to do whatever it takes."

As we talk, I feel a sliver of hope. Later, I prepare for bed and call Matt.

"Hey Jahi," he answers grumpily.

"Hi Matt. You sound surly. Is Jane nagging you?"

"Nah. It's not Jane. It's Chrissy. She called over here complaining about you taking Susanne back. It went on for hours. I'm drained."

"Yeah, she blew up at me at dinner on Sunday."

"Well, I've got to admit I agree with her. I don't approve of Susanne either, but it's not my life. It's yours. Anyway, I support you no matter what."

"Thanks, Matt. You're a great friend. It's complicated and I've got mixed feelings, but I keep thinking I've got to give it one more chance, for Lily's sake."

"I understand, Jahi. And by the way, you're my best friend and don't you forget it. I'm always here for you," Matt says.

I've been unconsciously trying to gain Matt's approval, but

he admits he's secretly rooting for Rose and can't picture me with anyone else. *I don't think this is the entire story of his disapproval of Susanne, but I accept his explanation, anyway.* Failure to do so will make him keep explaining, and sometimes he talks like he's paid by the word.

CHAPTER EIGHT

ROSE

I have one thought in mind when I arrive at Jahi's house to tutor Lily. This will be my last tutoring session. Not because I'm moving, I'm not, but because gossip flies around this town, and that's how I know Jahi is getting back together with Susanne. I saw the vibe between them that day when I left for Fayetteville. There's a reason they married. *They must have loved each other.* I should have seen that coming, but I was so smitten by Jahi and his gentle ways I was blind to the truth.

Even through my mother's sickness, I still called Beatrice to tell her about the latest development with Jahi. She was concerned and repeatedly asked if I would be okay and visit Fayetteville to spend time with her and Mom. Unfortunately, seeing my sickly mom depresses me, but I thanked her for the suggestion.

I need to talk to Jahi.

As soon as he opens the door, I see Susanne sitting on the sofa watching a movie. She greets me with an inscrutable smile and calls out to Lily. Lily hugs me and we begin our session.

I sit across from Lily, watching her innocent face as she concentrates on her math problems. She's a bright child and tutoring her lights up my day. But this day is bittersweet. It will be my last.

I must tell Jahi the truth about why I'm quitting.

After we finish, I pack my things and give Lily a hug. "Keep up the good work, okay?" I urge her, trying to keep my voice steady.

As we walk out of the study, Jahi appears in the hallway. "Hey, Rose. How's it going?" he asks, a casual smile on his face.

I want to tell Lily this is our last tutoring session, but I decide to leave that task up to her dad. It's his daughter. Surely, he knows best how to talk to her about it. I hope so. After all, he didn't really know how to go about braiding her hair.

I take a deep breath, trying to prepare myself for what I'm about to say. "Actually, Jahi, I need to talk to you about something," I say, my heart pounding so loudly I can hear it in my head.

Jahi's smile fades. "Is everything okay?" he frowns.

Susanne is nowhere to be found. Has she retired into her bedroom? Is she waiting for me to leave so she and Jahi can enter his bedroom and sleep together? The thought makes my chest hurt, and I almost want to stay to prevent that from happening.

I nod, biting my lip and trying to keep my voice calm. "Yeah, everything's fine. It's just... I can't keep tutoring Lily anymore," I say, my eyes locked, unblinking, onto his.

Jahi's brow furrows. "Why not?" he asks, confusion spreading across his face.

I take a deep breath.

Because... I have feelings for you, Jahi, and I can't keep pretending like I don't. It wouldn't be fair to Lily or to me.

I imagine saying all that to him, but I say, "I just think it's the best decision."

Jahi's eyes widen, and he takes a step back. "Rose, if you're sure." He pauses and takes a deep breath, and I sense what is coming next. "I'm... I'm getting back together with Susanne. I want Lily to have two loving parents and a complete family."

Wracked with disappointment, my face tightens, but I force a smile. "I understand, Jahi. Honestly, I just want to be real with you. I wish you and your family the best," I say, trying to keep my voice steady. I fail at it but hope Jahi doesn't notice because if he does, I'll have no excuse to give him but to say the real reason I must leave.

Jahi looks like he wants to say more, but then just nods. "Thanks, Rose. I appreciate your honesty. I'm sorry it didn't work out," he says, his voice almost a whisper.

As he walks away, sadness wells up in my chest. But I know this is the right decision. It would be too hard to keep tutoring Lily while nursing a secret crush on her father.

I promise myself that day to focus on my happiness and find someone who'll love me back just as fiercely as I love him.

It won't be easy, but I have to try. I'll call Enid to see what's going on, because I need to know my next step. No use sitting around, waiting for a man. He decided and I hope he finds peace with that. I just pray I'll find peace, too.

Stumbling into my bungalow, I collapse on the couch, tears streaming down my face. Jahi's getting back together with Susanne. I don't know why I thought I ever had a chance, but my heart shatters into a million pieces.

I grab a bottle of Burgundy from the counter, pull the cork with a mighty yank and a resounding pop, and drink straight from it. I don't care anymore. All I can think about is how much I love Jahi, and how he never felt the same way about me.

Halfway through the bottle, memories of my marriage flash before me. It was a fiasco, from start to finish. Lee was abusive and controlling. I finally found the strength to leave LA when Lee filed for divorce after ten years of marriage, but it took a toll on my self-esteem. More than a toll, he stomped it flat.

Now, here I am, heartbroken once again. Life keeps kicking me while I'm down. I cry harder, wishing things could have been different with Jahi.

But then, I feel defiant—a change of heart. *I don't need a man for my happiness. I have to find it within myself.*

Wiping my tears, I stand, feeling more determined than ever. It's time to focus on my happiness and find joy in the little things.

I'll keep tutoring Lily after all and be the best tutor she's ever had.

And maybe, just maybe, I'll find someone else who'll love me back. Someone who sees me for me, not just as a tutor or a rebound relationship.

I finish the bottle at a more civilized pace, even fetching a proper glass. Jahi may have hurt me, but he doesn't define my life. I have the power to shape my destiny, and I'll use it to find happiness.

For now, though, I'm content to sleep and dream of a brighter future. Even though my life is in total shambles, and I teeter on the edge of falling apart, I don't want to think about that. I will focus on the positive. As my wine-filled mind convinces me of great things, I lean over and plop my head on a pillow. The empty wine bottle rolls under the sofa, escaping the snoring monster above.

CHAPTER NINE

JAHI

Matt says I have his support no matter what, but he seems not as friendly as usual. In constant motion, I can't get his attention as he finds ways of excusing himself. Something feels off. At first, I think Matt's just mad at me, but I realize that it's probably something else. Matt doesn't hold grudges and if he has an issue with me, he tells me immediately.

I figure it must be a personal problem. Frustrated with the charade, I surprise him at Living H.I. Coffee & Treats, devouring a cinnamon roll, scattering crumbs everywhere. I take a seat in front of him and wait. He acknowledges me reluctantly.

"Matt, come clean. You're going to tell me what your problem is, and you're going to tell me now."

His body arches back from my confrontation, and he wipes his mouth with a crumpled paper napkin. I never get confrontational. I avoid confrontations as much as I can. *What am I doing?*

Matt dons a contrived smile. "Homeboy, I do not know what you're talking about."

He sucks at lying. Of course, something is terribly wrong, and I won't stop until I find out. "I'm going to find out, anyway. Isn't it better for you to tell me now?"

He sighs. "It's Jane. She's upset with me about not spending enough time at home with her and the kids."

"Oh, yeah. That's still going on, huh?" While I'm not thrilled to hear Matt is struggling with marital issues, I'm relieved his troubles have nothing to do with me. We go back to the station to sign off from our shift.

He elaborates on the tension between him and Jane. Then the alarm goes off and we scramble to don protective gear. It's a house fire on the outskirts of town. Our whale of a fire truck careens out of the station, sirens screaming.

The fire is well developed by the time we get to the scene. It got an ample head start before the fire station received a call from passersby.

The sounds of the fire shock me with its cacophony of pops, snaps, and an all-encompassing roar like a military jet taking off. I'm never prepared for how loud it is. It feels like an assault on the center of my being, as if it's roaring inside me. Flames lick at the edges of the structure, like a living beast, while smoke fills the rooms in a deadly, unbreathable tide descending from the ceiling.

The heat burns my face as if I'm basking in the desert sun. Time is elastic. It slows down and stretches out. The dreamlike landscape is paradoxical with the simultaneous combination of sensory overwhelm and sensory deprivation, of time experienced as both fast and slow, of beauty and destruction. The beauty of the color, the light, the motion, and yet its deadliness.

Fire mesmerizes people when it's contained. With billowing, leaping, swirling flames, it's a dance with the devil. But now time is critical. This is not an environment hospitable to human life. Every minute decreases the chances of survival for inhabitants and firefighters alike. Hurry, but do not make mistakes. And know which threats to push through and which to retreat from.

We assess the situation, figuring out our best course of action. Unfurling the hoses and snaking our way into the house, we direct the water to extinguish the most critical flames. Smoke surrounds us as we navigate through unfamiliar territory to find anyone trapped inside. We don't know the layout of the house—

we never do—but we work intuitively. I worry we'll miss someone or find them too late.

We hear faint cries near us. My heart races, knowing people need us to extricate them and save their lives. I bump into a small shape crouched on the floor and scoop him up. Matt finds another small person next to mine and lifts her into his arms. Running outside, we deliver them to the paramedics. The little boy cries out for his mommy and says she's upstairs with his two little sisters.

We rush back in, the fire roaring, searching for the stairs, but they've collapsed already. Panicking, we retrace our steps back outside and yell at the team to deploy the ladder. We lean it against the house and clamber up the metal steps to the upstairs window. It won't open, so we break the glass with an ax and climb through. Blinded by roiling smoke, we crawl on the floor to get underneath it, feeling for bodies.

The smoke is a lurid orange lit by flames shooting up from where the staircase was. We find the mother and children lying on the floor, unmoving. *Are they unconscious or already dead?* I lift the woman over my shoulder and Matt holds the two babies in his left arm. As we climb out the window and descend the ladder, I have a bad feeling they won't make it. The paramedic team starts CPR, but it doesn't look good.

They're still working on resuscitating the mother and babies in the ambulances as they speed away to the hospital. Matt and I exchange knowing looks. What a rotten day. We tried everything we could to save them, but are afraid they'll die. The two children we found on the ground floor may end up orphaned.

I feel a deep sadness and dejection, despite knowing that sometimes we cannot save everyone. It's like a reflex. If I can't save everyone, I feel like a failure. I can't help it. It's the way I felt when Dad died—powerless and devastated. *I'll never get the image out of my head of standing there, frozen, when Dad collapsed.*

Matt's eyes are downcast as we return to the station in silence. Today's tragedy on the heels of his recent marital struggles tips him over the edge. We did everything possible to save the mother and her babies, but it probably wasn't enough.

There will be other fires to fight, but today was devastating. I have to remember we're firefighters, and we can't save everyone. The day's events settle like weights on my shoulders. We haven't heard news from the hospital yet, but I can't shake the sadness from my soul.

When I get home, Susanne is waiting for me. She senses something is off. I kick off my boots and slump on the couch, letting out a long sigh, and I tell her about the tragedy.

"Hey," she says softly, placing a hand on my shoulder. I flinch. I don't pull away, but I don't want her to touch me, either. She pulls her hand away, looking hurt.

"Hey," I reply, my voice gravelly.

Susanne sits beside me, her eyes scanning my face. "I know it's been a tough day," she says. "But you can't keep it all bottled up inside. You need to talk it out."

Shaking my head, I say, "I don't want to talk any more about it. Nor do I even want to think about it."

I see the disappointment in her eyes, but she doesn't push the issue. Instead, she leans her head against my shoulder and lets out a small sigh.

We sit in silence, neither of us saying anything. It's strange, being so close to her again after all these years.

"How have you been?" I ask her, breaking the quiet.

She shrugs. "Alright, I guess. Trying to rebuild my life."

"And how's that going?"

She smiles slightly. "Well, I'm here, aren't I? That's something, I suppose."

We fall into another silence. My thoughts drift back to the fire. I don't like feeling helpless, standing there watching as flames consume everything. *I did everything I could, but it wasn't enough.*

Susanne shifts her position, and I feel her gaze on my face.

"I know it's hard," she says softly. "But you're strong, Jahi. You've been through so much, and you've always come out the other side."

I scoff. "Strong? How can you say that? I couldn't save them, Sue. I couldn't save them." Somehow, deep down, I know the mother and baby girls didn't survive. Tears prick the corners of my eyes, and I fight to keep them at bay. I haven't cried in front of anyone since the day Susanne left, and I don't want to start now.

"It's not your fault," she says firmly. "You did everything you could. Sometimes… sometimes, things just don't go the way we want them to."

"Yeah." I nod. I want to believe her. I really do. But the guilt is so heavy, I can hardly stand it. I'm not sure I want to admit this, but the words spill out, anyway. "Sometimes you can do everything right and still lose."

"That's true." Susanne falls silent. "But you know, I've always admired your strength," she continues. "When we were together. I thought you were the strongest person I knew."

I turn to look at her. Her hair is shorter than it once was, and she has lines around her eyes I haven't seen before. But she's still the same person I fell in love with all those years ago.

"I didn't feel very strong when you left."

"I'm sorry," she says quietly. "I never meant to hurt you like that."

I shake my head. "It's okay. It's in the past, and we both made mistakes."

Susanne lets out a breath. "I'm glad we can be friends now, at least."

I'm not sure if I'm glad about that or not. Part of me is still angry at her for leaving, but another part is grateful to have her back in my life.

"Yeah," I say finally. "It's good to have you around for our daughter."

Susanne's face lights up at the mention of our daughter. "How do you think she's doing?"

"She's good," I reply, smiling slightly. "Growing up way too fast, though."

We talk a while longer, reminiscing about Lily's birth and the early years when we were a family.

As the conversation ends, Susanne stands. "I should probably get going. I don't want to overstay my welcome," she says, searching my face.

Susanne is staying with her mother for a few days, but I could use her company right now. I'm anguished, and I don't want to be alone with my thoughts. At every lull in the conversation, images of the woman and her two babies lying limp upstairs in that inferno intrude on my thoughts. My mind searches for what else we should have done to save them. I can't stop thinking we could have extinguished the fire sooner if we'd gotten there earlier. If, if, if.

"It's fine," I say, not wanting her to leave just yet. "You can stay a little longer."

She hesitates before nodding. "Okay. Just for a bit."

We sit in silence, her head on my shoulder. I'm not sure I can ever love her again, but I'm grateful for her friendship.

As she finally stands to leave, I stand, too. "Thanks for coming by, Sue. It's good to see you."

She smiles, a sad smile that doesn't quite reach her eyes. "It's good to see you too, Jahi."

I walk her to the door, feeling wistful as she steps out into the night. It's not just the loss of the woman I once loved, but losing the person I used to be. The person who thought he could save everyone, the person who used to feel invincible.

But seeing Susanne reminds me I'm just human after all, and sometimes it's okay to let go of the pain and sorrow, if only for a little while.

CHAPTER TEN

ROSE

My phone beeps.

"Hey, Rose, it's me," Beatrice says.

"Hi, what's up?" I ask, inhaling a deep breath, my spine rigid and unmoving, awaiting more terrible news to add to the list of losses in my tortured life.

"We just got back from the oncologist. The CT scan of Mom's lungs shows slight tumor shrinkage."

I exhale. Maybe our luck is turning. "Oh wow. That's absolutely wonderful news." Can this possibly be happening? I thought lung cancer was a death sentence.

"Yes, it is. Mom's color has been better the last few days. So, in some ways, this doesn't surprise me. She may turn the corner. The immunotherapy must be working."

Finally, some good news about Mom. Maybe she'll go into remission. I definitely need a win after Jahi devastated me with his decision to take Susanne back. I've been reeling the last few days, walking around like an aimless sleepwalker, not knowing what to do with myself. He was going to be my prince, rescuing me from all the losses in my life, but I guess that's not the case. *I'm not his Sleeping Beauty and he's not my prince.* He's moving on with his life, and I need to as well.

"I'd like to see you and Mom," I say, my tone cheerful at the thought of this minor victory for my mother's health.

"Yay! Why don't you come to Fayetteville this weekend? Mom's getting some of her strength back. She's able to walk a bit without using the walker. Maybe we can go to the Crystal Bridges Museum in Bentonville. There's a new exhibit of contemporary abstract painting with lots of artwork by women, and I'd love to see it. And their Sunday brunch is to die for."

"Oh yes, I like that idea. After that, we can drop by the Momentary Museum, and see who they're exhibiting, too."

"Let's do it. I'll talk to Mom."

"Okay," I agree, ending the call and filling my duffel bag with two tops, two pairs of jeans, a cute dress, and a pair of red and white striped espadrilles. This plan for the weekend with Mom and Bea gives me the structure I need. I've been floundering around, feeling restless and lost. Now it's time to wake up and start living. I can't wait to see Mom.

I get to Mom's house by ten o'clock in the morning. Beatrice swings open the door before I've had time to bound up the porch steps. Her eyes are sparkling and her complexion is glowing. She looks like a new person. In fact, she reminds me of the way she looked in high school. It's like she's drunk a youth elixir. *Is this because of Mom?*

She squeezes me so tightly I can't breathe for a few seconds.

"Bea. You look gorgeous. Radiant," I gush, after recovering my breath.

"Hey, you look beautiful yourself. You always do," she asserts, grabbing my bags from me.

"Thanks," I say, blushing. Anxiety rushes in when she says, "you always do." Beauty is a minefield between us. Smiling softly, I disguise my discomfort by keeping my hands relaxed, imagining holding a champagne flute as I stand with my hip jutted out, not a care in the world, as if I live a life of ease, like the character Daisy in *The Great Gatsby.*

There's a point of unspoken tension we've grappled with our entire lives, and I'm desperately trying to avoid it. Since childhood, my family constantly commented on my hair and how the strawberry blonde hue came from our paternal grandmother, the red-headed beauty, Emeline Tate. Dad made a big deal of it, likely because he had flaming red hair and was proud that one of his daughters carried on the genetic trait, even if muted by blondeness. I remember cringing any time the subject of red hair came up because I could feel my sister's pain of being invisible to certain members of the family because of her darker hair. It especially hurt Bea that Dad was one of the worst offenders, bragging incessantly about it.

I was extroverted and popular with peers—captain of the swim team, lead roles in the high school musicals, solo vocalist in the opera program—and Beatrice was more introverted. She preferred ballet and was brilliant at it, but never took it as far as her talent allowed because she didn't like an audience. Growing up in California, people constantly asked my sister about me. "Hey, are you related to Rose Aberdeen the swimmer?" they would ask and she would answer, slightly rolling her eyes, "Yeah, sure. She's my kid sister."

I downplayed our differences by wearing my "uniform" every day—tattered blue jeans and a white t-shirt and not messing with hair gel or rollers like most girls. I didn't wear makeup, which was unheard of in LA. But it didn't matter. People asked about me, probably because I was extroverted.

Bea cared a lot about clothes, shoes, hair, and makeup in high school, and Mom stretched her budget to make sure she had the latest fashions. She worked additional hours at the elementary school so she could give my sister the emotional lift and confidence these items gave her.

One day when I was a freshman, Mom took me aside. "Rose, you know your sister has it rough. She's shy. Is it okay if I give her extra clothes and shoes?"

"Of course, Mom. Bea loves beautiful clothes and I want her to be happy."

I'll never forget the look of relief on Mom's face. This was our secret. I've never said a word about it to Bea and never will.

My attention snaps back to the present when Bea asks, "You know how we were talking about going to the museum?"

"Yes. I remember and I love that idea."

"Well, do you think it would be okay if I invite Andrew to come along with us, too?" Bea's voice dampens into a whisper, as if she's embarrassed about asking permission from me, her baby sister.

"Of course," I reply, hesitating. This is what I call a pattern interrupt. I know Bea has been dating Andrew, but I have heard little about him since Mom's diagnosis. I wasn't even sure he was still around. He kind of went *incognito*. But maybe my sister avoided mentioning him these last few weeks as our lives crumbled around us.

"You don't sound… so sure," my sister prods, drawing out her words, never missing hidden signals or changes in vocal tone. She can read the spaces between the notes better than anyone I've ever known.

"No, no… it's fine. I just haven't heard you mention Andrew in a long while, and I wasn't even sure you were still seeing each other," I say, backpedaling.

"Well, we've been quietly getting together this whole time. When Mom slept, Andrew came over after work."

"Oh, that's so nice." I offer her a smile, still trying to recover from my hesitation.

"He's such a comfort—he's like a ballast in a raging storm,

keeping me right-side-up. In the last few weeks with Mom, I've felt like I'm sailing the Antarctic Ocean in a merciless gale, surfing mountainous waves that threaten to pitchpole me in an end-over-end capsize." Bea's voice is breathless and bubbling over with excitement. I suspect she's been watching sailing videos. I know she always wanted to learn. Me, I don't know a skeg from a halyard, much to Lee's chagrin during our marriage. Of course, Lee knew his way around yachts. He grew up in swanky Newport Beach and was on the sailing team in high school and got a sailing scholarship to Stanford.

"Oh, that's so good. I'm happy for you, Bea!" My voice is sugary as I try to sound sincere, even though I'm torn up inside. My sister is smitten. It's her first love. I've never heard her speak of any other man. There's nothing quite like the purity of first love, one not complicated by exes who disappear or children who miss their abandoning parents or a string of debilitating heartbreaks. Bea is looking to the future, moving on with her life, and imagining possibilities with Andrew. *What am I doing with my life?*

I feel paradoxically happy and envious. Those aren't two feelings that belong together, and I feel ashamed of the envious part. *This is my sister. Why am I so envious? Can't I just be purely happy for her with her good fortune in love?*

My chest tightens. My first deep love, Lee, was a disaster, a sharp contrast to Bea's experience. Oh, how I wish I could rewind time and go back to my early twenties. There would be no Lee in my new reality.

I was insecure with Lee from the get-go and never so radiant as Bea because there was always an underlying threat of the center not holding. It was only three or four weeks into the relationship before Lee's mask slipped. It was like sailing outside the Straits of Gibraltar and being stalked by a pod of orcas. Lee was the predator. I was prey.

How do I hold all of this so I don't inflict my suffering upon Bea?

I need to be here and be happy for my sister like she is for me. Bea's sweet, emerging relationship with Andrew, with its ease and enthusiasm, highlights in stark relief my history of failed relationships, dented love, abandonment, heartbreak—the whole gamut of bad luck that would put Las Vegas to shame.

Why are our love lives on such diametrically opposed paths?

Will I ever find my one true love?

CHAPTER ELEVEN

JAHI

I hold the peach cobbler in my trembling hands. *Fine, Chrissy may want to throw me into the flames, but she'll never reject a peach cobbler, made from the sweetest end-of-summer peaches from my tree, fat and fuzzy.*

I take a deep breath before knocking on her door. It's been two weeks since I last saw her, and she's still freezing me out. And she's not the only one—my mom is unhappy with me, too. They're all upset with me for trying to get back together with Susanne.

But I can't give up on her. She still loves me and I'm re-finding my feelings for her. It may never be romantic love, but she is still the mother of my child. We just need time to work through our issues.

The door opens slowly, and my sister peeks through the gap with a bewildered expression. I must have awoken her with my knocking.

"Jahi?" she says groggily, rubbing her eyes. "What are you doing here?"

"I just want to talk to you," I reply, swallowing hard. "Can I come in?"

Chrissy hesitates before nodding and stepping aside. I follow her into her small living room, taking a seat on the sofa. It's a mess, as usual, with books and fashion magazines strewn across the floor and a half-eaten avocado sandwich perched on the coffee table, turning brown and unappetizing.

"So, what do you want to talk about?" she asks warily, sitting in the armchair opposite me.

I steel myself and take a deep breath. "I know you're upset with me for getting back together with Susanne," I begin. "And I understand why. But I just want to explain my side of things."

Chrissy rolls her eyes. "What's there to explain, Jahi? She left you and Lily for years without a word. How can you even think about taking her back?"

I sigh, running a hand through my hair. "I know it seems crazy. But there's still a part of me that loves her, Chrissy. I always have since high school. And I know she loves me, too. We just need to work things out."

Chrissy looks skeptical. "What issues could you possibly have left to work through? She abandoned you, Jahi. That's not something you brush aside."

"I know," I say, my voice soft. "But she was going through a lot at the time, and I think she just needed to figure things out. She's different now, Chrissy. She's changed."

We sit in silence as my sister considers my words. Finally, she let out a deep sigh.

"You know I love you, Jahi," she says finally. "And I want you to be happy. But I don't want to see you get hurt again."

"I won't get hurt," I promise. "I know it's a risk, but it's one I'm willing to take."

Chrissy nods slowly. "Okay, I'll support you, but you need to promise me something."

"Anything," I reply eagerly.

"Be honest with yourself about what you're getting into," Chrissy says firmly. "And you must be honest with Susanne, too. If this is going to work, you both need to get real with each other."

"I will be," I say earnestly. "I promise."

Chrissy smiles slightly. "Well, that's all I can ask for, I guess. Just… be careful, Jahi. That's all I'm saying."

"Okay," I say firmly, preparing to leave. "Thanks, Chrissy. I really appreciate your support."

She shrugs. "What are sisters for?"

I skip to my car, feeling like a kid in grade school. My life has been out of kilter and now, getting Chrissy's approval, sets things in balance. I hope my mother will go along with her, but I'm not sure if she will. Chrissy's opinion matters a great deal to me. I can't wait to share the news with Susanne.

On the way home, I sing along with the radio and muse on how much has changed in the past year. Lily is no longer a baby. Yes, she's only seven-years-old going on twelve but getting more independent by the day. A new school year has started and Lily is doing her homework and her braids even look sort of ok. I'm almost afraid to think things are looking up. I'm even realizing I need to take care of myself, too. I can't keep putting everything aside for the sake of others.

When I get to the house, I find Susanne watching TV. The sight of her makes my heart skip a beat. She looks up, her face glowing.

"Hey," she says, standing to give me a hug. "How did your visit with Chrissy go?"

"Great," I reply. "She's on board with us giving this another chance."

Susanne's face lights up. "Really? That's amazing, Jahi!"

I nod. "Yeah. It feels good to have at least one person in my corner."

Susanne pulls away from my hug. "What about your mom? Have you talked to her?"

I sigh, the weight of my mother's anger and disappointment settling heavily on my chest. "Not yet. I think I need to give her time to cool off first."

She nods. "That's probably a good idea. But Jahi, you can't

ignore her forever. You need to talk to her."

"Yeah," I say, running a hand through my hair. "It's just… it's hard, you know? She thinks I'm making a huge mistake."

"But you're not," Susanne insists, placing a hand on my arm. "You're following your heart, Jahi. And that takes courage."

I smile at her, feeling grateful for her unwavering support. "Thanks, Sue. I don't know what I'd do without you."

She grins. "You'd be just fine. But it helps to have someone in your corner."

We sit together, planning our future. It feels good to be honest with her, to share my hopes and dreams without fear of judgment.

As I look at her, I realize I'm willing to spend the rest of my life with her if we can work through our problems. It will be a long road, with plenty of obstacles, but worth the risk.

Together, we can face anything. And then I get the call.

"Mr. Adams. This is Miss Locke," she says, her voice cracking. "It's Lily. She's at the hospital…"

My stomach drops. "What?"

"I'm so sorry. She ran into the street to get a ball during recess and a school van taking kids on a field trip hit her." Miss Locke's words tumble out breathlessly.

The world stops turning. Time stretches in slow motion.

I don't recall hanging up. I remember bolting out the door with Susanne trailing. The road blurs, my mind racing through possibilities of what I'll face when I see my little girl.

My heart throbs as I run towards the hospital's entrance, not even pausing at the front desk.

We run to the ER and a nurse stops us.

"Are you Lily Adams' parents?" she asks.

"Yes. Where's my daughter? What happened to her?" I ask, frantic.

"She's in surgery right now," she says.

My mind can't even comprehend what that means. "What? Surgery? How badly is she hurt?" I ask.

She deflects my question. "Come. Let me take you both to the waiting room," she whispers as she leads us down the hall. Once we get there, she says, "Wait here. The doctor will come out of surgery and update you soon." Her voice is soothing before she leaves.

The waiting area feels cramped and claustrophobic. I can't sit still. I'm pacing back and forth, checking my phone every five seconds.

After an eternity, a doctor emerges through the double doors that lead to the operating room. My heart stutters like an arrhythmia as he approaches.

"Mr. Adams?" he ventures.

I nod and my throat catches as I speak. "Is my daughter okay?"

The doctor hesitates. "She's stable, but we need to watch her closely."

I'm stunned, my knees threatening to collapse. Stable. She's stable. At least she's alive.

"What happened to her?" I ask, my mind grasping for details.

"It looks like she ran out in front of a school van. It was moving relatively slowly, but still," he says gravely. "The driver didn't see her in time. She suffered blunt force trauma, and it ruptured her spleen. We had to operate to stop severe internal bleeding. We had to resect part of the spleen, a partial splenectomy."

I gasp for breath, like someone has kicked me in the stomach. My little girl, so full of life and energy, lying on the operating table, fighting for her life.

"We need to watch for any postoperative complications, but I think she'll be okay. The bleeding was bad, but we got in there quickly and took care of it," the doctor assures me.

I nod. I'm numb, unable to form any coherent thoughts. Susanne wraps her arms around me, keeping me from collapsing on the floor.

The next few hours are a blur of panic and anxiety. We pace the waiting room endlessly, jumping at every sound and voice.

Finally, after what feels like a lifetime, a nurse appears and says in the kindest voice, "You can come see her now."

I feel nervous as we follow the nurse through the hospital corridor with its plain walls and smell of rubbing alcohol. The door to Lily's room is ajar, and I see her slight form lying on the bed.

She's tiny, lying there on the hospital bed, hooked up to IVs and monitors, her body bruised from the trauma. But she's alive.

I exhale as I approach, reaching out to touch her tiny hand. Her skin is baby soft—tender and velvety. Her hand doesn't respond to my touch, but there's something in her face, a stubborn set to her jaw, that remains even through heavy sedation. I watch her rhythmic breathing and know she's determined to recover.

As we sit by her bedside, reality hits. One moment of carelessness, one moment of inattention, and I feel my entire world torn asunder.

It's painfully obvious Lily has a long road ahead. The doctor says even once she leaves the hospital, it can take up to twelve weeks to fully recover. But I'm confident Susanne and I will be there to nurse her through it.

As the hours drag on, the waiting room slowly fills with family and friends offering prayers for Lily's recovery. Their glazed, unblinking expressions mirror the shock and trauma of my own.

Even with so many people around us, I can't shake this feeling of dread—a bad omen, like a witch has placed a hex on us. A devastation that can't be reversed.

Our lives will never be the same.

The doctor assures me Lily will recover. My fear is she'll have a postoperative complication that will kill her. It's irrational, but I can't help it. Losing my dad in the blink of an eye makes me realize how thin the veil is between this life and the next.

Lily remains in the hospital for days. I lose track of time. In the back of my mind, she's slowly recovering while machines and tubes surround her small body. Every day is a painful reminder of the accident that has torn our lives apart. I try holding it together for Lily's sake, but feel helpless and terrified.

The first days are interminable. It's like we're sailing a passage in the southern Indian Ocean, just the two of us, isolated as we navigate the battering waves and gales, praying for time to speed up. In my dreams we're on a fast, skittish sailboat, barely outracing the rogue wave looming astern that can sink us. The stress and grief cause a rift between Susanne and me. Fights erupt out of nowhere. We're both raw. It's like we're two drowning people clinging to one another for dear life, but the harder we hold on, the more we sink beneath the surface. My decision to let her back into my life is premature. I'm wondering if I've been wrong to place my confidence in her.

My family is no better. They associate all bad things with Susanne, almost as if she caused Lily's accident somehow. And honestly, I do, too. Whenever she's around, it's only a matter of time before there's upheaval. This trauma is no exception. It may not be fair or logical to think of it this way, but I do. I'm not superstitious, but this woman is bad luck.

Chrissy and Mom are pressuring me to kick Susanne out, and I understand this, but I can't handle the stress. It's all I can do to stay strong for Lily.

They transfer Lily to the postoperative unit. The surgeons round on her every day and tell me the surgical incision is healing and her vitals and labs are looking good. They say it's a miracle she survived the blunt abdominal trauma, and that surgery saved her life.

Lily is out of the woods in terms of life-threatening danger, but my mind obsesses on Susanne and whether giving her a second chance is the right decision. Something in me still loves her, but resentment is souring the relationship. It feels like a burden and one I don't need on top of everything else.

Susanne and I take turns sleeping on a cot next to Lily. She's too young to be left alone overnight in a big, scary hospital. Susanne stays with her during the day while I work a shift at the station. Since Lily's accident, I've been on administrative duty. I'm not called out for emergencies, in case Lily needs me.

There's been little time to talk to Susanne and I'm feeling distant. All I care about is Lily healing and our life returning to normal.

When I finish my shift, I go directly to the hospital. Susanne sits beside Lily's bed, but for the last week or so, I've noticed something looks off. I can't quite put my finger on it. Susanne looks drawn—her eyes empty, like the spark is gone. She has dark circles and puffiness under her eyes and a red flush on her cheeks and nose I haven't noticed before, but then again, I'm preoccupied with Lily.

One day, the doctors pronounce Lily is ready to go home. They will discharge her tomorrow after lunch.

Susanne perks up. "Yay! This is so exciting, Jahi. I'll take care of it. There's no need for you to take time off work. Let me pick her up after lunch tomorrow and bring her home."

Reticent to miss out on Lily's big day of homecoming, I say, "Hmm… I can take time off."

"No, no, no… you've taken so much time off already and it's no big deal. It's logistical. Lots of papers to sign and it won't be fun. Let's celebrate when you get home from work."

"Ok, but I want cake, ice cream, and balloons. This is a pivotal day in Lily's life." As I say this, I can't quite figure out why I feel uneasy, because Susanne's words make logical sense. Susanne seems proud of herself to be the one present for Lily's hospital discharge, like she's the magnanimous heroine. It ticks me off. She sees herself this way, and it makes me feel left out.

The next day, I go to work after sleeping beside Lily in the hospital.

"Hey, today's the day our babydoll comes home," Matt says, giving me a high five.

"Yeah," I say after a long silence.

"You're not saying much. I get worried when you go silent. You seem preoccupied. What's going on?"

"I don't know, Matt. I've got a bad feeling."

"Uh oh, you're not going all woo-woo on me are you?" he teases, trying to bring levity to the conversation.

"No, I just can't shake this ominous feeling."

"What do you mean?"

"I've been waking up in a cold sweat on the nights I stay home." I pause before confiding, "I'm having nightmares about Lily dying." Beads of sweat form on my upper lip as I say this.

"Jahi, you're overthinking this. Nothing's going to happen. Lily's on the mend and doing great," he insists.

I file reports and sweep and mop the floors of the station, but my hands tremble.

"Hey, Jahi. You need to eat something. You're shaking. You've probably got low blood sugar." Matt offers me a turkey sandwich, but I can't eat. My stomach coils in knots. I watch the clock. They'll be discharging Lily soon. *Why am I so nervous?*

I keep looking at my phone for a text from Susanne, but there's nothing. At two o'clock, there's still no message. I call, but it goes to voicemail and my texts go unanswered. Matt watches as

I pace the floor, checking and rechecking my phone.

Finally, forty minutes later, my phone rings and I jump.

"Hello," I say.

"Jahi?" a man asks, his voice gravelly, and I slowly recognize who it is. It's the sheriff, Brett Hamilton.

An electric shock rips through my body. *What in the world is going on? Surely nothing has happened to Lily.*

"Brett, is Lily okay?" I ask, my voice trembling. I hold my breath, praying he says she's fine.

"Lily's okay, Jahi. Don't worry. She's still at the hospital," he says.

"What? She's supposed to be home by now."

"She's safe. They're holding her at the hospital. You'll need to pick her up," he says. After a long pause, he continues, "The issue is Susanne."

"What do you mean?

"She was driving erratically on the road a mile from the hospital."

"What?"

"Yep. I pulled her over and administered a sobriety test. You know, the whole shebang—walking in a straight line, finger to nose, standing on one leg, and the horizontal gaze nystagmus test. She failed miserably. The breathalyzer reading was 0.15. I arrested her for a DUI. She's spending the night in jail."

I fall silent.

"Jahi, can you hear me? Are you still there?"

"Uh... yeah. I'm just... in shock. I have no words."

"I'm sorry. You've been through so much with Lily's accident and now this."

"Yeah."

"I arrested her, Jahi. She's a danger to your daughter and others, as well as to herself."

"Yes, I understand. I'm so glad you did. I'm just shocked, that's all. I can't believe she did this," I say. *What was she thinking, putting Lily's life in danger?* "Did she say why this happened? Did she try to explain herself?"

"Yeah. She confided she started drinking again after Lily's accident. According to her, stress drew her back to the bottle. She's been sneaking a bloody Mary or tequila sunrise in the mornings right after you leave for work. I went through her backpack, the one she takes to the hospital, and found airplane bottles of tequila and vodka. Upon questioning, she admitted sneaking swigs of liquor in the hospital. By the time you see her in the late afternoon, she's sober."

"I'm surprised the nurses didn't notice."

"Yeah, and Jahi, this means on the days she drove to the hospital, she probably drove under the influence. She put many people at risk."

"Yes, you're right," I agree.

Brett confides in a low voice, "She begged me not to tell you."

"What did you say?"

"I told her you'll find out, anyway. A group of people from town saw her erratic driving and noticed me pulling her over on her way to the hospital in Fayetteville. Word gets out in Eureka Springs. Everybody knows about Lily's accident and hospitalization."

"This is so alarming, Brett."

"Yeah, I don't know what to say. I can't believe I missed this. She seemed okay when I saw her after work."

"Exactly. That was strategic on her part. She's a master of deceit. She begged me not to tell you, but I asked her, 'Who's going to get you out of jail, if not Jahi?'"

"What did she say to that?"

"She said nothing. She just looked at me, horrified."

As I rush to the sheriff's office, my mind races. I imagine all the tragic ways this could have turned out. *What if she had gotten into an accident with Lily in the car? What if someone got hurt or killed?*

I'm so disgusted by her betrayal, I can barely stand to look at her face.

Susanne's eyes are downcast, her shoulders slumped. She can't look at me. With a swollen face, disheveled hair, and sweat-soaked shirt, she looks like a homeless woman.

"Jahi," she whispers, her voice thin but not slurred.

I remain silent, contempt curling my lips.

"Please, Jahi. I'm so sorry. Please don't be angry," she begs. "Please don't leave me."

I can't look at her. A cold, gnawing rage is eating me alive, and I want it to stop. I think of the legend of Prometheus earning the wrath of Zeus for stealing fire and giving it to humankind, which we as firefighters know was a bad idea. In the story, they chained Prometheus to a rock where an eagle ate his liver as fast as it regenerated, condemning him to eternal punishment. My relationship with Susanne feels like Prometheus' imprisonment.

How can she be so reckless? So selfish?

I go through the motions of bailing her out, but I have a sinking feeling this is the end for us. In a flash, Rose's face comes to mind. *I can't believe the mistake I made in letting her go.*

PART 4

CHAPTER ONE

ROSE

"So, you don't want to come? You know, back to Los Angeles?" Enid's voice has a barely audible quiver, and I know she's a bit hurt.

"Nonsense. Who told you that?" I ask my friend. It must be because of my delayed response and the letter I sent. Maybe the clinic thinks this is not the attitude of someone who truly wants to work with them.

"I don't know, Rose. You're not in Los Angeles yet. Is there something you're not telling me? Are you in love with Eureka Springs now?" She pauses, and I sense a subtle shift in her energy. "Am I being pushy?"

"It's not that I don't want to come, it's just that... Well, as you know, my mother has cancer. What you may not know is the situation is unstable. We've had a bit of a respite, but at any moment the cancer can come back like a wildfire burning out of control. We didn't catch it super early."

I feel her horror over the phone. She says something, but I interrupt her. "I still want to work in psychology, but I need something nearby so I can be close to Mom."

"I get it. Of course! I'm so sorry she's struggling with this terrible news. I definitely wouldn't want to move away if I were you," she soothes.

Enid sounds like she wants to cry for me, but there's nothing she can do to change the bleak reality.

"I wish I could be there to comfort you, Rose."

"Thanks Enid, I know… it's awful. And there's more…"

"There is? What is it?" she asks.

"You know the little girl I tutored… before I went to Fayetteville? Lily?"

"Yes." Her voice takes a distinct note, one full of curiosity. "Jahi's daughter?"

"Yeah, Ja… Jahi's daughter," I say, my voice breaking, hot tears welling up in my eyes just from saying his name. I wonder what he's going through. And Lily?! Oh, poor, sweet Lily.

"It's okay, Rose, take your time," Enid says softly, sensing I'm about to tell her something critical.

I push back tears and speak after a long silence. "Lily was in an awful accident. A school van hit her when she ran after a ball during recess."

"Oh, no!" she gasps.

"Yes. She had emergency surgery for a ruptured spleen. There was internal hemorrhaging and she would have died without emergency surgery," I say.

"Oh dear! I'm so sorry to hear this. You know she's going to be fine, right?" Enid is a superb therapist, and I'm already feeling soothed by her words. Without thinking, I nod as if Enid can see me over the phone. "Rose? Do you understand?"

"I'm not so sure, Enid. The doctor says there can be postoperative complications. She lost a lot of blood, but they stanched it when they removed part of her spleen."

"Poor girl! Let's just be glad she survived and hope there won't be any long-term problems. What about her father?" she asks.

"Oh, Jahi. I feel terrible for him," I say, deciding not to mention the gossip flying around town that he and Susanne are divorcing for real this time. "It's a tough situation for Lily. Her parents tried to make their marriage seem better, for her sake. But she still has a lot to process about her mother, who abandoned her as a toddler and drinks excessively."

Susanne's an evil woman and doesn't deserve Jahi. There's a chance for Jahi and me to be a couple, now that he's kicking her out. The baffling thing is, if I'm completely honest, I feel a little guilty about taking her place, as awful as she is.

I'm too conflicted to continue talking about Jahi and his daughter with Enid, so I end the call, promising to keep in touch. After a bath, I dress and leave my house instead of being alone and letting my feelings eat me up from the inside out. Stopping at Eureka Market, I fill my car with groceries for Mom and Beatrice because I'm visiting them for the weekend. I don't know how much time Mom has left. The doctors are being cagey about her prognosis.

I get to Fayetteville within an hour and just in time for lunch. My heart is heavy with worry for Lily, and I can't shake the feeling I should be there with her and her family, but I can't abandon my family who needs me, either. Especially since Beatrice is the only one taking care of our mom, and she never complains. The least I can do is to be here for them as often as I can.

Not that Jahi has called to ask for my help. This makes me sad, but I'm not dwelling on it. The man is going through so much already.

Beatrice beams, her black eyes sparkling when I enter the house, her luxurious shoulder-length auburn hair bouncing as she walks towards me in her white, dotted swiss sundress and matching white espadrilles. She looks like a Greek goddess, her olive skin contrasting with the bright white sundress and her hair looking like she had it blown out at a salon. "The prodigal daughter," she exclaims, taking my first bag of groceries from me as I drop my weekend bag by the front door. Seeing my athletic sister so stylish, I feel shabby in comparison with jeans and a plain white t-shirt, my pale, freckled skin and strawberry blonde hair pulled back in a casual ponytail.

Mom is on the sofa with a book on her lap. Her eyes light up when she catches sight of me.

"Hello, Mother," I say as I hug her lightly, afraid I'll break her ribs.

She looks brittle, her birdlike bones bulging out at odd angles—the muscles of her limbs wasting away. Cancer is a silent marauder, storming my mother's body and strangling her life force. Mom has donned a crocheted hat, and I stare at it, unable to look away. Noticing a flutter of movement in the corner of my eye, I look over and Beatrice is silently signaling me to follow her.

"Let me put my bag away in the bedroom," I say to Mom, snapping out of my trance and mustering a smile. Still dazed, I grab my bag and follow Beatrice down the hallway.

Beatrice grabs my elbow, pulling me into her bedroom. "Just so you know, Mom's wearing this hat all the time because she's ashamed of her thinning hair."

"Oh, dear. I'm sorry… I couldn't take my eyes off the hat," I say, embarrassed by my staring spell. "I just can't believe this is happening. Mom never wears hats. Who would want to cover up such a thick, gorgeous mane of auburn hair?"

"Yeah, I know, but she doesn't have a headful of hair anymore. She lost it in the first few weeks of chemo. Whatever you do, mention nothing about hair—yours, mine, hers, or anyone else's. It's a sore spot."

"Absolutely," I agree, dejected by my mother's hair loss.

"Cheer up, Rose… or try to. We can't let her suspect we've been talking about her. It'll make her sad," Beatrice warns in her "big sister" way.

I murmur assent and follow her back to the living room. I

retrieve the rest of the groceries from my car and as I carry them in, Mom looks up at me.

"Oh Rose, you shouldn't have. It's too much." My mother's eyes are watery as she thanks me. "You're such a wonderful daughter, Rose," she says, giving me a weak smile. "Beatrice, get your sister a bowl of the asparagus green chile soup you made. She looks like she's starving and needs fattening up."

"Mom, I eat just fine. I don't need to gain weight," I answer, laughing.

"Hmph…" my sister huffs while she sets the table. I shoot her a look.

"Nonsense!" my mother exclaims, gesturing towards the kitchen table. Beatrice and I help Mom into her wheelchair and my sister wheels her to the head of the table.

"Sit down, Rose, and eat your soup while it's still hot. Your sister outdid herself on this one. You'll love it."

"Okay, Mom. And thanks, B," I say, sitting down to eat. Beatrice says grace and we eat. The soup deliciously combines asparagus and potato in chicken broth, with green chile, onion, garlic powder, and salt. It's creamy and spicy and served with crusty sourdough bread crisped in the oven topped with cold, unsalted butter and a glass of sweet iced tea. The soup is savory and comforting, reminding me of all the times my mother made it for me when I was young. Now Mom's too sick to cook, but Bea steps in to continue the tradition.

After lunch, Beatrice and I sit in the living room with my mother. We talk about everything from work to our love lives to Lily's accident. I share my thoughts about Jahi and how I've grown to love his daughter.

"I feel like I need to be there for her," I say, tears in my eyes. "I should help her family through this trauma."

My mother puts a hand on my shoulder. "Rose, you can't

blame yourself for what's happening to Lily. You've done everything you can for her, and she knows this. The best thing you can do is to be with us and take a break from everything else."

I know she's right. As much as I want to be there for Lily, I need to take care of myself, too. Being with my mother and sister reminds me of what's most important in life.

Later in the evening, as we prepare for bed, I still feel the need to talk to Beatrice. After becoming close again, my sister is my confidante and dearest friend. I knock on her bedroom door, my hands trembling. When she opens the door, I look away as my eyes threaten to fill with tears.

"Hey, you okay? You're shaking." Beatrice searches my eyes.

I raise my shoulders and let them fall. "I—I don't know. Everything is overwhelming me right now."

She comes closer and pulls me into her arms. "It's alright, Rose. Take a deep breath. You'll be okay. Tell me what's on your mind."

After my sister holds me for a few minutes, I sit on her bed and shift closer as she strokes my back. Her touch comforts me, and I let out a long, shuddering sigh.

"It's just everything," I say in a choked whisper. "I don't know what to do with myself, and Lily's situation isn't making anything better."

Beatrice says nothing for a moment, and I wonder if she heard me. Then she speaks, her voice gentle, "I know it's hard. But you must remember this isn't your fault. You can't control everything. You can't fix everyone's problems, as much as you want to. And Lily knows you care for her. That's what matters."

It's not like I don't know this, but hearing it from my sister, someone who's always had such a profound influence on me, feels like the reality check I need.

"I know," I say, my voice breaking. "It just feels so heavy sometimes."

Beatrice pulls back and looks at me with a soft expression. "It's okay to feel like this. Just remember, you don't have to carry it all by yourself."

I smile, feeling a bit defeated but somehow lighter. "Thanks, Beatrice. You always know how to help me."

She hugs me, and we both become weepy all over again. It's a moment of vulnerability, and I feel lucky she's my sister.

The weekend is a whirlwind of watching movies, playing bridge, and wheeling Mom in her wheelchair through the local parks. I take countless photos, a sort of "museum of Mom" as if it will ward off her death, and I imagine one day showing them to Lily and Jahi. I should memorialize these moments. There may not be another chance.

As I prepare Sunday evening to leave Fayetteville the next morning, my mother pulls me aside. "Rose, I want you to remember I love you more than life itself and I'm so proud of you. I always have been. You're doing amazing things with your life, and I know you'll continue to do great things. I just want you to be happy."

I hug her tenderly, tears filling my eyes as I recall the beautiful letter she gave me the last time I visited. "Thank you, Mom. I love you, too."

Leaving my family is difficult, but I must return to Eureka Springs. As far as I know, Lily is still in the hospital, and I need to show that I'm here for her. Being with my family reminds me of what is important in life. No matter what happens, they'll always be here for me.

CHAPTER TWO

JAHI

After I bail Susanne out of jail, she disappears. History repeats itself and she goes AWOL. This is her *modus operandi*. It's predictable. She's pretty good at it, so I was relieved when I received an email from her lawyer regarding the divorce. If Susanne disappeared for good, it would have thrown a major wrench into the divorce proceedings.

My family stands by me, though. I expect a bunch of "I told you so" comments, but I don't get any. They just feel bad for me, especially Chrissy.

Chrissy's empathy toward me on the topic may have something to do with her marital struggles over the IVF issue. She now misses a lot of work. Sometimes she comes to my house and sits on Lily's bed, mumbling to herself. I want to bust through her troubles and ask her to sit down and tell me what's wrong, but I know this isn't the way Chrissy works. She must come to me with her problems, not the other way around. If I push her to talk, she'll pull away in retreat and be angry besides.

She doesn't like anyone placing demands on her, despite being a demanding person herself. My sister's an odd duck. We're a flock of odd ducks in my family, but we love each other and that's what matters. We fly together.

This time, when I wake up, Chrissy is already at my house, flipping pancakes. I smell chocolate chips—that singular aroma with notes of vanilla and undertones of cocoa butter, evoking memories from childhood of laughter and sugar-fueled chaotic exuberance. I stare at her in disbelief, not sure how she got into my house.

"It's for Lily," she says, as if that explains everything.

"Okay." Lily loves her chocolate chip pancakes, but I know my sister has a husband and a job, so her presence here is a little odd.

"Don't you have to go to work?" I ask my sister, who apparently thinks it's fine to skip work whenever it suits her. I'm not a disciplinarian, but I won't sit by and watch my sister sabotage her life.

"Yeah, I'm supposed to be there today," she says, with an air of nonchalance.

"But what?" I ask. My sister turns off the burner on the gas stove to face me.

"I've taken paid leave. Some of my vacation days." She shrugs.

I look at her, incredulous. "What vacation days? You're still here."

"Yeah."

"And how did you even get into my house?"

"I have the keys."

"I gave them to you?" I question my sister.

She raises a brow. "Do you want to send me out of your home, Jahi?"

I laugh a little at that. Chrissy's one of a kind. She gets defensive whenever someone calls her out on something or wants her to get real.

"Chrissy, let's talk." She needs someone to talk to. Maybe she thinks she's alone with her problems, but I want her to know I'm always here for her, just like she is for me.

"I don't know, Jahi. Your daughter still needs bed rest, and it's time to proceed with the divorce. So help me God, if you don't get a divorce, I don't know what I'll do, but it won't be good. Anyway, I don't want to bother you with anything."

"Bother? You're never a bother to me, Chrissy. You're my sister and probably my best friend," I say, winking at her, trying to lighten the mood.

"Okay, that's kinda nice. I think I'm going to tell you what's up," she says, sighing heavily. "I imagine you'll try to fix this, but I just need someone to listen to me."

"Sure, I can do that. I can be anything you want me to be. I'll do my best to just listen, but my nature is to jump in and extinguish fires." All that matters is she knows she can rely on me as much as I rely on her.

She pulls a cigarette out of her green leather Chanel handbag, lights it, and takes a drag—her eyes squinting like you see in those classic 1950s movies. "Chrissy, what are you *doing*?" I ask, frowning at the cigarette.

"I know, I know," she says, after inhaling and exhaling deeply. "It's a bad habit—a new one, I might add."

An image of our dad gasping for breath, his lungs strangled by the saddle embolus, his heart collapsing, flashes before my eyes. *What is she thinking? Has she gone mad?* I look at her intently, fear gripping me. I keep my tone light and say, "You need to quit before that thing kills you, you know that. They don't call 'em coffin nails for naught."

She nods, cigarette smoke curling around her face. "I know. But right now, it's the only thing keeping me sane."

I erupt. The memory of Dad's death cuts too close to home. "Bull! You won't care about your sanity anymore when you get emphysema and you're gasping for every breath in the ICU."

"Whoa! Jahi?" She recoils in shock at my anger.

I stand next to her, feeling bad about my outburst. Staring at my rose garden beyond the kitchen window, I realize I need to tone it down, to change tack, or I'll unwittingly run her off.

"What's going on, Chrissy?" I ask, my voice soft again.

She shakes her head, her eyes filling with tears. "I can't handle it, Jahi," she says. "It's too much. Lily... she's just a little girl. She doesn't deserve this."

Finally, we're getting somewhere. I put my arms around her, feeling a pang of sadness in my chest. "I know, but we have to stay strong. For her."

Chrissy lets out a laugh. "I'm supposed to be the one consoling you," she says, wiping her eyes with the back of her hand.

"Well, maybe we can console each other."

We stand in silence for a moment, toxic cigarette smoke swirling around us.

"I believe Lily will be okay," she says, her voice firm. "I have to believe that."

I look at her, surprised by the conviction in her voice. "Why do you say that?"

"Because I have to," she replies. "Because the alternative is too terrible to consider."

"The surgeon said she'll be okay. She got through surgery and the postoperative period without serious complications and now needs time to regain her strength. We must believe she'll fully recover, for Lily's sake."

There's nothing like having my sister in my corner, the one who weathered the storm of losing Dad alongside Mom and me. And now she's here again—for Lily and me.

"There's something else I want to tell you, though," she says, drawing out her words.

"What is that?" I ask in a coaxing manner, remembering my sister doesn't like to be pushed, and I will not be the one to push her.

"I don't want kids, Jahi."

I'm struck by the forcefulness of her voice—the tone of finality. I respect her decision, but is it premature? I hope this isn't an impulsive reaction to arguments with her husband. Of course, it's her body and her right to decide. She's the one who'll raise the child. Her husband is nice but not mature, so the decision belongs solely to her. I don't blame her if she thinks she can't handle it or if it's just something she doesn't want.

"That's fine, Chrissy. It doesn't matter."

"I love Lily so much. I adore her. And I thought I loved kids. I just don't think I love them enough to want one of my own. It's just not something I'm into."

"That's okay. No one cares. Do what you want."

"You suck at consoling people. You know that?" she scoffs and tries kicking me lightly on the shin, but I move too fast, and she misses.

I shrug, but she already has a small smile and while that might sound a bit like I'm bragging, I'm happy I'm able to cheer her up.

"Thanks, Jahi. You're the best."

"You might have to warm up the pancakes later, though. Lily doesn't like them cold."

She shakes her head and goes back to making pancakes when my phone rings—Susanne. She's been calling incessantly the last few days.

I don't answer. A few minutes later, my phone rings again. My sister and I sit on the sofa, staring at the wall, exchanging incredulous glances at the audacity of my soon-to-be ex-wife.

She's left many voicemails and texts, begging for a third chance. I'm trying to move on from her betrayals, but hearing her voice on these messages upsets me so much it's causing nightmares. I'm sleep deprived from her drama, but I must stay strong for Lily's sake.

I try to revisit the conversation with my sister about having children, but the phone rings again. I'm getting increasingly irritated by this nonsense. It's Susanne, of course. I look at

Chrissy for strength, but she pointedly looks away.

"Don't look at me, Jahi. You're gonna have to deal with her at some point."

Knowing that she's right, I exhale in exasperation. I steel myself and answer the call.

"What do you want, Susanne?" I ask, trying not to sound too harsh, but not too nice, either. I don't want to give her false hope.

"Jahi, please, just hear me out," she pleads. "I know I messed up again, and I'm trying to get better. I promise you this time will be different. I miss you and Lily so much. Please give me another chance."

For a moment, I almost cave. I'm such a softie, it's sickening. *Why do I keep giving her another chance?* But this time, something is different. I have some kind of newfound fortitude. It even surprises me. It grew while I wasn't looking, but there it is, solid like a foundation of concrete and steel.

Chainmail forms around my heart, preventing her from penetrating it with sad childhood stories to excuse her egregious behavior as an adult.

She's like a television station, and this is one of her four channels—the pity channel. The other three are seduction, criticism, and rejection. She's played me with all four channels so many times it is head-spinning. It's like she works from a playbook. It's predictable. She wants me to feel sorry for her, so I'll give her another chance. She promises to change and fails every single time. I'm privy to her games and simply sick of it.

"I'm sorry, Susanne," I say, my voice firm. "I can't keep giving you second and third chances when you continue hurting us. It's time to move on."

Chrissy grabs the phone out of my hands, the vein on her forehead so dilated it looks like it will burst. "Stop calling my brother, Susanne," she yells. "Get out of his life. He's done with you and your antics. We're all done with you. You put my niece's life in danger with your drunk driving. What kind of mother are you? Not to mention disappearing on my brother as soon as he got you out of jail, despite him giving you a second chance against every voice of reason. Your behavior is despicable. It's unforgivable. You should be ashamed of yourself. Look, it's over."

I hear Susanne crying, but Chrissy hangs up on her and demands that I block her number.

I'm like a bee caught in Susanne's spider web, struggling to escape but wearing myself out in the meantime. I flip back and forth between outrage at Susanne and guilt that I'm finally saying no, finally ending the marriage.

But as much as I wish things could be different, I'm convinced deep down it's impossible. It's futile, like trying to resuscitate the dead—it may have worked for Lazarus, but it doesn't for Susanne.

Sometimes, the hardest thing is letting go of the person who will destroy you.

"Goodbye, Susanne," I whisper to myself. My soul silently slips its moorings from this toxic land and drifts away on the outgoing tide with nary a ripple.

CHAPTER THREE

ROSE

I'm back in Fayetteville for a few days, determined to spend more time with Mom and Beatrice. Fighting back sadness, I stay busy talking to them, going to stores, and cleaning the house. We thought Mom's tumor was shrinking, but she became short of breath last week and the doctors think the tumor is growing again. Mom's face is pale, with a slight bluish cast. Sometimes, in the middle of the night, I hear her puking her guts out and praying to God for relief. I've started praying, too. *Please, God. Let her live.*

Beatrice is constantly by Mom's side, holding what's left of her hair so it stays out of her face, offering sips of water, and saying she'll get better. It's almost like I'm an impingement, like I don't belong, like I'm just one more person for my sister to worry about.

It's a full-time job taking care of Mom. Beatrice barely has time for anything—for herself, for Andrew, or for anyone else. It's devouring her life, and it's unfair.

How do I voice my concern that all this caretaking is ruining her life without rubbing it in her face? I'm free to do whatever I want, but she isn't. *Does she resent me for that?* I don't want to imply our mother is a burden and I'm not sure how to articulate my concerns, so I say nothing.

After packing my bags and saying goodbye to Mom and Beatrice, I drive back to Eureka Springs. Shunning my car's AC for fresh air, I roll down my windows and breathe in the spiciness of early fall, leaves not yet turning, but they know they're on notice. *I think of the cycles of life and the inevitability of death. The trees know it. Nature knows it. Why is it so hard for us humans to accept it?*

The buzzing of myriad insects is so loud I hear it over the car's engine and the rushing air. It smells like life, but with a poignant tinge of impermanence. I think about Beatrice's predicament of twenty-four/seven caregiving, and there seems to be no obvious solution in sight.

Listening to sad songs from my phone, I end up sobbing. Blinded and unable to see the road through my tears, I pull over. I don't want to get in an accident, and this thought makes me burst into tears again, as it reminds me of Lily and Jahi. I blow my nose, wipe away my tears, and get back on the road.

When I get to my bungalow, I'm sweaty from the ever-present humidity, even in the fall, so I have a quick scrub and put on a white linen dress. I got two books for Lily from a children's bookstore in Fayetteville. It might be good to introduce some fresh stories to her. I hope she likes them.

I haven't texted Jahi for a while, so I pull out my phone and message him.

"I'm back in town. How is Lily? Hope she's resting and recuperating well? How are you, too?"

He responds within minutes. "Lily is feeling better. I think it would boost her spirits if you have time to come see her while you're here. She misses you."

The thought of seeing Jahi again gives me goosebumps all over.

I write back, trying not to portray overexcitement, "I would love to see her."

I make my way to Jahi's house with the books and a basket of fruit for Lily. She must still be feeling loopy, even though the hospital cleared her. I'm concerned about her full recovery. Did she have a head injury? Jahi has mentioned nothing about it, but it's significant to be hit by a school van, even one moving relatively slowly. I worry about how this will affect her life and schooling, but remain hopeful. If there are any long-term complications from Lily's injuries, I'm prepared to deal with them. I'm hoping for the best, but bracing myself for the worst.

Jahi breaks my daydream and opens the door before I knock, flashing his brilliant smile. I take a moment to study his face. He's lost some weight. His eyes look weary and don't match his smile, and he sports a couple days of stubble. Although he tries to mask his fatigue, I see through it.

"Bet you're getting tons of these," I say in a wry tone as I hand him the books and basket of fruit.

"Nah, just peach cobblers. You're the only one bringing books for Lily. Even Jolene didn't," he answers, ushering me in.

I want to joke around and ask if he's calling me a nerd, or even smile at him, but I'm nervous and don't want to say the wrong thing.

"Is Lily awake?" I ask instead.

"No, she's asleep. The medications knock her out."

"Oh dear. Pain medications?"

"Yes, they are," he answers. "She's recovering from her surgical wound, but she's doing well."

"Oh, that's wonderful news." I exhale. Maybe my worst fears won't come to fruition, and Lily is doing better than I thought.

"So, how are you? How was your trip to Fayetteville?"

"My trip was okay," I reply, my voice trailing off as I replay the events of the last few weeks in my mind. I stare blankly at the wood floor, overwhelmed by the reality my mom and sister are facing every day.

"Hey, you don't look like it." He gives me a look of concern.

"Jahi, I feel guilty," I confess, my voice barely above a whisper. "My sister is taking care of my sick mother, day and night. I feel like my sister's life is being snatched away alongside Mom's."

Jahi guides me to his sofa, sits beside me, and places his warm hand on my shoulder. "I know what you're going through is awful, Rose," he says as tears fill his eyes and his lower lip trembles. "I want you to know I'm here for you, and you can tell me what's on your heart."

Touched by his vulnerability and emotion, I go further. "I feel like it's so hard to explain why I'm riddled with guilt, Jahi. And I don't know how to express it to my sister without it being awkward."

"You don't have to explain it to me, Rose. I understand. I know about guilt because I've lived with it my entire life since Dad died," he says, breaking eye contact, his eyes deflected towards the floor.

"What do you mean?"

"After Dad's funeral, I avoided the house. I couldn't stand it there. It was too painful and gloomy. Mom and Chrissy cried all the time. I was a pimple-faced fifteen-year-old. Well, I had bad acne, and got distracted by Susanne's attention and all her friends. I regret that. I'm ashamed that I abandoned Mom and Chrissy at such a terrible moment in our lives," he says with a long sigh.

"You were so young, Jahi. Don't blame yourself for what happened. Most teenagers wouldn't know what to do in that situation. But me, I'm a psychologist, I'm thirty-seven years old, and I know better. I'm a grown woman, yet I'm not stepping up to the plate for my sister and Mom, and this reminds me of my dad and how much I'm like him. This is my chance to redeem myself, to be here for my family, to make up for all those years in LA when I visited rarely. I allowed my troubled relationship with Lee to disrupt time with Mom and Beatrice… and now I'm doing the same thing, except my excuse is my career, even though it's on hold at the moment."

"Rose, you have a lot of big changes going on. You're reinventing your life, post-Lee. Things will settle into a new reality, perhaps one you don't see yet. From what you've told me, your sister and your mom know this and want you to blossom in your new life."

"Well, maybe you're right. I think they've always wanted the best for me, but I still feel guilty."

"In some ways, it may be inevitable to feel guilty, Rose. Some things in life we have no control over. I have so many regrets about Dad's death, but it's too much to get into. As for you, you hid your talents for years because of Lee. I imagine your family doesn't want to do anything that causes you to sacrifice your life for someone else's."

"Yeah… I think you're right," I answer, amazed by Jahi's insight and also his revelation about his own guilt. "You know, it's a knotty problem, this issue of guilt. Sometimes, we have to work out an uneasy truce as we come to terms with it."

"That's true. I think I've got work to do on that account, Rose," he says, his eyes sad as silence falls between us.

Jahi is right. I don't have to feel guilty for not being there every second. I realize I need to have the difficult conversation with Beatrice, of letting her know I struggle with guilt. It troubles me to not be there all the time like she is. I must promise her that if she's ever feeling overwhelmed or just needing support, I'll be there within an hour.

"Hey, let's play chess. What do you think? Maybe it will lift your spirits," he deftly changes the subject, trying to look cute by raising his eyebrows. I feel he doesn't want to deep dive into Lily's medical situation yet. His burden has been so heavy lately, too.

"Uh, I don't know," I say with hesitation. I've got a lot on my mind, and I don't really feel like doing anything. Besides, I'm not much of a chess player, apart from the time I played Jahi, and I don't want to embarrass myself in front of him. "I'm not good at chess, as you know. I don't remember all the nuances."

"Come on. I promise to show you the ropes and teach you the secrets of getting better at chess. It'll help get your mind off your mom. Besides, it'll help me, too." He pulls my hand, cajoling me.

"Ok." That last part clinches it for me—helping Jahi. It's my Achilles heel to help others.

"So, let's review the rules. You have eight pawns in the front," he says as he sets up his own pieces and shows me where to place pawns on my side of the board. "It's the least powerful piece. For its first move, you can move it forward one or two squares. After that, it only moves forward one square at a time. It attacks the enemy diagonally to the left or right."

"Ok," I say as I set up the pawns.

"Now, you've got two bishops, one on a dark square and the other on a light square. It moves like an X shape with as many squares as it likes." His hand, with its strong, competent fingers, gently places the bishops on the board. I'm entranced, that old flicker of desire for him burning strong in me.

"Got it."

He has a calming voice and presence, and I relax under his spell.

"Now, for the knights. You have two of them, a king's knight and a queen's knight. It's the only chess piece that can jump over another and it moves in an L shape. You can move it one square horizontally, left or right and then two squares vertically, up or down. Or the opposite, two squares horizontally and one square vertically."

"Wow. I like the knight. I've always loved horses," I say, admiring the curvature of the horse's head.

"Yeah, it's pretty cool. Ok. Now you have two rooks on the corners. It's a major piece and can move as many squares as it likes horizontally or vertically as long as it's not blocked. You can think of its actions as a plus sign."

"All set."

"Ok, now for the queen. She's the most powerful chess piece."

"Oh, I like that—a powerful woman." I smile at Jahi, and he grins.

"Yes. She's like you—she can do whatever she wants." He glances at me with a sexy grin. "She can move as many squares as she likes and in all directions: vertically, horizontally, and diagonally. A good way to think of it is that she moves like a bishop and a rook combined."

"Great. I'll remember that," I say, blushing in delight at his comment about me.

"Now for the grand finale. The king. He's the most important piece—sort of like me—because the goal of chess is to checkmate the king." Jahi puffs out his chest. "Paradoxically, he's not powerful. He can only move one square in any direction, but he's pivotal in the game."

Boy, is that right. You're certainly pivotal in my life.

We play chess for hours, joking and trying to outsmart each other while Lily sleeps peacefully in her room. I'm laughing and smiling more than I have in weeks. Losing myself in the game and forgetting my problems for a bit, I honestly haven't felt this good in a long time.

Jahi is an impressive chess player, and I'm wowed by his strategic moves. But he is also patient and kind, letting me take back moves and explaining things I don't understand. How refreshing to be around a man who doesn't judge me or make me feel inferior. He's like this with his daughter, too.

"Thanks for showing me how to improve my chess game. I feel like I got a lot better," I say, smiling at him.

"Anytime," he replies, returning my smile. "You've got a quick mind, Rose. Next time, you'll probably beat me."

I laugh. "I doubt it, but I'll definitely try."

As we put away the pieces, a faint cry startles us.

"Daaad."

It's Lily. She must be awake. My heart leaps. I'm excited but also nervous about seeing her. *Will she still be the same Lily I know? Or will she be irreversibly changed?*

"Yes, babydoll. I'll be right there!" Jahi springs out of his chair like he's responding to a fire and is halfway down the hallway in seconds.

I'm not sure what to do, so I wait, wringing my hands in my lap.

Jahi returns, carrying Lily in his arms. She's paler and thinner in her flowery nightgown than I remember. Her eyes look hollow and haunted, but they light up with surprise when she recognizes me.

"Miss Rose," she exclaims, her voice scratchy and thin. *When they intubated her in the hospital, did they damage her vocal cords?*

"Lily," I gush, my heart bursting with love and goosebumps prickling my arms. "I'm so happy to see you."

Lily reaches out her arms for a hug and I rush to her, throwing my arms around her as Jahi holds her. We stand there in silence, hugging one another, as three become one.

Jahi carries Lily to the sofa and says, "Lily, Miss Rose brought you a gift."

"I sure did," I say as I present the basket of books and fruit to her.

Lily unwraps the two shiny packages in the basket and smiles when she sees the books, *The Yearling* and D'Aulaire's *Book of Greek Myths.* "I saw these books in the library and I've been wanting to read them."

"Wonderful," I exclaim, relieved she's excited by the books I selected.

Lily and Jahi thumb through the gorgeous N.C. Wyeth illustrations in *The Yearling,* oohing and ahhing over them. I hesitated buying it for her, because it's an advanced book for Lily's age, but she's an old soul and reads at a high level, so I figured she would enjoy it. She also looks through the D'Aulaire book, mesmerized by the drawings.

"Daddy, read *The Yearling* to me," Lily says.

"Okay, here we go," Jahi says. "A column of smoke rose thin and straight..." Jahi begins in the sing-song voice of a storyteller.

Jahi rivets Lily and me with his velvety, spellbinding voice. He spins the tale of a child who suffered under the care of a cold, abandoning mother who could not form a meaningful bond with him. A fawn appears, and I imagine a story of redemption. Within two paragraphs, I look at Lily, and she's sound asleep in her father's arms with a beatific smile, the kind that says everything is going to be alright.

Jahi looks at me and lifts his index finger to his lips. I watch silently as he carries his daughter to her bedroom. When he returns, he says, "Thank you for the gifts. The illustrations in those books are fabulous. Lily loves them. I think the medication causes her to be drowsy. She usually lasts at least a page."

"Yes, I noticed. I'm so happy to see her, Jahi."

"She loved seeing you, too, Rose, and it means the world to me you're here," Jahi says, his voice soft. "Hey, would you like to see my rose garden?"

Heat threads through my body. He wants to spend more time

with me. This feels intimate. Something about the way he invited me to his garden differs from the energy he gave me during our chess game and even after seeing Lily. I wonder if Jahi notices my flushed face and chest.

"Oh, I'd love to," I answer, my voice breathy as my heart gallops like a wild horse across a landscape of untethered possibility.

"Be careful, Rose," Jahi says as he takes my hand like an old-fashioned gentleman. He guides me as I descend the uneven stone steps to his garden in my espadrilles, holding my long linen dress in one hand to make sure I don't trip.

"Thank you, I will," I say, swooning under his spell. It makes me realize how hungry my heart is for love… maybe even for Jahi's love.

Our walk through the garden unfolds like I'm in a dream sequence. Time slows down. I'm walking in slow motion. Jahi's otherworldly smile, his tender gestures, and the warmth of his hand mesmerizes me. Some part of me is witnessing this, as if I'm watching a silent movie.

These first moments before you become a couple are the ones you remember forever… these precious moments when you know something amazing is forming. There's a quickening. Your heart knows. It's that spark of these earliest moments when two beings merge and create something new—like an embryo becoming a full-formed being. The birth of a relationship.

It's an experience beyond words. A treasure. The greatest joys in life are these magical, ineffable moments.

I think of the great loves from history and literature who exemplify this—Romeo and Juliet, Anthony and Cleopatra, Napoleon and Josephine.

Some part of me registers this moment as a story I'll recall and recount for as long as I live.

"You seem lost in thought, Rose. I was telling you about the

Big Momma rose, but I'm not sure you heard me," Jahi says in a tender voice.

I'm shocked out of my reverie. Oh dear, what did I miss? I don't want to miss anything Jahi says. "Oh, I'm sorry, Jahi. I'm stunned by the beauty of your garden, and I lost myself in it for a moment."

"No worries," he says, his gaze lingering on me just long enough to cause hope to surge through me. I didn't know seeing him again would awaken so many closely held feelings. "This is the rose named after my grandmother," he says as he shows me a gorgeous, plump white rose and I nod in appreciation. "But what I want you to see is this rose…"

Jahi takes my hand and walks me a few steps down the path to a rosebush with pale pink petals and white flecks. "This is a rose I've bred and not yet named," he says.

I'm astonished by the singular beauty of this tender rose with its delicate petals and sweet scent of lilac and rose oil, like the familiar soaps my mother kept in her bathroom when I grew up.

"Oh, it's exquisite," I gush. "I imagine someone special will feel honored to have it named after them."

"Oh, yes. Indeed," Jahi says with a knowing look in his eyes.

We pass the rest of our time in his garden together peacefully. I push my attraction to Jahi deeper into my heart, knowing I can't overwhelm him or me with these feelings, not when so many things are uncertain in both our lives. Our goodbye is polite but sweet. I promise to visit again, and I mean every word.

I walk home and see on the sidewalk in front of an old Victorian house a game of hopscotch chalked in by a child's hand. I hop in the squares like a six-year-old and giggle. Something in me has lifted. I have chased away some darkness that was devouring me. Sometimes the best way to overcome sadness is to be present, to embrace moments of joy, to keep moving one square at a time, like a chess piece on the gameboard of life.

No matter what happens to Jahi and me, I'm lucky to have him as my friend, and I'll always cherish this one precious, unforgettable day.

I know my life isn't magically fixed, but something has changed, something I can't explain. Maybe it's the simplicity of being together and playing a game of chess or the kindness of a friend, but something is shifting inside me. My mind calls him my friend, but maybe it's because I'm scared it will be nothing more.

CHAPTER FOUR

JAHI

It was devastating to hear of Rose's mother's cancer. I felt so bad for her and that's why I asked her to play chess, hoping it would take her mind off her troubles. It certainly does for me.

I want to see her every day, so I contrive ways to invite her over again, without making her feel coerced. She has an ailing mother to consider, and as much as I want to acknowledge my growing feelings for her, I keep them to myself. The timing just doesn't feel right.

I could ask her to watch a movie.

She agrees to my invitation and comes over the next day, a little earlier than the last time, which I'm happy about. I want more time with Rose. Welcoming her, I serve her sweetened iced tea since the weather is sizzling. She grasps the glass as soon as I set it on the table. My fingers brush hers and we chuckle nervously.

"Thanks Jahi," she murmurs, after gulping the tea and placing her empty glass on the table. I refill it, and she smiles half-heartedly.

"Are you okay?" I ask after a stretch of silence.

"I just… I feel so bad about the other day, telling you all my worries with everything that's going on with Lily. I mean, she's lying on her bed one room away and all I'm talking about is me and my foolish problems."

"Your problems aren't foolish. Your mother is gravely ill. That's not foolish at all."

"Yeah, I know. It's not a good idea to vent to you, though.

It's not fair. You know what I think? I think we should get a therapist."

I laugh at her. She's pretty funny sometimes. Not that I don't believe in therapy, but this is humorous.

"I don't mind if you vent. We're friends, Rose," I say to her, but my mind says something else. Friends? I don't want to be just friends. What I want is way more than that. I want her to direct her blinding smile at me. I want to touch her flirtatiously. Heck, I want to see her in my bed every morning. But I don't know how to tell her that, yet. Besides, men don't always get everything they want.

"Yeah, thank you for that," she nods, giving me a close-lipped smile.

We sit in silence for a few minutes before I ask, "Hey, do you want to watch a movie?"

I've been sort of lonely since the accident, with Susanne leaving and then my sister staying away as she faces her problems. The silence is haunting. Susanne is selfish and has proven to be dangerous for my daughter, but she was another living soul in my great expanse of a house. I don't miss her, per se, but I miss the idea of having a whole family in the house—a mom, dad, and my little Lily.

"No, I don't want to watch a movie," she almost barks out, her jaw muscles rippling.

I wonder why she's clenching her teeth. This turn of events is sudden. *Did I say something wrong?*

"Why? I'll let you pick." I offer her a smile.

Rose shakes her head like she's trying to tell me something, and I'm not understanding what she's getting at. I'm not good at decoding body language. Well, maybe I'm okay at it.

"It's not about picking. I can watch literally anything, even a commercial, with my eyes taped open multiple times. I'm not picky," she says, her voice rising to high soprano territory.

Uh oh. As a man, I know that tone and it means I'm in trouble. Something's wrong and I need to figure out what it is. Then, I need to solve this problem fast. Maybe I should set off a large firecracker from my secret stash as a distraction while I collect myself.

Trying to appear calm, I ask, "Then, what's the problem? Is this because you feel bad about venting to me about your mother and sister? I already told you I don't mind, and I mean that, honestly. Don't worry about it. I'm always here for you as a friend."

"There's that doggone word. Jahi, I don't want to be friends with you. That's not what we're cut out to be." Her porcelain skin mottles with radiating red streaks on her delicate chest and neck. "I refuse to believe that's it for us. Do you understand?" She stares at me, unblinking, her emerald eyes bulging and inflamed. "If we can't be more than friends, I can't be in your life. It hurts too much. It's not my heart's desire to only be friends."

A cloudburst breaks open in my head. This is it. This is the moment I've been waiting for.

"Rose…" I say, my voice cracking. She feels the same way about me, and I can't believe it. "I need to tell you something."

"What? That I shouldn't have said that, right? I forgot. You're still a married man, but rumors are going around that you're divorcing Susanne. I thought maybe we have a chance, but you keep calling me your friend. It's simply more than I can bear. I can't stand by and be your friend, waiting for you to divorce your wife. It's desperate and I don't want to be like that, but I can't help how I feel, either. I'm sorry."

This is my chance. It's one of those moments you imagine all your life. The kind you've read about in great works of literature and seen in films, and it's hard to believe it's finally here. This is the pivotal make or break moment. It's time to confess. This is where the soundtrack calls for a full symphony orchestra, not just someone noodling on the piano in the background.

I take a deep breath, moving my gaze from the hardwood floor to Rose's emerald eyes and her doll-like vulnerable face. My heart is bursting out of my chest. "I want you to know something, Rose. Something I've held in all this time, because I didn't know how to tell you. I… I've always liked you."

Her eyebrows raise and her pupils dilate in a wide-open gaze. "Really?" she asks, incredulous.

I nod, my heart galloping in my chest like a herd of mustangs in the Nevada desert. It's so loud and thunderous I wonder if she can hear it, too. I can hardly believe the words coming out of my mouth. Finally, I've said it. "It's true," I say. "But I never had the courage to tell you because I always felt like the timing wasn't right."

Rose leans forward, her eyes locking onto mine. The intensity of her gaze bores into me as she waits for me to continue.

"The time right before you got that job opportunity was when I was going to confess my feelings to you," I explain. "But then I realized if you got the job, you'd have to move away, and I just couldn't bring myself to do it. I couldn't stand in the way of your future."

As the words leave my mouth, I feel a weight lift off my shoulders. A part of me, hidden away for so long, is finally being expressed.

Rose sits in silence for a moment, processing this revelation. A radiant glow spreads over her velvety skin. "You do not know how happy I am to hear this," she says, her lips supple, forming the gentlest smile I've ever seen. "I've always liked you, too, Jahi. I just never knew how to tell you."

Rose leans in and brushes her lips against mine. I lean towards her, my hands trembling as I touch her cheek. She closes her eyes and tilts her head up towards me. Our lips meet and a bolt of electricity explodes through my body like Zeus has struck me.

Her lips are soft, and I feel her tongue tentatively flicking against mine. I deepen the kiss, wrapping my arms around her waist, pulling her closer to me.

Her fingers run through my hair, and a low moan escapes her lips. I pull back for a moment, looking into her eyes and seeing the love in them. I want nothing more than to make her feel cherished and desired, to be the one to make her heart sing.

Passion builds as we continue kissing, and I feel as though time is standing still. Our bodies move together, like two stars in a constellation meant to be together for all time, and the world fades away as we lose ourselves in this moment.

Reluctantly, I break the kiss and press my forehead against hers. She smiles up at me, and I know no matter what happens, we will always have this moment, this kiss, this love between us.

It's a tender kiss, one that conveys all the love I hold for her in my heart. Cradling her in my arms, I know this is just the beginning for us. Confessing my feelings to Rose is one of the best decisions I've ever made.

While we nestle in each other's arms, I share details of what happened with Susanne. How she's a reckless drunk and I'm divorcing her because she's broken my trust for the last time. I can't let my daughter be around her destructive mother. It could do damage and affect her psyche as a child. Rose agrees but looks sad for Lily, and who wouldn't? Susanne took away any real chance for Lily to stay with her biological mother.

After much discussion, we fall silent, and I know it's now or never. "Will you date me? Be my girlfriend?" I ask Rose.

She laughs uproariously as she nods, saying, "Yes, of course." We kiss again.

"Under one condition though…" She trails off mischievously.

I nudge her to continue.
"You must let me see your rose garden again."
I nod eagerly.

CHAPTER FIVE

ROSE

The first thing I do is call Jolene's number. I've got to tell her the news.

She answers snippily. She must have been busy and now I feel bad about interrupting her. Whatever is making her peevish must be more significant than what's happening to me.

"What do you want?" she asks when she registers my silence. Now I'm regretting calling her and wonder if I should tell her anything. Maybe I should call Beatrice instead.

"Don't worry. It's a mistake. We can talk on another day," I say, but Jolene is intuitive, and sniffs out lies on the spot.

"I know that's not true. You want to come to my house?" she asks.

I stop myself from screaming in frustration into the phone. Not wanting to alienate her and cause her to revoke her offer, I take a deep breath so I don't blurt out in anger. I wouldn't forgive myself if I caused a schism with her. "Are you sure you'd not rather be doing something else?" I ask gingerly.

She exhales and finally replies, "Rose, do you want to come over or not?"

Of course, I want to. Why would she even think I wouldn't? This time, I don't hide my eagerness to tell her yes because I need someone to talk to.

"Yes."

"Sorry for answering like that earlier. This meal isn't going as planned."

It must be one of her Korean dishes. "Is it a new one?" I venture.

"Just come over, Rose."

I nod over the phone like she can see me. I take my bath and throw on one of my casual sundresses and strappy Grecian sandals. If I dress like a slob just because I'm coming to see her, Jolene will have something to say about it, and it might not be nice. The last thing I need is criticism from her or anyone else.

I drive to her house even though I live nearby. I sing along to sappy country songs about boots and bars and lost and found love, my lips tingling. It's more than a physical thing, it's an emotional reminder of that singular moment between me and Jahi when he revealed his heart to me. It's one of those stories I'll tell my children and my children's children if I'm ever lucky enough to become a mother. I can't help it—I giggle so much my stomach aches. Jahi is a miracle worker and I laugh at how giddy and silly I'm being. Finally, I pull into Jolene's driveway.

She appears at the door in seconds and ushers me in. She scrutinizes me for a few seconds.

"Why are you grinning from ear to ear? Your cheeks must be aching with the effort already," she comments as we settle down on her velvet sofa.

I simply can't hide my smile. "Jolene," I start. She raises a brow as if telling me to continue, but I'm bursting forth with my goofy smile and giggles, making it hard to talk.

"My, you're being a silly one today," she begins, as if talking to a kindergartner. "I don't mean to sound negative, but when you called, I thought you had bad news, and needed me to console you, but it seems to be just the opposite," she says, then trails off.

I snap out of my silliness and look at her. "It's not bad news," I say, and then the ringing doorbell startles me.

Jolene pads over to the door. *Who is she expecting? Why did she invite me to her house when visitors are coming over?*

I crane my neck to see who it is when Jolene walks in with a box of pizza. Pizza? The Jolene I'm familiar with likes to eat healthy. It's why she's drawn to fermented Korean food like kimchi.

"Pizza?" I vocalize my disbelief.

Jolene shrugs. "I know you like it and besides, I ruined the meal I was cooking, so it's only right." she says, placing the pizza on the small round table in her living room as I look at her, dazed. She frowns, then settles down beside me.

"So, Rose, tell me what's going on."

I clasp my hands on my lap as I recount the events of the past week. Jolene leans forward, her chin resting on her hands as she listens intently.

"So, let me get this straight," she says. "You and Jahi are finally getting together, and he's divorcing his wife because of her behavior?"

I nod, a small smile curling the corners of my lips as I think about Jahi. "Yes, we shared a kiss on his couch, and it felt right. Susanne has been erratic lately, drinking while driving, and abandoning their daughter at the hospital while doing so. I think Jahi finally realizes he needs to get out of that situation."

Jolene lets out a sigh of relief. "I'm so happy for you, Rose. You deserve to be with someone who treats you well."

A warm flush spreads across my cheeks at her words. "Thank you, Jolene. It's just... it's been a long time since I've felt this way about someone. I know it's silly, but I feel like a high schooler again."

Jolene chuckles. "We all need a little teenage romance in our lives, Rose. And you and Jahi have been dancing around each other for so long, it's about time you figure it out."

I nod, and we both fall into a comfortable silence, the only sounds coming from the jazz tunes playing softly from Jolene's stereo.

"So, what's the plan now? Are you and Jahi going to move in together?"

I shake my head. "No, not yet. We both want to take things slowly and make sure we're ready for this. I don't want to rush into a living situation."

Jolene nods, taking a bite of her pizza. "That's smart. And what about Susanne and their daughter?"

I let out a long sigh. "I don't know. Jahi is trying to figure out the best course of action. He's looking out for his daughter. He wants to be sure he's not enabling Susanne's behavior anymore."

Jolene chews thoughtfully, contemplating my words. "It's a tough situation. But I trust Jahi to do what's best for his family."

I nod, grateful for Jolene's support. "Yeah, he's a good guy. And he's been through so much with Susanne. I just want him to be happy."

Jolene reaches out and pats my hand. "You deserve to be happy, too, Rose. Don't forget that."

"Thanks, Jolene. I won't forget."

We finish our pizza in comfortable silence, the music playing softly in the background. As I look around Jolene's cozy living room, I realize how much I've missed spending time with her. Life has been so hectic with Lily's accident, my mom's illness, and the drama with Susanne that I forgot to slow down and enjoy life's day-to-day pleasures.

"Hey, Jolene?" I say, breaking the silence.

She looks up from her plate, a questioning expression on her face. "Yeah?"

"Thank you for having me over. You're a wonderful friend

and you mean the world to me. I've missed hanging out with you like this."

Jolene smiles warmly, her eyes crinkling at the corners. "Of course, Rose. You know you're always welcome here. It's been great catching up with you, too."

I grin back at her, feeling content. "Yeah, it's been too long. We should make this a regular thing."

Jolene nods in agreement, finishing her pizza slice. "Definitely. And maybe next time, we can do something a little more adventurous than eating pizza on my sofa."

I raise an eyebrow in curiosity. "Like what?"

Jolene lets out a mischievous laugh. "I don't know, maybe go to a concert or try that new Korean restaurant that just opened up. Something fun."

I can't imagine Jolene at a concert, but it sure is something I'd love to see.

"Sounds like a plan. We'll have to make sure Jahi can come, too."

Jolene's expression softens at the mention of Jahi. "Yes, of course. He's part of our little group now, too."

I nod, feeling pride bubble up inside me. Jahi has become such an important part of my life in a short amount of time, and it feels good to have Jolene accept us as a couple.

I'm grateful for the simplicity of this moment. All the drama and chaos of the past few weeks fades away, leaving only the warmth of friendship and the comfort of a familiar place.

When it's time to head back home, Jolene walks me to the door, giving me a tight hug before I step out into the cool night air.

"Thanks for coming over, Rose. And congratulations on finally getting together with Jahi. You deserve all the happiness in the world."

"Thanks, Jolene. And thanks for being such a good friend."

She waves as I walk down the path to my car, the sound of her laughter echoing in my head all the way home.

Life is far from perfect, but in moments like this, surrounded by the people I love, it's pretty sweet.

CHAPTER SIX

JAHI

I'm dissolving my marriage. It's long overdue. I have doubts about my lawyer, Chad Murphy, being convinced that the dissolution of my marriage will go smoothly. He doesn't know Susanne like I do. She's like a scorpion—grasping victims with her pincers and whipping her tail around to strike and sting them with her poisonous venom. Wouldn't you know her moon is in Scorpio? It's a fact she bragged about our entire marriage. People tell you what they're really like. All you have to do is listen carefully.

She loved to go on about how, as a Scorpio, she's the most intuitive sign in the zodiac and can size up a roomful of characters in seconds. I don't know about that, but she sure picked up on how smitten I am by Rose. I could almost hear her neurons yelling, "Battle stations! Battle stations!" It was just like years ago, when she knew the curvy gal in paramedic school was a threat to our relationship.

As far as the divorce goes, I don't mind negotiating if Susanne demands a reasonable settlement. I just need this marriage to be over.

Susanne is broken from the drunk driving arrest, ashamed to show her face in town. It's possible she may not pursue a settlement, but just skulk out of Eureka Springs, that scorpion tail tucked between her legs. Maybe she'll take her poison and drama elsewhere. We were once in love, but now I sort of hate her. *Who wouldn't? She almost ruined my life and my chances with Rose.*

I talk to my lawyer daily. At the end of our last conversation, he muttered, "This is long overdue." I wonder if that's even professional. I don't think so, but my lawyer is brash when he's out in public. He's a leather-lunged bellower, his voice filling up any space like a carnival barker, but he knows his stuff. Some people thrive on conflict, and I'm glad he's running interference for me because that's not my personality.

"So, what are you doing today?" he asks, trying to make small talk. Maybe it's not advisable, but Chad and I are sort of friends or actually acquaintances. Sometimes, he calls out of the blue to check up on me.

"I'm going on a date," I tell him honestly.

He pauses momentarily, and I brace myself for his response. "Does Susanne know about this?"

"No," I say. I've been dreading him finding out about our dating.

"You better keep it that way, Jahi. If she finds out, she might try to claim alienation of affection."

"What? Chad, aren't homewrecker laws no longer recognized in Arkansas?" I ask.

"Well, supposedly they're not, but you never know. Sad sack stories from spurned hags can sway some of these judges, those old coots sitting askew on the bench because of hemorrhoids. So, even though it's no longer on the books doesn't mean it's not still playing out in courts. The bias is there."

Political correctness is not my lawyer's strong suit and actually, I'm glad. "Oh, no," I say.

"Yeah, you get the wrong judge and he'll decide you're shoving Susanne out of the marriage, inflicting mental and emotional anguish. You're not divorced yet, so you're at risk."

"Why do you say that? That's ridiculous. Susanne put my child in danger. She's got a DUI on her records and she abandoned us for years. What more do they need? Why would the courts side with her?"

"Because people will say anything to come out victorious. She'll do anything to win, mark my words."

"I don't care about the victory. I just want her gone."

"Maybe you need to care about it, Jahi. Look, just be careful, okay? She's probably seething with rage that you're divorcing her. If she's as primitive as you say, she'll seek revenge until her dying day."

"That's true. She's envious and holds grudges," I say, dread slithering up my spine like a cottonmouth snake.

"Meanwhile, the judge may see this as a betrayal of marital vows, that you're cheating on your wife. If that's the case, she would have a legal claim and could recover compensatory and punitive damages. She could clean you out financially."

"But Chad, can't we contest it if this happens? These archaic laws are no longer in the books in this state."

"Yes, we can. But it will cost you dearly. It may not be worth it, depending on how much compensation she asks for."

"Right," I say, my mind racing.

"I'll update you when I have something to report. And on that note, enjoy your date."

He's right. I need to be careful. Even if I wasn't before, I need to be cautious now, not only for me but for Rose as well. I won't do anything to put her in any sort of danger or embarrass her.

I call Matt. He promised to stay with Lily at my house because he claims to be Mr. Cupid—always doing everything within his power to aid young lovers, even if they're older than he is. He's so funny. I laugh at his antics and he takes it hard, so I apologize.

"What's up, bud?" Matt asks, his voice chilly.

I wonder why he sounds like that. Did he have a fight with Jane?

"You good?" I ask.

He shakes his head, his shoulders slumping. "Jane is mad at me again for not helping her out enough. I'm genuinely tired of this."

"Okay. You want to stay at home and help her out today?" I ask.

"No. You've got your thing with Rose, and I want to spend time with Lily. It's been so long since I've seen my girl. I'm sure she can't wait to see her favorite uncle."

"Yes! Indeed," I say sarcastically, but I assure Matt that in case he needs a rain check, I understand. Even though this date with Rose is something I've wanted for a long time, I don't mind pushing it back a bit to help my friend.

I admire his and Jane's marriage. They're a cute couple and make me envious sometimes. They seem to take the inevitable bumps in the road with grace, but nobody ever knows fully what goes on in somebody else's relationship.

Matt says he plans to arrive earlier so he can make sure I'm not wearing something disastrous to the date. I pretend to be offended, but deep down, I want his advice.

I lean against the kitchen counter, my arms crossing tightly over my chest as I survey the mess before me. Lily's toys are scattered all over the living room floor, and the sink is piled high with dishes from dinner.

I let out a long sigh, feeling the weight of exhaustion settling heavily over me. It's been a long week, between work and taking care of Lily, who's still recovering from the accident. I'm so distracted, I temporarily forget about my date with Rose tonight, and I'm far from prepared.

Just then, the doorbell rings, and I nearly jump out of my skin. Thankfully, it's Matt. He's here to help me with Lily while I get ready.

"Hey," he says as he walks in, taking in the chaotic scene around us. "Looks like you could use some help."

I let out a relieved laugh, feeling the tension in my shoulders ease up. "Yeah, I'm a little behind tonight. Thanks for coming over."

Matt nods, looking towards the living room where Lily is playing with her dolls. "No problem. It's good to see you guys again. How's Lily doing?"

I smile at the thought of my little girl. "She's doing really well, actually. Her surgical wound is healing, her energy is coming back, and she's acting more like herself again."

Matt claps me on the back, his expression warm with pride. "That's great. She's a tough kid, just like her dad."

I grin, feeling our camaraderie. Matt and I have been through many traumas together as firefighters and paramedics, and it's comforting to have him here on this pivotal day. As I head to my bedroom, Matt trails after me, eyeing my wardrobe with a critical eye.

"Alright, it's time for an instant makeover, Jahi edition," he says, rummaging through my closet. "What are you wearing tonight?"

I shrug, feeling a sort of impotence. Grooming to attract a mate isn't my forte. "Don't know. I haven't really thought about it. I've been so focused on Lily and work."

Matt shakes his head, clucking his tongue disapprovingly. "Well, we can't have that. We've got to get you cleaned up and looking sharp for Rose."

I follow him to the bathroom, where I run a comb through my hair and he smooths out my wrinkled shirt. It reminds me of being fourteen and Dad helping me get dressed for my eighth-grade step-up ceremony. I feel like a teenager, but that's okay. Matt is always here for me, just like Dad was before he died.

"So, tell me about you and Rose," he nudges me, breaking the silence.

A smile spreads across my face as I think of her. "She's amazing, as you know. It's hard to believe we're finally getting together, just like you hoped. The more time we spend together, the more I'm falling in love with her. Being with Rose makes me feel like everything is going to be okay."

Matt nods thoughtfully. "That's great. You deserve someone like that."

My heart clenches at his words. I'm grateful for the validation. "Thanks, Matt. It's been a long time since I've felt this way about someone."

He claps me on the back, grinning. "Well, you better hurry and get ready, then. You don't want to keep your princess waiting."

As I finish dressing, I realize how excited I am about tonight even though I feel unpracticed with dating. But with Rose, I know it's going to be special.

I come downstairs and Lily is sitting at the kitchen table, her art pad and markers spread out in front of her. Matt is sitting next to her, a proud smile on his face.

"Look, Daddy!" Lily exclaims, holding up a picture of a horse. "I drew it all by myself!"

She didn't. Matt held her hands as she drew. But she's recovering little by little and that's all that matters.

"That's amazing, Lily. I love your horse. He's got a lot of personality. Like one of those many-colored horses in your favorite movie."

"The Wizard of Oz," Lily exclaims with excitement. "It's a girl horse, Daddy." Lily giggles.

Matt stands, clapping me on the back. "Alright, bud, you're all set, and it's time now. You look great, and Lily's in excellent hands. Now, go have fun on your date."

I thank him profusely, kiss Lily, and walk to my car to drive to Rose's house and pick her up, as nervous as a seventh-grader taking a date to my first school dance. I feel a giddy nervousness, like I'm breathing helium and I worry that when I talk to Rose, my voice will sound high and squeaky.

When I get to Rose's house, I stand on her porch, summoning the courage to press the doorbell. To my surprise, the door swings open to reveal a breathtaking apparition. Rose is wearing a breezy, floral sundress that hugs her curves and shows off her delicate collarbones. Her cascading strawberry blonde hair is curled and blown out, and her face has a light layer of makeup, causing her skin to glow and highlighting her broad cheekbones.

"Wow," I breathe out, my eyes roaming over the luscious landscape of her body. "You look gorgeous, Rose."

She blushes, her eyes sparkling with happiness. "Thank you, Jahi. You look pretty darn good yourself."

I grin, loving the way she's looking at me. "Thanks. It's because of Matt. He's a miracle worker."

Rose laughs, taking my arm and leading me out the door. I open her car door, and I can tell she loves this gesture. We arrive at Ermilio's, the best Italian restaurant in town, and settle into a window table near the back. Smells of garlic and basil waft over us, and my mouth waters with anticipation.

"So, how's Lily doing?" Rose asks, sipping Chianti.

The tension in my shoulders dissipates. "She's okay, all things considered. She's getting her energy back, and she seems more like herself. I'm optimistic she'll heal completely."

Rose reaches over and squeezes my hand, her eyes shining

with warmth. "That's wonderful, Jahi. She's such a strong little girl. I adore her."

We peruse the menu and order the same thing—Tuscan Chicken with a Caprese salad. We joke about having similar tastes and I love this. I have a feeling it's a good sign.

"That's a beautiful song," I say, noticing the Italian aria playing in the background.

Rose's face lights up. "Oh yes, that's Puccini's *O Mio Babbino Caro*, one of my favorite soprano arias, and it was one of my dad's, too."

"What's it about? I don't know Italian."

"Well, it's an opera set in Florence, Italy, in the late 13th century. It's powerful because it's about a child's relationship with her father. It starts with the lyrics, 'Oh my dearest Papa. I love him. He is handsome. I want to go to Porta Rossa to buy the ring,'" Rose begins.

"What happens?"

"There's tension between her family and his, sort of like the Montagues and the Capulets from *Romeo and Juliet.* She warns her father that if he doesn't allow her to marry him, if her love is in vain, she'll walk on the Ponte Vecchio and throw herself into the Arno. Back then, people didn't have swim lessons, either," Rose says.

"Whoa. That's intense," I say, loving discovering hidden aspects of Rose that are meaningful to her. She's a multi-faceted, beautiful woman. I have a feeling I could be with her for a lifetime and never get to the end of her brilliant mind. I feel at ease, as if we've been together forever.

As dinner winds down, I realize how much I don't want the night to end. I'm smitten by Rose, and I don't want to let her go.

"Hey Rose," I say, feeling my nerves kicking in. "I know

I probably sound repetitive, but I just want you to know how much I enjoyed tonight."

"I had a great time, too, Jahi. You're a wonderful guy."

"Thanks. I know things are still new between us, but I really like you. A lot."

To my relief, she doesn't seem shocked by my admission. She just smiles at me with a gleam in her eyes. After dinner, she suggests we take a walk.

I saunter alongside Rose, holding her hand and feeling content. Dinner was yummy. Ermilio's restaurant has the best Tuscan Chicken I've ever tasted. The candlelit ambiance and operatic arias playing in the background created a special romantic atmosphere, especially given Rose's love of opera and works by Puccini, in particular.

Rose looks beautiful, her strawberry blonde hair bouncing as we walk. The cool breeze is redolent with the scent of sandalwood from rows of blue hydrangeas lining the path. Velvety red-violet spikes of ornamental sage dance as we pass by. We play a game of naming as many flowers and plants as possible. I surprise myself by knowing a few of them.

"Hey, there's supposed to be shooting stars tonight. You know what we do if we see one, right?" Rose teases as we turn our attention to the sky.

"Yeah, make a wish. But technically, it's debris from the comet Swift-Tuttle. It's the Perseids meteor shower, and it comes every year around this time."

"Oh, impressive, Herr Professor Adams. So, I'm not the only nerdy one around here," Rose says with a wink.

I blush, enjoying the moment. "So… What's your favorite food?" I ask, desperate to keep the conversation going.

"Pizza," she answers emphatically.

"Wow! Decisive. I love how quickly you answered that.

Okay. Maybe we'll have a pizza date next time. Then, I get to have you all to myself alone again, like tonight," I say, leering at her in a humorous way.

She laughs and gives my shoulder a slight push.

"What's your favorite color?"

"Colors," she corrects me.

"Oh, you have more than one favorite color? That's cool."

"Yes, I love white because it represents purity. And then I love red because it goes in sync with my name, Rose," she says wistfully.

I'm amused. She's a fascinating woman and there's no way I'll ever get bored with her. "Cool. What about traveling? Places you'd like to see?"

"I'd love to visit Italy again because of opera, especially Florence. And then there's Paris for the food and wine and culture. I'd love to explore parts of Asia and Africa, too," she says with a dreamy expression.

I make mental notes, because I want to remember everything Rose loves. All the while, I steal glimpses of the sky. It's getting late and I'm about to give up on seeing a shooting star when, out of the corner of my eye, I see a flash across the sky, a ball of fire burning brightly before disappearing—ephemeral, like life, bright, bright, then gone. It feels like a good omen as I make a silent wish to be with Rose forever.

As we get up to leave, I wrap my arms around Rose's slim waist, pulling her in for a hug as she rests her head on my chest.

"Thank you for an unforgettable evening," she says, her voice muffled against my shirt.

"I had a great time, too," I reply, running my fingers through her hair because I can't resist it any longer. She has beautiful, silky hair. "It was wonderful, and so are you." Burying my fingers deeper into her hair, I mentally add it to the growing list of things

I love about Rose.

I lift her chin. We stand there for a few more minutes, wrapping our arms around each other. Her body is a perfect fit for my arms. I wish we didn't have to be apart tonight, but I have to take it slowly.

We drive back to her bungalow in comfortable silence. I relish these silent moments as much as the lively ones.

When we arrive, she turns and says, "Goodnight, Jahi."

"Goodnight, Rose," I reply, leaning in to plant a gentle kiss on her lips.

CHAPTER SEVEN

ROSE

Autumn house cleaning. Energized by last night's first date with Jahi, I deep clean and rearrange my bungalow as if possessed—possessed by an overwhelming desire to make everything right.

Two days after our first official date, Jahi calls and invites me over to his house.

"I was thinking you should come over to the house today so we can spend time together." Jahi's voice sounds breathless, and it excites me.

"Is that all you have in mind? You act like there's more," I tease.

"Not really. I just can't wait to see you again, my beautiful girlfriend," he says emphatically.

"Come off it, Jahi," I reply, chuckling.

"Come on, Rose."

"Fine, I miss you, too."

I choose a dress from my freshly laundered stack and throw it on after bathing and eating two slices of pizza from my fridge.

When I arrive at Jahi's place, he says, "Come inside. I've unlocked the door." My heart rate quickens and I become slightly apprehensive, so I give myself a little pep talk.

It's just Jahi. No need to be nervous.

Entering Jahi's living room, I see that he's wearing a form-fitting polo shirt and khaki shorts. His legs are taut and tan and he looks handsome talking to someone on the phone. I stand there mesmerized until he raises his head and reaches out his muscled arm for me to come closer. I go to him as if in a trance.

"Mmmm, you smell so good, Rose," he murmurs in my ear as he gives half his attention to the caller. He pulls me deeper into his embrace, and I snuggle closer. I haven't felt this safe and at peace in a long time. Jahi is perfect for me. I hear a gruff, booming voice, even though the phone isn't on speaker. He mouths the word "lawyer" to me in between breaks in the conversation. After a few minutes, he ends the call.

"I'm sorry she's at it again," I tell Jahi, referring to his wife as I could deduce from his conversation that her actions are still hurting him.

"It's okay. I'll be fine." He shrugs. "Come, let's watch a movie. I remember promising to let you choose."

"Haha, that's quite noble of you. Let's see what you have here."

I sift through his streaming account on TV and eventually choose *The Sound of Music*, a classic I love and never tire of watching.

"Excuse me for a minute. Let me get the popcorn and sodas." He returns with a bowl of popcorn and two Cokes in cold glass bottles dripping with condensation. "You know, I should have seen it coming. But I'm too optimistic for my own good."

"Nobody would have seen it coming. Besides, I can't fault you for trying to rebuild your family, for Lily's sake. I respect how much you love your daughter and will sacrifice for her."

"You're just saying that to console me. Everyone knows and saw it coming from a mile away. Everyone except me."

"I don't agree, Jahi. I wouldn't have. You did it for Lily and nobody can fault you for wanting to do the right thing for your daughter. If anything, you should be applauded because you're a wonderful father. You know that, right?" I wonder if what I'm saying is lifting his spirit or if he just thinks I'm saying it only because I want to make him feel better. I hope he believes what I'm saying.

"How'd I even get so lucky? Darn, we danced around this for so long. I wish we'd gotten together earlier." He flashes his handsome smile at me, and it's like all is well with the world again.

I snuggle up next to Jahi on the couch as the opening credits of our movie starts rolling. It's Saturday afternoon, Lily is with Granny, and we have nothing else planned except to relax and spend time together. It's moments like these that I cherish the most—just Jahi and me, alone and happy together.

We've come a long way to get to this point. This past half-year of knowing each other has been fraught with tension—my move to Eureka Springs, teaching for the first time ever, an ex-spouse reappearing, the breakup of Jahi's marriage, Lily's life-threatening accident, and my mother's cancer. We've been through so much together and yet slowly but surely, we've found our way to each other.

As the movie plays, I feel Jahi's hand slip into mine, and we intertwine fingers. I smile to myself, feeling the warmth of his touch.

The story intensifies, and we mirror this intensity with our bodies. We tease each other mercilessly—thumb wrestling a dozen rounds with me winning all but one match, arm wrestling five rounds with Jahi redeeming his losses, and making funny toddler faces to see who can stick out their lower lip, mimicking the poutiest face. We're laughing so hard my stomach aches and happy tears stream down my face. But soon, our folly develops into something serious. Jahi leans in for a kiss and our lips lock.

As our make-out session sizzles, Jahi carries me to his bedroom, the droning dialogue of the movie growing fainter. I won't go into detail, but let's just say we're both satisfied and euphoric when we finish. Jahi is a kind and tender lover, which doesn't surprise me. He took everything slowly, making me feel treasured.

A man like him is all I've ever dreamt of. While some people might call this the honeymoon phase, since it's only the beginning of our relationship, I don't think that's the case with Jahi and me. I think we'll always be in love with each other.

The next day, I stop by again to check on Lily and see Jahi. She's tired after spending time with her grandmother, but Jahi tells me she was in high spirits before falling asleep just after lunch.

Jahi lets me in and says, with a glimmer in his eyes, "I've got a surprise for you." He's holding his hands behind his back. "Pick a hand."

I pick his left hand, and he reveals it to be empty. Then, I pick his right hand and the same thing happens. I keep trying his hands—and it's the same thing. "Ah… you're funny and clever… but come on!" I say, pouting again like a three-year-old.

He laughs and tells me to keep trying. We go through several more rounds of his "pick a hand" game when he finally reveals a gold box. He tricked me by shuffling the box from hand to hand behind his back. I open the box and it's filled with petite chocolates. My heart melts.

"Oh, I love these dark chocolates," I say. "How did you know this is my favorite?"

"Well, remember that time we walked into the village and stopped at Sweets Fudge Kitchen?" he asks, and I nod. "You only chose dark chocolates, and I made a mental note of it."

"Wow. I love that," I say, feeling special and important to him, and proud that I have a surprise for him, too. "Well, guess what? I've got something for you."

"Really, Rose! You didn't have to bring me a gift."

"Keep saying sweet stuff like that and I'll get emotional and start crying."

He smiles at me kindly. "I'll lick your tears away, but please don't cry."

"Then stop talking and close your eyes. I'll tell you when to open them," I shoot back.

"Ok," he says, raising his arms in surrender. He closes his eyes and patiently waits.

He's so cute with his eyes closed, like a little boy. "Alright, open your eyes. Now... pick a hand," I say, with a mischievous smile.

Jahi laughs and pretty soon we're replicating his "pick a hand" game, only this time I'm the one bearing gifts. After more than a dozen empty hands and just before the game gets old, I surprise Jahi with a mesh bag.

"Wow!" he says.

"I picked up some of your favorite Japanese gardening tools last time I was in Fayetteville."

I watch his face light up. "That's amazing! You really know me so well." It's such a simple gesture, but it pleases me immeasurably to see Jahi delighted. I'm learning that it's the little things that matter most. Jahi's love for gardening is no secret. In fact, I've heard him talk about spending countless hours tending his roses. I'd like nothing more than to watch him trim his heirloom roses.

We sit on the porch, sipping coffee and enjoying the cool breeze. "Thanks once again. I can't wait to use these tools. I'm thinking of starting up a range of hibiscus flowers. There are some varieties that will grow here. Maybe some veggies, too. I have the land for it, anyway."

"That'll be so nice, Jahi. Your roses are doing great. You should give sweet peas and veggies a shot, too."

"Come with me," he says, leading me to the patch of land where he intends to start his new projects. He takes a long stick and marks out where he'll build a partition for the new plants. I admire his hard thighs and muscular body. Jahi works out at the station, maybe not as much as Matt from what he says, but his body is still an exquisite specimen, like granite.

Watching him work in his garden is like watching an artist painting in his studio. Every stroke of his hand is expressive—his own personal lexicon, his unique signature of meaning. His moves in the garden are deliberate and measured, with a gentle touch that shows how much he cares. As he works, he hums quietly to himself, lost in his own little world. It wouldn't surprise me if Jahi believes, like I do, that plants are much more aware than we give them credit for.

I'm grateful for his passion for gardening. It's a reminder that there is always room for beauty and growth, even in life's darkest moments.

The garden becomes a source of joy and connection for us. As we continue to date, we spend lazy afternoons sitting among the flowers, reading or chatting about our dreams and plans. It's our own little retreat, a place of peace and tranquility.

One evening, when the sky is painted a deep ultramarine blue with hints of cerulean, peach, and apricot cloud streaks, Jahi asks me to come look at his garden. As I approach, I see he has set up a small table and chairs by the colorful flower bed, with a warm blanket draping over the back of the chairs.

Sitting there, enjoying a warm cup of tea and the cool autumn breeze, Jahi thanks me again for the gardening tools. "You give me the gift of joy, Rose," he says, looking at me with his sparkling eyes. "I will never forget this."

My heart overflows with love for this man. I know it's not just the gardening tools that bring him happiness, but that I take the time to notice and appreciate his interests. Love isn't just about grand gestures, but about the everyday little things we do for one another.

Surrounded by the beauty of nature, I know Jahi and I will always find solace in the simple moments of life, and our love will continue to grow, just like the flowers in his garden.

Afternoons are my favorite. Jahi and I curl up with a book or watch a movie, and Lily sometimes joins us. I love seeing her strength as she recovers to be even more joyful than ever. I've thanked her more than once for sharing her dad with me. It's like a secret pact for us. We both want to see him happy, her as his daughter and me as his girlfriend.

Hours turn into days, and days turn into weeks. I shuffle between sleeping at his place and sleeping alone at my bungalow. Our love for each other deepens. It feels meant to be—like we're on the same wavelength in just about every aspect of life.

Sometimes, I stop and look at Jahi and Lily, mesmerized by this beautiful man and his beautiful child, and realize how lucky I am. I hope our happiness continues for a long, long time.

CHAPTER EIGHT

JAHI

We're sitting in the kitchen, making pancakes and eggs, when my phone rings.

"Hey, Matt. Good morning. Hope all is well. What's up?" I ask, while sneaking looks at Rose.

"Work is overwhelming. There was an incident yesterday with a teenager. We're short of men at the station." Matt's speech is breathy. I know this voice. He needs me.

Rose looks at me with questioning eyes and I whisper, "I'll tell you in a minute."

"Matt, I got it. I'll be there," I say. "It's not a problem."

He voices his relief and thanks me. "That's great, Jahi, see you soon."

"Alright, bye." I hang up and face Rose to break the news to her, but I feel like she already knows what I'm going to say.

"I'm needed at work, back to my regular schedule from before the accident." The thought of leaving her alone makes me sad, but I have little choice in the matter.

"Jahi, that's ok. You should go, or don't you want to go?" Rose asks, raising her eyebrows as if dreading my answer.

"Of course, I do. I love my job. I love helping people and giving back to the community in my own little way. It's you I'm worried about." I walk around the counter to stand in front of her.

"Why are you worried about me?" She scrunches her face in the special way I adore.

"Well, you'll be alone most of the time. You haven't begun your therapy practice yet, and you're not working right now. I'm afraid, with that big, brilliant noggin of yours, you'll get bored or fall into sad thoughts," I answer.

She smiles, placing her palms on both sides of my face, and my heart melts a fraction more. "I'll be fine, Jahi. You don't have to worry. I'll surely find something to occupy me."

"Let me make it up to you." I must sound like a worry wart because she gives me a bemused smile.

"Although you don't have to… but how?" she asks playfully.

"I usually go to my mom's house with Lily once a month for dinner. Will you come with us? We're getting close to Thanksgiving. I want Mom and my sister to meet you before the holidays. I'm sure they'll love you," I say hesitantly, hoping I'm not rushing things and scaring her off.

"You want me to meet your mom? Jahi?" Her voice rises a whole octave.

"Calm down, Rose. It's nothing serious. My mom is nice, I promise. She didn't like Susanne, which in retrospect is an accurate read on her, but Mom was still decent to her. But as for you—Mom has heard great things about you, and she's going to welcome you warmly."

"Oh. I don't know…." Her voice trails off.

"Trust me, Rose." I take her palms and place them on my heart, wordlessly willing her to see into me and hoping what she sees is enough to make her agree.

"Alright! Now go get ready for work, then. I'll be fine."

"Are you sure?" I ask again, still worried.

"I'm sure. Go, Jahi." She shoos me into my bedroom and continues cooking. When I finish getting ready, I come back to the kitchen to say goodbye, and I'm surprised when she hands me a packed lunch from the first batch of pancakes she made.

"I packed enough for you and Matt and some extras. There's maple syrup, breakfast sausages, and strawberry jam. I added a chocolate spread, too, just in case that's what Matt likes. There are some apples and hard-boiled eggs, too."

I'm touched by her thoughtfulness, so I pull her over to me and kiss her with every emotion I'm feeling. I'm lucky to land myself someone like Rose. She's a breath of fresh air compared to Susanne.

Still breathless from the kiss and feeling on top of the world, I head straight to the station, because that's where Matt and the team are. When I arrive, the men welcome me. Some of them are smiling as they eye the lunch box I'm holding.

I look for Matt and find him in the storeroom. I tap on the door to get his attention, but he doesn't hear me. He looks lost in thought, which concerns me.

"Matt? Hey, buddy," I call softly, using his favorite word for me so I don't startle him, but he doesn't look up.

I step forward and wave my hands in his line of sight for a few seconds before he blinks and raises his head. He looks disoriented for a moment but composes himself.

"Hey Jahi, when did you get here?"

"Just now," I answer, sitting beside him and placing my lunch box on the table. I consider how best to approach what's gotten him so deep in his thoughts.

"I know I look awful. Don't say it," he says, waving his left hand at me.

"What's going on Matt?"

"Jane. I understand nothing again, Jahi. I feel like I'm walking on eggshells in my home. She's so prickly. Anything I do offends her, and she nags me. She snarls and curls her lips at me," he laments.

I give myself a mental smack on the head. Matt has mentioned this change between him and Jane for weeks, but I've been so preoccupied with my own problems I haven't taken time to talk with him about his.

"Matt, I'm so sorry for everything you're going through right now, and I'm not an expert in women's matters, but have you tried to speak with her? Maybe she's bothered by something and she doesn't know how to tell you."

"What could bother her?" he asks, exhaling in exasperation.

"You won't know unless you ask. Women are funny creatures, and they have a knack for making a simple situation complicated. It's best if you approach her with love and concern. I'm sure she'll open up to you, and you guys will sort out whatever it is." I pat his shoulder gently and use my other hand to grab the lunch box.

"I'm worried we're growing apart, to be honest. I hear that happens a lot."

I nod, choosing my words carefully. "You two have been together for a decade, including dating, right?"

Matt nods.

"From what you're telling me, it sounds like she may have been holding on to resentment for a long time. I say this because I've learned the hard way with Susanne that even if I suppress my annoyance or anger in the moment, it shows up eventually. Usually in passive-aggressive ways or through bickering."

"Yeah. That's exactly right. You hit the nail on the head with the passive-aggressiveness and the silly little fights." Matt runs a hand through his blonde mane, thoughtful. "If that's the case, then the more I sit on it and try to let it pass, the worse it's going to get."

"I'm afraid so."

He slaps his hands on his thighs. "Well, she's still the love of my life, so I just need to get her to open up so we can figure this out."

I smile, relieved he has a plan. "That's the spirit. Tell her exactly what you just told me. Just do a lot of listening and be honest with her."

"What's that?" Matt asks to change the subject to something lighter.

"Rose packed us some food. Pancakes, sausages, and four different spreads, eggs, and apples. There's maple syrup, mustard, and strawberry jam. She doesn't know which one you like, so she packed them all. But she threw in a chocolate spread just for you because she thinks you'll like it." I shake my head and chuckle.

"She did? Wow! She's definitely a keeper."

"I know, thanks, Matt. Let's dig in." We attack the food with gusto, spreading the toppings on the pancakes and placing eggs onto our plates. Two of our colleagues pass by the door, and we invite them to join us for the feast.

We clean our plates and I pack the dishes back into the box. The guys thank me and leave Matt and me alone in the room.

"That was delicious, thanks. Pass my gratitude to Rose, too."

"I will."

A call comes over the intercom, and we run to the fire truck.

Time to work…

CHAPTER NINE

ROSE

When Jahi gets the call to return to work, a feeling of dread comes over me. I know it's not rational, but I feel abandoned. It's like when Dad left that day in October so long ago, never to return. I feel sick to my stomach like I did that day. It's as if I knew I'd never see him again. And maybe there's some kind of seasonal resonance that gets triggered every fall.

Jahi must sense this because he's torn and reluctant to leave me alone. He finally leaves, and I'm left on my own. It's terribly still without him here and with Lily in school. My mind goes into overdrive, which is sometimes not a good thing.

When I was a young girl, my mother called me a big dreamer. I dreamt of being a superhero, of being Barbie and living in a pink-themed house, of being an opera star and singing at Carnegie Hall, of being a doctor and saving the lives of cancer patients. I dreamt of many things.

After eating, I go to my bungalow and make myself a cup of chamomile tea, something I'm coming to love, and I realize I'm about to face endless hours of free time. *What will I do?*

I've been hanging around with Jahi or staying at home with Lily. I think about Jahi's invitation for dinner at his mother's house and feel nervous. He thinks it's an excellent opportunity for me to get to know his mom and sister. We've only been together six weeks. I think it's a bit too fast, but I'm willing to do anything for this man.

As I sip the tea, my eyes fall on a dusty book lying on a table in the corner of my house. It's a psychology book. My brain takes this as a sign to write the book I've been dreaming about since I started my psychology practice in LA. After all, what harm is there in this?

Nobody has to see it. For all I know, it'll probably rot in draft form until the end of time. It won't hurt to try, and it's a good way to pass the time. I still have no significant news from Enid since our last call. I get occasional texts from her, though, where she asks if there's something new with me. Apart from that, she hints that she's going to help me talk to her boss about creating something worthwhile near Eureka Springs.

Here I am in Eureka Springs with not much to do and a lot of free time. So, I turn to writing, something that's always been a passion of mine. It's surely a good idea for me to write the book, and that's how I forget about my tea. I research the topic, remembering stories that animate the clinical manifestations of the disorder. Anxiety disorders, particularly panic disorder, fascinate me. I gained extensive experience treating patients with this condition during my time as a therapist in Los Angeles.

I remember one of my psychoanalytic mentors saying that at the root of most cases of panic disorder is an underlying death anxiety. Fear overwhelms these patients and they often believe they're dying of a heart attack. There's something about the combination of psychological pain and physiological reactivity that interests me.

I think it reminds me of how I felt when Dad disappeared. I had terrible nightmares and couldn't sleep alone. I would slip into Mom's bedroom in the middle of the night and lay down on the carpeted floor, wrapping myself in a blanket while she snored. Mom says I refused to separate from her to attend school. *Was I afraid she'd disappear, too?* I saw a child psychologist for several years. Maybe that's why I became a psychologist, to work through the trauma of paternal abandonment and realize that helping others through their predicaments helps me as well.

Looking up from writing, the sky is dark. The day slipped away and I despair at how little I got done. I put the project aside and call Jahi on a video call. I want to see his handsome face. I want him to lift my mood. He's still at work, and I miss him terribly.

"Hey, beautiful," Jahi beams.

"Hey, you," I reply, grinning from ear to ear. "Guess what? I've been working on something all day."

"What's that?" he asks, looking intrigued.

"I started writing a book about panic disorder," I say with a laugh. "I know it sounds nerdy, but it's fun." This is news to him because I haven't mentioned it. I'm kind of minimizing it in case it flops. I make it seem like I'm just doing this for fun and it's no big deal.

I know Jahi. He's going to support me no matter what. I take care to make it not sound serious, like it's a one time thing and I'm writing this because I'm bored without my teaching job or psychotherapy practice. It's important to me, but I don't want Jahi to know that. The question is—am I gifted enough to write this?

"I bet it sounds nerdy because you're so brainy," Jahi says, looking genuinely interested. "What are you saying about panic disorder?"

"Well, I'm exploring the underlying psychological issues driving irrational fears. I'm fascinated by how anxiety can drive all kinds of physiological responses, like how a panic attack can masquerade as a heart attack. The person has shortness of breath and chest pain, just like a heart attack."

"Oh, yes, I think I've seen that out in the field."

"Yeah, panic is mercurial. It can manifest as derealization, a surreal feeling of detachment from your surroundings, as if they aren't real. The person may not even recognize family members. It's literally terrifying. Also, the person can experience depersonalization, an uncanny feeling of dissociation, of being unreal, as if detached from one's own body. Anyway, there's more."

"Wow. That's fascinating. I've been on a few paramedic calls where the person thought they were dying. After a full medical evaluation in the ER with an EKG and cardiac enzymes, the doctors determined it wasn't a heart attack, but a panic attack. Of course, it's important to rule out cardiac events. Anyway, this is an important topic, and I'm sure your book will be outstanding." He gives me a thumbs up over the screen.

I carry the laptop to my bedroom and lie down as we continue talking.

"I wish I could be there next to you, holding your lovely body," Jahi says.

"I wish you were here with me, too," I say, looking into his eyes through the laptop screen. "I miss you every second."

"I know, babe," he says, his voice full of longing. "But we'll be together soon. I promise."

"I can't wait," I say. Even though we saw each other this morning, it feels like forever.

"There's a new inn that just opened up in Bella Vista by Beaver Lake. Maybe we can go there this weekend to get away. Just to spend time together. Lily's doing better and can stay with my mom."

"Oh yes, Jahi. I love that idea."

"Alright, I'll let you know the plan tomorrow."

"Sure. I think I'll get ready to go to sleep now. But I've got to change and freshen up."

"Should I come wash your back for you?" he asks, wiggling his eyebrows suggestively.

"You're impossible!" I laugh. It's always like this with Jahi. He has a way of making me feel content and calm, no matter what's going on in my life.

Someone yells out his name in the background and he tells me he must go. We say our goodbyes and I end the call.

I prepare for bed thinking about how life can be chaotic and stressful, but how moments like these—talking to Jahi, writing my book—make it worth it. I drift off to sleep, the satisfaction of beginning my book project and a loving conversation with Jahi still in my heart.

As I brush my teeth, I notice swollen gums and a tinge of blood on the floss. That's odd. I've never had this issue before and I don't want gum disease. Besides, there's been enough medical drama for a year already, with Lily and Mom. I climb into bed, snuggling under the covers.

But as soon as I close my eyes, something feels different. I'm hot and sweaty, and my stomach churns. It's probably just a fever. I try ignoring it, but it worsens. Nausea overcomes me and I run to the toilet, vomiting violently, barely making it in time. My heart races as I sit on the cool tile of the bathroom floor, trying to catch my breath.

After a few minutes, my body calms down, and I scuffle back to bed. I lay there, trying to fall asleep, but the thought of feeling that sick again keeps me awake.

I toss for hours, feeling increasingly uncomfortable and anxious. I can't shake the feeling that something is seriously wrong. Finally, I drift off to sleep, hoping I'll feel better in the morning.

The next day, I'm weak and depleted. Struggling to get out of bed, my body is heavy and my head pounds. I can't work on my book while feeling like this, so I crawl back under the covers.

In the early afternoon I wake up, and my condition is worse. My stomach cramps. Looking down at my abdomen, I see it is bloated. Checking my temperature, I have a low grade fever. *Something serious is going on. Could it be appendicitis?* A cold sweat breaks out on my forehead. I'm terrified because I don't want to be a patient in the hospital and I certainly don't want surgery. I've heard too many horror stories from Lee, and he's an eminent surgeon.

I call Jahi feeling helpless and scared. It's almost like a false alarm because later that afternoon, I'm much better and I wonder if I'm just imagining things and worrying about nothing.

CHAPTER TEN

JAHI

The next day, Rose calls me in the afternoon and the minute I hear her voice, I know something is wrong. Her voice has an edge that sounds like she's in great discomfort but trying to hide it.

"Hello, Jahi."

"Rose, what's wrong?"

"I've been sick since last night."

She's sick? But I spoke with her yesterday evening via video call when I was at work, and she looked fine. I'm good at eyeballing patients and I saw nothing alarming. "What's wrong? You were okay last night when we talked."

"Yes, I was. I don't know what's going on, Jahi. As soon as I laid down to sleep last night, I felt nauseated. I vomited three times before daybreak," she tells me.

Nausea? My only experience with nausea in a woman this age means one thing. Could she be? I push away the thought before it takes root. I can't think about the implications of the possibility of her being…?! Catching myself again, I shake my head twice as if to rid myself of the thought.

"Rose, could it be what you ate?" I ask patiently.

"Jahi, I ate the same thing I packed in your lunchbox, and I made it myself. I drank a cup of chamomile tea before I started working on my book. By the time I got ready for bed, I was still full, so I didn't eat again."

"I'm sorry to hear this. How about now? Do you still feel nauseous?"

"No, not anymore. I'm just weak and hungry," she says in a thready voice.

"Why haven't you eaten then? Or don't you have groceries?" I ask, ready to provision her with food. She outdid herself yesterday at my place, cleaning the entire house. It delighted me, and I haven't had time to thank her yet.

"I do, but I'm scared to eat. I'm afraid I might throw up again."

"I could bring some of the soup you made for Lily and me yesterday. Thank you so much for the beautiful note, too. It made me feel important and cared for." I felt more than cared for. Another fraction of my heart melted.

"It's my pleasure. You don't need to bother, though. I don't feel like eating soup. Once I'm strong enough, I'll make myself something to eat."

"Rose, it's not a bother. I don't mind, even if I have to wait on you and feed you," I add with a chuckle to lighten the topic. She laughs, too.

"Don't worry Jahi. I'll be okay. After our call, I'll make a cup of tea and eat some bread. That will hold me for now."

"Are you sure?" I'm not convinced she doesn't need me to look after her, but she says she'll be fine. I assure her I'll call her soon to check on her again and then I end the call.

I go in search of Matt. We haven't had time to talk today, and he promised to talk to Jane last night, to get to the root of the issue and sort out their differences. I intend to follow up and see how it went. I look for him in the storeroom and the lobby, but he's not there.

Two colleagues are arguing about something inane, and I interrupt them. "Hey, have you seen Matt?" I ask the skinny one and he says Matt went home to drop off something for his wife. I thank him and move out of their earshot to call Matt.

"Matt, where are you?" I ask.

"Hey buddy, I'm on my way back to the station. I bought some peace offerings for Jane and delivered them myself," he answers.

"Peace offering? Why did you need to buy her something? Are you trying to bribe her? Didn't you guys sort out your differences last night?"

"Oh, we did. Look, I'm almost there. I'll give you the full story when I get to the station."

"Alright, no problem. I'll wait for you in the storeroom."

Five minutes later, Matt arrives and sits beside me, looking weirdly happy for someone who's having issues with his wife. I raise my brows in question.

"You're a lifesaver. Turns out you're an expert in women's matters, after all."

"The only thing I know for sure is that flowers work better than they have any right to. I'm as clueless as the next guy. Maybe that's why I ensure I have an infinite supply of roses. But anyway, why do you say this?" Whatever magic I worked for Matt and Jane, I'd like to understand because I could use some of that magic myself.

"Well, I did the very thing Jane begged me not to do before our marriage. She was adamant about this issue. In my defense, I did it unintentionally."

"What did you do?" I ask, bracing myself for some awful revelation.

"Well, I forgot one of our anniversaries. I got the date mixed up with another event and it totally slipped my mind. Instead of her reminding me so we could celebrate, albeit belatedly, she started nagging and picking fights, hoping I'd get the clue. I didn't." He hits his forehead with his two palms, looking contrite. "You were right. She's been holding onto this resentment for months, and I didn't even know."

"An anniversary? Really, Matt," I exclaim, giving him a hard time. I release the breath I didn't know I was holding.

"Yeah, I know. And she felt like I didn't care about her anymore. I felt so bad, man. Here I am, more in love than ever, and she's feeling the exact opposite. I'm glad she told me that's what's been bothering her, so I bought her a pendant and chain to commemorate the occasion."

"Oh, that's brilliant."

"I think what really clinched it, though, was this crazy idea of mine. I bought two dozen roses, picked all the petals off, and put them between the sheets of our bed. We're all good now," Matt says, the giddy grin returning to his face.

"I'm so relieved to hear this. But I won't sign up to replace a psychologist just yet," I joke.

He laughs and thumps me lightly on the shoulder. "You don't need to when you've got Rose. How's she doing and how's Lily?"

"Well, Lily is back in school, fully recovered. It's Rose I'm concerned about." I frown, remembering that Rose's cause of illness is yet to be determined.

"What's wrong?"

"Nothing serious. She was sick last night, but she's not this morning. I'm wondering if she's caught a bug or something." That's another possibility—it could be the flu. I mentally huff out a breath.

"I'm sure she'll be fine, but she needs to go to the hospital to get checked if it doesn't resolve itself," Matt says.

"Yeah, if the illness persists tonight, I'll take her to the hospital tomorrow morning."

We both spring to action when we hear the alarm.

Time to get moving.

CHAPTER ELEVEN

ROSE

It's consuming my entire being—this book taunting me in my draft pile—one more failure to add to the graveyard of unlived dreams and unfinished projects littering and haunting my life like a backyard full of broken-down cars covered with blue tarps to save them for a later that never arrives.

I don't share news of the book because it's like a tender shoot and could be mown down by the locusts of life's misfortunes and wanton critics. I don't even tell my sweetheart Jahi the full details because I'm not so sure of it myself.

I don't need another failure—a failed marriage, a failed career, a failed family. If I can barely acknowledge its existence, how can I let anyone else know about it? I downplay the whole thing to Jahi, so he won't think it's a big deal. It's easier that way.

It's a bad habit I have, but it's pretty easy to talk myself out of something if I think failure is a possibility. No amount of love or support mediates this destructive tendency. Someone might unknowingly say something that discourages me, and I brood for months. I don't want that to happen, so it's better if I avoid telling anyone. I don't even say anything to Enid, even though she mentioned the idea once when she was drunk at a soirée in LA.

I'll never forget the moment. "You are 'best-selling author' material, girl. You're so incisive," she exclaimed with authority years ago. I still hear her voice in my head whenever I write. Psychologically, she was invoking me to internalize her belief that I'm not only an author, but a successful one, so I could incorporate her conviction into my psychology.

I think of Enid as I write the book, even as self-doubt rears up like a cobra, threatening to kill me with its paralyzing venom.

A text comes through, interrupting my thoughts. It's Jahi. We see each other almost every day and he comes to my house sometimes, but today is D-day—the day I'm meeting his family. It's a big deal for both of us, or maybe just for me. I'm so nervous. Jahi is a family guy. What if they don't like me? Will he change his mind, abandon me, and never speak to me again? It seems like a palpable possibility. *How can I get out of this? Maybe I can tell him a blimp hit me.*

I see his text message.

"Are you ready? Coming to pick you up in twenty."

I scramble around the bungalow. "Ready?" I haven't even had a shower today. Consumed with anxiety about my book, I lost track of time. Surely, that's why I've been feeling a little sick lately. Riddled with anxiety, I search my closet and find a simple but elegant flowy blue dress. I haven't worn this dress in a long time. I lay it on my bed and take a shower.

The doorbell rings as I emerge from the shower, wrap myself in my bathrobe, and open the door for Jahi.

"Hey. What's wrong?" As soon as he sees me, his smile disappears and a look of concern replaces it.

"I'm okay," I say, trying to muster a smile. "It's this on and off nausea I've been feeling."

He enters and closes the door, taking my shoulders in his hands and checking my body from head to toe like he is looking for something in particular.

"Sorry, babe. Do you feel the nausea right now?"

"No, it's passed," I answer petulantly.

"If you don't feel like going, it's okay. We can stay in. I'll call and cancel."

I see so many emotions pass over his face—fear, worry, love, and concern. But I can't muster the courage to tell him to cancel. I don't want his mom to get the wrong impression of me.

"It's okay, Rose. I'll explain it to my mother, and she'll understand. She won't hold it against you, nor will my sister."

"No, we'll go. Just give me a minute so I can get dressed."

"Are you sure?" He looks conflicted.

I don my brightest smile and say, "Sure! It'll only take a minute. I have my dress picked out already."

I pull out of his arms and get dressed in my room. It doesn't take long for me to return, ready to go.

"You look beautiful. I love your dress," Jahi says, trying to calm me down on our way to his mom's house. "I think we'll have a wonderful time. Mom and Chrissy can't wait to meet you," he promises, but it's not working.

This is a terrible idea. Why do I ever think I can impress anyone? His mother is surely going to find fault with me, just like Lee did. I feel like crying. I want to reverse this, to order Jahi to take me back home because I'm not ready for this. Why are my emotions all over the place? This isn't like me.

I remember the bout of sickness two days ago and this morning. This could be my excuse to beg off. But it's too late. We're already on our way and there's no going back, so I push it out of my mind.

When Jahi and I pull into his mom's driveway, I'm still on edge. This is the first time I'll officially meet his family as his girlfriend. He's been talking about this visit for weeks, and I must admit, I was initially excited, but now I'm second-guessing it. I don't feel ready. The last thing I want is to put a foot wrong in front of his family.

Lily is sitting in the backseat, chattering away about school and friends. Children have a way of cutting through this nonsense we adults get hung up on. Her infectious energy shakes out my tension and makes me laugh. I remind myself to breathe, soften my belly, and imagine something beautiful happening tonight.

We walk to the front door, and Jahi gives me a reassuring smile. "You'll do great," he whispers before he opens the door.

His mother is there, reaching out and welcoming me with a big hug. My body softens in her embrace, and I feel my heart rate slow down. His mom's warm, dark chocolate eyes are just like Jahi's. Lily squeals when she sees her granny, and they run off to play with toys kept there for her in the living room.

Jahi's sister Chrissy approaches me, while her husband, Lucas, stands behind her.

"You're the famous Rose," Chrissy exclaims. "The one who captured my brother's heart." My face flushes scarlet. I glance at Jahi and his face is red, too. "Ah… you two are so cute. You're both blushing."

This makes us even more self-conscious, and we both fall silent for an awkward moment. "Yes, that's me, I guess," I say, my cheeks still hot.

She laughs and I join her. Something about this exchange, perhaps the levity of it, causes my body to relax. I almost wonder if she senses this, and it's her way of helping me and Jahi out? She's psychologically savvy from what I gather.

After we chat for a while and drink iced tea, we sit down for dinner. As we eat, we talk and laugh. As soon as Jahi's mom brings out her famous lasagna, the conversation flows effortlessly, and I feel like part of the family. We discuss everything from work to travel to our favorite movies.

Uncle Jed is there visiting for a week. He's Jahi's dad's brother and lives in Toad Suck, Arkansas. He keeps the conversation going, making everyone laugh with stories about his travels.

Uncle Jed begins his yarn. "Then I thought, is he not going

to ask for the money? If this is free, then I'm definitely gonna come here a lot. I didn't pay that day, the next day, and until the end of the month, when I was expecting my paycheck. Imagine my shock when I didn't get any?!" Uncle Jed says in his drawling voice.

"What? Why?" Chrissy asks.

"Apparently, all the food I'd eaten for free was being charged to my employer directly, who paid the man feeding me. Your Uncle Jed used his whole paycheck to eat like a pig, and I already owed half of my salary for the next month."

All of us laugh uproariously. I can see how Jahi got his sense of humor from that side of the family. His sister, Chrissy, is also great fun to be around. She has a contagious energy and tells some of the funniest stories about her life with her husband, Lucas.

"Rose, tell us more about yourself and your job," Jahi's mom says, passing me the garlic bread.

Inhaling a deep breath, I say, "I'm a psychologist and had a practice in LA. I moved here for a fresh start after my divorce and to be closer to my mother and sister, who live in Fayetteville. My sister told me about the position for a first grade teacher here and that's how I met Lily and Jahi." I see genuine interest in everyone's expressions, but I wonder how much of what I'm saying they already know. It makes me proud to tell them I'm a psychologist, and I notice Jahi beams with pride, too.

"My work as a psychologist focused on helping people with anxiety, depression, and relationship issues. For me, it's existential—it's about helping people live their most meaningful lives. In some ways, it's sort of like being in the clergy."

"Wow, that's impressive," Jahi's mom says.

"So, for now, you're taking it easy, right? Because I know you no longer teach at Lily's school," Chrissy says.

"Right, I don't teach anymore. I'm trying to set up a clinical practice in Eureka Springs. I've contacted a few clinics, and I'm still awaiting their response."

"That sounds great. I'm sure they'll snap you up," Chrissy says, cutting her eyes at Jahi with a knowing look as his mom nods.

As we finish the meal, Jahi's mom brings up an embarrassing anecdote from Jahi's childhood. She tells the story of how Jahi had once eaten a bottle of ketchup when he was three years old, thinking it was chocolate syrup. We all erupt in laughter as Jahi turns ketchup red.

Chrissy shares a story about how she got stuck in her own suitcase while trying to hide from Jahi. These moments of laughter make me feel part of something special.

"Can I just say, Rose, you're fitting in perfectly with our family," Jahi's mom says, raising her Champagne flute. "We're lucky to have you."

A lump forms in my throat as I smile at her. I didn't expect Jahi's mother to fully accept me.

"Cheers to that," Chrissy says, clinking her flute against mine.

A chorus of cheers ripples down the long oval table and I feel close to tears.

We sip Champagne and chat away. It's clear that Jahi's family is close knit and cherishes one another's company. I grow quiet as sadness overtakes me. I hate that what should be a joyous occasion gets marred by the dark cloud stealing over my thoughts. Their conviviality highlights, in stark contrast, the deprivation I've felt in my family. Everything fell apart when Dad disappeared. It haunted us—it still does.

Dad's actions were ruinous for my family, setting off an out-of-control nuclear chain reaction of relative abandonments. And there were no control rods to mitigate the nuclear disaster, no extended family to step in, no big circle of friends. Nothing. The reaction just continued until it ran out of fuel. I don't know if we'll ever be fully in the clear.

It led me to overvalue the self-absorbed narcissistic Lee and sacrifice my life and family for him. It made my sister suspicious of men and unable to live a life independent of taking care of my mother. And it widowed my mother. She's never had a proper relationship with a man since.

A sharp pain in my head interrupts my thoughts. Uh oh, I'm getting a headache. My stomach churns and I'm feeling ill. I try to ignore it, but it doesn't let up.

Jahi notices something isn't right and asks if I want to go home. I nod, embarrassed and anxious all at once about having to leave. His family is so welcoming, and I don't want to ruin it by seeming to be rude or ungrateful.

Jahi's mom notices my discomfort and helps me exit gracefully by whispering in my ear, "Thanks for coming tonight, Rose. You're such a sweet girl, and I'm glad Jahi found someone like you. You're always welcome in my home," she says, hugging me gently.

Tears prick my eyes as I hug her back. I'm so lucky to have found Jahi. His mom is so proud of him, and I can see why.

Getting into the car, Jahi can tell something is wrong with me. "Are you feeling okay?" he asks, putting his hand on my forehead.

"I think I'm just coming down with something," I reply. "I'm sorry."

"Don't apologize," Jahi says, starting the car. "You don't have to be sorry for being sick."

The ride home is quiet. I rest my eyes, feeling the ache in my head subside a bit. We get home, and Jahi puts me to bed, bringing me a glass of water and tucking me in.

"Two days ago, you said you thought you were sick. You

think you might need to go to the doctor?" Jahi asks, but until I confirm my suspicions of whatever the heck this is, I can't go anywhere.

"It's the flu, I'm sure. I took nothing for it two days ago, so it probably came back."

"Okay, babe." Jahi kisses me on the head and heads back to his own house with Lily. After they leave, I drive to the pharmacy.

As a woman, I know my body and I know this isn't the flu. I need to confirm my sneaking suspicion. *Oh Lord, please. Don't let it be what I think it is.*

Jahi is a good man, but I don't think, if this happens, that either of us is ready for it. I can only hope the result is negative. I slink around the pharmacy, making sure no one recognizes me. It's a small town and word gets around. I buy the pregnancy test kit at the cash register where the cashier doesn't know me. I drive home like a maniac, running into my bathroom to test my urine.

This is surreal. It feels like I'm out of my body, hovering in the ceiling's corner, watching myself like some sort of déjà vu.

Time stretches out forever. Didn't Einstein write about time's elasticity? Maybe I'm in one of those vortices, like a black hole. I could get sucked in and never come out. That might be the best thing and it sure would solve my predicament.

I imagine leaving Earth for another planet and traveling near the speed of light, and time slows down in some strange way. I'm barely aging, but those left behind—my peers, my friends, my family—are aging in a sped up fashion relative to me.

When I return to Earth, my loved ones are decrepit or dead, and I'm barely older than when I left on the space mission. Talk about abandonment—this is the ultimate non-negotiable abandonment, to lose your peers, to lose your history. In these minutes of waiting, I feel years rush by. What will greet me at the end of this round-trip voyage?

Literature saves me when life fails and all hell is breaking loose—I reference my favorite books as a kind of hymn, a journal speaking to me across time, of the ineffability of life. I feel like a character in Waiting for Godot, Samuel Beckett's existential play. Lessons from that play never abandon me in moments like this. Though experiencing Beckett's play was an excruciating two hours of waiting… for nothing. But now I'm waiting for something.

The reality of pregnancy tests is it only takes a few minutes to get my results. In these few minutes, I feel like I travel between worlds—the Before World and the After World. But, I stare at that stick like my life hangs in the balance for what seems like hours. Talk about relativity!

Come on, come on. What's the result?

Two pale pink lines appear.

I'm doomed.

PART 5

CHAPTER ONE

ROSE

My phone rings for the third time today, but I ignore it. It's Jahi and I don't feel like talking to him yet. The confirmation of pregnancy is still a shock. Being with Jahi for such a short time and then getting pregnant by him feels far too soon. How could I be so careless and not use any form of contraceptive?

What was I expecting? I'm probably not the first woman in this position, but that doesn't excuse my carelessness.

But we've only been intimate twice. I didn't envision getting pregnant so easily. I had terrible luck getting pregnant when I was with Lee. So, I had no reason to believe it would be any different with Jahi.

When were you expecting to get pregnant? Three years after sleeping with him? Realizing how silly that sounds, I scoff at myself.

I take deep breaths, trying to focus on my options. I'm keeping my child. That is not in question, but I need to figure out who to tell and who not to tell. I feel threats lurking everywhere, like walking a forest trail at nightfall, where every boulder becomes a bear.

I know one thing for certain. I can't just dump the news of a pregnancy on Jahi so soon. He hasn't completed his divorce. He's still married to that woman! And with Lily's recent recovery, he needs a break from emotional turmoil.

Jahi is a good man who would do the right thing by me, but it feels wrong to drop this in his lap without a plan in place first.

Slumping onto my bed, my mood sours. *Who should I call?* Two people come to mind, Jolene and my sister. I call Jolene first, since she lives nearby and I can see her in person.

"Jolene." I all but grunt out her name, surprised at myself because she's usually the grumpy one.

"Rose, what's wrong? Are you okay?"

"Not really," I admit, feeling sorry for myself. I place a hand on my stomach protectively.

"Come on, what is it?" Her tone is urgent, sensing I'm not myself.

"Well, Jolene I..." I trail off, not knowing how to break this kind of news to her.

"You, what? What happened to you?" Her voice turns sharp, as if she's about to drop everything and come check on me.

"Oh Jolene, I've made a big mess of things. I wasn't thinking… and I didn't expect this outcome. Now, my carelessness is about to ruin me. I honestly don't know what to do. How am I going to tell Jahi?" The words pour out of me like torrential rain.

"Rose, you're confusing me. You're talking so fast I can barely understand you. What happened between you and Jahi? Can you calm down and explain it to me so I can know how to help you?"

"I'm pregnant," I blurt out, my voice a strained whisper.

"Excuse me?"

"Jolene, I'm pregnant."

"Oh, Rose! How could you do this to Jahi with everything else he has going on? He loves you!" Her voice has taken on a harder tone.

"I didn't intend for it to happen. It just happened." I rush to defend myself, shocked at her attitude.

"Oh, I see." She pauses. "I've known Jahi for a long time. He's a good guy. He'll take care of you and the baby," she asserts in a no-nonsense voice.

"Thank you, Jolene. I needed to hear that. Trust me, I've beaten myself up about this already. I'll tell him soon. Just not yet," I promise, tears pooling in my eyes.

"I understand. Why don't you come over to my place? We can talk."

"Okay," I sniffle, noticing how unkempt I look and feel. "I need to shower and change. I've been in bed crying since I took a pregnancy test and confirmed the pregnancy yesterday."

"You need to stop crying. It will change nothing," Jolene says firmly, ever the logical one. "We'll think this through together. Everything will be fine."

"I'm so glad I don't have to handle this by myself."

"You certainly don't. I'm here. Start by getting out of bed, freshen up and get dressed. Then come over so we can talk about this."

"Okay. I'm coming," I agree meekly.

"Alright. I'll see you soon."

I take a minute to regain my composure before pushing off my bed and getting ready. Within half an hour, I'm standing at her door.

Jolene opens her door before I knock, and I breathe in the scent of ginger. "Rose, come in. Sit." Jolene takes my hand and guides me to her red velvet sofa, the one I've cried on many times before as if I'm her patient. She looks at me with the inscrutable expression of a psychoanalyst.

"Thanks." I'm on the verge of crying again, but hold back tears, not wanting to create a scene.

"Okay, that's better. Here, have some tea." She hands me what smells like chamomile tea in one of her Japanese-style tea cups. She settles on her couch next to me. "Tell me everything."

"Well, we've spent the night together twice. I didn't use contraceptives because I didn't imagine I could get pregnant so easily."

Jolene looks at me oddly.

"Let me get this straight..." She peers at me, aghast. "You had unprotected sex, but you didn't think there would be any consequences?" She lets out a huff. "In a town this size, you think you know everyone's business, but apparently, you don't. I never saw it in you, Rose."

I gape at her. Why is she judging me for sleeping with my boyfriend? I shake my head. Maybe coming here was a mistake.

Jolene looks at me with somber eyes. "You can't tell Jahi. It will break him. With everything he's been through with Susanne and Lily... and now this. This is going to hurt him so badly."

I sit back and wonder at her words. This is the second time she's mentioned how much this will hurt him. What does she know I don't? "Is another child such a bad idea for him?" I furrow my brows. It's not something we've spent a lot of time talking about, but I felt certain he'd accept his own child.

"I can't believe this, Rose! How could you do this to Jahi?" She looks at me so accusingly it hurts my heart.

"I didn't do it alone, Jolene. Stop blaming only me!" I cry.

"Yes, I blame the other man, too, but you'll take most of the blame when word gets out. Because you're with Jahi."

I stare at her, my eyes drying up for a moment. My gut clenches as her words hit me. "Wait, what other man? What are you talking about?" I reach out to hold on to her arm.

"The other man," she repeats. She gestures to my still-flat stomach and I look down at it in confusion. "The one who got you pregnant." She raises her eyebrows at me as if I should know what she means.

Realizing what she thinks, I place a hand on my heart, not sure whether I want to laugh or cry. "Oh my goodness, Jolene!" I look at her incredulously. "There is no other man."

"There isn't?" she asks, searching my face. Slowly, understanding crosses her features.

"There isn't. I swear. It's only Jahi."

"The pregnancy is Jahi's?" she asks for clarity one last time.

"Yes, it is." Taking a deep breath to calm my racing heart, I try not to get upset with her. "I would have hoped you'd have known me better than that, Jolene." Swallowing hard, I try but can't keep the hurt out of my voice.

Her own face has softened into a rueful smile. "Sorry, Rose. On the phone, you kept going on about making a mistake, being careless, and making a mess of things. You said you didn't know how to tell Jahi. Then you said you were pregnant. I assumed the pregnancy was not his because of the way you were talking." She reaches over to pat my knee, as if her explanation clears everything up.

"What a mess that would be. Honestly, I wouldn't hurt Jahi that way. He means too much to me. And I'm not that kind of woman. Throughout my marriage to Lee, I didn't cheat on him, although he was a horrible human being to me most of the time."

"I'm sorry, Rose. I jumped to conclusions. If it's Jahi's baby, why are you worried? Jahi is not attached to any woman aside from you, so I'm sure he'll accept the child."

"Yes, but he's not exactly a single man, either," I say, feeling warm with all the anxiety I'm dealing with. Distracted, I push a strand of strawberry blond hair out of my face.

"What do you mean, 'he's not exactly a single man'? He's not with Susanne anymore," she points out.

"Yes, but on paper they're still married," I huff out the words, absently running a shaky hand over her soft velvet couch.

"Really? The last thing I heard was that he had already served her divorce papers, and she signed them. Jahi cornered her and made her sign before she could disappear from town again. That's why he's been free to pursue his love interest in you."

"Where did you hear that from?" My eyes widen as I face her.

"Um, I think it was from Karen Knight…"

I quirk a brow at Jolene, my gaze skeptical. Karen Knight is a kind woman, in her own way, bless her heart. But she delights in keeping tabs on everyone's business, even if her information is only hearsay. I rub my forehead. A wave of nausea simmers deep in my throat, but I suppress it.

"Jolene, I'm not sure Karen is the best source of information. What she told you and God knows who else is not true. I remember a story from Jahi about one firefighter walking up to her and saying, 'Hey, Karen, I found your nose. It was in my business.'" Jolene laughs and I continue, "Jahi served Susanne divorce papers, but it's not completed yet because she's nowhere to be found. After Sheriff Hamilton pulled her over for drunk driving, Jahi bailed her out of jail and she disappeared. She's called Jahi twice, but doesn't ever reveal her location. They're still in the middle of the divorce."

"Oh, I didn't know. So, what are you going to do about the pregnancy now?" Jolene casually sips her tea, but looks nervous as she tries to help me figure things out.

"I don't know, Jolene, but I can't tell Jahi yet, and you can't tell him, either." I move closer and grab her hand.

"Rose?" she says cautiously.

"Jolene?"

"It's none of my business… but why can't I, or you, tell Jahi about this pregnancy?" She's pacing now. She stops before me, standing with authority, her strikingly lean silhouette peering at me quizzically. She pulls a lock of hair behind her right ear, her pale complexion a sharp contrast to her long, blue-black hair and electric blue eyes.

"Because I just found out yesterday, and I'd like to have a

couple of weeks to think things through before breaking the news to him."

"I understand, but he deserves to know as soon as possible, and he needs to hear it from you." She narrows her eyes at me, and I smile at her in return.

"Of course he does, and I'll tell him. I just need to process the news myself first."

"Alright, no problem. Just don't put it off too long. Babies don't wait."

"Yes, I agree. Please don't breathe a word to him about this until I do. Do we have an understanding?"

"Yes, yes…" She waves me off. "How are you feeling?"

"On and off nausea. Dizzy spells and weakness. And constipation just joined the party."

"Sounds like fun," she deadpans. "How far along are you?"

"I think I'm a few weeks pregnant, but I don't know for sure yet. I have to visit the clinic to find out."

"You know, Rose. I'm sorry you're in this situation, but the prospect of a baby is getting me a little excited." Her normally serious face softens a bit at the thought.

It makes sense. Jolene works with children every day. She has her quirks, but she is a remarkably caring person deep down. I see Jolene suppressing a smile, and I give her a little smile in assurance.

"Thanks, but don't get too excited yet, Jolene. We don't know how this is going to work out."

"Yes, yes. I understand. Have you eaten anything today?"

"No, I don't think I can stomach anything yet, but thanks."

We chat a bit more, and then I bid her farewell. I go back to my bungalow, still undecided about what to do. I make a cup of tea and try to work on my book. My first step is continuing my research on panic disorder and its various clinical presentations. I work into the afternoon before my phone rings again.

My heart pounds in my throat and my palms feel sweaty. Maybe this is because of what I'm working on and it's the power of suggestion—sort of like how first-year medical students believe they have every disease they're studying. I think I'm having an anxiety attack. The phone rings and rings, and I sit there frozen. When I don't answer, my phone buzzes, notifying me of a text message from Jahi. I can handle a text message, but I can't handle a call.

"Hey babe, what's going on? I've been trying to reach you since yesterday, but you're not answering any of my calls. Is something wrong? Please call me, I'm worried. J. xxxx"

My heart rate slows long enough for a new malady to set in—guilt. *Why am I acting like I can't handle my boyfriend's texts? I better text him back.*

"Hi Jahi, I'm sorry I haven't taken your calls. Believe me, it's not intentional. I'm just deep into research for my book. And I want to stay focused. But I'm fine."

If I pick up his call, something is bound to give me away. He'll know I'm hiding something from him, so it's better to communicate through text messages. I send the message and hold my breath for his reply. I don't have to wait long.

"I need to see you for myself to be assured you're fine. I miss you. Is it okay if I come to your house? I can be there in thirty minutes."

Oh, no! He's coming over?! I can't let him see me. He'll know I'm keeping something from him. Scrambling to think of an excuse to keep him away, but coming up with nothing logical, I decide to flee before he gets here. I hurry into my room, throw a few clothes and toiletries into my travel bag and pack my laptop and chargers inside another bag. I lock the front door and speed out of my driveway into the morning's cool dampness.

After a few miles, approaching the town's boundary, I text Jahi.

"Oh no, I forgot to tell you. I'm not in town right now. I'm headed to Fayetteville to spend time with my family. I should be back in a few days. Going to work on the book and take care of Mom."

Without waiting for his reply, I drop the phone into my purse and drive to Fayetteville. I try not to lay rubber leaving the driveway. I don't stop until I'm outside my mother's house.

CHAPTER TWO

JAHI

I may not have an inkling about women's minds and their actions, but I have a strong hunch there's something happening with Rose and I'm determined to discover what it is. I drive hurriedly to her bungalow and park outside.

Her car is gone, but maybe she's here. I'm so upset, I'm not thinking straight. Did she really flee to Fayetteville? I knock on her door, but I'm met with silence. I try the doorknob, but it's locked. Disgruntled, I go around the house to check if there's a sign of anyone inside, but it's eerily silent. The blinds are drawn and there's no sign of life inside the house. *Where has she gone?*

I go around to the front of the house and sit in my car, wondering what's going on. This is strange. *This isn't the Rose I know, but then, I haven't known her that long. We're just starting to go deeper with each other, and I'm not liking this evasive side of her.* I call her again, but the call goes straight to voicemail, so I send her a text message.

"I hope everything is okay. What's so urgent that you had to leave without telling me? Are you avoiding me? Should I be worried?"

I send the text message but I'm not satisfied when I don't get a reply after ten minutes, so I fire off another one.

"Rose, I really hope nothing bad has happened. Please call me, okay? Jahi xxxo"

Thirty minutes go by, and I don't get a reply. Realizing I probably won't hear from her soon, I call Matt to rant. The phone rings, and he doesn't pick up, so I try again and he answers on the second ring.

"Hey buddy? What's up?" He sounds like he's half asleep, even though it's ten o'clock in the morning. I feel bad for waking him up, but I need to talk to someone before my head falls off from the weight of overthinking. I didn't envision myself being in this situation with a woman so soon after what I went through with Susanne.

"Jahi? Buddy? Are you there?"

His voice startles me out of my spinning thoughts.

"Yes. Yes, Matt. I'm here. Sorry, I kinda zoned out."

"Why? What's wrong?"

"It's Rose."

"Rose? What happened to her?"

"That's the problem. I don't know. She disappeared!" My voice grows harder as I say the words, and reality hits me. Of all the things Rose could do to destabilize me, disappearing is at the top of the list. That's exactly what Susanne used to do, and Rose knows how much it hurts me. Why is she doing the same thing now?

"Calm down, buddy. Take a deep breath and control yourself."

Doing as he tells me, I take a deep breath, not only to follow his instructions but also because I'm finding it difficult to breathe. My chest is constricting and I rub it to relax my airways, then I clear my throat and take another breath, releasing it slowly this time. I've got to get a better grip on myself.

"I'm fine. I'm okay."

"Good, that's good. Please explain what happened. Give me the full story."

"Remember how I told you she wasn't feeling well?"

"Yeah, I remember. I advised you to take her to the hospital, and you said you will today if there's not any improvement in her health."

"Exactly. I've been calling her all day, and she wasn't picking up my calls. So, I sent her a text, and she replied vaguely that she's knee deep in research for her book and she's fine. I told her I'm coming over to her house to check on her, only for her to say she's not in town. I went over there anyway. True to her word, she wasn't home."

"Wow." After a thoughtful silence, Matt says, "Something is definitely going on. You need to find out what it is."

"I know, Matt, but I feel like she's avoiding me. The feeling is strong. It started drizzling this morning before I got there, and there's a dry spot where her car was. Which only tells me one thing..."

"That she just left her house. She left immediately when she got your text that you were coming over. That's not cool. Where did she say she was going?"

"She said Fayetteville, to her mom and sister's house. She said she wanted to go there a couple of days before her planned visit to spend time with her mom and help her sister."

"Maybe something truly came up, Jahi."

He's trying to pacify me, but I'm not buying it. He doesn't know how sick Rose's mom is, but if he knew, he'd probably use it to back up his argument. No use telling him now, because he'll just hammer on my hunches with inconvenient and obvious facts and make me feel crazier than I already am.

"Yeah, maybe." I pause. "But I feel it's more."

"This is eating you up. Why do you think she's acting like this?" Matt is pensive. I can imagine him in his thinking pose with his hands clasped behind him as he walks slowly back and forth, placing each foot gingerly as if traversing a minefield.

I exhale forcefully, then blurt out, "I think she's pregnant."

"Whoa...!" Rarely at a loss for words, Matt whistles.

"That's why she's been so sick. I think it is morning sickness. Don't breathe a word of this to anyone, not even Jane," I whisper, looking around furtively, a shiver running down my spine. "Promise?" I emphasize, holding my breath.

"Promise," Matt says solemnly.

"You know why, right?"

"Yup, I sure do."

"Okay, thanks. Listen, I've got to go. We'll talk later."

"Sure. See you later."

I head back to my house but change my mind and decide to make a detour and drive to my mom's house instead. When I get there, I take two giant bounds up onto the porch, covering three steps at a time as I look for Mom. I know where she'll be, either in her bedroom or in the sunroom where she sews or knits on afternoons like this.

My childhood home is a two-story Victorian house, softly decorated in a French country style because of the love my mother and sister have for everything French. My mother designed the interiors herself when she got married. The Gustavian chairs and rustic vintage table, Toile de Jouy valances and drapes, crystal chandeliers, antique mirror, wrought iron hardware and hanging copper cookware, French doors, understated console table, and the gallery of gilt-framed portraits all have a story.

My mom enjoys running her fingers tenderly over her prized possessions as she recounts tales of how she collected each piece and why each one is meaningful to her. It's as if each item is a character with a life of its own, sort of like the characters in Pirandello's *Six Characters in Search of An Author.* She wasn't always like this, but I think she developed a love for objects because they stuck around and wouldn't die and abandon her like Dad did. Sometimes it seems over the top, but she probably feels the same way about my obsession with roses.

I check the sunroom first, passing through the living room where her Louis XVI-style settee sits proudly near the center of the room, decorated with Schumacher velvet pillows in cheerful pastel tones. I'm still walking along the long corridor lined with family portraits when she calls out.

"Who's there? Jahi? Is that you?" I hear her voice from a room deep in the house.

"No, just a robber," I call out jokingly. She knows the sound of each of our footsteps. How she does this, I don't know. She just does. Maybe it's pheromones she's picking up unconsciously? She heard and smelled me before she saw me, as usual. "Yes, of course Mom, it's me. Where are you?"

"In here." Her voice is coming from the suspected sunroom. I stride through the corridor and I'm at the interior French doors when I see her sitting on her special single seater sofa she uses for sewing. Attached to the chair arms is a woven basket, padded with a handmade quilt filled with needles, threads, scissors, and other sundry sewing tools.

There is a short cushioned stool my father added to the sofa on their two-year marriage anniversary. My mother declared the chair her sewing and knitting chair. Dad screwed the stool to the chair so it wouldn't shift positions when she rested her legs to avoid leg cramps. It works famously except for those times in my childhood when I tripped over it at a dead run and it didn't move. I think the scars on my shins are still there. There is a bookcase filled with catalogs, books, patterns, skeins of yarn, knitting needles, yards of fabric, and a pincushion that looks like a tomato.

I give her a half hug because she's sitting, and she's got a load of sewing materials on her lap. Seeing her comforts me, and I need it.

"Good to see you, Mom. How are you?"

"I'm fine, dear. How about you?"

"I'm okay. I've come so you can feed me. Don't feel like eating my own boring cooking." I chuckle softly. She has a calming aura, and I relax.

"Oh. You silly boy. I've got leftovers from last night's dinner—Wiener schnitzel, garlic cheddar mashed potatoes, sauteed Romano beans, and sweet iced tea. I'll get you some, or do you prefer to eat at the kitchen table?"

"No, Mom. I prefer to eat here, so I can watch you work. It's been a long time since I did that. I'll come with you and carry the food. That sounds like an elaborate feast for one person! Did you know I was coming over?"

She smiles at that comment. I follow her to the kitchen and watch her heat the leftovers and pile my plate high. She must think I've got a tapeworm and need lots of calories, even more than the standard hefty firefighter's quota. She stands on a chair and pulls down Big Momma's 1940s Shawnee Pottery cookie jar, a white pudgy pig in black pants and a red scarf who holds the treats. I've stared at that pig with yearning since I was a toddler.

"Have some. I baked these yesterday afternoon. It's a new white chocolate chip cookie recipe with peanut butter, raisins, oats, and candied ginger that I tried and it came out beautifully. I call them 'Raisin Detras,' a take on the French *raison d'être*, meaning reason to live or reason for being. Lily couldn't get enough."

I love that about my mom and my sister, too, how they appreciate anything French. "I see why, Mom. It's superb," I mumble, my mouth full of the cookie. I'm surprised she's feeding me dessert first, but maybe she can tell I'm famished. There's something to that saying, "Life is short. Eat dessert first." I realize I've been so worried about Rose that I have eaten nothing of substance all day.

"Sorry, I should have asked—iced tea, wine, water?"

"Wine is fine. Pour some for yourself, too. You'll have a bite with me." I wink at her and she laughs, batting me with a towel.

"Oh, you know how much I like that. Your sister always denies me. Naughty girl."

"Right, and that's why I always offer mine." I smile in return, a full-blown beam, one that charms her and gets her to do my bidding, no doubt learned as a toddler with my heart set on cookies. But this time, I'm smiling to hide inner turmoil. I'm frantically thinking how to avoid the inevitability of her sensitive radar as she carefully peels the cork cover from a bottle of Beaujolais and uncorks it with a satisfying pop. Some people say this is the sound angels make when they burp, if you are fortunate enough to be in their company.

She pours the wine and carries both glasses into the sunroom. I grab a jug of water, two water glasses, and my tray of food and follow her. I settle the tray on the center table in front of the sofa. She sits beside me and watches as I cut into the Wiener schnitzel.

"Good?" she asks.

"Excellent. This is yummy," I say between swallows and give her a thumbs up for good measure. She smiles and takes a bite. We eat in silence, sipping our wine. Mom hums an old tune from babyhood, *You Are My Sunshine,* and looks at me, saying nothing.

I finish eating and get up to return the tray to the kitchen when she stops me.

"Jahi, my dear. What's wrong?" she asks in a soothing voice.

Dang, caught by her radar. You almost have to fly underground to evade it.

"What's wrong? No, Mom, nothing's wrong," I answer, wondering why she let me eat the entire meal before dropping the bomb.

"Mmhmm, Jahi. You're my son. If I say something is wrong with you, it's because I've seen that something is wrong. I can tell. I know you like the back of my hand, so don't pretend." Her voice is kind.

"Just how do you know something is wrong with me?" I raise my brows at her, and I yelp when she spanks the back of my head.

"Don't raise your brows at me, boy! Call it a mother's instinct, but I just know. Now, answer my question."

"Mom, talking of instinct, I'm having this feeling. I've been trying to downplay and ignore it, but I feel it strongly today more than ever."

"What is it? Tell me," she prompts.

"I think Rose is pregnant. With my baby," I admit, holding my breath as I await her reaction. It feels good to get the swirling thoughts out of my mind, finally, and into the open air.

Mom's mouth goes lax and her eyes widen.

Invisible weights pull down the corners of my mouth. "Yes, Mother, your son has done it again."

"How do you know this, Jahi?" My mom's face remains calm, but I can see her eyes glowing with excitement.

"I don't know, Mom. She hasn't told me anything, and I don't know if she knows it herself yet, but I feel it. Strongly."

"Where is she? Take her to the hospital for a test. That's the only way to be sure." Mom reaches out to put a firm hand on my arm, letting me know how serious this is. She's right. If Rose is pregnant, the sooner she's under a doctor's care, the better.

"Yes, well, she's not in town. She left before I got to her house this morning, claiming she needed to help her family in Fayetteville."

"Thanksgiving's coming right up and maybe her mom needs help, but such a hasty departure is suspicious. Maybe she knows. How long have you been suspecting?"

"Since that night when we came over here for dinner. She said she was having dizzy spells and nausea in the evenings and mornings, then told me she was better in between that period."

"Jahi, do you love her? How much do you love her?" Her mouth has drawn tight in a thin line. She knows how rough my time with Susanne was and how hard I tried to keep the love alive with her.

"I love her, Mom. I really do. But I haven't told her yet, and I don't know if she loves me in return."

"Then you have to make sure you tell her. Let her see that you're willing to fight for her. If she doesn't love you in return, then at least you'll know the truth. I know you can handle her rejection, if it comes to that. You're an amazing man, my son, and any woman would be lucky to have you."

"Thanks, but there's still Susanne. What am I going to do about her?" My voice rises in a desperate plea, as if my mother might deliver the solution to my predicament.

Life's a trap. How did I get myself into this one? It's like some kind of Gordian knot I can't unravel.

I squeeze my hand around the cushion of the sofa in frustration. "What am I going to do about Susanne?" I implore my mother.

"Oh Jahi! If not because of Lily, I would have said I wish you never met that devious woman. Divorce her. If you ever want to have a peaceful life with Lily, and a happy ending with Rose, you need to divorce Susanne."

It was on this note that I thanked my mom and went back to work at the station. I asked her to pick up Lily from school and keep her there tonight because I might be on call all night. She accepted without question.

CHAPTER THREE

ROSE

"Hello, who's home?" I say in my most cheery voice. I suppress the bile in my throat until I'm able to exchange pleasantries and escape to my room.

"Rose! What a surprise!" Beatrice beams as she hugs me.

"Where's Mom?" I ask, looking around for her.

"She's in her room, sleeping."

"Oh, okay. I need to use the restroom. I'll be out in a minute."

Racing to the bathroom, I lift the toilet seat, and promptly empty my stomach's contents of water and yellowish green fluid into it. I have not gotten used to the pregnancy, but it's already controlling me. Rinsing my mouth, I silently give thanks for living in an age with indoor plumbing. Then I go back to the living room to look for my sister.

She's sitting where she was before I came in. One of Mom's crossword puzzle books is spread out on her lap. She looks content, and I wonder if Andrew is the reason. My heart drops as I realize the secret I'm keeping may push Jahi and me apart, robbing us of such contentment.

"What's going on, B? How are you?" I ask, pushing my worries away.

"Nothing much. I just woke up recently. Today is my day off from work."

"Okay, how is Mom's health?" I look around the room, glad to see it's tidy and everything looks like it's in its place. They both seem to cope well. Burdened with my secret, I have an overwhelming need to keep busy and be helpful. If I'm busy, then I don't have time to overthink anything.

"She's a little better. She's eating more lately and keeping it down."

"That's good news. I'm here to check on you guys and spend a couple of days before going back to Eureka Springs. So, is there anything I can do for you to help while I'm here?" I ask eagerly, too eagerly, by the skeptical look on B's face.

"Nothing much, really. Maybe when Mom wakes up, she might have something she'll want you to do for her." She quirks an eyebrow at me. "You good, Rose?"

I nod vigorously. "Okay, she's in her room, right? Can I go check on her?"

"Sure, but you have to be quiet so you won't wake her."

"Yes, I'll be quiet. Be right back." I give her another too-bright smile.

I slip off my shoes and head to Mom's room in my argyle socks. I gently open the door and slip in, closing the door quietly.

Taking a minute, I observe the way she decorated her room. I notice the blinds are drawn, but there's a table lamp with a dim bulb turned on, allowing me to see around the room. On the wall is a large photograph of my mom standing in front of a baby blue '57 Chevy, the colors a bit faded. I haven't seen it before. She looks melancholic in the picture. I wish I could ask her why, but she's asleep and too sick to answer such questions.

The cream paint and butter colored linens give the room a warm look. The flowery flannel bed sheets and pillows look cozy. On the bedside table is a small frame with a picture of Bea and me from grade school, looking like we've been told to sit still for the sixth time.

I had one missing tooth and braided hair, as we both stood there smiling in Sunday school taffeta dresses, wearing little white gloves. Bea had her hair fixed into a permanent. Was it Easter? I wonder who took the picture. Dad? I can't remember.

Childhood slips away like a receding wave. I'm haunted by Rilke's words. I say them over and over in my mind.

Oh, hours of childhood, when behind each shape more than the past appeared and what streamed out before us was not the future. We felt our bodies growing and were at times impatient to be grown up, half for the sake of those with nothing left but their grown upness.

Those hours are gone. Memories fade. I've lost so many memories of our lives, especially since Dad disappeared and Mom is now too ill to remember. *Why can't we ever think of the important questions to ask our parents when they're still alive and well?*

I sit on the floor and watch my mother sleep. Being in her presence soothes my anxious heart. She looks gaunt and frail. Her neck muscles strain with every breath, as if breathing is the most difficult thing in the world. I realize how I take for granted this vital act. A knot swells in my throat and I can't swallow as sadness fills me. I fight a wall of tears threatening to burst through the dam of my defenses and spill onto my cheeks. A bottomless sorrow holds me captive as I sit there, numb and transfixed, unable to wish it away.

I move and notice the pins and needles in my legs from being crouched in an awkward position for too long. I bury my head in her duvet and inhale her smell. Some of it is familiar and some of it is not. It's the familiar aroma of her shampoo and face cream mixed with the unfamiliar metallic odor from her body's reaction to the chemotherapy, foreign molecules like unwelcome party crashers.

Seeing her weak and vulnerable breaks me. I bend my head and cry. After a few minutes, I feel her hand on my shoulder, then I raise my head to look at her. She's awake and staring at me.

"What's wrong, baby?" She searches my face, her eyes blinking, attempting to get up. I quickly stand to assist her, plumping pillows to cushion her back.

"Mom, are you okay? Should I add more pillows?"

"I'm fine, babydoll. Stop fussing over me. Why are you crying?"

"It's just a little man trouble I'm having, Mom. It's about Jahi."

"Have you told your sister about it?"

"No, I just got here. I wanted to see how you're doing first."

"Oh…" Her voice grows faint as she draws out the word, as if she has more to say but doesn't finish the thought. Mom's eyelids descend like a heavy curtain as she yawns. It must be the treatment making her drowsy. Her eyes close, and I watch her chest rise and fall. My precious mother. She's like a baby now, sleeping day and night. I lay her back gently into a more comfortable position on her bed and tiptoe out of the room to talk to B.

"B?" I call out when I don't see her in the living room. She's not in the kitchen, so I check her room, being careful not to make too much noise and disturb my mother.

Beatrice isn't in her room. I'm about to rest in my room when I hear the toilet flushing.

"Beatrice, I'm in your room," I say so as not to surprise her.

"Rose? Coming," she calls back. She appears at the door, wiping her hands on a small towel. She's changed into a blue chiffon evening gown. It reminds me of Christine's gown in *The Phantom of the Opera,* the last show I saw with Dad when I was six years old.

"Going somewhere?" I ask.

"Not really. I'm just trying on this gown to see how it looks."

"Ah, come on. There's more to it than that. I've never seen you so dressed up. Are you going to a ball?"

"Well…" she hesitates. "Andrew invited me to the season opening of Opera Fayetteville at the Walton Arts Center."

"It must be pretty highfalutin'."

"Yeah. Opening night is supposed to be fancy and brings out the high society of not only Northwest Arkansas, but Little Rock, too."

"Wow. I bet there will be a lot of doctors and lawyers there. It's almost as if attendance is required and they'll get demerits if they don't show up. I didn't know you were into opera. You never went with Dad and me to the Pavilion in LA. Heck, my opera productions when we were teenagers bored you to tears," I joke but an embarrassed look comes over B's face, so I scramble to add, "But hey, you look lovely. You'll have a wonderful time. I'm so excited for you."

Bea forces a smile that tells me she's stung by my remarks, and an awkward silence descends between us like a scrim on an opera stage.

Why did I make this churlish comment to my sister? Am I so envious of her love life that I can't be happy for her? It's like the tables have turned. I was Daddy's golden girl, and now my life is a mess. I'm pregnant, and my lover is married.

I break the stalemate after what seems an eternity. "Mom looked better than I thought she would. She woke up while I was there but quickly fell back asleep."

"Yeah, she sleeps all the time, but she's stabilizing. Thank God for that." Bea's voice sounds clipped and I'm desperate to undo the damage I've done.

"You're doing a great job, B. Well done. I'm proud to be your sister, and I love you," I say in my softest tone, praying she forgives me. She's still avoiding my eyes.

"Thanks Rose. I'm just doing what needs to be done." The spell is broken, and I sigh. She rubs my arm, looking at me, her face softening. "Alright then, what's happening with you? Talk to me."

Can she read me so well? I avert my gaze, shifting in my seat, and then I let the words spill out.

"I ran away from Jahi, from Eureka Springs." I bow my head in shame.

"Why? What happened?" She squeezes my arm, letting me know I have her support.

"I'm pregnant. And I don't know how to tell Jahi." I raise my wide eyes to hers. To her credit, she hides her reaction well and goes back to rubbing my arm as she processes my uncharacteristically blunt words.

"Oh dear! Rose!"

"I know. I was careless, I wasn't thin..." I cut my words short when she throws herself at me in a big hug, laughing and congratulating me in my ear.

"Beatrice, calm down. I don't know how everything is going to pan out yet."

"What do you mean?" she gasps, her eyes widening.

"I haven't told Jahi yet, and I don't know if he's going to accept it. Or if he will leave me the same way Lee did... and then," I pause, sadness coming over me, "and then there's my history of miscarriages."

"Stop talking nonsense, Rose. From what you've told me, Jahi is not like your no good ex-husband. Of course he'll accept you and the pregnancy... and it's all going to work out," she assures me with a big grin and begins dancing around the room.

"B, he's still married to his wife, Lily's mother." That catches her attention. "I don't want to be a baby mama."

"Oh, Rose." She draws me to her big bosom like a loving mother and hugs me tenderly. I soak in her warmth and strength for a minute before withdrawing. I realize that she's stepping in as a mother figure, as my mother's once vibrant health is deteriorating.

"I don't want to be a baby mama," I repeat adamantly.

"According to what I've heard and seen about *that woman*, she seems like a vindictive person. She will not divorce him if she hears about this pregnancy." I rub at the stress headache in my temples.

"You've seen her? When?"

"Yes, well, I saw her before Lily's accident. She came to town and moved back into Jahi's house. He let her come back. She began playing the mistress of the house, trying to stop me from coming to his house and tutoring Lily. I had to stop going there altogether during that time. That was before Jahi and I started dating properly."

"Rose, you shouldn't let her threaten you," Beatrice says firmly.

"She didn't. Not outright, anyway. She pretended to be nice while throwing subtle hostility my way. I didn't feel comfortable at all."

"Okay. So why hasn't Jahi divorced her since they're not together anymore and he is now with you?"

"Well, after Lily's accident, the sheriff caught Susanne driving erratically toward the hospital on the day Lily was being discharged. The sheriff pulled her over, and she was drunk. He detained her, then Jahi had to bail her out of jail, and she disappeared. She's not been back in town since. Jahi and I got together after all this drama."

"What a mess. Wow! She must have been a thorn in the flesh to Jahi, poor man." She gasps. "Rose, didn't you say the first time things went south between Jahi and that woman, she disappeared?"

"Yes. She just left town without a word," I answer, not knowing where she is going with this.

"And this time again, she did the same?"

"Yes, she did. Why are you asking me this, B?"

"Rose, you're doing the same thing, don't you see? You disappeared on him, too. What is he going to think?"

A sick, sinking feeling sets in and I feel like throwing up again, but there's nothing left in my stomach. I'm so torn. Will Jahi reject me because I'm pregnant? I feel terribly guilty that I fled and left him in the lurch. It's not only like Susanne... it's like my dad. I don't want to be like either of them, but I can't tell Jahi what's going on. I'm too afraid. Self-preservation takes over. Maybe I don't have as much empathy as I imagine. Maybe I'm just selfish, and so I defend my actions.

"I didn't disappear without a word, Bea. He knows where I am. I just need more time because I only confirmed the pregnancy yesterday. I'm avoiding him because the moment he sees me, he'll know the truth, and I'm not quite ready to face this."

"I get that, Rose, but think about Jahi. From his perspective, you vanished without explaining why. Imagine how much hurt he's experiencing and remember his history. Remember yours, too, and how it felt when you were six years old and Dad disappeared and we never knew what happened to him. We still don't. This is a deep wound, and the unconscious doesn't care about logic or utilitarian concerns. You know this as a psychologist. The unconscious knows what it knows and wants what it wants. So in that way, it's still the same thing, it's still abandonment. You need to go see Jahi and tell him about the pregnancy, Rose!"

I grunt and flop onto Bea's bed. Not my sister, too! That is the same thing Jolene told me. They should allow me to at least wrap my head around the news before telling Jahi. Bea taps me, and I use both arms to cover my face. I don't want to look at her, and I don't want her to see me. Only for a minute do I have this respite from her angry look, because she grabs both my arms and yanks them away from my face.

"Seriously, Rose, you need to tell the man! He deserves to know!"

"I deserve time to process this monumental life change happening in my body, don't you think?" I say, my voice small.

"Yes, you do. But you need to talk things out with him. ASAP. You can't know what his reaction will be until you tell him, but I'm sure he will stick with you."

"Fine, I will," I shoot back petulantly.

She raises her brows in disbelief.

"Seriously, I will. I'll go back to Eureka Springs in the morning. But first, I'm starving. Is there anything to munch on? Something light that I can easily throw up, just in case."

"Having morning sickness already?" Her face drops in concern.

"Midmorning, afternoon, and evening sickness, too." I sigh.

"Oh dear. I'm sorry. Don't worry, I'm sure it'll all go away before you know it."

"Will it?" I ask myself.

CHAPTER FOUR

JAHI

I call Rose again, but her number still goes to voicemail. I'm going out of my mind, but I try to hold myself together.

I call again, but this time I leave a voicemail when she doesn't pick up.

"Hi Rose, it's Jahi. I'm worried about you. Did you arrive safely at your mom's house? Hope all is well. Call me, I need to hear your voice. I... take care, bye." The call feels awkward and I hang up in a hurry.

This total mystery with Rose is eating me up, so I decide to focus on work and take on more hours at the station over the weekend. Maybe this will distract me from my worries, at least for the hours I'm here. Matt thinks it's a good idea, so that's what I'm doing.

Near the end of my twelve-hour shift, just when I'm imagining my soft bed, a call comes in about a forty-week pregnant woman who says she feels strange, and she's afraid some part of the baby is coming out of her body... maybe the umbilical cord. She's terrified and in discomfort. She's two blocks away, so she calls the fire station. As we race to her house, I get on a call with her.

"Get down on your hands and knees and get your head near the floor. Make sure your hips are higher than your head," I instruct her.

"Okay," she replies, her voice trembling.

"Don't push the cord back in and don't eat or drink anything.

We'll be there in a moment," I say, trying to keep her calm. Matt calls the ambulance to back us up.

Matt and I burst through the door, and we find her on all fours. I examine her and see the prolapsed cord.

"I'm supposed to have a Cesarean in two days… my Thanksgiving baby. My doctor told me my baby is sideways."

"Ah… I see," I say with my most soothing voice, willing my pulse to stay steady. As they say to ER doctors and paramedics, "When you deal with an emergency, check your own pulse first." Stay calm so you can help your patient. *I'm not doing an excellent job at this, but I hope she doesn't notice.*

My mind scatters in a welter of diverging thoughts. *A transverse lie presentation. You cannot deliver a baby positioned sideways. And it's late in the game. She says she's forty weeks pregnant. It's unlikely the baby will turn and get into a head-down position at this point. That's why they told her she must deliver by Cesarean section. If this were the Middle Ages, both she and the baby would flounder and die. But now we've got another complication—a prolapsed cord. This is a surgical emergency.*

A deep sadness comes over me and I think of Rose. *What if my fragile, beautiful Rose found herself in this situation? What if she lived in the 1400s like Simonetta Vespucci, the gorgeous muse for the great artist Sandro Botticelli, who fashioned his most famous painting, The Birth of Venus, after her? Rose is my Venus. I'll never forget the first moment I laid eyes on her that day when she arrived at my door.* I imagine her like Simonetta, dying too early—Simonetta of tuberculosis and Rose of childbirth. Haunted by that thought, I shiver.

"Yes. We've got to get you to the hospital immediately," I say calmly but decisively, mustering professional demeanor and snapping out of my reverie. I glance at Matt, who is already on a call with the obstetrician for an emergency C-section.

"What's going to happen? Will my baby be okay?" the woman beseeches me, her voice high and panicked, her eyes filled with desperation.

"We've got it under control, but we need to get you to the hospital to get your baby delivered," I say as the ambulance arrives. We transfer her to a gurney, have her lie on her side and start an IV and fluids to prepare for surgery. The ambulance crew takes over and drives away as I look on, praying her baby will be okay and not suffer brain damage or worse, death.

Matt nods at me, and we leave her house in silence.

"Hey, Jahi. You okay?"

"Yeah… I just… seeing this pregnant lady made me think of Rose," I say quietly, tears filling my eyes. "What if something like this happens to her, and she's alone like this woman? You saw the terror in this woman's eyes."

"I know, Jahi. But it will not happen to Rose. You'll be there for her, no matter what."

The phone awakens me with incessant ringing. I pick it up on the thirty-eighth ring, hoping to hear Rose's voice, but I'm bitterly disappointed when I see it's Susanne. I decide at the last minute to take her call.

"Hello," I grunt out after taking a minute to compose myself and harden my voice.

"Hello, Jahi. How are you and Lily?"

I'm sure she's up to one of her games. She hasn't called since the last time I hung up on her, so why is she calling again? Despite Chrissy's directive, I didn't block Susanne's number that day.

"We're fine. Why are you calling?" I'm not in any mood to play her game today, so the earlier she says why she called, the better.

"Why are you being so hard on me, Jahi? I'm truly remorseful. Does my apology not count? I'll apologize a million times if that's what it takes."

"Yes, you apologized, but how am I to know you will not do something like that again, or something worse? I gave you the benefit of the doubt, and you betrayed me. I can't trust you anymore. My stance will not change."

"I was under so much pressure and was looking for an escape. I felt bad about Lily's accident. She'd been fine under your care until I showed up and I felt guilty about that. I wasn't thinking right, and I was sleep deprived, so I behaved rashly. I'm sorry, Jahi. Please forgive me."

Is she reading from a script?

She's crying, but I don't feel an ounce of pity for her. Even on the phone, her cries don't sound genuine. Something strikes me as odd. I've been looking for a way to divorce her, and here she is begging me to forgive her. This is my freedom from her served on a platter, but now she's desperate to come back and I'm desperate to get rid of her. I have to think of how I can get her to sign the divorce papers. Knowing Susanne, she won't just sign the papers and leave willingly.

She'd rather disappear again without signing or force me to use the legal system to serve her with papers, leaving me tied to her so she can torture and manipulate me at will. She wants to undermine my life, my free will, and I have to outsmart her in this game. I've got to turn this around for my benefit. Even if I don't end up with Rose, I still want to be free from Susanne.

"If I forgive you, then things are going to be on my terms from now on. And you don't have a choice but to agree, otherwise you can hang up now and disappear."

"No, no, I don't want to hang up." She sounds too enthusiastic, not knowing what I have in mind. "I'll take whatever conditions you decide, as long as you give me another chance to be with you and Lily."

"That's a condition, or didn't you hear me? I'm the one who sets the conditions, not you," I insist. "Where are you, anyway?"

"I'm at a friend's place. I can come and meet you at home."

"No, Susanne. This time, I won't let you call the shots." I speak to her so forcefully she gasps over the phone. In my mind, I can see her recoiling in shock.

"Oh, sorry. I understand. What do you want?"

"Where are you, Susanne?" I grit out the words while trying to calm myself.

"I'm at Cherry's house. We went to high school together. Do you remember her?"

Cherry was one of her lap dogs masquerading as a friend when we were in high school. She was a spoiled brat whose parents would do anything for her and let her get away with snotty behavior. I didn't like her then, smacking bubblegum and all, so I'm not sure I'm going to like her now. There's something smarmy and sycophantic about her. She's a total suck up and her front teeth remind me of a horse.

"Yes, I remember her. Where does she stay?"

"I'll text you the address."

"Text it to me, and I'll meet you there." I don't wait for her to respond. I hang up abruptly. No more "nice Jahi" for her. I tried that for decades, and it never worked.

I splash water on my face, brush my teeth, and make a cup of coffee strong enough to dissolve the spoon I stir it with. I take a few sips before driving off. I call Susanne when I get to Cherry's house.

"Hello, Jahi."

She's using her breathy, seductive voice. How can she imagine this turns me on? "I'm here. You can come outside and meet me in my car. We'll talk then." I don't have much of a game plan, but my suspicion about Rose's pregnancy makes divorcing Susanne urgent.

"Alright. I see your car, Jahi. I'm coming outside now."

She traipses outside and to my car, opening the door and plopping in the seat next to me. Instantly, I gag at the strength of her cheap perfume.

"Oh, Jahi, I'm so sorry. Please forgive me." She has tears in her eyes, but she's a cold-blooded reptilian, spilling crocodile tears. She reaches over and buries her face in my shoulder.

What an actress. She must think I'm falling for this. My body stiffens, so I force myself to relax. I don't hug her back. I just wait for her to sit up straight and look at me.

"This is the last chance you're going to get. You understand that, right? After this, I'm cutting you off totally." I keep my tone stern.

"I promise, Jahi. I'll do my best to earn your trust and prove myself. Just give me another chance."

"You were my first love, Susanne, and you'll forever be in my heart," I say through clenched teeth, steeling my nerves for the bad news I'm about to deliver.

"Thank you, Jahi. That means so much. You're such a good man. That's why I chose you so many years ago."

She thinks she's victorious and is coming back to live with us. Little does she know what's in store for her. In her mind, I'm gullible and softhearted. That's why she chose me to manipulate. Few men let a woman toy with them the way I allowed her to toy with me. Even my family expresses outrage on my behalf. They never liked her. Well, that's in the past. I'm in charge now. This time around, I have too much to lose—my daughter's safety and Rose's heart.

She sees me lost in thought and places her hand on mine. "How's Lily?"

I jerk my hand back. "She's fine. Her recovery is almost one hundred percent. She's gaining her strength and energy back. She's scheduled for a checkup in two weeks to see if there's anything that needs to be addressed."

"I feel so bad I almost put her in danger. I miss her."

"Well, you disappeared, so it doesn't seem like you've been that concerned. You'll get to see her soon, but not until I say so."

She lowers her head in shame. I look away because I can hardly stand these charades. It's time to harden my heart against her if I'm going to win this game.

"Alright, Jahi. If you say so."

"I do," I say, losing my nerve to confront her. I need to think this through, think about exactly what I'm going to say to get rid of her. "Listen, I've got to go now, but I'll be back to see you. I'll let you know when, but until then, stay here and don't get into more trouble. Do you understand, Susanne? No more trouble!"

"I understand. I've changed, Jahi. Believe me."

Yeah right. She's made me so cynical. Rose says cynicism comes from a heart that's broken. I'm ready to have my heart repaired, and to be with my beautiful Rose.

"We'll see," I say, not sounding convinced.

She cups my cheek, looking into my eyes. She's probably searching for something. I soften my gaze, staring back at her, smiling and giving her a nod to signal her to get out of the car. She smiles and opens the door. When she's in the house, I head home.

A few miles down the road, my phone rings and it's my lawyer, Chad Murphy.

"Hello, Chad. I had it in mind to call you."

"Good thing I called then. How's it going?"

"Everything's okay. Susanne's been calling and begging again."

"Really? What did you say to her?"

"What do you think?" I sigh.

"Jahi, don't mess with me. Just tell me what you told her."

"I told her things are on my terms now."

"How did she respond?"

"She went along with it. She thinks she can woo me back. Little does she know her gig is up. She's always been able to weasel her way back in, no matter how egregious her behavior."

"This time she's shot her wad," Chad remarks.

"Yup, she sure has."

"What are you going to do now?"

"I told her the relationship is on my terms now. She pushed back on my boundaries, but I set her straight. I've got her where we need her to be to complete this divorce. The next time we meet in a day or so, I'm going to take her on a picnic."

"Don't you think that's sending the wrong message?"

"Nope. The message is we can maintain a friendly relationship for Lily's sake, but we absolutely must divorce in order to do that."

"Uh-oh. Brace yourself for the fireworks."

"I know, Chad. I know."

CHAPTER FIVE

ROSE

My stomach growls with emptiness. I barely slept last night. I search for remnants of the wheat bread my sister gave me earlier in the evening. I had some bacon at dinner, but this time I'm eating a bread sandwich, a slice of bread between two slices of bread. It's true what they say—you'll eat anything when you're pregnant. If there were pickles and ice cream, I'd have that, too.

What am I going to do if Jahi decides he wants nothing to do with me, after all? He might think I'm trying to tie him down and trap him with the pregnancy.

What if he decides he doesn't want me anymore and goes back to Susanne? After all, they're still married and have a child together. I guess I have to face this possibility and find out the truth because I'll never know unless I speak with him. I had this thought on my mind when sleep took over and lured me into dreamland.

Waking at midday, I pull on jeans and a t-shirt and look for my mom and sister. They're in the living room. Beatrice is beside Mom, doling out medications like a nurse, while Mom pops them in her mouth and swallows them with water, catching her breath after each swallow.

"Hey B. Hello, Mom. I'm glad to see you looking better."

"Yes, yes. I'm fine. It's you who is losing weight. What's wrong, Rose? Do you ever eat in that town of yours?"

I look at Beatrice in a questioning way, and she shakes her

head negatively. She hasn't told our mother about my pregnancy yet. I won't tell her. She needs to focus on her recovery and not worry about me.

"I'm okay. I was just sick for a couple of days and wasn't eating, so I lost weight. But I'm almost fully recovered." I glance at my sister. She is keeping a straight face with some effort.

Mom notices me looking at Beatrice and glances her way. It's an awkward moment, but Beatrice gives nothing away with her blank expression.

Mom turns back to me. "Alright, have you eaten anything today?"

"Nothing yet, Mom. Gotta rush back to Eureka Springs. I have to see someone, but I'll be back for Thanksgiving, so I'm not taking my luggage."

"Will you at least pack something to eat on the way while driving? It's quite a distance and you might get hungry. You said you're recovering from being sick, so you need as much nutrition as you can get," she argues, and I relent, since I don't want her to worry about me.

"Okay, I'll pack something." I turn towards the kitchen.

"Beatrice, can you help me push the wheelchair to the kitchen?" Mom asks. "Open the cabinet right beside your leg, Rose. I have something for you there."

Inside the cabinet are two boxes. She directs me to open the one on the top. I cut open the box and see a blue thermal food jar set and gasp.

"Mom, this is beautiful. Hey B, come see." I beckon to my sister.

"Rose, this is Mom's favorite food container, a beautifully designed insulated jar with a wide mouth. She bought it three years ago, and she's never used it. Whenever I ask her, she keeps saying it's not time yet."

"Wow! Mom, is this true?" I look at my mom, looking so fragile in her wheelchair, but her eyes sparkle as she smiles at the two of us.

"It is true, my dear. Beatrice?" she calls, facing my sister.

"Yes, Mom?"

"The second box is yours. It contains the same food jar set but in a different color and it has your initials. Yours too, Rose. When I saw the first set, I thought of you girls, but they had only one. I ordered the second set for Beatrice, but kept it as a surprise for both of you."

My sister and I look at each other. These insulated sets must have cost a lot. My mother is not one to spend money like that. She rarely shops except for essentials, so her buying these thoughtful gifts for us means so much.

We both kneel beside her wheelchair and hug and thank her profusely. She hugs us back and a few tears escape our eyes.

"That's okay, now. Rose, you need to pack your food so you can leave while it's still daylight. If we keep on with the hugs, you might not leave today."

"Yes, I better get going." I release her and pack my meal in my new food jar, a white bean and chicken stew. Looking back, I bid them farewell. They're still there at the door, Bea standing and Mom sitting in her wheelchair, waving goodbye as I drive away into an uncertain future.

When I arrive in Eureka Springs, I head straight to Jahi's house, but he isn't there, so I drive to my bungalow and call him. He picks up on the third ring.

"Rose? How are you?" he asks tentatively.

"Hi Jahi. I'm doing *fine*," I say, my voice lifting on the word *fine*, surprising me, as the three-word sentence takes on a sing-song quality similar to the language patterns I saw in the eating disorder patients I treated at UCLA. We called those patients repressors because they repressed and minimized their feelings and avoided conflict, just as I'm doing now with Jahi. I stay on the surface and act like everything is fine because I don't want to face the truth of my fears and ambivalence about the pregnancy. I continue with my utilitarian questioning to keep Jahi off center so he won't see how vulnerable I am. "I drove to your house, but you weren't there. Where are you, Jahi?"

"Wait… what? You… you're back in town?" Jahi hesitates, as if he's having trouble registering the fact that I've returned. "You're here? When did you come home?" He's seemingly not registering my question.

"Yes, today. I just got back from seeing Mom and Beatrice in Eureka Springs. Where are you?" I ask again, wondering why he's deflecting my question of his whereabouts.

"I… I'm at the station. I'm not supposed to be at work today, but I needed to drop off something for Matt."

"Okay, how long will that take you?" I ask, feeling shy about inviting him over and hoping he's picking up on the hint that I want him to come see me.

"I'm done already. I'll come over to your place from here," he says, finally making things easy for me.

"Great. I'll wait for you." As I sit in my living room, my foot shakes uncontrollably as if a grand mal seizure is coming on.

I don't have a seizure disorder, but it feels like I'm going into an altered state. The bottom of my foot itches, my personal strange reaction to extreme stress. I kick off my shoes and rub my arch on the top of my other foot. Unable to sit still, I boot up my computer to review my manuscript, but I'm unable to write. I can't concentrate, so I shut it off. The walls feel like they're collapsing in on me, and I'm worried I won't be able to conceal my apprehension. *What if I have a panic attack?*

This is when he arrives at my door. He walks in and we lock gazes. There's a new line on his forehead and he looks weary, even resigned. I wonder if I caused this. He hugs me, but his body is rigid. The silence is unbearable, so I break it, like an insect walking on the surface of a pond who finally pierces through the surface tension.

I clear my throat. It comes out rough and edgy.

"Hey," I say, softening my voice after that unfortunate throat clearing.

"Hey. How are you?" he asks. He looks happy to see me, but perplexed. I can tell my evasiveness has put him off over the past few days.

"I'm okay. I mean, not totally okay. Not in a bad way. It might be in a bad way. It depends on how you see it. I mean, I'm sorry." I shut up, realizing I'm rambling and not making sense.

"You've lost a bit of weight. The nausea?" he asks, standing frozen, like a sculpture, hard as granite.

"Yes, the nausea. Will you come in and sit down? I've got something to tell you." I gesture towards the sofa, a surprising awkwardness coming over me.

"What do you want to tell me? I'm all ears." He sits facing me, staring into my eyes.

"Before I go on, I want to apologize to you in advance. I didn't know what else to do." I bow my head in shame, saying a silent prayer, hoping this doesn't go off the rails. *Please God, help me. Help us both.*

"I don't understand you, Rose. First, you deliberately ignore my calls. Then you avoid me and disappear. And now you're back and apologizing. What exactly are you sorry for?" He sounds peeved and petulant. Not the effect I want at all.

I risk a glance at his face, and he looks cross. Normally he has a gentle gaze, but now he looks hurt, causing him to sit stiffly away from me as if to protect himself. "For everything, Jahi. I'm sorry. You might not understand why I behaved the way I did, but you will soon."

"Alright. Make me understand." He crosses his arms. This single action makes him look menacingly hot and for a moment I'm aroused, a temporary reprieve from the secret I'm about to reveal.

"Umm, never mind. You look handsome Jahi, I'm happy to see you." I didn't just say that, did I? Where did that come from? I shake my head, as if shaking out the words that went lateral, trying to recompose myself.

"Okay, thanks, but you still haven't told me why you're sorry."

"Yes. About that, well I..." I trail off, looking at him to gauge his mood.

"You?" He raises his brows.

Swallowing hard, I decide to just say it. "I'm pregnant. I'm pregnant with your baby, Jahi."

His face is a tapestry of shifting emotions. A cloud descends and his face freezes. Like he's in shock. I sit still as the Sphinx, allowing him to process the revelation for what seems like an eternity before I touch his arm.

"I'm sorry I didn't tell you as soon as I knew. Although I only found out three days ago. I've been worried about how to tell you the news." I barely get out the last bit before he jumps from the chair as if someone has released him from invisible chains.

"Rose, this is not bad news. Why do you think I can't handle it?" Jahi's eyes are unblinking, his face etched in hurt.

"Please, calm down, Jahi," I say, taken aback by the intensity of his reaction.

"Calm down?" His voice is louder than usual. "You've just told me you're carrying my baby in one breath and telling me you don't think I can handle it in the next!"

"This is so hard, Jahi. I don't want to become a baby mama, entangled between you and your wife. We still need to get to know each other better. It hasn't been long since we started dating. Bringing a pregnancy into this kind of picture is not a wise move if you ask me," I admit slowly.

"What about trust? You could have trusted me, Rose! All this only proves you don't." He steps away and shakes his head as his eyes darken. I can't tell if it's because of tears or anger or both.

"Well, I… look, Jahi, I'm sorry. Can we talk about this?" I step near him and place my hands on his arms, but he recoils, his body snapping back from my touch. He must feel betrayed by me. It's as if he's allergic to me, and his body reflects his truth perfectly. No need for words. I retract my hands, and there's a terrible feeling of emptiness hanging in the space between us. *I just want to vanish.*

"I can't do this, not now." He looks away from me, his downturned lips betraying deep disappointment.

"I'm sorry..." I whisper to his back, but he's already gone in an air-swirling door slam that flutters the candles I had lit on the coffee table.

I collapse on the floor, releasing the tears threatening to fall since the moment I knew I had to tell him.

God, where were you? How could this have gone so spectacularly badly? Now I've alienated him.

After crying for what seems like an eternity, my phone rings. Despite my depleted energy reserve, I retrieve my phone and answer the call without looking at the screen.

It's my sister. She's psychic. She probably feels the ripple in the force.

"Rose? How are you?" Her voice is anxious.

"B, I told him."

"You did? That's great. How did it go?" She's trying to sound excited as if she can, through the force of will, make this turn out wonderfully, but I can tell she's worried.

"Hell. It went to hell." I break down again.

"What do you mean, it went to hell?"

"He blew up when I told him. He thinks I betrayed his trust by keeping this from him, and by running away."

"Didn't you try to explain yourself to him? I'm sure if you explained to him why you acted the way you did, he'd understand."

"I didn't articulate it well. Anyway, he was too angry to hear me and to understand the nuances of why I acted as I did. I was trying to get him to calm down so we could talk things out, but he left in a huff. B, what am I going to do? I've ruined my chances for a happy life with him, just as I've ruined all my relationships with men."

"That's not true. You've been unlucky in love in the past, but that's not your fault. Stop crying, Rose. This is different, and I'm sure he'll come back and talk things out with you."

"What if he doesn't? What if he's gone like Lee? What if he'll only come back to taunt me with the pregnancy?"

"None of that is going to happen. Besides, you can always come to Fayetteville and live with us if things get to that. Mom and I will always be here for you. You know that, right?"

"Yes, I know, B, thanks." Blowing my nose noisily and wiping my face, I imagine I look pitiful right now.

"What are sisters for? Don't worry, honey. It will all work out. I'm sure of it."

I cut the call. My stomach growls. I have eaten nothing all day, so I devour the stew I packed at Mom's this morning, but I hardly taste it.

CHAPTER SIX

JAHI

I storm out of Rose's house and drive home, gripping the steering wheel like a life ring in a flood. If anyone ever told me I would react this way over something I already suspect, I wouldn't believe them. It's the fact that she ran away, not trusting me with this wonderful news, that devastates me. This baby is part of us, something we created together, a reflection of our love for one another… a part of touching eternity. Why does she not trust that I'll be there for her and our baby? Why would she imagine saying no to this sacred bond?

She could have come to me first when she discovered she's pregnant instead of evading me. I'm so distraught I do something I haven't done in a long time. I stop at the store and buy a bottle of whiskey. Karen Knight, the town gossip, accosts me on the way out of the store, trying to get me to talk and wondering what I have in the brown paper bag. I brush her off and depart hastily, but I can feel the conniving in her brain even without looking at her.

When I get home, I open the bottle and pour a shot for myself. I imagine Mark Twain's ghost saying, "Whiskey's for drinking, water is for spraying on fires."

I sip it but don't get the buzz I want, so I throw the remnants down my throat. It burns, but I like the sensation. It feels like the compression stroke of a diesel engine. That's what I want… I want to start the engine of my departure from Susanne.

I move from one corner of my house to the next, thinking of what to do, and how best to go about it, fighting with myself.

Susanne mustn't get wind of Rose's pregnancy, or she'll unleash the hounds of hell and use it to her advantage.

I like Rose...

I love her, in fact. She's the type of woman I can build a life with. She loves and takes care of Lily like her own. And Lily has bonded with her in the short period they've been together. If I'm able to divorce Susanne, marrying Rose will be the best decision of my life. *We'll be one little happy family.*

I pour a third shot and swallow it in one gulp, the rough, peppery liquid warming my gut.

With newfound determination to confront Susanne, I put the bottle down and phone her. She picks up immediately, as if she's been expecting my call.

"Where are you?" I ask, my mind buzzing.

"Jahi? I'm still where you left me earlier. Why? What's wrong?"

"Nothing's wrong. Stay there. I'm walking over to meet you."

"Okay, I'm here."

I lock the front door, the bottle of whiskey sitting on my dining table.

I see myself knocking on the apartment's door, like one of those out of body experiences people talk about when they're dying. Before I can stop myself, she opens the door, garbed in a dressing gown that hugs her shape. I haven't seen the gown before. She catches me staring and smiles.

"Do you want to come in?"

She doesn't wait for my answer before she grabs my hands and pulls me inside. I close the door behind us. She leads me to a lounge chair and we sit beside each other in silence for a long while.

"Why have you come back, Jahi?" she asks, looking directly at me.

"I came here to invite you to join me on a picnic," I say,

buying time. I'm not in any state to get into a heavy conversation about divorce at this moment.

Her lips curl up, and her eyes shine in a look of delight. *She thinks her seductive ways are effective, and she's drawing me into her web.*

"Oh, I love it, Jahi. Where are we going? When?"

"It's a surprise. How about I pick you up tomorrow at four o'clock? We can talk and eat and go for a walk and watch the stars when they come out."

"Oh, that sounds so romantic," Susanne gushes.

I have to suppress my feeling of disgust, so I smile tightly, hoping she doesn't notice my insincerity. Abruptly, I get up and walk home, taking my time by walking the long way back, feeling my buzz die a little more with each step.

Returning to my house, mindlessly watching videos while lying on the sofa, I laugh despite myself. Just after midnight, I get an urge to see Rose, so I go to her house. As I knock gently on the door, it opens slightly, so I let myself in and lock the door behind me.

Rose is curled up on her sofa, loosely wrapped in a blanket, her small toes peeking out under the woolen mass. The heater is running full blast as I kneel beside her and cup her cheek, which is cool to the touch. Her eyelids flutter and she sniffs as if she's been crying, and I feel sad about being the one who put tears in those dreamy eyes. She whimpers and I instinctively wrap my arms around her.

"Shh, shh. It's okay. I've got you." I repeat the words over and over until she wakes up.

"Jahi?"

"Yes, baby, it's me."

"Am I dreaming?" She raises her head and looks at me.

"No, you're not. Rose, I'm here." I scoop her up from the

chair and sit, cuddling her in my arms. I'm at peace. This is who I want.

"Oh, I'm so sorry, Jahi. Please forgive me," she apologizes profusely, her eyes unfocused.

"Shh, it's okay. I'm the one who is sorry. For leaving you in a vulnerable state. I promise I won't do that again. I got triggered, and handled it poorly."

"Okay, please don't leave me," she pleads, tears slipping out of her eyes.

I can't bear it, so I hug her tightly. "I won't. We'll work things out, okay? I'm not going anywhere again," I say fervently, meaning every word. I love her, and I have to tell her.

"But how? How are we going to work things out?"

"Just trust me. I have everything under control. Look at me, Rose." I wait until her eyes meet mine. "I love you. Do you hear me? You're the light of my life, and I love you very much, Rose."

She swallows and nods. Then she burrows back into my arms, burying her face in my chest. I let her take comfort in my body. I hold her, tenderly caressing her back.

After what seems like an hour, she tries to stand, but I hold her back, only allowing her a fraction of space. I look down at her; her eyes a reflection of her acceptance and readiness.

I bring my lips to hers, and we both withdraw on a gasp almost immediately. Her lips feel like a raw electric current I tap into. I feel the jolt travel over my body. This is what I've been missing. Her wide eyes search mine for a second and, as if pre-planned, we approach each other with a ferocious hunger.

I kiss her like a starved lion, drinking her in and taking more.

"Oh, Rose."

"Jahi..."

I go for her clothes and fling them into a crumpled pile on the floor. She tears at my shirt and slings it over the back of the sofa.

I take a minute to admire her beautiful body in lace underwear.

I kiss her with all the passion I've been keeping at bay all day.

"So beautiful. Too precious," I murmur, kissing her lips and down her neck.

"I love you, too, Jahi. I love you." Her words at this exact moment make me shiver.

"This is where I belong," I tell her as I embrace her sweet body.

When I awaken, the sun is already up. We're in Rose's bed, and she's sleeping softly beside me. Her chest rises and falls with each breath. I shift to my side, supporting my head with my hand, and I watch her sleep, mesmerized by her radiant beauty.

She opens her emerald eyes some minutes after and stretches her body. She watches me watch her for a full minute before talking.

"Good morning."

I smile. "Good morning, beautiful. Did you sleep well?"

"Better than I've slept in the last couple of days," she says, sincerity written on her face.

"Did your sound sleep have anything to do with last night?"

She blushes and looks away. With my free hand, I turn her face towards mine, chuckling. I brush her lips with a light kiss.

"There's nothing to be ashamed of. Our passion heightened because of our temporary separation and growing love for each other," I tell her.

"I'm not ashamed, just shy. A little." She smiles.

"A little. Okay. How are you feeling this morning?" I ask her with a raised brow.

"You mean morning sickness?" she returns, pointedly.

"Yes."

"I feel it at the back of my throat, but it's not strong."

"Have you ever been pregnant before?" I know this can be a sensitive topic for a woman, but I want to know how best to proceed, so I can be there for her.

"Yes. Three times. They all ended in miscarriage." A haunted look flashes in Rose's eyes, then disappears. I know we're in tender territory.

"Okay. I think you need to see a doctor to give you a full checkup."

"Yeah, you're right."

She opens her mouth to say something else, but I guess she decides against it. I draw her closer and we cuddle.

"Rose?" I say after a while.

"Hmmm?"

"Will you be my wife?"

"Excuse me?" She pulls out of my embrace, her eyes searching mine.

"I'm asking you to marry me. Please marry me, Rose," I say, letting her see the truth in my eyes.

"How long have you been thinking about this, Jahi?"

"A while now, but I know what I'm doing. I want to be with you."

"This is so soon." She sits up, putting distance between us. Her face is soft as she looks at me.

"Is it, though? We both love each other, and I don't want to lose you."

"I don't know what to say..."

"Very simple. Yes." I smile at her, moving to sit in front of her.

CHAPTER SEVEN

ROSE

"I ... No. I can't, Jahi."

"What do you mean, you can't?" He frowns.

"I can't marry you," I repeat.

"No, I heard you the first time. My question is why?" he states, staring at me.

"Because a part of me feels like you're only asking me to marry you because of this pregnancy. I can't do that."

His face becomes clouded. "No, baby. That's not true. Wasn't it clear last night? I love you, Rose Catherine Aberdeen. I want to be with you and make my home with you. You *are* my home."

"But we don't know each other all that well yet." I feel the claws of uncertainty dig into my mind.

"What do you need to tell me about yourself? I'll tell you everything about me right now," he says, looking so earnest that it's adorable. Even so, I raise a questioning brow.

"But still..."

"Rose, don't you love me?"

He's hurt. I feel it. "Yes. I love you, Jahi."

"Then why are you saying no?"

"I just can't, Jahi. You're still married to Lily's mother."

"Oh, Susanne. Is that why?"

"Yes," I answer and he sighs.

"I'm handling that, baby." He cups my cheeks and waits for me to look at him. "I love you, truly."

"I love you, Jahi. So what are we going to do?"

“First, I have to get divorced, since you won’t accept my marriage proposal without that,” he says, teasing me with a smile.

“Yes, you do, but how do you intend to do that?” As far as I know, he hasn’t seen Susanne since she left town, and he hasn’t been in touch with her.

“You leave that to me,” he says with such confidence I become suspicious. I voice the question lingering in my head.

“When did you see her last, Jahi?”

“You mean Susanne?” I notice his voice takes on a weary tone.

“Yes, I mean Susanne. When was the last time you saw her?” I ask again.

“Promise me you won’t take this the wrong way.”

My hackles rise when he says that. In my experience, when someone tells you to make a promise blindly, run. You never know what they’ll divulge that could take a hunk out of your hide.

“I can’t make any promises, Jahi. You need to trust that I’ll make the right judgment,” I answer resolutely.

“Okay, can you at least promise you won’t leave me?” he insists. What he is about to tell me must be terrible. Am I sure I even want to hear it?

“I’m not going anywhere, Jahi. Just tell me.” Even if I’m going to run a mile after hearing whatever he wants to tell me, I think I deserve to know.

“Okay. I saw her yesterday.” I try to speak, but he holds up his hands to signal silence. “Actually, I saw her twice. She called me yesterday morning saying she was sorry, and she wants to see me. I wanted to brush her off but realized I’m never going to be free of her if I do that, so I went to see her.”

“What happened when you saw her the first time?” I prompt when he stops talking.

“Well, she texted me the address of where she’s staying, and

I drove to see her. We sat in my car and talked. Then I left and came back to Eureka Springs, but I went directly to work."

"Do I want to know what you both talked about?"

"Believe me, Rose, it's not relevant. She apologized, and I said whatever next steps we take will be on my terms. I'm going to befriend her. I have to, if I want her to sign the papers without a protracted legal battle. It's the only way."

Even though I don't like the idea of Jahi befriending her just so he can get her to sign the papers, there's nothing I can do about it, and I don't have any better ideas. I ask the second important question.

"Why did you have to go there again? Wait, what time did you go?"

"After I left you here in anger, I went home. Then I went to meet her." He looks at me, searching my face. "Rose, nothing happened. Read my lips. Nothing happened. I was confused and slightly intoxicated. I just wanted to put the rest of my plan into action."

"And did you?" I ask him, spellbound by his eyes.

"I did. And then I came back to you," he replies and pulls me in for a hug.

He holds me for a while, and then I go to the toilet to freshen up. As I'm brushing my teeth, a wave of nausea comes over me. I swiftly remove the toothbrush and retch violently into the toilet.

He hears me and rushes to my side.

"Oh my goodness, Rose?" He holds my hair while I throw up. He stays with me and caresses my back. When the nausea subsides, he leaves the room and I call him back.

"I'm not going anywhere. I'm just getting you water." He returns and places the glass to my lips. "Drink."

I swirl the water in my mouth and spit. We repeat the process a few times before I'm able to swallow a sip. Then he scoops me into his arms before I attempt to stand. He carries me to my bedroom and places me on the bed.

"How do you feel?" he asks, concern written all over his face.

"Awful," I answer.

"I'm sorry. I hope it'll pass soon. Meanwhile, what can I do to help?"

"Nothing. I'll be fine."

"Are you sure?"

"Yes, don't worry. It's only morning sickness. I'll feel better in no time," I assure him.

"Okay. Is it okay if I spend the day with you?"

"Yes, but I'm not sure how fun I'll be until the nausea passes."

"It's okay. I just don't want to leave you alone."

"But what if you're needed at work?"

"Don't worry. I'm not supposed to go in today. And if they need me, Matt will call."

"Alright. That's fine then. What are we going to be doing indoors all day?" I ask him with a suggestive smile. And he bursts out laughing.

"Ha, someone is getting frisky," he teases me.

"Come on, Jahi. I have said nothing yet."

"*Yet* being the operative word here, so quit giving me that look. I intend to use today to take care of you."

It's my turn to burst out laughing at the tone he uses to scold me. I stick out my lower lip like a child. I'm feeling better already and in a lighter mood.

"Take care of me? Isn't that part of taking care of me?" I ask.

"Rose, don't toy with me. We'll have plenty of time for that, but not today. I just watched you puking in the bathroom. You must be feeling weak."

He's right. I am weak. It's time I quit this little game before it gets more serious. "I was only playing."

"You're cute when you tease me. Come on, scoot over to the middle and get comfortable. Let me pamper you for the rest of today."

And pamper me, he did. He brought me breakfast in bed. Toast, eggs, hash browns, and fresh berries, but we discovered that eggs in any form make me sick. He made me another breakfast, this one without eggs. He steamed ginger slices in water and made ginger tea to help curb my nausea.

Later, I show him the book project as we eat lunch. Somewhere in the conversation, it turns to my recent past, which inevitably leads to the subject of my ex-husband, Lee.

"... that's how we grew distant. Most of my friends stayed away because no one liked Lee. If Enid, who is quite bullheaded, hadn't intervened, I would have become isolated."

"That's pretty sad. I'm sorry you had to experience that. I'm glad at least one person stuck with you, and I'm happy you're now bridging the gap that was created between you and your mother and sister because of your ex-husband."

There's something about sharing with Jahi about my deep disappointments and failures in my marriage that feels cathartic and healing.

We play games, one similar to Tic-Tac-Toe in four dimensions, another involving making up silly languages, and a round of chess. Afterward, he makes love to me, our passion as fierce and deep as last night. We fall asleep wrapped in each other's arms.

CHAPTER EIGHT

JAHI

Rose is sleeping beside me when I wake up at dawn. Her porcelain skin is radiant in the morning light. I slip out quietly, leaving a sweet note on her nightstand. Driving home to shower and change into work clothes, I feel a lightness and a sense of possibility I haven't felt in years.

At work, I chat with Matt all day. There are no emergencies. Our paperwork is minor, and there isn't much to do, so I call Susanne.

"Hi, Susanne. Are you ready to go picnicking?"

"Yes. I'm still at Cherry's house, ready to go. Where is this place?" she asks, already intrigued.

"You'll see. Get ready, and I'll be there in an hour," I tell her and hang up. I jump into the car and drive, all the while thinking about Rose.

I pick up Susanne and take a hard left at the town's major intersection. When we get to the end of the paved road, it turns to gravel and we drive another few minutes.

I turn off the ignition. "Come on, let's go. Can you grab the last bag?" I ask her, carrying the first two bags that contain hamburgers, fries and two bottles of Coke, her favorites.

"Oh wow, Jahi. Bella Vista," Susanne coos. "It's so romantic."

I cringe, but try to hide it. We walk to the meadow and inhale the aroma of freshly mown hay rolled into round ton bales that look like gigantic Quaker Shredded Wheat strewn across the land by God. This awakens a memory, transporting me to childhood when Big Daddy cut hay in late spring on his 286-acre farm just outside of town. A wistful feeling comes over me, and I wish Rose were here to share it instead of Susanne.

We make our way to a clearing and lay down my tartan blanket, a gift from Big Momma, and I spread out the food.

"Oh Jahi, I love this," Susanne enthuses as she sinks her teeth into the juicy burger and munches with gusto. I watch with growing disgust as she licks her lips and fingers. I open her bottle of Coke and pass it to her. She gulps the drink and stops cold when she realizes I'm staring at her.

"Jahi, you're staring at me. Is something wrong?

Considering how best to answer her, I only come up with, "Nothing. I'm just enjoying watching you eat. I know it's your favorite food."

Later, we sit on the blanket, staring at the sky. I'm wondering how to broach the subject of divorce when she speaks up.

"Jahi?"

"Yes?" I answer.

"Why can't we make love? It's not like we haven't in the past."

"Because I don't have those types of feelings for you." I give it to her as straight as possible, emboldened by my determination to get rid of her. It's like I'm channeling Big Daddy. He let no one run over him.

"Why is that? Is it because of what I did?"

"Yes, it is. I feel you're a stranger, not the woman I fell in love with in high school. We're adults now and it's time we act like it. So this picnic is me reconnecting with you differently, as co-parents of Lily." I glance inconspicuously at her and see tears slipping from her eyes. I look away and continue talking. "I still care about you. But it's different. I'm not in love with you the way I was in the early years."

"I'm sorry, Jahi. I know it's my fault." She's sobbing now. I don't affirm it's all her fault. We both know that already.

She says nothing for a long time. When she finally realizes I'm waiting for her to speak, she looks at me and lowers her eyes in shame, nodding.

"If we're going to work out our differences and do the best thing for Lily, meet me halfway. Are you ready to do that?" I repeat.

"Yes. I'm ready, Jahi. I'll do anything to be with you," she confirms.

"No, you don't understand. This is not about being with me. That isn't an option."

Susanne looks at me, stunned and frozen, as if she can't believe what I just said.

"We can be friends for Lily's sake, Susanne, but we have to get a divorce." She stares at me blankly for a full minute, then her eyes widen with fear.

"What? Divorce?"

"Yes. We have to get a divorce." I repeat it so she knows she heard me correctly and I mean it. She grabs my arms and cries hysterically.

"No, no. Jahi, you can't do that to me. You can't ask me to divorce you. Please, Jahi."

"Listen, Susanne. It's important we get a divorce from this sham of a marriage."

Seeing her cry is getting to me. I don't desire to hurt her, but I've got to get this divorce, and this is proving harder than I thought it would be. I steel myself and state further, "Because this one is a lie, Susanne. It's been wrong from the onset. We both know that."

Seeing that I have her attention, I continue, "It's over, Susanne. But we can still work together to co-parent our child. Work with me on this, and I'll be sure you receive what is fair to you."

She howls like a hurt animal. It's otherworldly, and frankly, scaring me. It's worse than the growling sounds she made during natural childbirth with Lily. *What is she going to do next?*

Her face distorts into a mixture of anguish and rage, and she looks like a monster. *Why did I ever marry this monster? The biggest mistake of my life.*

"No," she bellows. "*Non, non, non, non, non! Absolument pas!*"

Oh no, she's speaking French! I want to say one of a very few choice French phrases I know, *merde alors!*, but I think better of it. Susanne only knows a few phrases and butchers those with her Southern accent and poor pronunciation. She thinks she sounds sophisticated and always competes with Chrissy, trying to one up her with her French. She pulls out the French words for *absolutely not* when she's enraged. This is going to be bad, terrible. It feels like a tornado touching down out of a bilious green sky.

"I will NOT give you a divorce." Now her voice is rising, and she's screaming at me.

I sit silently, unmoved by her rage. This makes her madder, and she pummels my chest and arms, but she's pretty weak.

"I'll ruin you, Jahi Adams, and sue you for everything you've got. I will take away your house and drag your name through the mud, and that little wench's name, too."

My body hardens, like wet plaster drying into a solid sculpture. I know there's nothing I can say now. She's gone bonkers. There's no use trying to talk sense into her. She's not rational.

I think about how I'm going to wrap this up and drive her home. I need to get away from her. She's got so much rage, like Medusa, she could kill me. And Rose. Terror comes over me when I think of Rose and her safety and the safety of our precious baby. Everything in my body is silently screaming: *Get out! Get out!* Or like those old submarine warfare movies with klaxons going off, boots clanging down metal corridors, and amplified voices yelling, *"Dive! Dive!"*

And then she drops the nuclear weapon.

"You're cheating on me with Rose. Everybody knows it. It's the talk of the town. Considering that you're messing around with Rose, it wouldn't be surprising if you got her pregnant."

My heart hits my throat, and I feel like throwing up.

"Don't look so sickly, Jahi. You're guilty as sin. I can read your face any day. You're committing infidelity. Alienation of affection."

Her eyes go wild like a raging lunatic as she drops the biggest bomb of all.

"I'll sue for sole custody of Lily."

PART 6

CHAPTER ONE

ROSE

A knock at my door startles me. I'm not expecting Jahi yet, nor anyone else. It's late, but the suspicions I once had in LA of a knock on the door have dissolved in my year of small-town living, so I open it.

There stands Susanne, glaring at me with cold eyes, her mouth pinched, her posture stiff. She's dressed up like she's ready to go clubbing in a low-cut scarlet red knit top with a push-up bra, black leather miniskirt, and six-inch red stilettos, though I doubt they're Louboutin heels like Chrissy's. She doesn't have the money. I try closing the door on her, an intuitive reaction, but she has a hold on the doorknob and one foot across the threshold. It's pointless. What am I going to do? Get into a physical fight? Not a good idea since I'm pregnant, and besides, I've never in my life pushed or hit anyone.

"May I come in?" she spits out the words arrogantly, smirking as she speaks.

"I prefer you didn't," I say, mustering a smile, but resentment fills my eyes.

When she roughly pushes past me, I take a step back, deciding to be polite. *What other option do I have?*

"Please, sit. Can I offer you anything?" I ask, wishing to get rid of this vindictive woman, but not sure how.

"No, you don't need to. I'll only be here for a minute." Her eyes have the look of a predator on the hunt. It unnerves me.

"Okay. Why are you here?" I ask, squaring my shoulders

and returning her stare.

"I won't beat about the bush, Rose. You need to forget about Jahi. Don't see him. Don't call or visit him, and don't associate with my daughter, either. No contact. I'm back in their lives fully, and there's no space left for you."

"I see." Surveying her wild eyes and frantically gesturing hands, I don't believe a word she says. "Why are you here in my house at night telling me this?"

"Because Jahi and I are getting back together, and I don't want you to distract him or try to take him away from me. I know you want him, but you can't have him. He doesn't want you. He wants me back, despite everything."

"And how do you know he doesn't want me?" I give it right back to her, my tone calm because she and I both know she's lying. Her face blanches and her eyes look dead. I can almost predict what's going to happen next and my stomach curdles.

"Oh, so you want to play dirty? Let's get down in the dirt, then. It's time to knock that coy smile off your precious little face," she taunts and continues, "How else? He told me about it today. He took me to a beautiful garden at Bella Vista. We had a picnic, and we made love under the sky after he announced he cut ties with you. He said you both got together a few times, but it was a fling. It was with no strings attached. I believe him, but it's you I don't trust to let him go. So, go look for your own man elsewhere and take your eyes off mine."

I sit there, annoyed and a little dumbfounded. Would she so blatantly lie about them having sex, or did she manipulate him so much that… I don't want to think about it.

"No. That's not true..." I assert, but my heart sinks as part of me wonders if it is.

"What's not true?" she counters smugly. "That we spent the day together in a secluded spot, or that we settled our differences and made love? Or maybe it's you not meaning anything to him and he told me as much. Whatever it is, it's clear you can't have him. He only entangled himself with you because he was lonely, and you were up in my matrimonial home, cooking my husband's meals and washing the dishes, acting like you're the lady of the house. He doesn't love you. He told me that. So move on." She gives me a hard stare to drive her point home.

"I don't believe you, Susanne. It saddens me to see you this desperate."

"Hey, when I told Jahi I don't want to fight another woman for his affections, I meant it, but it doesn't mean I'll hide and watch another woman have eyes for my man. If I let it go, you'll lay a claim on him. I know it and I feel it. I'll go to any lengths to make sure I get rid of any opposition against me getting back with my family and, little Miss Rose, you're no exception, even though you've been good to my daughter."

"You've spewed enough lies for one day. It's time for you to leave my house," I say firmly, standing and gesturing to the door.

She walks out and zooms off in a spray of gravel, taillights careening around the bend. It occurs to me she doesn't even have to be drunk to drive crazily.

I stand by the window watching Susanne drive off, wondering what had just happened. How did she know where my house is? Did Jahi tell her? Of course he did. How else did she get this kind of information if he didn't tell her? I haven't seen him today at all. He isn't at his house because I drove by on my way back from the doctor. Is he at the fire station?

When I call him, he doesn't answer, but I think little of it. If Susanne is to be believed, this means that yesterday when Jahi told me nothing happened between him and Susanne when he saw her two nights ago, he lied. He told me she's staying near Bella Vista and Susanne confirmed it tonight.

I'm emotionally drained. If Susanne isn't lying, then Jahi betrayed me, despite all his promises and proclamations of love. I lock my door and switch off the light. For some strange reason, I don't feel the urge to cry. Maybe I'm too numb. I sit on my sofa in the darkness and rock myself to sleep.

Nausea wakes me the next morning. I run to the toilet and get there just in time to throw up all over the linoleum, like I'm trying to win a contest for force and volume. I wonder how I'm still able to vomit since I barely ate yesterday. The last time I ate well was two days ago, when Jahi fed me. It's almost like my stomach is a space-time portal and I'm throwing up meals from the future that I haven't even eaten yet. I wish God had made my esophagus out of stainless steel so I could remove it, wash it out, and click it back into place, all spiffo-kleen.

After cleaning the floor and toilet and taking a shower, I go back to the sitting room and start up my laptop. Then, I open my email, and there's a surprise. It's from the company I wrote to about starting my practice in a remote location. They're offering me a lucrative contract but at a location of their choosing. Although they say it won't be far from my family and loved ones, they can't set up a location in Eureka Springs yet because the venture won't be favorable.

I read the letter again.

Dear Dr. Aberdeen,

We hope this email finds you well.

We received your letter about opening a remote counseling/psychology office. We're ready to move forward on this venture with you, but when we surveyed Eureka Springs and Fayetteville as you proposed in your letter, we discovered the projected patient numbers for

Fayetteville and Eureka Springs don't reach our minimums. We have looked into Little Rock, Hot Springs, Russellville, or Conway as alternative locations.

Check the attached file to learn more about these locations, budget, your remunerations, and our contract plan.

Warm regards,
Sally Brode
Yarbrough Medical Group

I call Beatrice as I stare at the email. She doesn't pick up at first, so I call her back. She answers on the second ring.

"Rose?"

"Hi B."

She clears her voice before answering. "Good morning. How are you?"

"You sound like you're just waking up?" I ask.

"Yes, I was out late last night working. What's up?"

"I've got good news."

"Really? What is it?"

"Do you remember my friend Enid?" I prompt.

"Yes. I remember her. She's helping you get a job with her organization."

"Exactly. I got an email from the organization this morning. They want to employ me and the offer is good. I can start up in a new practice, but not Eureka Springs or Fayetteville, though. They said Eureka Springs is too small, so the opportunity will be somewhere else in Arkansas. They've sent me a list of four cities to choose from."

"That's a lot."

"Wait till you see my yearly salary and contract. That's

what's a lot."

"Oh my goodness, a contract? That means they're serious. Mom! She got the job!!!" she squeals.

I laugh at her excitement. My sister's always been like that. She celebrates wins more than the actual winner does. I'm glad and lucky to have her.

"Congratulations, Rose. Mom's here, and she wants to talk to you."

"Thanks, B. Of course, give her the phone."

My mom comes on the line, her voice stronger than the last time I saw her.

"How are you doing, dear?"

"I'm alright, Mom."

"Congratulations. I'm happy for you, and your sister is, too."

"Thanks, Mom. I really appreciate it."

"What are you going to do?"

"I don't know yet. They say they can't choose to establish themselves in Eureka Springs or Fayetteville. But somewhere nearby because I told them I don't want to be far from my family."

"Where exactly, then?" she persists.

"I'm not sure yet. I'll forward the email to Beatrice, and she'll show you."

"Okay, since it's somewhere nearby, take it. We don't mind coming over to visit with you. It'll work out."

"But Mom, what about Jahi?" I ask sadly.

"What about him?"

"I can't just leave him."

"Of course you can." Mom's response surprises me. I thought she was happy about my relationship with him.

"What?" I ask, puzzled.

"Tell him of your job offer and carry him along. If he loves you, he'll come with you," she asserts reassuringly.

Mom is saying this because she doesn't know I'm pregnant yet. I don't know how to tell her now, especially with Jahi's wife coming here last night to capsize the boat of my relationship with the man I love, the father of my child.

My mom's voice cuts into my reverie. "Take the job offer, Rose. It will all work out. You'll see."

CHAPTER TWO

JAHI

"Well, Chad, your prediction was right. When I told her I want a divorce, there were fireworks, except not the kind for the Fourth of July. This was more like an atomic bomb in a sewage treatment plant."

"Uh oh. Well, you told me she's an atomic borderline, whatever that means," he chuckles, trying to bring levity to a serious situation. "Anyway, what did she say? I imagine she threatened you?" he asks, his voice turning solemn.

"Yup, she sure did."

"Jahi, you're sighing. Spill."

I exhale loudly. "She says she's going to ruin me and blab all over town, dragging my name and Rose's through the mud, taking me for all I'm worth financially, like the house."

"Oh, that's pretty standard. Predictable."

"Yeah, well, that's not the worst of it." A dropping sensation in the pit of my stomach makes me nauseous.

Sitting at my kitchen table, Chad braces himself, though his face is impassive. I imagine as an attorney he's seen it all, the terrible things humans can inflict on one another. What I'm about to tell him is no exception.

"Susanne is threatening to sue for sole custody of Lily." I shudder, my voice metallic and unrecognizable.

"I see… she's going for the jugular." His eyes narrow, and the muscles of his jaw twitch furiously like he's grinding his teeth.

Silence looms between us, and I can't sit still, so I pace the kitchen, clenching and unclenching my fists.

"What am I going to do? She's like a madwoman, something out of *Grimm's Fairy Tales,* almost supernatural. There's no telling what she'll say or do. She's unencumbered by the truth."

"That's what I'm afraid of, Jahi. She's got no filters, no stops. This reminds me of an old *Star Trek* episode of an enormous interstellar robot, a doomsday weapon, let loose by its creators. The desire for vengeance was so strong it started with the suicidal destruction of the civilization that created it. Then the robot traveled to other solar systems, gobbling up planets one by one, even though its creators were long dead. Their hatred was literally all-consuming. The force was so destructive it even destroyed the planet they were on, as well as their enemies and lots of worlds they had no connection to. The robot looked like Satan's cornucopia, kind of an embodiment of Susanne's character."

"Yes, that would be Susanne." It worries me that Chad is so concerned. For the first time, I realize how treacherous it is to pursue divorce with Susanne.

She's a vengeful beast. Could she really get sole custody of Lily, my precious Lily?

"She'll annihilate us all, just like the robot," I continue, wanting Chad to grasp the gravity of the situation. "Even herself. She'd rather go down fighting, even dying, and take everyone down with her, even Lily, than give me the divorce. She has to win, at all costs."

"Perhaps not surprising that somebody named Sue is threatening legal action," Chad quips, ever the wisecrack.

"Yeah, that's for sure," I laugh half-heartedly.

"Honestly, I don't think she has a leg to stand on, Jahi, because of her history of child abandonment and endangerment and her recent DUI. But I'm worried she's got something up her sleeve. She's a loose cannon. What did she say to back up her threat of going after sole custody? Does she have something on you I don't know about?" He leans forward, squinting his eyes at me.

"She said I'm committing adultery and called it alienation of affection. That's all she's got. Is that a problem?"

"It shouldn't be… but, depending on the judge, it could pose a problem. That's why I said to be careful. We don't need her sniffing around and finding things about you that look bad."

"Uh… there's one more thing…" I say, hesitating, debating whether to tell him about Rose.

Chad's eyes widen, his eyebrows lifting. "Yes?"

I let out another long exhale. "Rose is pregnant," I blurt out in one breath.

"Oh dear God! You're kidding me, right?"

"No, I'm not."

"How far along is she?"

"A few weeks."

"Does Susanne know? Does anyone in town know?" The words come tumbling out in rapid succession.

"No, not that I know of… only her sister and I know," I say decisively, but a sharp sliver of worry lodges in my mind. *Could she possibly know or suspect Rose is pregnant? Susanne is preternaturally intuitive. It's part of her nature. Sometimes she even seems psychic. What if someone saw Rose buy the pregnancy test at the drugstore?* An image of the nosy gadfly Karen Knight flashes before my eyes. I don't know why, but since childhood I've called her Karen Spoon in my mind. There seems to be no reason for it, but that's what my mind does when I see her. *Surely she didn't see Rose in the store?*

"We have to hide the pregnancy, Jahi. Susanne cannot find out or we're in *big trouble*. Getting a woman pregnant while you're still married is a grim situation. Judges and juries have unconscious biases and this is a no-no. This could undermine our entire case."

"I can talk to Rose and ask her to stay in Fayetteville. That way, as the months go by, no one will know she's pregnant."

"That's a stellar idea, Jahi. We've got to outsmart this witch… but it's going to be tricky. We've got to watch every single thing you do."

CHAPTER THREE

ROSE

I work on my book, but I'm restless. Unable to focus on the document, I pace back and forth in my living room. No wonder I'm losing weight… between pacing, throwing up, and barely eating, I'm down ten pounds. Soon I'll need ankle weights to avoid floating off into the upper atmosphere. Everybody's commenting on it, at least the ones who know I'm pregnant: Jahi, Bea, and Jolene. I hope they're the only ones who know about it.

Could someone have seen me in the drugstore buying the pregnancy test? It felt like someone was watching me, but maybe I'm being paranoid. I remember looking around the store and it was empty except for the pharmacist in the back who didn't see me and the cashier who I'd never seen before.

Dread comes over me at the thought of being outed. This would look terrible… a single woman impregnated by a married man. And that married man is a town hero. If the news leaks, people will probably treat me as if I were a witch in medieval times, doomed to be burned at the stake. I shiver at the thought.

My phone rings as if someone is reading my mind. *Is this an omen?*

It's my sister. *Of course it is.* She's like a breastfeeding mother whose milk lets down when she hears a baby crying, only I'm not a baby and she's not my mother. But we have that kind of connection where it's like her heart is outside her chest and it lives in me.

"Hi Bea, what's up?" I try to sound nonchalant, but I'm sure my sister isn't buying it.

"Hey Rose. That's what I'm wondering. I feel you. What's wrong?"

"Whoa, Bea. You never cease to amaze me," I say. *I realize telepathy works, even though I've been told many times it's nonsense. I hesitate to tell her about Susanne's visit because I'm not ready to relive the nightmare.*

"Something's wrong, Rose. I hear it in your voice." Bea states with the authority borne of complete confidence.

"What do you mean?" I ask, playing dumb, hoping I can insert some breathing room before the full confessional. Like a shark, she gobbles down the chum and swims in for more.

"Come on. I've known you all my life. You can't keep a secret from me. What is it?" she demands, growing petulant.

I exhale loudly and silence hangs between us.

"You're sighing. What's going on?" she persists.

Exhaling again, I confess, "Guess I'm sighing a lot these days. I'm having trouble sitting still and I can hardly eat. I can't hold anything down," I parry, hoping to deflect the onslaught of questioning about what's really going on.

"Yes, I noticed. But that's not the entire story..." she insists, sensing I'm skating on the surface of something ominous. She's not swayed. My answers bounce off of her like hailstones off a tin roof.

"Yeah, there is," I finally relent.

"What is it?"

"Susanne," I spit out the name in disgust, like it's sulfuric acid and could kill me. "A surprise visit from that witch."

"What in the world... why? What does she want?"

"She threatened me. She told me to back off, to leave her husband alone, to never see Jahi or Lily again. To get out of their lives. She says she and Jahi are back together for good."

"It doesn't surprise me. Of course she would say that. Who

cares? Jahi is divorcing her," my sister counters adamantly, as if that's the end, as if it's a done deal.

"But that's not all." My voice is trembling, tears filling my eyes.

"What else did she say?"

I can barely say the words. "She said… he wants her," I gasp as a big feeling of fear ripples through me. "Then she said… they made love." I choke on the words and they come out broken like I've lost my ability to be articulate.

"What!?"

"They went to Bella Vista. They had a picnic… she said he told her it's over with me, that our relationship meant nothing, that it's always been no strings attached… and he's over me." I tremble, collapsing on my bed, my body convulsing.

"Oh, Rose. Oh dear," my sister soothes me with the gentlest, kindest voice.

"The thing I feared is coming true. He's abandoning me, just like Dad and Lee. This is my fate."

"Rose, no. Absolutely not. Besides, we don't know whether this is true. Have you thought of that? You know how manipulative Susanne is. You told me. She'll do anything to get her way. She could be lying through her teeth. In fact, I think she is. She's a pathological liar," my sister states with authority.

"I don't know, Bea," I say, not convinced of her interpretation because Susanne's words cut me to the core. She got under my skin and now I'm doubting everything… but then, borderlines and narcissists are experts at undermining people. *Why am I allowing her to do that to me?* "Jahi says he plans to maintain a friendship with her for Lily's sake, which I'm not happy about, but I guess I understand. He's got to maintain the peace. But maybe something more happened between them, and he's hiding it from me. Maybe things got out of hand."

"Rose, I don't mean to sound harsh, but I think you're being paranoid. Jahi is an honest and good man. There's been no sign to the contrary, and why would that change now? Besides, how in the world could he want to be with that hag when he has you, the beauty?"

A brief laugh escapes my lips and surprises me. "B, you always have a way of cracking me up, even in my lowest moments."

"What are big sisters for, sweetie?"

After the call with my sister, I take a nap. I'm sleepy most days and my mind is soupy, like a fog bank descending over my cerebral cortex. Rest helps me and the baby, but it worries me. I need to work on my book and think about my future, especially if I have no future with Jahi.

What am I going to do about the clinical position? Just thinking about it makes me anxious. I don't want to leave Jahi and Lily and Eureka Springs, but I guess I have to if nothing changes in terms of the divorce or if what Susanne says is true.

If I want to go back to psychology, I've got to decide, but I'm torn. I'm afraid it will take me away from Jahi at a critical time and besides, Mom and Bea need me near them because Mom is so sick, but the closest position is in Russellville, 116 miles away, almost a two-hour drive under the best of circumstances. I don't know anyone there. This will mean a full life reboot, just like when I moved from LA, starting over again from scratch. I'm afraid I'll be lonely and depressed. I don't know how many full life reboots I have left in me.

I look at my phone to check messages because I turned off my ringer after Bea's call. Sure enough, there are three missed calls from Jahi and a text from two hours ago. I look at the text.

"Hey babe, what's up? Let's get together tonight for dinner.

I could cook you something mild and rub your shoulders. XOXO, J."

Is Jahi the real deal? Is he the man I think he is, or is he playing with me? Susanne's words injected poison into the watery depths of my mind, and you can't un-poison a well, that's for sure. I hate her and everything she stands for. All she does is wreak havoc, and she ruins everything she touches. Susanne has vengeance in her blood, and she focuses it on me. She's eaten up with envy because she sees how smitten Jahi is with me. Her rage knows no bounds and somebody always has to be the target. Unfortunately, it's me, and she's on a vendetta to take me out.

I'm feeling so fractured, so vulnerable by this situation, that I'm not sure I'm up for seeing Jahi. He'll know something's wrong the minute he sees me, and I'll have to bring up Susanne's visit and what she said. *Am I ready to confront him and possibly see something I don't want to see? What if he cheated on me? I'm not sure I can handle it.*

I've got to put him off, so I dash off a response:

"Hey, love, I'm not feeling great, and I think I'll just go to bed early tonight. Let's talk tomorrow and set something up. Love, Rose."

There. That will buy me some time to think through this and maybe talk to Bea again and even Jolene.

I look at my phone and see a moving waveform as Jahi writes back. I hope he doesn't insist on coming over.

"Ok sweetheart. I'm sorry you're not feeling well. You know I'd love to come over and rock you to sleep, but if you'd rather I wait until tomorrow, I can do that. XX, J."

"Thanks, love. Yeah, let's wait until tomorrow. I'm about to fall asleep now. XX, R."

The next morning, Bea calls and her voice is upbeat.

"Hey, baby sister. How are you feeling today?"

"I'm okay. I went to bed early and slept fitfully, thrashing around all night in a stormy landscape. It was quite symbolic of my life at the moment. Jahi texted and wanted to come over and cook me dinner last night, but I put him off and said we could figure it out today."

"Hmm... why are you avoiding him? We've seen this movie before." I hear disapproval seeping into her voice, and I exhale loudly. "Oh no, you're sighing again, Rose."

"Yeah. I'm sighing a lot these days. I can't seem to catch a break. My life is falling apart and every relationship I'm in gets ruined."

"What do you mean? You've got a glorious life and a great relationship with Jahi. You're in love with a dreamy man and he worships you and treats you like a princess. What could be wrong with that?"

"You know what I'm talking about. Don't sugarcoat it. I'm pregnant, I don't have a job, my lover is married, his wife won't give him a divorce, and she came to my house to intimidate me and claim that Jahi is cheating on me."

"These issues are solvable, Rose. I know it feels overwhelming, but these problems are merely temporary nuisances. One by one, you'll work things out, you'll see. "

"What do you mean?" I ask, grateful for my sister's encouragement, but not convinced I'll find a workable solution for the predicament I'm in. My sister is always there for me, but I'm afraid this situation is beyond repair and my sister can't fix it for me. She stepped in and solved a lot of my problems growing up, like helping me get to Florence by giving me money for the opera program there. But this is different.

"You're in the middle of what seems like a mess. It's like

you're trapped in a thicket of thorns in a foggy forest and can't see beyond it. You can't see the brilliant light of possibility just beyond these problems. You just see the twigs and the thorns and the darkness."

"That's true. I'm in a mess and I've made a mess of my life. I've ruined it," I say, overwhelmed by the enormity of the issues I'm facing and feeling like a failure.

"No, no. You just can't see your way out of the thicket… *yet.*"

"I guess," I say dejectedly, unconvinced, and sighing heavily.

"It's true. Think of it this way, Rose. You're thirty-eight, you're beautiful, you sing with the voice of an angel, you have your PhD in psychology, you've got a great man who is madly in love with you and would do anything for you, and you're pregnant. It's a miracle! What more could you ask for? There are women who desperately want to get pregnant, who try everything, including putting themselves through the emotional and hormonal trials of IVF, all to no avail, who would give anything to be in your position… man or no man. Besides, you'll have a gorgeous baby, that's for sure."

"Oh, Bea." I sigh, still feeling like giving up.

"No, I mean it. And Jahi wants out of his marriage. He'll find a way, mark my words. You've got to believe this."

"But what about his wife?"

"She'll be history before you know it."

"I wish I could be so sure."

"Trust me on this. She will not win. She's a nightmare, but she'll eventually disappear, like she did before. It's her pattern."

"I know you're intuitive, sis, but what if you're wrong this time? What if he can't or won't get rid of her?"

"We'll deal with that if it comes. But I think I'm right."

"Hmm, I'm just not sure, B. I'm overwhelmed and not

thinking straight. Pregnancy is scrambling my brain."

"This will pass. You've just got to hang on and get through the worst of the morning sickness."

"Well, what if I don't? What if I decide this is too much? It's a complication, and impeding my life and my relationship with Jahi?" I venture, daring to give voice to the ambivalence riddling my mind.

"Oh Rose. Please. Please hold on." Bea urges, sensing my emotional instability, but also knowing from our history that she has a profound influence on me and my decisions. "This is like the messy middle you've told me about when you're writing books, far from the beginning and far from the end. You know life is like this… it's not always pretty, but life can be beautiful, even so."

"I'm just not sure about continuing with the pregnancy," I say with hesitation. *Did I just say that?* I grit my teeth, bracing for her reaction.

"What? Rose, please. Don't act rashly. I beg you. You've always wanted a baby. In fact, when you were a child, you said you wanted six children! I always thought that it was cute and humorous that you imagined having a big family. Do you remember being elated when you got pregnant when you were married to Lee? I know that didn't work out, but Lee is a troubled man and it was a terrible marriage. Jahi is different and this time, it's going to work out. So don't give up on your dream, little sister. You're not getting any younger and it's a miracle you've gotten pregnant so easily with Jahi. This is your chance to live the life of your dreams with your true love. I know you're upset with the circumstances, but this is temporary," my sister pleads.

"It's not how I imagined my life would be." My shoulders slump. I still can't embrace my sister's encouragement.

My life isn't turning out like I thought it would when I was a starry-eyed teenager singing arias in LA and Italy, imagining living a glamorous life like Maria Callas. My life would be a victory over operatic tragedy. I would find my one true love. It sounds corny now, but deep down, it drives me. I'm still searching for my happily ever after. In opera, the main characters either die or live happily ever after. Since I'm not dead, where's my happily ever after?

"You're an idealist and always have been, and I love that about you. You've dreamt of a perfect relationship for as long as I can remember. When you were a little girl, after Dad left, you played with your dolls every day and I remember hearing you role play, finding love, getting married, having children, and creating the perfect family. But sometimes, dear sister, life gives us unexpected gifts and they don't look like our dreams. And the danger is we might reject them before we give them a chance. I think Winston Churchill said something like, 'When people stumble over the truth, they usually pick themselves up and carry on as if nothing had happened.'"

I sit there on my bed, stunned, taking in my sister's wisdom. She probably should have become a psychologist. She'd be a great one.

But the doubt hangs on. "Meanwhile, B, the man I love, the daddy of my baby, could be a cheater. He may not be all he seems. I've gotta wonder what he's hiding. Maybe he's got skeletons in his closet we don't know about."

"Well, he is from Eureka Springs, after all. You know, the whole town is into the ghost thing. Heck, they've got ghost tours at the Crescent Hotel and then there's the Zombie Crawl in October. Maybe ghosts, ghouls, and long-leggedy beasties infest the town," she jokes, trying to lift my mood.

"B, what am I going to do with you?" I laugh.

We chat for a while and when I hang up, I hold my belly tenderly.

"Little baby." I exhale. "What am I going to do with you?"

CHAPTER FOUR

JAHI

"You will not believe this," Chad announces triumphantly.

I wonder what he's found. I imagine it's about Susanne. Chad fancies himself as something of a sleuth, a modern day Sherlock Holmes, though most of his cases are pretty standard and boring, like negotiating settlements for shoddy house repairs. There aren't a lot of big time cases in Eureka Springs. Thank God he's on my team and not Susanne's.

"Go ahead. Try me," I counter.

"I asked myself, 'What are Susanne's motives for staying away all those years?' and I became suspicious. So the next question I asked myself was, 'Why would she do that?'"

"She doesn't have a maternal bone in her body," I interrupt.

"Yeah, well, there's more to it than that. I've got sources all over the country from my days at Yale Law. I've been sniffing around and making calls to my colleagues."

"What have you got?" My interest piques.

"Remember, you told me she went to beauty school in Hot Springs for a year?"

"Yeah. It was intense, living so far apart. I was at Fayetteville studying pre-med while she was in Hot Springs, three and a half hours away, and we didn't get to see much of each other."

"Well, she had no shortage of company—*male* company, that is. She didn't waste any time crying over you. She hooked up with a blonde hunk from Chicago. He had a lot of money and was visiting Hot Springs to bet on the ponies at Oaklawn Racetrack."

I sit there, speechless. My muscles stiffen and ice enters my veins. *How could she do that to me?*

"What?" I say, stunned and blindsided by this revelation. I get up to pace, but dizziness overtakes me, and I sit back down.

"I'm sorry to give you the bad news, Jahi, but it gets worse. Remember that girl's weekend she took in Vegas?"

"Of course. That's when she left me and Lily and never came back... until recently, years later."

"I don't know if he's the reason she went on the trip, but when she got to Vegas, she hooked up with him again. I'm not the betting type, so I've never been to Vegas, but I doubt this brief encounter of theirs was by chance."

A sick, hollow feeling overtakes my gut, and I have difficulty forming words. "Are... are you... are you sure?" I stutter. *Why am I upset? I don't even care about her. I think I'm just shocked. It sucks to be betrayed, even if it's long ago and even if it's your estranged wife who you now despise.*

"Yes. I'm sure. I know this is hard to hear. Do you need some time to process it?"

"No... go ahead. It's just hard to believe she did that. She acted so in love with me then. She was so jealous of me. We were just kids. We weren't even twenty."

"She's not who she seems to be on any level, Jahi. I'm almost afraid to tell you the rest."

"Oh dear, what in the world has she done? And how do you know this?"

"I have my sources." He's pacing, jingling his keys in his pants pocket.

"You're making me nervous, Chad. Rip the Band-Aid off and give it to me straight." I sit erect, bracing myself for untold horrors, because Susanne is capable of treachery.

"Okay." Chad draws out the word and exhales loudly. "She was smitten. She never got over the blonde hunk from the time she met him at beauty school. He moved back to Chicago and built a real estate empire. They communicated secretly for years, with her plotting how to get back together with him."

"But... but she was married to me, and we had a baby." My voice rises as if I'm still that young father with a baby, and I feel like screaming. Now I know why I'm so upset. It's because she could betray her own child for this bozo.

"Well, apparently she told him her life as a stay-at-home mother was boring. She wanted the rich life in the big city, to live in his 10,000 square-foot stone lakefront mansion north of Chicago, to vacation in Italy and France, to lark about on yachts, to be unburdened. To be free. That's what she wanted, Jahi."

I blow air out of my mouth through pursed lips, my cheeks ballooning from the pressure. Mom and Chrissy were right all along. I should have never married her, but then, I wouldn't have Lily, and that's unthinkable.

"She always complained about Eureka Springs, saying it was too small, too provincial," I say.

"Yep. She has contempt for this town."

"And that's not the only thing she has contempt for, Chad. She has contempt for me to this day... the fact that I blew it in organic chemistry, ruining my chance to be a doctor. She never forgave me and never let me forget I failed to be the rich doctor she wanted me to be."

"But you're a town hero. You're a firefighter and a paramedic."

"She looked down on that. She said, 'you're just a paramedic, not a doctor. Why couldn't you be a doctor?' I couldn't win with her."

"Well, she's a loser, Jahi. You will not believe the rest of this."

"Try me. I think nothing will surprise me."

"Oh, this will. Guaranteed," Chad says decisively.

I stiffen. My body feels like I covered it in chainmail and I'm wearing an iron helmet, with eye holes the only vulnerability. "Okay, I'm waiting," I say, holding my breath for the blow of the broadsword.

"The man swept her off to Chicago. She got pregnant in short order."

"Wait. What?" I yell, my mind spinning, not comprehending Chad's words. It's like when a doctor tells a patient they have cancer. After that word, they typically can't hear anything else. I wrap my arms around my torso, holding myself together as if the broadsword is tearing through the chainmail, ripping apart my guts. I feel as if my bones have liquefied and offer no support. My weight feels heavy on the chair. Squinting to focus, I try to concentrate. Suddenly there's no oxygen in the room. I must hear whatever terrible news he has left to tell me.

"She has a daughter with that guy, Jahi. She's almost two, I think."

Silence weighs heavily in the air between us. I can't speak right away.

"Wh… where is the little girl now?" I finally say. I'm short of breath, struggling to absorb this news.

"*That man* has her."

"Why?"

"He got sole custody of their daughter," he says finally.

"How did he do that? Isn't that impossible? How do you take a baby away from its mother?"

"He consulted all the top attorneys in Chicago so she wouldn't have access to the best counsel. He's mega wealthy and connected, remember? They play rough in the big city."

"But I still don't get it. She's the mother. How did he get the baby?"

"After the birth, she did okay for a bit, but a few weeks later, she was acting strange, staring off into space, not eating, not taking care of the infant, not able to breastfeed, crying day and night. He got scared she would kill the baby, so he hired twenty-four seven in-home care."

"Oh no, that's awful."

"It gets worse." Chad pauses, squinting his eyes at me as if he's analyzing whether I can handle the next batch of bad news.

"What?" I ask, but wonder if I can handle what he's about to reveal.

"She ended up in the hospital for a few weeks and seemed better, but it didn't last. When she returned home, she wasn't any better. She was secretive and muttering words under her breath, and he couldn't figure out what she was saying or what was wrong. And then…"

I hold my breath, waiting. Surely she didn't murder the baby?

"And then?" I mirror him after gulping enough air to speak, my voice cracking.

"One day she was driving to the grocery store with the baby girl…"

"Oh, no!"

"And they pulled her over for drunk driving. She got a DUI, Jahi. They took her to jail."

I gasp, horrified.

CHAPTER FIVE

ROSE

I wake up and caress my belly. *What am I going to do with this pregnancy? Can I handle this as a solo parent if Jahi stays with Susanne? How will I support myself and the baby in a new town where I don't know anyone?*

I've got to decide soon. Letting this go on too long will only complicate things more.

I glance at my phone and see a text from Jahi.

"Hey beautiful. What's up? Sleep well? I can't wait to see you for dinner. I'll come over and cook you something special. Love, J."

I clutch my arms around my chest, my shoulders curving forward as I rock myself. My stomach roils, and I crumple back on my bed. *What am I going to say to Jahi? How do I tell him I need to leave town, go to Fayetteville and stay with my family while I sort out my decisions about work and the baby?*

I realize I need to pack. I won't take everything, because I haven't yet decided exactly what I'm going to do, whether I'm going to stay here or leave for good. He may feel disappointed or even devastated, but I keep reminding myself: *Don't structure your life around a man.* I repeat it like a mantra.

I text him back.

"Hey handsome. I'm good. Yeah, I slept well. Look forward to our dinner. You're such a superb cook. XX, R."

I feel some relief even though a part of me doesn't want to see him. There's something in me that wants to sneak off without a word, like I did before. But that wouldn't be fair. That would be just like Dad… running off secretly.

Thinking about Dad throws my mind into a tailspin. *There was a secret between him and me. A big, devastating secret. That day I got out early from grade school, a few minutes earlier than he expected, and saw him and that black-haired woman as I rounded the corner. He was leaning into her beater car, her window down, and kissing her on the lips. He must have felt me staring. I stood there, frozen, and he looked up, his widened eyes locking onto mine, unblinking. He froze, too. I broke our gaze and ran into the house. He came in a minute or two later and said nothing. He didn't look me in the eye for days. We never spoke a word of it, as if that made it not exist. As if we erased it. It was our secret.*

But I don't want to live a life of secrets. And right now, I'm keeping one. At least one, but probably more. I'm not telling Jahi what happened between Susanne and me. Is that fair? And I'm not telling Jahi what my decisions are about work and the baby. But I really don't know for sure what those decisions will be, so do those count as secrets?

I spend the rest of the day ruminating as I quietly pack. It all seems so surreal, like a dream. Am I really doing this? Am I sure I want to leave the love of my life just because his wife is threatening me? And what about the baby? Can I imagine not having this baby who is part of me… and Jahi?

Jahi arrives at six o'clock sharp, always punctual, and I love it. He's as handsome and sexy as ever, with a slight stubble on his chiseled jaw. He knows I swoon over his manly jawline. I'm sure he did that on purpose. I prefer this look to his clean-shaven look. Part of me wants to throw myself into his arms and another part wants to run away.

He picks up on my ambivalence. "What's wrong, Rose? You seem distant."

"Sorry, but I have a lot on my mind. I'm trying to figure things out."

"What's there to figure out? You know I love you. I want us to have our own little family. You, me, Lily, and our baby."

I let out a loud sigh. I didn't mean it to be so loud, and I feel embarrassed.

"Why are you sighing, Rose? You look troubled."

"I am, Jahi. I am."

Jahi's brows furrow and his eyes darken. I'm not sure if he's about to cry or blow up. "Tell me what it is."

"I don't want to keep secrets from you. I really don't," I say with hesitation.

"What do you mean? What secrets?" He searches my face, a look of alarm etched on his.

I sigh again. I can't seem to stop myself. My arms tremble and I feel cold, like I'm in the Arctic. My jaw locks up and my teeth chatter. This is what my body does when I'm anxious and panicky. I don't want to tell him, but I have to. I can't see a way out.

"I'm so cold." I don't recognize my voice because it's coming through gritted teeth.

"Here, let me hold you and wrap you in a blanket," he says soothingly, wrapping his muscular arms around me, pulling me onto the sofa, and covering me with an afghan. After a few minutes, he says, "I'm going to make you some hot tea with a little ginger to warm up your gizzards." He gives me a slight smile.

A laugh escapes me. When he returns, I sip the tea until the cup is empty. By that time, my body is warm. I sigh again. I'm sighing so much I wonder if something's wrong with me. Jahi holds me in his arms, waiting patiently for me to speak.

"Jahi, I've got some bad news," I start and his body hardens, but he remains silent. "Susanne came to my house the other day."

His eyes widen, and his face blanches.

I wonder if this means what she said is true, and he's horrified I've found out and caught him red-handed? I'm quite good at reading body language and the look on his face disturbs me. He's swallowing a lot, and I notice his Adam's apple moving up and down. He looks guilty.

He's silent, so I continue, "She barged into my house and told me to stop trying to steal her man."

"That sounds just like her," Jahi says, his voice dripping with sarcasm.

"She went on and on, threatening me." My voice gets shaky and I cry. "She said," I gulp and the words gush out of me like a torrent. "She said you took her on a romantic picnic in Bella Vista and told her it's over with me, that I'm nothing to you, that there's always been no strings attached between us…"

"No, no, no. That's not right."

"She said… she… you… made… you made…" My voice is hysterical.

"No!" Jahi yells, a wild look in his eyes, like he knows what's coming next.

"... love to her."

"She's a liar. She's a pathological liar! That witch." Jahi's voice is booming so loudly I wonder if the neighbors can hear him even though all the windows are closed.

"But Jahi, you said you wanted to just be friends with her, but that's not what she's saying."

"She's lying, baby. Don't you know that? Susanne just wants to win, and she's humiliated that I'm demanding a divorce. She threatened me, too."

"She did?"

"Yes, at the picnic. The picnic was my attempt to get her away from the gossips in town, show her we can communicate respectfully, and insist that we divorce. I was worried she would explode and make a scene… and she did."

"What happened?" I ask, sniffling.

"When I told her we can be friends for Lily's sake, but we can't be married, she didn't register it at first and I had to repeat it. When she realized I meant it, she flipped and threatened to ruin me in every way possible—take me financially, take the house, drag my name in the mud in town and yours too, and worst of all…" Jahi chokes up and falls silent.

"What?" I ask softly.

"She said she would… she'd try to get custody… of Lily. Sole custody."

"Oh, no!"

"Yes. She's eaten up with vengeance, Rose. She'll do anything to tear us apart. And not because she even cares about me. But because she wants to be in control. The only person she loves is herself. She's a madwoman."

"I know," I agree. Then I can't stop myself from saying, "But maybe you like that kind of woman. Or maybe she scares you enough that you just go along with her and let her intimidate you."

"Rose! That's not true," Jahi's voice booms, and his hold on me tightens protectively.

"Something about what she said and how she said it got under my skin. I'm having trouble believing you're totally innocent here, Jahi."

"Rose. What else did she say? You're being illogical. This doesn't sound like you. It must be…"

"My hormones?"

"Yes," Jahi says sheepishly.

"Oh, come on, Jahi. That's a cheap shot," I say, suddenly angry. "And even if what you say is true, that you weren't with her… she's still stopping us from being together as a happy family, and this is wrecking my life."

"You've got to believe I love you, Rose, and that I'm working hard and fast to outsmart her and get divorced. I've been talking with my attorney and I've come into some legal information that, if you knew it, would remove all the doubt you're having."

"Oh, that's convenient. If only I had this information, all would be hunky dory. It sounds like a fairy tale and I'm not buying it. You don't think you can pull that on me, do you? That doesn't wash."

Jahi exhales loudly. Now he's the one sighing. "I can't tell you yet because I'm bound by confidentiality… but Rose… I'm going to win this battle. I'm going to get a divorce, I promise you. Please, I beg you to believe me."

I collapse onto the sofa in tears, pounding the throw pillow. "I can't take it," I cry out. "This is tearing me apart. This is ruining my life, putting it on hold. I've got decisions to make, Jahi. I don't have time for this long, drawn-out battle."

"We're almost there, Rose. This new information will seal her doom in court. Please, don't do something impulsive at the cusp of victory."

"But Jahi, I don't have the luxury of time. A baby is growing inside me. A clinic position just opened up, and I must decide whether to take it."

"Where is it?"

"Russellville. There are others, but it's the closest one."

"Russellville? That's two and a half hours away. It's not in the middle of nowhere, but you can see it from there. Can't you get a position in Fayetteville?" he asks desperately, knowing our lives will change in big ways if I'm working in Russellville.

"Fayetteville already has a thriving clinic. I had my eye off the prize dealing with this nightmare and waiting for you to get a divorce from Susanne. But now, I have more than just me to plan for financially, and I've got to get a job."

"I'm sorry, Rose. It's been a lot, I know."

"I have to take the position in Russellville, Jahi. Nothing else is available closer to here."

"But you'll be leaving us."

"You've given me no other option."

"What do you mean?"

"Susanne's unannounced and unwelcome visit to my home was so traumatic, it made me wonder if she's capable of murder. I had a client years ago, a twenty-eight-year-old woman, a doctor, who got involved with a married man who was her colleague. She got pregnant. One day, she missed her appointment with me. I found out why she never came to that appointment. I saw it online," I say, my voice trembling.

"The wife of the cheating man murdered my patient. She stalked my patient, followed her home, and stabbed her to death in blind rage." I shiver. "I'm creeped out, Jahi. Who could imagine the unassuming doctor's wife, sweet and mild-mannered, whose job it was to look beautiful at galas and academic dinners and serve canapes on her veranda overlooking the Pacific, would end up dying in a hail of bullets from a SWAT team after she barricaded herself in her house with her daughters?"

"I'm so sorry," Jahi says soothingly.

"Susanne had a psychotic look in her eyes that day she came to my house. She must have stalked me… or you, to find out where I live. Then she waited until I was alone before she pounced."

Jahi's face looks horrified at the thought.

"The way she looked at me made me wonder if she suspects the pregnancy. You said she's intuitive. Women can often tell, long before anyone else, when another woman is pregnant. It's a sixth sense. *This* is the reason I have to walk away."

A look of understanding crosses Jahi's face. He bows his head and rubs his eyes. And then looks me straight in the eyes. "I've seen that look, too. On the picnic. Murderous rage. She's like Medusa. You told me that once."

"She may plot my demise, Jahi. As extreme as that sounds, I think she's capable of it. I don't think she'd kill you, because that would ruin her plan to stay married to you and stay in control. I'm the one she has the vendetta on. She wants to annihilate me. The consequences will be catastrophic if she discovers I'm pregnant. It will be the *coup de grâce*, the final blow that crumbles your life. She'll win the case if she finds out."

"I agree with you. Chad and I have spoken about how this pregnancy would look to a judge who doesn't know the full facts. We think it's best if you stay away from Eureka Springs for now. Go to Fayetteville and get an obstetrician there. Susanne won't know where you are. Maybe she'll think she ran you away, and she'll believe she's won. "

"Oh, that's convenient, too, Jahi. Now you get me out of the way, and you can be with your ex." The words spill out before I can stop myself.

"Rose, that's not it at all. Please believe me. Please," Jahi begs, looking desperate.

"Jahi, I don't know who to believe."

Jahi runs a firm hand through his hair and slowly nods.

"I think you need time, baby, to process all this. Let's talk more later?"

He's right. I'm in no frame of mind to continue this conversation. I'm agitated and ready to lash out at him for Susanne's misdeeds. My emotions are running the show for me right now, and that's not fair to him.

"Thank you," I say quietly, after a long pause.

He kisses me softly, then gets up and walks lightly to the door, closing it softly behind him.

I'd almost rather that he slammed it.

CHAPTER SIX

JAHI

"Jahi? Jahi, you're not saying anything. You've been sitting there silent for a long time."

Chad's words snap me to attention. I'm reeling and dazed, having been through hell with Rose. She thinks I cheated on her with Susanne, and nothing I said convinced her otherwise. I hope once she thinks it through, she'll see that Susanne has lied to her. When will I get this train wreck of Susanne out of my life once and for all? I need to shunt her off onto another track that leads far away with no return ticket.

"Yeah," I finally answer.

"I'm sorry. I've shocked and upset you with this news, but actually it's good news from our point of view."

"How so?"

"It shows a pattern the judge won't like: abandonment and multiple DUIs."

"But she didn't really abandon her daughter in Chicago."

"That's not the point. It's a relative abandonment, Jahi. Because of her DUI, they took the baby from her. Her DUI was child endangerment, which is worse. Add that to the fact she got a second DUI here while on the way to pick up Lily and you see she shot herself in the foot."

"And how do you know this? You were evasive when I asked you that before."

"I have my sources. Like I said, I made a lot of connections at Yale. I spread my network all over the country. Heck, some of them are international."

"You're still not telling me who told you."

"My, you're a persistent one. You'd make an excellent attorney or maybe even a private investigator," Chad jests. I stare at him, unblinking. "Okay, okay. I got a surprise call from my old law school buddy, Phil Beckham. He's the one who told me."

"How does he know Susanne? Should you be telling me what he said? Isn't it confidential?"

"This is crucial for our case, and I trust nothing about this conversation will leave this room. Anyway, whoever let legality stand in the way of pursuing the truth?"

"I don't know what you mean," I say, dubious.

"Oh Jahi. You're such a goody two shoes," he jokes.

"Yeah? That's exactly what Susanne said to me many times."

"Hmm... sometimes there's a fine line between the criminal and the prosecutor. They're opposite ends of the spectrum. They're like a snake coiling around to bite its tail, the *ouroboros*."

"What the heck is that?"

"It's a symbol from ancient Egypt where a snake eats its own tail. Medieval alchemists took the symbolism over."

"Great, not only did I fail organic chemistry, I failed medieval alchemy as well. Anyway, so they're just different aspects of the same thing."

"Exactly. Okay, so let me tell you what he said. Here's the gist of it."

"Okay," I say, still not sure this is wise. *Is there more horror ahead? I'm still recovering from the last nightmare.*

"I haven't seen Phil in eighteen years, so I asked him why he's in Eureka Springs, of all places. He said he's counsel for a woman here and the strange thing is, he was on the opposing side of a case in Chicago she was involved in."

"Ooh," I say, drawing out the word. "I think I see where this is going."

"Yeah. And it turns out the lover boy is a billionaire real estate developer in Chicagoland. That's how he had so much sway with the courts and how he bought out all the law firms."

"She threatens him," I say.

"Yeah. She's a nutcase. He had to get rid of her and fast," Chad agrees. "Phil said she's bonkers. She's petty and seductive and manipulative, and she sucked this guy in and got herself pregnant. She's a baby mama, desperate for a baby daddy with a fat checkbook. That's pretty much what he said, from my recollection."

"What happened next?"

"I wanted to take him out to Legends Saloon, but he declined. I joked that he always enjoyed going out in New Haven even though the neighborhoods were sketchy, but here we are in *Smallville* and he won't take me up on the chance for a beer."

"What was his reason?"

"He said that once I hear the story, I'll see why he needs to be discreet. That's when he informed me about what you already know—her going psycho after the birth, her hospitalization for postpartum depression, and lover boy being appalled when she got the DUI with the baby in the car. That's why he sued for sole custody and made sure he won. And that's when Phil dropped the bomb of why the woman never married the Chicago dude."

"It's because she's already married," I interrupt. "What's the clincher?"

"I inquired if his client's name is Susanne. When he nodded, I told him I'm counsel for the man she's planning to sue."

"Unbelievable. What are the odds?" I ask.

"I don't know, but I think it's more like dumb luck and I'll take it. No conflict, no interest. Then again, you've heard of six degrees of separation and that the world seems to have only four hundred people in it, so maybe it's not so improbable after all."

I sit in silence, and Chad says nothing.

"So, your friend Phil unwittingly ruptured client privilege by blabbing to you, divulging sensitive information, not realizing you're opposing counsel."

"Yup, that about sums it up."

"What happened when Phil realized his error?"

"His face flushed bright red. He looked shocked and embarrassed. I felt sorry for him. He knew it was a rookie move, but nobody bats a thousand, so I cut him some slack."

"And what does this mean for us?"

"First, it buys us time. She'll have to find another attorney, and it may not be easy to find one of Phil's caliber. Second, it verifies that Susanne is harboring two secrets. She has a baby girl she abandoned because of her actions, just like she abandoned Lily so she could be with this guy. And she has a previous DUI that put her baby at risk, child endangerment."

"Plus, she's a cheater. She committed adultery," I add.

"Bingo," Chad affirms.

Maybe my luck is changing. Because luck matters, whether it involves Vegas or not.

CHAPTER SEVEN

ROSE

I'm ashamed I treated Jahi so badly. When he left quietly with such grace, it left me with a mirror of my behavior. I wasn't kind. In fact, I was condemning him. I kept acting like he was guilty and that was totally not fair. I know better than to do that.

Before I met Lee, I briefly dated a first year UCLA law student. He told me something I've never forgotten. He said when people assert someone is guilty as if it's the truth; the person accused will, of course, defend their innocence. Just as Jahi did. And the more they defend themselves against these assertions of guilt, the guiltier they look. It's impossible to prove innocence; therefore, a cardinal principle of our legal system is the presumption of innocence. You're presumed innocent until proven guilty beyond a reasonable doubt.

The moment the guy told me this, I knew intuitively it was true. I had my own experiences with this, in middle school, when a bunch of girls who were jealous of me couldn't think of anything else to defame me other than to assert I was a lesbian. I'm not sure they even knew what that meant. They must have heard it somewhere. It was so painful and absurd, but there was nothing I could do to unring that bell. If I argued, it would look like I was guilty. I had to be like Britain's Royal Family with their motto: *Don't complain. Don't explain.*

I never told my mother, or anyone, about this. It would upset my mom too much, and what would she be able to do? You can't stop mean girls. This lie, instigated by a band of girls who hated me, followed me throughout high school. I'd see, here and there, my name scratched into a wooden desk saying, *Rose Aberdeen is a homo. Rose is a lesbian. RA loves girls.*

Poor Jahi. I was relentless. The more I doubted him as if he were guilty, the more he tried to defend himself, and the guiltier he looked. I pushed him to the brink. He probably gave up. You can't win this battle, and I put him through it, knowing full well what I was doing, knowing more about blaming and guilt than most people. I understand now why our legal system has the presumption of innocence.

It sickens me to think about it now. Am I cracking up under the stress? Is it hormones? I was harsh when Jahi mentioned hormones, and he was probably right. It's just never okay to hear a man say it.

I may not know what I'll decide regarding the job offer and the baby, but one thing is clear. I've got to disappear and not be findable by Susanne. If I give her any surface area by being visible, she'll try to destroy me. She might even kill me, just like the aggrieved wife killed my patient in that love triangle. *How in the world have I gotten myself into this mess?*

I call Jolene because I need to see her in person and let her know what's going on before I leave town. I don't trust getting on a call with her, in case it's tapped.

Am I being paranoid? I don't think I can stay one more night in my bungalow. Last night, I had a nightmare. I was on a river rafting trip, and the group left to scout the next rapids. I sat on the bank, peeling and eating an orange. My fingers got sticky, so I bent forward and rubbed my palms together in the cold water. A thin branch floated in the river five feet away. As it drifted in the sparkling water, I fell under its spell, mesmerized. It was like a mirage. A calmness came over me, like I was meditating, with no thoughts, no monkey mind. As it moved closer, now three feet away from my hands, the still branch transformed into a serpentine, dancing movement on the surface of the water. My mind registered the shift. How could the branch move like that... maybe... maybe it's not a branch! Is it a snake? Do snakes swim in these frigid waters? I snatched my hands out of the water and leapt onto my feet, backing away from the bank. An icy reptilian eye stared back at me, unblinking, like a sociopath. I shivered and tried to scream, but no voice came out. I woke up sopping wet.

I've got to get out of here. Gotta go to Fayetteville and hide out. As far as I know, Susanne knows nothing about my family. The only way she could find out is if she asks Lily. Surely she won't do that and come hunt me down.

I call Jolene, and she picks up on the first ring.

"Hey, that was fast. You must have been near your phone."

"Hi Rose. I was scrolling online for recipes. Seriously, I've been worried about you. I haven't heard from you. How are you doing?"

"I'm sorry, Jolene. I'll tell you about it when I see you. Okay if I come over now?" I say, not wanting to divulge anything on the call, in case someone listens in.

Is that even possible? This isn't the '50s in rural Arkansas with nosy neighbors listening in on party lines. When did I become so paranoid? Oh, right? After Susanne threatened me. The nightmares don't help, either.

"Uh... sure. Okay. You sound like you're in a hurry."

"I am, Jolene. I'll tell you about it when I see you."

I pack up my car with the bags I prepared yesterday, check the stove burners, turn on a dim light in the living room and in my bedroom so it looks like I'm still here. Then, I drive to Jolene's. I'll tell Jahi to get my mail. I don't want to contact the post office to forward it because it would give away my location.

Jahi can send the mail to me using my mother's maiden name, Ethel Ferguson. Mom's not from Eureka Springs, she's from Tomahawk, so no one knows that name here.

Jolene lets me in, her dark eyebrows raised, a look of concern on her face. She knows I'm being secretive. I smell something yummy boiling on the stove.

"What are you cooking?" I ask, trying to act calm.

"Smoked salmon kimbap."

"What in the world is that?"

"A yummy smoked salmon dish that's crunchy and tastes like seaweed. It's addictive. It's like sushi, and it's one of my favorites, but because you're pregnant, I don't think it's a good idea for you to eat it. When you've delivered the baby, I'll make you some."

"Sounds good," I say half-heartedly. Delivering the baby seems a long way off, almost unreal.

"I'd also love to make you Ganjang gejang. It's crab marinated in soy sauce. I'll have to get a hold of some crab, probably frozen," Jolene gushes, ignoring my non-committal response. "Anyway, you'll love it. It's tangy and spicy, totally yummy. But for now, I made you a goat cheese sandwich to fortify you before you leave town."

"Thanks, but how do you know I'm leaving town?" I ask, perplexed.

"Rose, I know you. Your voice was furtive on the phone. You're paranoid about something, and I think I have a pretty good idea of what it is."

"Tell me."

"Okay. You're pregnant, and you don't know what to do about it because you're worried about not having a job. Jahi's still married, though he's trying to get a divorce, and Susanne is lurking in town."

"All true."

"And you're worried she'll find out you're pregnant, am I right?"

"Yes."

"And the longer you stay here, the more likely it is she'll figure it out."

"You're right, Jolene. And there's one more thing."

"What is that?"

"She threatened me." Jolene's eyes widen as I say this. "She came to my house and told me to leave Jahi alone, that he's hers, that they're in love and they made love."

"Oh, that's bogus," Jolene scoffs. "She's a known liar. Believe nothing that comes out of her mouth."

"That's what Jahi told me."

"You sound unconvinced. Why doubt Jahi?"

"I don't know, Jolene. She got under my skin, and I can't get it out of my head."

"It may be the hormones, Rose."

"You sound just like Jahi. That's what everybody and their dog says." I laugh ruefully.

Jolene laughs, too. "Well, I've known Jahi all my life, like a brother. He's a good guy, Rose. Don't underestimate him. He comes from excellent stock. He's as honest as the day is long."

I exhale. "Jolene, there's more."

"What is it? You look worried."

"I am. I'm afraid she'll murder me if she gets half the chance."

"You're kidding." Jolene's eyes go wide.

"No, I'm not. When she barged into my house, her eyes were wild with fury, like she was psychotic. She's primitive. She could do anything and get off for it being a crime of passion. We're talking about a love triangle. Even people who are more rational than Susanne can do ruinous things when their relationship is in jeopardy. It's dangerous. It could be lethal."

Jolene sighs loudly and I'm relieved I'm not the only one sighing these days. After another exhale, Jolene says, "You're right. We've got to be careful. We've got to get you out of here, Rose. She could become unspooled as things erupt with the divorce. If she sees you pregnant, she'll go nuts. She could hurt not only you, but Jahi and even Lily, and herself. I've seen those cases of murder-suicide on true crime shows. This is treacherous territory."

"I'm going to Fayetteville," I announce. "I'll stay there with my mother and sister. This will buy me time to decide what to do about the job offer and the baby," I say, relieved that Jolene understands my predicament.

"Just be careful, Rose. I'll keep my eyes peeled for anything suspicious, and I'll watch out for Jahi and Lily."

"Thanks, Jolene. You're a genuine friend. A gem."

"This, too, will pass. One day, it will be over, the divorce will go through, and Jahi will be free. You two will be together. You'll have your baby, and you'll have a happy little family—you, Jahi, Lily, and the baby."

"We'll see, Jolene. We'll see."

CHAPTER EIGHT

JAHI

"You can't breathe a word of this, Matt. Not one word. Understand?"

"Of course, I promise." A solemn look comes over Matt's face.

"I haven't even told Rose. She's so fragile with the pregnancy and all. I don't want to upset her and risk causing a miscarriage."

"What in the world is it, Jahi?"

"I'm just going to spill it out, Matt. Susanne cheated on me years ago on that Vegas trip she took where she never came back. She got together with a billionaire from Chicago. They had a baby girl together." Matt's eyes look like saucers at this news. "She got postpartum depression, was probably psychotic, hospitalized, got out, acted strange again, and was secretly drinking."

"Wow. This sounds familiar," Matt interrupts.

"Yup. Drove drunk with the baby in the car, got pulled over, got a DUI, went to jail. The father became enraged and got sole custody of the baby girl."

"Whoa. So, she cheated on you, had a baby, and got a DUI."

"That about sums it up."

"And the recent DUI is her second."

"Yeah, at least. Maybe there's more."

"And she committed adultery and has a baby she left behind." Matt whistles.

"Yes, exactly."

"Well, this should be a slam dunk for you to get a divorce, Jahi."

"It should," I say hesitantly.

"You don't sound convinced." Matt raises an eyebrow at me, looking puzzled.

"You know Susanne. She finds ways around the rules. There's no telling what she's got up her sleeve."

"Right."

"The thing is, I'm worried. When I took her on a picnic to insist on the divorce, I tried to be nice. The moment I said we could remain friends, she blew up. She threatened to ruin me, take my house, slander me and Rose, and even get sole custody of Lily."

"What? No way. She's nuts."

"She had a crazed look in her eyes. And then she went to Rose's house."

"No." Matt looks alarmed. "I don't like the sound of this."

"And she threatened Rose and told her we're back together. That I wanted Rose to leave us alone. She lied, saying we made love on that picnic."

"I'm not surprised she would say that, Jahi."

"Neither am I, but the thing is, if she gets wind that Rose is pregnant, all hell will break loose. It could hurt my case legally. A judge may not look fondly on a man who impregnates another woman when he is technically still married. She can't find out. If she does, she could become deadly. She has murderous rage." I rub my aching temples.

"As they say, hell hath no fury…"

"Like a woman scorned," I finish his sentence. "Exactly."

"Jahi, we've got to protect Rose and the baby."

"Yes, we do. Rose is going to Fayetteville to stay there while she figures things out, and also to get out of sight of Susanne."

"And what about you, Jahi?"

"What about me?"

"She could come after you, even Lily."

A shiver runs up my spine. "We've got to be prepared. Maybe we should have Lily stay with Chrissy while we're dealing with divorce proceedings."

"Yeah, you could do that. The biggest danger is probably for Rose and the baby, though. Susanne wants to be married to you, and Lily is her blood, so it's probably okay for you and Lily, though not a hundred percent."

"Better to be safe than regret not protecting Rose, Lily, and the baby."

"And yourself," Matt adds.

CHAPTER NINE

ROSE

I pull over on the side of the road in Garfield and call Bea. In my hurry to pack, see Jolene, and get out of town, I never got around to calling my sister to tell her I'm coming to stay for a while, not just for Thanksgiving.

"Hey Rose."

"Hi Bea. I'm coming over." I take a shaky breath and say, "I need to go *incognito*. Things are intense here. I'm about forty minutes away. I'll tell you about it when I get there."

"Are you okay?" Bea asks, trying to sound calm, but I hear the alarm in her voice.

"Yeah," I say, my voice clipped. "See you soon."

When I arrive, B rushes to my car breathlessly. Her face is flushed, her eyes expectant.

"Hi B."

"Hey Rose. Let me help you with your bags."

"How's Mom?"

"Hanging in there. She's asleep, so we'll have time to talk, but first, let's get you settled into your room."

I inhale the familiar scents of home—that lovely combination of natural coconut and citrus in the living room and the hint of floral, spicy Rose Absolute oil in mom's bathroom where she keeps bars of old-fashioned rose soap. For a moment, I forget my troubles. I'm home. I'm safe. No one can reach me here. I can fold into myself like a chrysalis in a cocoon, protected by the silken casing of my sister's and mother's embrace, transforming my life into something new, something beautiful.

Realizing I'm here for a respite and to get away from my fraught situation, I take my time unpacking. I want to soak up every moment with Mom and Bea, to slow down, to stretch out, and to give myself a chance to breathe and just be. I need to decompress from the turmoil and drama. My heart needs to heal.

"Rose." Bea's voice at the door interrupts my thoughts. "I just want to check on you. You've been here for over an hour and haven't come out of your room. I wondered if you'd fallen asleep," she says gently, sensing my fragile state, and not wanting to agitate me.

"Oh, I'm sorry, Bea. I'm lost in my thoughts."

"Don't apologize, love. I know you're going through a painful time with Jahi. When you're ready to talk, just let me know." She smiles softly. There's a warmth in her eyes as she touches me gently on my shoulder, and it brings tears to my eyes. Seeing my sadness, she rushes forward and holds me in her arms, rocking me as I weep.

I'm taken back to childhood when Bea would comfort me like a mommy, when it felt like my world was coming apart. Years later, a psychoanalyst in graduate school called these experiences "calamities of childhood," moments of despair. Like the time my best friend Lucy Bentley and I fussed over our dolls, and she stuck her tongue out at me, exclaiming with the force of a tantrummer, "You don't have a daddy. He left. That's what my mommy says. I don't want to play with you anymore." Devastated, I turned to Bea to comfort me, because only she understood.

Bea sings my favorite childhood song as she rocks me. "I love you, a bushel and a peck, a bushel and a peck and a hug around the neck. You bet your pretty neck I do," she continues and I sing the verses in my mind, remembering Dad singing to us every night as babies.

Her voice drones on, out of key, and I don't care. Just like Mom, who is tone deaf, Bea never sings, but she's singing now. That says it all. She must be worried about me. She knows I love to sing, heck I'm classically trained in opera, but that feels like four lifetimes ago. I'm soaking it up, soaking up her vulnerability, soaking up her love. I feel drowsy, like she's reading me a bedtime story, her voice carrying me to a dreamland place of possibility. That's the power of music, the power of art in our darkest moments.

My body relaxes into the steadfastness of her love. I'm safe. This is my sanctuary.

"Bea," I say faintly, my strength ebbing. I fall asleep before I finish the thought.

I wake up, and it's late. The sun is at a steep angle. A shaft of light illuminates the base of the closet doors across the room, dust motes dancing like a constellation of little stars, flickering in and out of the light. It feels like my life—one moment illuminated, the next moment dark.

I look around the room and realize I'm at Mom's house, not my bungalow. Everything comes roaring back, tearing into my mind, the confrontation with Susanne, Jahi's explanation, my doubt of Jahi's innocence, the threat of annihilation. But I feel safe here, away from that. The things that happened the last few days feel like news of a battle fought overseas. Yes, there were casualties and much destruction, but there's a numbness I feel in the face of it all. Outside, the sun is shining and the birds are singing.

I sit in my room for hours, avoiding the difficult conversation I need to have with Bea. After a while, I realize my sister is waiting for me to talk, but she will not force an agenda on me. Oh, how I appreciate her kindness and marvel at her innate gifts of sensitivity and intuition. It's up to me to share my troubles, and it takes as long as it takes.

Bea's patience is like Job's in the Bible. She's a healer. She's got the gift, the one from our great-grandmother, Hattie Osborn, the Quaker from Friendsville, Tennessee who married our brilliant great-grandfather, the inventor, Isaac Whitestone. Family lore says people came from miles around to be in Hattie's presence, the healer who healed through the laying on of hands.

I never knew Hattie Osborn, but I've felt her presence my whole life. She's with me now. I feel her in my bones. Her kind eyes reach across decades in silent black and white photos, half-burnt at the edges. But I hear her voice. No, I feel it. A woman from another time who prayed for her family. She'd said: *"I pray for my family here now and all those I'll never meet."*

I've felt her prayer my whole life. She surrounds me. I was born with this gift, and Bea, too. It's our lineage and my sister is every bit as good, if not better, than me as a therapist.

I weep silently. It's time to talk to B.

I tiptoe into Bea's bedroom and find her flipping through a fashion magazine. She looks up, her eyes soft. "Hey."

"Hi," I mirror back.

"You look pale, like you've seen a scary movie," she ventures, careful not to push me with questions.

"You're reading my mind. I'm scared, Bea." Goosebumps rise on my arms. It's uncanny how my sister can read my mind.

"Is it the baby?" she queries.

"Not exactly. Though that's something I need to figure out. There's something else that's scaring me more than being pregnant." I pause. It's now or never. Can I get the words out? Can I tell my sister what I'm deathly afraid of? I stand there, mute.

Bea waits, but I remain silent. Finally, she pushes a bit. "Rose, what is going on? What are you afraid of? It isn't like you to go mute on me."

"Susanne." I exhale in relief from finally saying what my genuine fear is. "I'm afraid of Susanne. Do you remember the story I told you years ago about the murder of my patient in a love triangle in LA?"

"Yes," Bea draws out the word, her brow furrowing and her mouth slack. "You don't think that is going to happen to you, do you?"

"I don't know. It's possible."

"Why do you think that? Has something happened? Is there something you're not telling me?"

"Yes. I didn't want to worry you. Susanne turned up at my place and surprised me. I thought it was Jahi, so I opened the door. She pushed her shoulder and foot in before I could close it. She forced her way in, Bea."

"Oh no," she says, biting her lip, her eyes wide and staring at me in alarm.

"She threatened me, telling me Jahi is hers, to leave him alone and Lily too, and she said I'm nothing to Jahi, that they went on a picnic and made love under the stars. I can't remember if I told you that before, but that's not the problem."

"What is, then?"

"Her eyes looked psychotic, Bea. They were bulging and inflamed, and she reminded me of *Medusa,* the painting by Caravaggio that depicts the moment Medusa's head is severed by the demi-god Perseus. Remember when I got the scholarship to sing opera in Italy and I told you about the painting I saw that hangs in the Uffizi Gallery in Florence?"

"Yes, yes. The wild eyed monster, the one Athena cursed to live as a monster, whose head was full of snakes and who could turn anyone who looked at her to stone. I've seen pictures of it in art books. It gives me the creeps."

"Exactly. Murderous rage." I shiver, recalling it. "Absolute fury."

"You don't think she would try to hurt you, do you?"

"Yes, I do. I got the same reaction I get when I meet psychopaths. You know the feeling I've told you about? Remember the story about the man they asked me to evaluate in the emergency room at four o'clock in the morning at UCLA? And how I stopped at the threshold of the doorway? My body wouldn't go into the room because it knew danger lurked there, even before my mind registered it."

"Yeah, your body knows the truth. It knows when something dangerous is about to happen. I remember. Didn't you have security come and check him out?"

"Yes, I did. And he went bonkers when they asked to check his backpack. He ran out of the emergency room and I had the officers place him on a seventy-two hour hold. We found a loaded Glock in his bag and so we shipped him off to the county's locked psychiatric facility."

"So, you had the same feeling with Susanne? That you were in harm's way?"

"Yes. The hair on the back of my neck stood up. My body was on high alert, my heart racing, cortisol coursing through my veins. It was a fight, flight, freeze response, Bea, and I felt like fleeing."

"If she was that bad the other day, imagine if she finds out…" My sister stops, her body freezing mid-gesture, her eyes wide and staring.

"…that I'm pregnant," I say quietly, finishing her sentence. "It will unhinge her."

"Rose, you can hide out here. She won't find you. She won't know where you are."

"Right. She'll never suspect I'm here because she doesn't know about you and Mom," I begin, but then another thought crowds in. "Unless… unless she questions Lily. I'm not sure if Lily knows about you two, but she might, though I don't think Lily knows exactly where you live."

"She may think you high-tailed it back to LA."

"She might. Meanwhile, I hope it's not too much of a burden for me to stay here. You've got a lot on your hands with Mom's care."

"No, no. I want you here." She rushes in to assure me. "I want you safe. You and the baby, my niece or nephew. Mom's grandbaby."

"Bea, I'm not sure about the baby." I hesitate, not sure whether to continue. Emotionally exhausted from the danger and the drama, I decide not to elaborate further.

"Well, don't make any sudden decisions. Not now. Rest. Recover. You've got time. It's still early," my sister assures me.

"Thanks, Bea. I will," I say, relieved to push that big decision off for now.

Everyone who loves me wants me to continue with the pregnancy. Mom, well, she doesn't know, but if she knew, she would. But yes, Bea, Jahi, Jolene, and Matt, I'm sure, if he knows. I'll have to ask Jahi if he's told him.

But I'm not sure what I want. I'm the one who'll be responsible for the baby. Can I take on motherhood as a single parent? I don't want to have a baby, only to have it in daycare from dawn to dusk while I work and barely make ends meet. It's amazing how fast even a big salary dwindles when you have to pay a roomful of people to do the things you can't do alone. What kind of life is that?

The fear subsides a bit as I get into the quotidian rhythms of cooking, shopping, cleaning, eating and sleeping, away from my life in the fishbowl of Eureka Springs. We go for walks in the park, Bea insisting that exercising is good for me. I'm anonymous here, and no one cares if my pregnancy is showing. Bea helps me find an obstetrician. I like her. Her name is Dr. Lea Mason, and she looks like she's in her late fifties.

She's six-feet tall with long, gray-streaked jet black hair, an angular face, and soft doe eyes that emanate kindness. People say she's Cherokee and I believe it. She wears band t-shirts from the '60s, shorts, and Birkenstocks in her office. She's my hippie doctor, but I've heard she's the doctor's doctor. All the doctors go to her—the women doctors and the wives married to doctors. She's delivered the most twin vaginal births in the Northwest Arkansas region, which apparently is a feat, and she's a fantastic surgeon which is relieving if I turn out to need a Cesarean. But I'm getting ahead of myself. I'm not sure about this pregnancy. I'm not sure of much of anything anymore.

My morning sickness has subsided since I've been here, so the three of us go on frequent excursions.

One day, Mom is napping and Bea asks, "Hey, do you want to take a short walk to the Greek Theatre on campus?"

"Sure. I'd love to."

We hike up Dickson Street, past Walton Arts Center, and up the stairs to Old Main, stepping on the names of alumni stamped into the concrete. We approach the chemistry building, that infamous stone fortress that burned Jahi's dreams and left them in ashes like some chemistry experiment gone awry when he failed the Herculean feat of passing organic chemistry. He told me the story. How he took the B.S. Organic Chemistry class, the exclusive one with only twelve serious students aiming to be scientists, rather than the B.A. class, the one filled to the brim with 462 cutthroat pre-med students. He was in over his head with Dr. Friar, and it fell apart in the first eight weeks. It saddens me to imagine the devastation Jahi must have felt at the tender age of nineteen, his plan of becoming a doctor ruined before he even started.

We cross in front of the biology building and see the white marble glimmering in the bright light, and Greek letters carved into the walls. The exquisite Greek amphitheater with the wide green lawn is littered with students sunbathing on one of those rare sweet warm November days.

As I stare across the steps, the stage comes into focus and I think of Shakespeare's words, "All the world's a stage." *Is it? Are we actors with entrances and exits, playing out different roles as our lives unfold? And do the people in our lives, both those close to us and those we briefly cross paths with, show up for a reason?*

There are so many people in my head these days, I feel they could fill this Greek amphitheater like the Greek chorus in mythology. The obvious ones, like Jahi and Bea and Mom, but fanning out in concentric circles are countless others, ones I've only seen in grainy photographs or ones I've never seen at all. I'm just a little bud on the top of a magnificent tree and today I feel that.

And then there are the ones in the shadows, the ones I can't see, the ones long gone. My grandparents: Granny, Papa, Mawmaw, and Pawpaw, and Jahi's grandparents: Big Daddy, Big Momma, Grammy, Popeye, and Jahi's dad. Even my dad, though he's not here. And there are the ones I came across fleetingly in my life. The woman at the five and dime who gave me a free lollipop when I was ten and had run out-of-pocket change. My best childhood friend down the street, the one I fussed with every day, Lucy. The opera director at the Academy in Florence. I'll never forget him. He called me to the front of the class when I was a self-conscious fourteen-year-old, and asked me to sing an aria. I picked my favorite, "O Mio Babbino Caro" and squeaked it out, my voice thin, reedy and breathless. And he said, "Let it out, Rose. Let your voice out."

What does my voice say now? Can I hear it over these remembered and imagined people?

The voices in my head are intoning the same message, "Have this baby, Rose."

Bea and I make a habit of taking short walks around campus while Mom naps after breakfast. It's a warm day for late November, and we take off our coats and carry them.

"I think we should go back," I complain.

"Hey, it's good for us. Mom said the key to life is to keep moving. We're sweating out toxins," she says, laughing.

I roll my eyes, about to say something sarcastic and maybe a little funny, when I feel a twinge in the back of my left calf. "Ow," I grunt under my breath, trying to hide the shock of the pain throbbing in my calf.

"What's wrong?" she asks, never one to miss anything subtle.

"My calf hurts suddenly. This is strange," I say, half disbelieving what's happening, clutching my calf, rubbing it to see if it subsides. My neck feels stiff. I don't want Bea to see that I'm worried, but I am. As I walk, the dull pain worsens. "This isn't good," I mutter.

"What? What is it? You're worrying me."

"It's getting worse," I grunt.

"Uh oh. Rose, your leg looks red and swollen," Bea says, her voice rising in alarm. "We better get you to the doctor."

Bea braces me, and I limp back to the house. Mom is still asleep. We leave a note telling her we're at the doctor's office, and we'll be back soon.

Dr. Mason breezes into the room, ever cheerful, but when she sees my leg, she frowns. She touches my calf, noting its warmth and measuring its circumference, comparing it to my other leg. "I'm afraid you've got a DVT—what we call a deep venous thrombosis. A clot in your vein. We need to start you on a blood thinner, just in case. It's injectable, just under your skin. Let's do it now."

I nod, shocked into submission. *Is this what it's like to be an obstetrical patient? I don't like this passive position I find myself in.* The nurse wheels in a cart. Dr. Mason smoothly picks up the syringe with the tiny needle. She pinches my skin, but I don't look.

"Bee sting," she warns. "There. It's done. Now we'll check your leg with an ultrasound, but I'm sure it's a DVT. I'll send you to Radiology, and we'll know for sure. Meanwhile, I'll call the internist, Dr. Martin, to get him involved in your care. We'll need to figure out what to do. You'll likely need heparin, the standard blood thinner, for about three months just to be sure you don't clot again. We can work with this. Don't worry," she states reassuringly, like someone used to dealing with nervous women.

"Is this odd? Is it concerning?"

"Well, pregnancy is a hypercoagulable state. Meaning, there's a tendency to clot easily so you don't hemorrhage during childbirth, but this shouldn't happen, and we need to treat it. You had three previous miscarriages, correct?"

"Yes."

"Did your mother have any medical problems during pregnancy?"

"Not with me, but she did with my sister." I look at Bea, who is staring, wide-eyed, uncharacteristically mute. Bea nods.

"What did she have?"

"Pre-eclampsia that progressed to eclampsia. Her kidneys started shutting down. She almost died. But she had no problems with me, her second child."

"Oh, I see," she says, as if carefully choosing her words. "Does she have anything called Factor V Leiden?"

"Not that I know of, but I'm not sure they tested for many things then."

"Right. Yeah, we didn't even know it existed until 1993, so she probably hasn't undergone testing."

"What is it?"

"A clotting disorder. It's inherited, and it causes a person to clot easily. We need to test for it. I suspect you might have it."

"And what happens if I do?"

"We'll watch you closely."

"Why? What does this mean? Am I in danger? Is the baby going to be okay?"

Dr. Mason exhales and hesitates before continuing, seeming to ponder whether and what to tell me. "It predisposes you to… complications," she says, then stops.

"Like what?" I ask, breathless. My heart is racing. *Am I going to be like Mom and almost die in pregnancy or childbirth? This is more than I bargained for. In fact, I had no inkling I could become pregnant so easily. I was so smitten by Jahi, I wasn't thinking clearly. It's like I stepped into quicksand. It's a trap.*

"Like more clots, low birth weight, problems with the placenta where it can break away suddenly before birth and," she hesitates, searching my face and then adds quickly, "stillbirth, but that's unlikely." She pauses again and says, "And it increases the risk of pre-eclampsia."

"By how much?"

"Fifty percent," she states in a matter-of-fact fashion, her tone calm.

I gulp. "So, this means I'm in the high-risk pregnancy category?"

"Yes. You are, anyway, being thirty-eight. We consider this advanced maternal age, but you'll be fine. You're strong and in good shape," she reassures me.

"But this makes it worse?" I ask, shaken.

"Yes. But we'll take care of it. I've dealt with many high-risk pregnancies. Women and babies come through this just fine all the time."

She says "all the time," not "most of the time," or "sometimes," or, heaven forbid, "occasionally." I'm sure she doesn't want to alarm me. I feel like I'm in a trance. Her mouth is moving, but I hear nothing. It looks like Bea is listening intently. She can tell me about it later. I'm feeling woozy. The outer world is rotating on its axis inexorably while my world is falling apart, spinning off onto a new unforeseen trajectory.

I don't remember the ultrasound or the internist. It's like I was in an accident, and all I remember is the time before the injection. I look around and I'm home. Bea is rocking me in her arms. Mom is soothing me, saying, "It's hard to be pregnant. It can be traumatic. Rest, dear."

I sit up abruptly. "You know?" My eyes are wide open.

"Yes. Your sister told me all about it. Don't worry, dear. You've been through hell. I just want you and the baby to be safe."

I take that as permission to go to my room and collapse on my bed. I hear mumbling and garbled speech coming from the living room. It reminds me of being a child, falling into slumber and barely making out what the adults are saying.

Bea appears at my door twenty minutes later. "Are you okay, Rose? That was scary. It's been a tough day."

I'm silent for a long while and Bea waits.

"Bea?"

"Yes, dear."

"What if I don't make it? What if it almost kills me like it almost killed Mom when she was pregnant with you?"

"Oh, love, you will be okay. You're strong as a horse. Always have been. Nothing will happen to you. You'll come through this."

"But Bea."

"Yes?"

"What if… what if the baby survives?"

"It will."

"What if the baby survives and…" I ask, choking out the words.

"And?"

"And I don't?" I look up at my sister, like one of those forlorn children I've seen in documentaries on orphanages across the world.

Bea is quiet for a moment, taking in my ominous question.

"I would take care of the baby as if it's my own. You have my word. But that will not happen, Rose," she assures me, as if she can will it not to.

CHAPTER TEN

JAHI

Rose has been gone only a few days, and I miss her like a heart-sick puppy taken from his momma. Only, Rose isn't my momma, thankfully. She's my love and the mother of our baby. Rose is already a mother! I'm not sure why I haven't thought of it this way before, as if you only become a mother or father once the baby is born. Whoa, I'm a father of two! I let that happy thought soak in when my phone rings. It's Matt.

"Hey Matt, what's up?"

"Just checking in on you. It must be hard with Rose out of town."

"Yeah, it is. I was just thinking of her. You know this means I'm already a father of two!"

"Wait, what?" Matt's voice hesitates.

"I forgot to tell you. It's confirmed. Rose is definitely pregnant."

"Woo hoo!" Matt yelps with joy.

"Yeah." I smile, my eyes soft, imagining our little infant safe in Rose's womb, and then the moment I hold the baby in my arms for the first time. My vision blurs as I blink back tears. "Hold on, just a second. Something just popped up on my phone. Hopefully, it's Rose," I say as I scan the screen, my heart sinking when I discover it's a text from Susanne. "It's Susanne," I spit out, disgusted.

"Yuck. What does that hag want?" Matt's tone turns to fury.

"Let me read it to you."

"Sure."

I read, "Jahi, we need to get together. I've got something to share with you."

I shake my head. "Can you believe this? She won't take no for an answer."

"I imagine she's going to pull some stunt," Matt snarls.

"Yeah. It's always a trap with her," I say, and then an idea comes to me. "I better let Chad know."

"Good idea, Jahi. Swim cautiously in those shark-infested waters," he warns.

"Exactly. Ok, let me text Chad," I say, already writing.

"Hey Chad, something's up with Susanne. She wants to meet. Says she's got something to tell me."

Chad texts back within seconds, like a leopard ready to pounce on prey.

"Careful, Jahi. It's a trap. Gimme a sec…"

Chad pauses, and then I see a waveform showing he's writing again.

"Okay, I've got an idea. Tell her to meet you at the park. In case she goes ballistic, we want it to be public. We don't want to put you at risk in a private setting. Tell her to meet you at two o'clock and to sit on the bench by the lily pond. I'll go with you, but I'll wait in the car. This might be our moment."

My heart rate speeds up as I think about all the ways this can go nonlinear.

I text back, "I'll pick you up fifteen minutes before two."

"Alright. See you then. Ciao."

Turning to Matt, I tell Matt about the plan. "Hope it works. I need to be free of this woman," I say, as if praying to the gods. "Let's talk later, after the showdown," I joke.

"Okay, bro. Don't overthink it. Just stand up to her."

"Will do." I salute him on the video call, and he returns it. Good soldier that he is.

I take a deep breath and text Susanne.

"Okay. Meet me at the park at two o'clock, on the bench in front of the lily pond."

"Alright. See you soon."

I swing by Chad's office, dread coursing through me like an IV dripping poison in my veins. Is this when everything changes? What terrible news is she hiding? Does she have something on me? Some kind of leverage I don't know about? Chad and I sit in silence as I drive the familiar road to the park. I feel dizzy, like my fate teeters on a ledge between the safety of home and the plunge into annihilation.

Out of the blue, Chad asks, "Didn't you used to ride horses?" I told him I had a horse as a kid. "I'm no equestrian or biologist, but I've always wondered why there are more horse's asses than horses," he deadpans. Chad is a miracle worker. He makes me guffaw in this gut-wrenching moment, and I relax despite myself.

I park the car and see Susanne sitting on the bench. Her hair looks freshly cut and coiffed. It's *déjà vu*, like the time she returned years after abandoning Lily and me, that time when she needed money. Now I know why she got involved with the loan shark.

"Break a leg," Chad says, which sounds abrupt and jars me after fifteen minutes of silence.

Wordless, I get out of the car. My body feels like a wooden marionette, and someone—God?—is manipulating the strings. The sunlight is harsh and bright as I squint without sunglasses. The distance between Susanne and me is about twenty-five yards, but feels like a hundred. As I walk towards her, towards whatever the fates bring, a breeze caresses my cheek, and I smell honeysuckle, that beloved scent from childhood carrying memories of Chrissy and me playing by the creek on Big Daddy and Big Momma's farm, catching tadpoles and looking for crawdads, and eating watermelon. It was a time of infinite summer and endless childhood, no reality beyond creeks and woods, food, sleep and play.

Childhood memories come rushing back as I make my way to the bench by the lily pond where Susanne sits. My high school sweetheart turned into Judas, still not aware of my presence. Moving closer to her, my mind snaps back into what awaits me. My body stiffens as I gird myself for something ominous, something I haven't considered, some trap she'll ensnare me in. Each step is like the Bataan March, like I'm a half-dead man walking one step closer to my doom.

When I'm at the bench, she looks up, one eyebrow raised. Maybe she was aware of my presence, but pretended she wasn't. I stand there, like a prisoner awaiting execution, remaining silent.

"I know what's going on, Jahi." Her voice growls like a mad dog rising on her haunches. She squeezes her fists so tightly her knuckles bulge and blanch, like she's preparing for a fistfight. "Don't think you can fool me," she spits out the words as if spewing venom, her voice lowering, like some kind of possessed devil.

She eyes me with hatred and boiling rage as I remain silent, determined to let her hang herself.

"Karen Knight. Karen saw Rose buy a pregnancy test at the drugstore. Your little innocent missus is a husband-stealer wreaking destruction wherever she goes, and now she's caught. That's why she disappeared. That's why you're hiding her. I'm going to take you for everything—alienation of affection and infidelity—if you don't come to your senses and drop your demands for a divorce. It's like you're in a cult, Jahi. You're entranced, brainwashed by *that woman*. Get rid of her. I demand you get rid of her!" She's screaming, and people in the park are staring.

I remain silent, and she starts in again, taunting me. "Has she muted you? Are you so far gone you don't have a voice, heck, a brain?"

"Enough." I bark the word through gritted teeth.

"I warn you. I'm coming after you if you don't agree and get her out of your life," she hisses like the snake she is.

"All right," I say, my voice so eerily calm it unsettles her. She looks at me with her reptilian eyes, startled. I continue dispassionately, surprising even myself by what I say next. "Sure. If you insist."

A glint of glee flits across her eyes, as if victory is near. Her demeanor transforms to the slithering seductress, like she switched channels on the television station, forever the actress. I swallow hard, relishing what's coming next. She looks at me, expectant, perhaps imagining I'll grovel and apologize, begging her eternal forgiveness, vowing to right the wrongs she perceives I've inflicted on her.

"Sure, if you insist," I repeat for emphasis. A smile forms on her ruby lips, and her eyes soften. "I have a question, Susanne. If you insist on staying together and continuing our marriage, does this include your other daughter?"

She recoils, her eyes bulging, and she's struck mute as she gasps.

I launch into a tirade. "You've been cheating on me for years. Years," I state firmly, emphasizing the word. "At beauty school." She shakes her head, her shoulders crumpling. "And Las Vegas? All those weekend girl's trips to Vegas? Wasn't that where you met up with your Chicago lover?"

"No, Jahi, no!" she screams, her hands on her face, her mouth wide open. "You don't understand. Please." She looks at me with desperation as her voice trails off.

I continue, relentless in my pursuit of taking her down once and for all. I have not one ounce of empathy left for her. "You have a daughter with that bozo, a *daughter* you abandoned just like you abandoned Lily. You drove drunk with your baby, just as you were planning to do with Lily, but you got caught in both instances. There's a pattern here, Susanne. A pattern of infidelity, child abandonment, child endangerment, and two DUIs, *two*, and those are just the ones where they caught you. You've lived a secret life for years. A life of lies and deception. You're evil. You're an evil woman and I want you out of my life."

"How do you know this? You're lying," she screams, changing tack, her eyes wild and desperate.

"We have evidence." I raise my hand in the air to signal Chad. She stares at my attorney, a rugged man rapidly closing in with his imposing stride. I get some small joy out of seeing her shocked by how he's marching toward her like a five-star general. "This is my attorney, Chad Murphy." Chad nods as Susanne stares blankly at him. "Let's just say he went to Yale Law School and has connections all over the country, especially in Chicago." As I'm saying this to her, her face blanches, and he steps behind her and signals me, waving the divorce papers. This is my chance. This is the moment I've been waiting for, for years.

She gulps, and her face turns even whiter, as if she knows what's coming. "Please, Jahi, please," she pleads with her eyes, like a prisoner on a death march, begging for mercy, but this is the moment of no return, and I go for the jugular.

"You don't have a case, Susanne. I suggest you sign these papers right here, right now, and bow out of my life."

"Yes, young lady, I suggest you sign off on this divorce," Chad says in his most menacing lawyer voice.

Susanne slumps forward, eyes downcast, her body shaking violently as if she's about to have a grand mal seizure. Chad shoves the papers and a pen at her, and she signs in her hen scratch signature, holding the documents on her thigh. She stands, the pen and papers dropping to the moist ground as she strides away without meeting my eyes.

CHAPTER ELEVEN

ROSE

The nightmares are increasing in intensity. Last night I was flying out of LAX across the Pacific and the plane was a Russian experimental aircraft, an ekranoplan, that flies ten feet over the water, riding the cushion of air compressed between wing and water. I must have seen this plane in a documentary because I'm not an aviation person at all. I was yelling at the pilot, "We're too low, go higher, go higher" and when he turned to me, his face melted into Susanne's and she laughed wickedly, making the plane pitch up and down, terrorizing me. "Stop it, Susanne. Stop it. You're going to kill us both!" I screamed hysterically. I woke up startled, anxiety breaking through, disrupting my sleep.

"Hey Rose," my sister says softly, tapping on my door. "Can I come in?"

"Sure, Bea." My voice is shaky as I wrap myself in my white cotton robe. "What's up?"

"I heard something last night, so I came into your room, and you were whimpering and breathing fast. It seems you had another nightmare."

"Yeah, I did. It was a nightmare about Susanne flying a plane over the water, taunting me. I've been having a lot of wild and wooly dreams lately. The common theme is my life being in danger."

"That makes sense," my sister says thoughtfully. "That DVT scared you and finding out about Factor V Leiden didn't help matters, either. I mean, it's good to find out you have this condition and can manage it, but it's also worrisome."

"What if I die in childbirth, Bea?" Beads of sweat form on my brow and upper lip. The room is hot and closing in on me.

"You're not going to. Mom survived, even though they didn't know why she had preeclampsia. You've got a brilliant doctor. She knows what she's doing. I've researched her. She's the best, one of the top in her field nationally. If you go down that path, she can manage it with medication."

"I don't know, Bea. I just don't know."

It's dusk. The wind is howling. The big black walnut tree is swaying and threatening to snap. I'm climbing over fallen branches, my swollen belly about to burst. I'm alone. My vision is a kaleidoscope of blurriness, flashing lights, and moving spots. I have a throbbing headache, and my ankles feel swollen, like inflated balloons. Oh no! This must be what happened to Mom when she was pregnant with Bea. Now it's happening to me. No one is here but me, not Bea, not Mom, not Jahi. This is it. It's what I was afraid of. Dying. I'm too young to die! I sit up abruptly, short of breath, and find myself in a dark room, disoriented. Where am I? Whose room is this? Is this the end? A light appears somewhere. Is that the light they talk about when you leave your body?

"Rose?" A voice reaches me, as if from some distant land. It's Bea.

"What?" I respond, confused. "Where am I?"

"Rose, you had another nightmare," she whispers as she caresses my forehead. "I heard you calling out again."

"Bea. I was dying. Just like Mom almost did when she was pregnant with you. This feels like an omen. Maybe our great-grandmother, Hattie Osborn, is sending messages to me, warning me."

"Rose, I don't think so. You told me about the Greek Chorus as you called it, and you said our ancestors, especially our great-grandmother Hattie and many others who passed before us, told you that you're meant to have this baby. It's your fate. You've got to have faith, Rose."

I'm terrified. I don't know what it is. Some factors that, alone, wouldn't stop me, but combined cause a state of overwhelm. It's everything. It's Dad's disappearance, the horrible marriage with Lee, the divorce, the feeling of failure, the move from LA, starting over in Eureka Springs, falling in love with a married man, Lily's accident, the surprise pregnancy, Susanne's threats and now this, the DVT and Factor V Leiden diagnosis, to top it off. I think it's all these elements combined that lead me to the conviction that I'm going to die.

I just can't shake it. No amount of support or encouragement or rational arguments from Jahi or Bea or Jolene can shake my fixed belief that I'm doomed.

Oh dear! Did I say fixed belief? Am I devolving into mental illness? I rub my temples and stare at the floor in a kind of trance. *Am I going to get postpartum psychosis?* I remember learning about delusions in grad school. A delusion is a fixed false belief based on inaccurate interpretations of what is real, what is reality, no matter the evidence to the contrary. *Great. Besides the ominous feeling of dying in childbirth, there's the added concern of mental deterioration. Will Jahi still love me if I become psychotic and can't take care of the baby? Maybe this happened to Susanne, too, but I can't think about her right now because she's dangerous.*

I could die. Maybe I should talk to Dr. Mason about whether this pregnancy is such a good idea, at my age and with my genetics.

Maybe Dad had some kind of mental breakdown, perhaps bipolar with psychosis, and I'm at risk for breaking down, too.

I call Dr. Mason's office. The receptionist, Deidre, says she can squeeze me in at four o'clock today. The rest of the morning and early afternoon I spend scrubbing the kitchen and living room floors, sweeping, mopping, dusting, doing laundry, and organizing my papers.

"My, you're a busy bee. I've heard about this nesting instinct of pregnant mommas," Bea says, bemused as she appears in the living room.

"Oh, I guess so," I laugh. "I hadn't thought of it that way."

"You're going to be a wonderful mother, Rose. I just know it."

"Hmm, I hope so." My voice drifts off, guilt eating at me. Little does my sister know I'm going to see Dr. Mason today to discuss whether I should continue with this pregnancy, given my risk factors.

"You seem preoccupied, sort of dreamy. But maybe that's part of pregnancy too, a kind of dreamland," she muses.

"Well, my dreamland includes plenty of nightmares," I joke.

My sister laughs and drops the subject. We eat a light lunch, a tossed salad loaded with garbanzo beans, mushrooms, tomatoes, pumpkin seeds, walnuts, and olives. Mom is napping, so she doesn't join us.

When it's time to leave for the clinic, I fib to Bea. I don't want to deceive her, but I need to face this alone. "Hey, I'm going to go out for a bit to get some fresh air. I'll be back in about an hour," I say breezily, not wanting my sister to suspect I'm seeing the doctor, because she'll want to come along.

"Oh, okay. Have fun. I've got to wake up Mom. She's been asleep all day. I'll see you when you get back," she says, distracted as she puts our dishes in the dishwasher and wipes the table.

"Thanks, B. I'll see you soon."

Dr. Mason sees me in her office in my street clothes rather than the generic patient gown. I'm wearing a flowered summer dress, lime green espadrilles and a white cotton cardigan because medical offices can be as cold as refrigerators. She's wearing a vintage Bruins t-shirt, shorts, and her signature Birkenstocks.

"Oh, that's a cool vintage t-shirt. That's from UCLA. Did you go there?" I exclaim, warming up for the conversation ahead and surprised to see my alma mater all the way out here in Razorback country, curious to know if she's an alumna, too.

"Yes, I sure did. Undergraduate and medical school. I finished thirty-three years ago. I'm an old lady," she laughs, lines wrinkling at the corners of her warm brown eyes, eyes betraying beauty and sorrow, having borne witness to moments of elation and untold despair. Birth is dynamic, mercurial. It takes a special doctor, a certain personality, to face these unpredictable elements. It's been this way since time immemorial. Even now, women die in childbirth and babies are stillborn. Heck, maternal mortality keeps rising.

"Wow. Small world. I went there, too, for undergrad and to get my PhD in Psychology. And my dad was a professor of chemistry there." My words get in front of my intention, and that last fact slips out before I can stop it. *Why did I say that?* My face flushes with embarrassment. I hope she doesn't know him.

"Oh, my gosh!" her face lights up. "I took biochemistry from your dad at med school. Dr. Aberdeen! I remember him well. I see the resemblance," she says, peering at me. "He was brilliant," she gushes. Meanwhile, my right leg rocks violently. I put my hand on my knee to force it to stop, which only tamps it down to a smaller tremble. Maybe she doesn't know about his disappearance. I brace myself, praying this conversation doesn't go off the rails.

I notice a shadow flit across her face so quickly I almost miss it, like the brief darkening of a sidewalk when an airplane flies in front of the sun. A dark flash. I search her face, but her expression is inscrutable, though I notice a flush of red on her neck. She's a pro. She knows not to break the glass shield of medical formality.

Dr. Mason takes a deep breath. "So, how are you doing?" she starts, pausing before continuing. Those first seconds with a patient can be awkward, as I've noticed in my own clinical experience. "It sounds like there's some urgency to see me today," she ventures, raising her left eyebrow.

I sigh. "I've been worried about my pregnancy," I begin, not sure how I'm going to describe to her in a few short sentences the complexity of how I'm feeling. I think about how to say this. I know words are everything. How you say something, how you frame it, makes it take on a life of its own.

"Tell me about your concerns."

"I'm having nightmares about dying, and I'm wondering if my body is trying to tell me something," I say with some hesitation. *Am I starting this conversation right?*

"I think it's natural to be anxious, Rose. Many women feel that way as pregnancy progresses, and they get closer to delivery. They worry about the pain of labor, how the delivery will go, and whether their baby will be healthy. For most mothers in a safe environment with a well-monitored pregnancy, things go well, no matter what the risks are." Dr. Mason leans forward, speaking softly but with authority. "You're not alone, Rose."

"What worries me is that my situation is risky," I assert, not deterred by Dr. Mason's soothing words and calm demeanor. "Not only am I older than most women giving birth, but I have a clotting disorder on top of it. And now I'm on a blood thinner because of a DVT. Doesn't that put me at a higher risk for potentially lethal complications?"

"Yes, technically it does," she says, speaking slowly, choosing her words carefully. "But we're going to take care of this. We've all heard horror stories, but the fact is, most pregnancies and deliveries go smoothly. I've treated thousands of pregnant women over the years, including women with pre-eclampsia and eclampsia. We can manage this in the hospital."

I don't mention my worries about postpartum psychosis. It's too close to the bone. She might put two and two together and make the connection between my obsession with thoughts of dying and Dad's erratic behavior at UCLA, leading to his disappearance. I don't want her to write me off and dismiss my concerns because she thinks I'm being neurotic, or worse, that I have a major mental illness and could become psychotic.

"Even with intervention, if I get pre-eclampsia or, God forbid, eclampsia, I could die," I say simply.

"That's true, but unlikely. You will not die, Rose," she asserts in her doctorly voice.

"Childbirth, even in these times, is risky business. The research shows this," I continue, not assuaged by her authority. I'm a doctor, too, though of a different kind, but I can analyze the data.

"But Rose, we deal with complications every day and most women survive," she insists, her voice rising.

"I had a colleague whose sister, during the birth of her second baby, went into shock. Clots formed everywhere. She had fulminating DIC—disseminated intravascular coagulation. All her platelets and clotting factors got consumed, and she ended up hemorrhaging. They kept her alive in the ICU until he could get there and kiss his sister goodbye."

Dr. Mason grimaces. I can tell she's surprised I know the

lingo, the medical language preserved for physicians. But I was married to a doctor for ten years, and I know the lexicon. "That's so sad. I'm so sorry for your colleague. That's devastating."

The room falls silent. Dr. Mason looks at me unblinking, her lips pressed together as if she doesn't know what to say.

"We both know I could die. There are no guarantees I'll survive this," I insist, ever the statistician, something that was drilled into me in graduate school. I'm sure I'm unlike most of her patients who defer to her judgment without question.

Understanding that she's dealing with an intellectual peer, she pivots to statistical logic. "You have a point about the risks, but Rose, your chances of dying in a car accident are much greater than dying in childbirth, even with all of your risk factors. If you want to reduce risk, stop driving," she drones on. This is getting tiresome, and I'm deaf to anything else she says, as last night's nightmare flashes in my mind.

"I can't continue with this pregnancy," I blurt, snapping out of my flashback.

Dr. Mason blinks at my eruption, her chin set, showing her disagreement with my words. This is a woman used to landing on her feet.

Her shoulders remain squared. She tried everything to assuage my fears and doubts, but to no avail.

Does she think she's failed?

I leave the office with an appointment.

The procedure will be in two days at the hospital.

PART 7

CHAPTER ONE

ROSE

"No! No. Rose, you've got to fight. Fight for your baby. Fight for Daisy, look at her Rose. Look at your daughter!" Beatrice is holding my hand and crying, but I can't react. I can't squeeze her hand back and tell her to stop yelling because I can't speak. I'm paralyzed.

"I'm so sorry, Beatrice. The bleeding was too much and the pre-eclampsia led to eclampsia. She's in a coma," I hear Dr. Mason explain to my sister. I turn my head to look at her, but my head won't move. I try to tell them I'm okay and not in a coma, but I can't move any part of my body. My sister throws herself at me, wailing and commanding me to open my eyes and prove them wrong.

My eyes are open, B, I try to tell her, but my mouth won't form the words. I decide I need to relax and process my environment. A nurse is holding a beautiful baby girl near me, cleaning and wrapping her in a blanket, my daughter. We decided on the name Daisy a few months back. Another nurse is cleaning me up and tidying the bed. *I must raise my hands.* As if by the power of suggestion, my hands move, but not the hands on the bed.

I'm no longer lying on the bed. This must be an O.B.E.—an out-of-body experience. This is my first time experiencing something like this, even though I know about it from my psychology studies at UCLA. A sound behind me makes me cut my eyes to the side, and I see Jahi burst into the room.

"Where is she? What happened? What about our baby?" he demands, looking at Dr. Mason.

"Please calm down, Mr. Adams. Your daughter is being cleaned and wrapped in a blanket by the nurse behind you. But unfortunately, Rose is not in great shape. The delivery had complications, and she's in a coma."

"Co-? Coma? What? Why? Oh my God, Rose." He falls to his knees and weeps, pulling at his hair from roots to tips.

I watch the scene below me, and I will myself to touch Jahi. Some sort of magnetic field pulls me into my body lying still on the bed and I settle in, disoriented for a minute as I wait for the cloud to lift.

I try signaling with my hands again, but they feel leaden. After many attempts, I'm able to raise my hand weakly, raising it only a few seconds before it falls back on the bed.

A nurse hears the dull thump of my hand hitting the mattress and alerts the doctor. Everyone in the room goes berserk.

"Rose?" My sister's high-pitched, anxious voice echoes as if we're in a dark cave.

"Rose?" Jahi's plaintive plea joins in with my sister and causes me to choke on my saliva. A nurse pushes a tube down my throat to clear out mucus, and I gag.

Dr. Mason touches my hand and studies the monitors. The world blurs as a distant voice calls to me. A powerful force pulls me to the unknown voice.

Wait. This voice is familiar. It's my sister. I squint and bring her face into focus and blink twice to clear the film over my eyes.

"Rose, are you awake? Are you okay?" Her voice is back to its normal resonant tone, not the squeaky one from a moment ago.

"Yes. I'm okay. What's wrong?" I ask her, stifling a yawn.

"You were whimpering in your dream, calling my name and Jahi's, too. I heard you while I checked on Mom."

"Oh. It's just another dream." I look away. I can't tell her about the nightmare. She'll just brush it away and pass it off as my fears of pregnancy playing tricks on me.

"Oh dear. Sorry about that. Do you want to tell me about it?"

"Not sure I can remember it," I hesitate, but continue throwing her a bone. "I guess you and Jahi were in the dream. That's why I called out your names." I have to explain that much, so she lets me off the hook.

"Okay." She looks unconvinced. "Do you still want to sleep more?"

"No. I'm awake now. I'll take a shower, then join you in the living room. After that, I might go for a drive alone to clear my head." I give her a wan smile. She purses her lips and leaves.

Of course, it won't be an ordinary drive. All the omens I've seen about this pregnancy are enough to tell me I can't continue with it. There are too many complications and uncertainties. It's not something I can risk. I take my shower and a half hour later, I'm out of the house driving to the hospital.

Hospitals have never agreed with me. During my clinical rotations as a psychology intern at UCLA, I preferred the outpatient clinics to the locked inpatient hospital wards. There's something about the cold architecture, antiseptic smells, and seeing sick people and families in despair wandering the fluorescently lit halls that makes me want to avoid it altogether. But I've got no other choice.

Only a hospital can perform the procedure I've come here for. I wish things were different, but Jahi's current situation, being married to another woman, is another reason I should go through with what I'm thinking.

I walk through the sliding doors of the hospital, like I'm walking through the gates of hell, but instead of fire and endless toil, I'm met with cold sterility, an updated, modern version of hell. Instead of sulfur and smoke, I smell isopropyl alcohol and iodine.

Robert Frost comes to mind. *Some say the world will end in fire, some say in ice. From what I've tasted of desire, I hold with those who favor fire.* I think of my desire for Jahi and how it has left me in this predicament, this place where *my world* is ending.

But if it had to perish twice, I think I know enough of hate to say that for destruction ice. Is also great. And will suffice. When I think of all the problems leading me to this devastating moment, Susanne's icy vengeance and unwillingness to give Jahi a divorce tops the list.

Entering the hospital, I begin a one-way trip from this reality to the next. Two of us are entering the gates, but only one will exit. As Dante said in *The Inferno*, "Abandon all hope, ye who enter here."

What am I doing? Should I turn back before it's too late? This is irreversible. Can I live with myself, with my decision? But then again, if I die in pregnancy, I won't be living with myself, either.

I'm cold to the bone and the frigid air-conditioning makes my teeth chatter. A sudden flush of heat rises in my face and my head feels heavy, like the walls are closing in. I grab the nearest chair and bend down to sit, feeling faint and nauseous. A young man with a mop of fiery red hair rushes to my side.

"Ma'am, are you okay? You look pale. I'm Tom. I'm here to help you." His name tag says Tom Barton, and he looks no older than eighteen, his light skin sprinkled with freckles over his nose, his electric blue eyes conveying warmth.

"I think so. Thank you, Tom. I'm just nervous." My voice is so faint, I hardly recognize it.

"Oh, are you here to be admitted?" His eyes widen as he scans my body. I'm healthy, and he's probably trying to figure out why I'm here.

"Yes, I am." My voice trembles as I realize everything I do from this moment forward is moving me closer to an irreversible action I may regret for the rest of my life.

"What's your name? I'll get you registered." Tom pats my arm like I need reassurance. He must sense my emotional state.

"Rose," I state, like a child, as if that's all he needs to know. A memory flashes in my mind of me at age four, telling a Sunday school teacher that my name was Rosie. When she asked for my last name, I thought about it and answered, "Posie. Rosie Posie." The woman stifled a laugh, and we carried on. I snap back to the present when the young man clears his throat and tilts his head, looking expectant. I realize he wants me to say my full name, something I'm reluctant to do. *Why am I hiding? Why am I avoiding saying my name?* Looking around before I move closer to his face, I whisper, "Rose Aberdeen."

"Okay, stay here. I'll be back in a moment." Tom whispers back as if privy to a secret. He retrieves a wheelchair from a utility room and returns. I stand too quickly and sway. He steadies me, helping me into the wheelchair before wheeling me to the front desk. "Yes, I see your name here on the computer. Okay. I'll take you to the fourth floor, and the nurses will get you settled into your room, room 402."

When I arrive on the fourth floor, the receptionist looks up and asks me to sign papers for the procedure. As I scan down the page, I see it includes a question about next of kin contact information, in case of an emergency. I panic. No one knows I'm here.

As I look over the paperwork, the receptionist peers over her reading glasses and asks if there's anyone to take me home after the procedure, and I answer yes a little too quickly. She raises a skeptical eyebrow.

I'm alone. Somehow, in the turmoil of the last two days, I

forgot about that detail of who will take me home.

I state Beatrice Aberdeen as my next of kin, though technically it should be my mother, but then again, Mom is terribly ill and I don't want them contacting her if anything happens to me.

My hands shake as I sign off with a scribbled signature, like I don't want anyone to identify me in the future. Being admitted to my room is a blur, but when I get settled, I think of Bea.

What if something terrible happens to me? I've been worried that the pregnancy and delivery will kill me, but what if the procedure does? Were all potential complications discussed with me? I can't remember. This isn't like me to be so impulsive. I better call Bea.

I call my sister and she picks up on the first ring, like she's waiting for me.

"Hey sis. How is your drive?"

"Bea, I'm in the hospital." I try to sound matter-of-fact, but my voice breaks when I think of Bea.

"Why?" Bea's voice rises and then she falls silent for a few seconds as she's taking this in. "What's wrong, Rose? Are you okay?"

"I'm fine, it's just that…" I hesitate. How am I going to tell her what I'm doing? She won't accept it, I'm sure. I shore up my courage and blurt, "I can't do this anymore, Bea. There are too many risks and I'm terrified."

"Rose! What are you saying?" Bea is shrieking. "You're not going to…"

"I'm having a procedure." I interrupt her mid-sentence, the words spilling out of me at high velocity as if this will set it in stone.

"No!" she growls, her voice deep, like she's some sort of wild animal.

I counter her emotion by sounding robotic, my voice strangely devoid of emotion. "This is a procedure. Something could happen to me. I need you to know, just in case."

Bea shrieks hysterically, "No, no!"

"Bea," I say flatly, my voice mirroring my numb and dissociated state. "I could die if I keep going... my life is at risk."

Mom overhears the ruckus and asks, "What's going on, Bea?"

Their voices become muffled, like my sister is covering the phone with her hand. "She's afraid she's going to get sick like you did when you were pregnant with me. She's terrified she'll die in childbirth. I'm afraid she's going to end it, Mom. I'm begging her not to, but she won't listen."

"Put me on the phone," Mom demands.

Uh oh. What is she going to say?

"Rose Catherine Aberdeen, it's your mother." *Oh no, this is bad—she's using my full name.* "You can't do this. Don't do this to me." *There's the guilt trip.* "I'm dying. This is my one and only grandbaby," Mom begs, her voice cracking in desperation.

"Oh Mom, I'm so sorry," I begin plaintively, my mother's anguish breaking through my numbness, tears spilling onto my cheeks. I'm sickened that I'm doing this to her at the end of her life. *Why am I so selfish?*

"Please, Rose. Please. Just come home. Walk out of there," Mom commands. She knows she's getting to me.

I almost change my mind and obey her, but my words betray the opposite. "I can't, Mom. What if I die?"

"Come home. You won't die. We'll take care of you and the baby. We'll figure it out. I'm sending Bea over there now," Mom states in her adamant voice, as if she's a five-star general, and she's taking over. I don't know where Mom found this sudden source of energy.

"No, Mom. Don't. I'm so sorry." Desperation builds, and now I'm the one beseeching her with my voice.

Mom switches gears and mirrors my desperation in her tone. "Please, Rose, I'm begging you."

"Mom, I love you. I'm so sorry, but I've got to go." Just before I hang up, I hear Bea mention Jahi. I can't decipher what she's saying, but it sounds like she's telling Mom she's calling Jahi. I hang up on my sister abruptly, or this call will never end.

CHAPTER TWO

JAHI

I miss my darling Rose since she moved to Fayetteville a week ago. My internal state matches the bare trees and brown landscape outside the window, the winter of my discontent. I didn't expect that being away from her would be so difficult. Every night since she left has got me tossing and turning, wishing I could share my bed with her, dreaming of holding her and breathing in her scent. It's funny considering I can count the number of nights we've spent together, but I've kinda gotten used to her. She's addictive.

But I'm glad she's away from the prying eyes and meddling busybodies of Eureka Springs. Especially those one or two nosy residents who wouldn't think twice about giving Susanne updates about the pregnancy and my relationship with Rose. *Don't they have anything better to do?*

Even though I call Rose every night, it's not the same as seeing her in person and holding her in my arms. Lily misses her too and asks after her. I cross my fingers that rumors don't leak out about her pregnancy. Even though Susanne has gone *incognito* since she signed the divorce papers, I need to keep this news about the pregnancy hush-hush until the judge signs off on the divorce.

One thing concerning me is how tired she sounds when I call. I assure her she'll feel better when she's in her second trimester, but she doesn't seem convinced. Her voice is faint. Sometimes I don't know what to say since she isn't confiding in me much.

She's mostly monosyllabic whenever we talk.

It's Friday and I'm sitting in the reception area munching the blueberries Matt brought from home. I look up when I hear the clomp of heavy boots approaching.

"Hey buddy. How's it going?" Matt asks as he plops onto the chair beside me and makes a grab for some berries. I slap his hand away with a raised brow.

"Hey, I brought those, remember?" he grumbles, furrowing his blond brows at me.

"Yes, well, you brought them for me. They're mine now, so you've got to ask permission before pawing at my berries." I smirk at his slack jaw.

"You gotta be kidding me."

"No kidding. Ask permission first," I return, pulling the plastic bowl containing the berries away from him and hiding it behind my back, out of his reach.

"Oh, you sneaky caveman! Fine. May I have some berries, please?" he finally agrees.

"You can't," I assert, doing my best to maintain a straight face.

He guffaws and sputters incoherently. I'm sure he's wondering what has gotten into me. I burst out laughing when I can't contain it anymore.

"I'm just toying with you." I quickly dodge when he tries to smack the back of my head.

"You got me there, man. I wondered what got into you for a minute." He chuckles and takes the bunch of berries I offer him.

"Yeah, I'm just bored. It's a slow day. What's the update from the chief?"

"The chief says one of us can go home early." He stands and leans his lanky body on the doorframe, his arms crossed as he nods at me. "Why don't you go ahead?"

"What about you?" He's always got my back, so maybe I

should be the same type of friend to him. "It's Friday. Wouldn't you like to start your weekend early?"

"Nah. Nothing much going on at home." A mischievous grin forms on his lips. "Besides, I've got an idea."

"What's that?"

"Why don't you pick up Lily from school and bring her over to my house? Jane and I will keep her this weekend."

I raise my eyebrows, wondering if he's talked to Jane about this or if he's just making plans for her. If he is, I'm going to have to set him straight. "Does Jane know about your idea?"

"Oh yeah. I just called her, and she loves it," he gushes.

"I have a feeling you've got an agenda for me."

"What makes you think that?" Matt cocks his eyebrow and chuckles. "Yeah, well, I guess I'm easy to read, huh?"

"Like a book. So, what's the plot?"

"It occurs to me you haven't seen Rose all week. Why don't you surprise her?"

"That's true… but how?"

"Go see her. She'll love it. Take her some roses from your garden."

"It's not the season for roses, but I've got pansies and violets in pots."

"Or you could take her chocolate. You need to spend time with her, Jahi. It's difficult being pregnant. Jane reminded me of this. And it's her first pregnancy, right?"

"Right..." The word gets drawn out, and Matt notices my hesitation but says nothing. *Did I give it away? I don't like to lie, but this truth of Rose's past pregnancies is hers to share, not mine.* I don't mention the miscarriages and technically, she's never been this far along in a pregnancy.

"So, you'll do it, right?" Matt breaks the silence as if nothing happened. He never wants to cause me pain.

"Okay. Thanks, Matt. I'll do it." Matt's one of the best friends I've ever had, and sometimes he's like a father figure. Who knew a surfer dude from California would feature so largely in my life?

I wait outside Lily's school in the pickup line in my car, the only man amongst a sea of mothers. I hear about gender equality and house-husbands, but I'm not seeing it. Maybe that's only on the coasts, not here in the South. The bell rings and Lily skips outside, the sun glinting off her bouncing pigtails. She looks surprised when she sees me. Lately, Chrissy has been picking her up and keeping her until I get off work.

"Bonjour, Papa," she says in a soft voice and smiles coyly.

"Where did you learn French?" I ask, delighted to hear this from my little girl.

"Aunt Chrissy. She's teaching me."

"She's a fancy one, that's for sure. And you are, too."

"Yes! And I have sparkly shoes, too, like Aunt Chrissy." Lily squeals in delight.

"You sure do," I glance down and admire her red sparkly shoes, and Lily taps them together three times like Dorothy in *The Wizard of Oz*. "Guess what? I've got a surprise for you." I build suspense, and Lily's eyes widen in anticipation. "You're going to stay with Uncle Matt, Aunt Jane, and the kids this weekend."

"Yay!!" Lily jumps up and down, performs a happy dance, and gives me a big hug.

After delivering Lily to Jane, I drive home and change out of my uniform into a pair of jeans and a green polo shirt. I look in the mirror to see if I need to shave, but decide against it. Rose likes it when I have a bit of stubble on my face. She says it rubs her the right way.

I step out into my garden. This is rosehip season. I collect rosehips for their seeds and for breeding future roses. Rose loves rosehip tea, so I snip seven of them for her. Seven is one of Rose's favorite numbers, along with the number two, but I've heard that even numbers of flowers or buds are bad luck. Prime numbers are best, signaling indivisibility in relationships. Two is a special case, both prime and even, enigmatic, like love relationships. I like that idea. That's Rose and me. But seven wins out because it's more generous.

I walk back into the kitchen and see the copies of the divorce papers. Chad made ten copies, just in case we need them, which I think is over the top, but that's Chad. I grab one copy and wrap it around the rosehips, tie it with a string, and head out for Fayetteville on the southern route.

As I drive along the winding, hilly road with its gentle rounded landscape of forested hills and sinuous valleys, the last of the fall color gone, it reminds me of Rose's glowing face and her voluptuous body, imagining it filling out as the pregnancy progresses. I sing *You Are My Sunshine*, the song Rose sings to our baby, and that Mom sang to me.

My phone buzzes, but I ignore it. It buzzes again. And again. I keep ignoring it, but I'm getting annoyed. I want time with Rose without interruptions. Don't they remember I'm not on call this weekend? The insistence of the buzzing causes me to pull over in a town called Claifty, on the slim chance there's any issue with Lily.

Hmm... I don't recognize this number. There are eight missed calls and a slew of texts from that same number.

I listen to the first missed call's voice message.

"Hello Jahi, I'm Rose's sister, Bea." I'm struck by the similarity of her voice to Rose's. The pitch is different, but they both have that same sugar-sweet drawl. I'm not sure how they maintained it, growing up in LA, but it must be because the mother is from Tomahawk, Arkansas. "It's about Rose. There's an emergency, and she won't listen to us. You need to call her." Her voice becomes more high-pitched and frantic. "Call Rose right now and tell her not to do it," she pleads. I sit there in my car, frozen, not sure what I'm going to hear next.

I listen to the next missed call and hear a mix of her voice and their mother's voice.

"Bea, you should be specific, so he'll know exactly what Rose is about to do." This must be Rose's mother.

"Yes, Mom. I'll tell him now." She pauses before continuing, "Jahi, Rose has gone to the hospital to have a procedure. It's all over. Please call..." There's a beep, beep, beep, and then the message ends.

I shiver, my heart in my throat, my hands shaking. I see darkness everywhere. My fingers shake violently as I tap the recent call and Bea picks up on the first ring.

Bea is sobbing hysterically, and I can barely decipher what she's saying. "Hello, Jahi! Oh, thank God. Mom?!! It's Jahi on the phone." Beatrice's frantic voice booms. I ignore the discomfort of my ringing ears and focus on the sound of their voices. "Rose... it's Rose... she's in the hospital."

"Oh dear God, no. Is she alright? Is she bleeding, is she conscious, is she stable, is the baby okay?" Panicked, my words tumble out in rapid succession.

"No." That singular word upends my world.

"What?!" I gasp, barely able to breathe, much less speak.

"She's ending the pregnancy."

There it is. The end. The end of everything that is precious.

"No! No!!!" The words echo, bouncing off the bony chamber of my skull, my mind wild with desperation, barely comprehending what she's saying, a waterfall of tears pouring down my face.

"Jahi, you've got to talk to her. Talk her out of this. She's not rational. She won't listen to me," she pleads.

"Please tell me she has the baby," I say, tears streaming down my cheeks without control.

"She says she can't continue with the pregnancy because of her health complications, so she's gone to the hospital. And she won't listen to any of us when we try to convince her to hold on and have faith. She's not being rational. The doctor assured her she can have a safe delivery, but she's convinced she'll die in childbirth. Call her and talk her out of this, Jahi. Oh God, I hope it's not too late," she cries, wracked with despair.

"Complications? Too late?! No!!! No, no, no! Oh God. I'll call her now." My paramedic voice kicks in, but inside, I'm terrified. *I can't lose Rose or the baby. I can't let what happened to Dad haunt me forever and live my life in fear of death, of the ones I love.* Time is of the essence. *I must get to her and stop this unfolding tragedy.*

My mind reels from the news. Rose didn't mention encountering serious complications because of the pregnancy, aside from morning sickness and weakness.

I hang up, my mind racing. I call Rose, but she doesn't pick up. And then I call again. Nothing. Again. Nothing. It goes to voicemail. I change tactics and text her.

Rose, please answer me.

I'm screaming inside.

Nothing.

I text her: *Rose, please keep our baby. Please don't end it.*

I write text after text, unable to stop myself. Frantic, my hands shaking so violently I can barely type the words. She's not answering anything. *Is her phone off? Is she having the procedure right now?*

I call Bea and tell her I'm racing to the hospital and that I'm already past Claifty.

"Bea, where is she? What room is she in?"

"I think she's on the fourth floor."

"Okay."

"Drive safely, Jahi."

I don't heed Bea's cautionary words. I race over the hills, tires chirping on the turns. Good thing I know this road and I got new tires last month. A siren screams behind me. I look in my rearview mirror and see flashing lights.

"Oh dear God, not now," I howl, as if my torso is being pierced through with a spear.

I pull over and roll down my window. My hand lands heavily on the horn, blaring it unintentionally. In my side mirror, I see a beefy man with an attitude walking stiffly towards me. When he peers in, I'm surprised to see Sheriff Brett Hamilton. He's just as surprised to see me.

He stares in disbelief. "Jahi, what in the *world* are you doing?" His voice rises an octave as he frowns.

"Brett, it's Rose. She's in the hospital in Fayetteville." I'm breathless and desperate, like a man suffering a heart attack. My facade of donning my paramedic hat falls away. Now, I'm just a heartbroken and desperate man.

He knows something terrible is happening. He wastes no time with further questions.

"Let's go. Jump in my cruiser. Leave the fast driving to professionals!"

I obey. I'm mute. The siren is blaring. A kaleidoscope of roadside shapes and colors illuminated by the police car's lights flashes and reflects off the asphalt like light shimmering on a river's rapids—a river that only flows forwards, not backwards. Forward, to wherever my life is taking me next. The first ten miles are a blur of tears, the landscape shifting, my world disintegrating.

I call and text Rose frantically, but she doesn't answer.

"I got the divorce papers signed, Rose. Please don't give up. Please keep our baby." I say this in case she listens to her voicemail.

No answer.

My mind flashes back to pivotal moments in my life. The little whimper Lily made when she was born that reminded me of a newborn foal, the moment I first saw Rose's face and how she looked like Botticelli's Venus, the day in my rose garden when I showed her my old roses and told her about Big Daddy and Big Momma, the chess games and the look of surprise on Rose's face when I defeated her, the moment Rose told me she was pregnant... and the terrible day Dad collapsed and died in front of me when I was fifteen and there was nothing I could do. I feel like that now. Helpless. It's a feeling I've tried to avoid ever since.

I snap back as we approach Shady Grove. We're almost there. My life is about to change, for better or worse.

CHAPTER THREE

ROSE

I stand in my hospital gown, peering out the double-paned window of the procedure room, waiting for Dr. Mason.

My hand wanders the contours of my stomach, caressing it, feeling the gentle swell around my lower abdomen. As a child, I always admired pregnant women and wondered how it would feel to be pregnant, to have a baby bump.

I think back to Mrs. Maryann Donors, my high school friend Loveday Donors' mother. I remember when she became pregnant that summer after trying to conceive for several years, to no avail. My friend was an only child until her mother conceived again, after she had given up hope around her fortieth birthday. *Why do some dreams only come true after you've given up on them?* It was a miracle, and Loveday was so excited. I still remember her joy, and how radiant she looked all summer.

Mrs. Donors gladly allowed me to touch her stomach whenever the baby moved, but by then, my friend's attitude changed and she was no longer so keen on the baby. Mrs. Donors took us with her to shop for the unborn baby, buying onesies, colorful two pieces, matching socks and hats, tiny shoes, so many dresses and diapers. After shopping, she treated us to pizza and Coke at the pizza parlor.

I remember Loveday confiding one morning that she changed her mind and wished her mother wasn't pregnant. When I asked her why, she told me, "Mom's attention is all on the baby that's not even born yet. When she gives birth, do you know what will happen then?"

"But your mom has been trying to have another baby for years. That's why she's so excited. And you also told me you don't mind having a sibling. I think this is your wish coming true."

"Yes, well, I didn't expect her to get hyper-excited. I feel like she doesn't love me anymore."

"Oh, come on. Loveday, how can you claim that a mother's love can be turned off like a water faucet? I'm sure she still loves you."

"Well, it's how I feel."

"You're just worried. Mothers don't stop loving their children no matter what," I reassured her.

The day Mrs. Donors went to the hospital for the delivery, we were all so scared when her contractions started despite being prepared for the delivery. She was in her early forties, so her doctor considered her pregnancy a high-risk situation, but she was determined to have the baby.

We waited with her during the first twelve hours, all of us doing our best to help relieve her of the pains until her water broke and Mr. Donors drove her to the hospital.

Loveday told me she overheard her mom tell her dad a week before the delivery to take good care of her and the unborn baby in case she didn't make it. She told Mr. Donors to always tell Loveday how much she loves her. My friend had tears in her eyes as she confided this to me.

After receiving the call about the safe delivery of the baby and the well-being of the mother and child, I vividly recall my mother and me hurrying to the hospital to visit them. But when we got to her room, we came to a halt. The door was ajar and Mrs. Donors was hugging my friend as she held the newborn, crying and telling the two of them how much she loves them. Loveday had her arm around her mother as she caressed the newborn. She seemed content, hearing that her mother still loves her, despite having another baby. We slipped away quietly, leaving them to their togetherness.

I wonder why I can't love my child, no matter the difficult situation we're surrounded by. *A mother's love is unconditional. Where are my own motherly instincts? What am I doing here, trying to stop the natural thing from happening?*

I should keep this baby, but I fear dying during childbirth. Does a mother's unconditional love entail having to die for the baby? The doctor told me about the risks I face while carrying and having the baby. I have dreams for my life aside from having a family and being a mother. If being a mother poses a threat to the actualization of my other dreams, then my decision to discontinue the pregnancy should be valid.

Why then am I feeling guilty? I pace and then go back to look out the window.

What am I doing? Should I keep the baby or should I not? I've dreamt of being a mother all my life. This may be my last chance. I turned thirty-eight this year in Eureka Springs, but I don't want to die in childbirth, like Mom almost did.

What would my great-grandmother Hattie Osborn do? She was a healer, so what would she say? I only know her from stories handed down through the generations and from old family pictures. As a child, and especially after Dad disappeared, I stared at those photos for hours, mesmerized by Hattie's kind eyes, warm countenance, and petite frame. I imagined her voice and her smile and what it would feel like to be hugged and held against her warm bosom.

One photo of her hung in my bedroom. It felt like she watched over me. Sometimes I could swear her eyes followed me around the room. What would Hattie do if she were me and living in these times? Did she have clotting problems too, like Mom?

And Mom... is this going to break her heart? This is her one chance for a grandchild and here I am, ending it. It might keep her alive longer if she has a grandchild.

And Dad... what would he say, what would he think if he were here? If ever there's a time I need you, Dad, it's now. *Where are you?*

CHAPTER FOUR

JAHI

Brett careens around the curve of the semi-circular driveway at the hospital entrance. I jump out of the squad car and race inside the building, but not before grabbing the divorce papers wrapped around the seven rosehips, forgetting my phone and backpack in the passenger seat.

I hear Brett calling out to me, telling me to wait, but I pay him no mind and race through the sliding doors that are opening in slow motion, making me want to beat them down. All eyes are on me as I burst into the lobby and run up to the receptionist at the front desk, a ginger-haired teenager, and say breathlessly, "Where is she? Rose Aberdeen? What room is she in?"

He knows the answer by heart and reels off, "Fourth floor, room 402."

I'm about to bound up the stairs when a battle-ax administrator appears out of nowhere, all prim officiousness, notices the ruckus, and interferes with my mission.

"Excuse me, sir, calm down so I can help you find who you're looking for," she asserts with an air of supreme authority, her eyes darting across the room and back at me. She's probably looking to see if security is not far away. I will not hurt her. I just need to get to Rose.

"I am calm. I just need to see Rose Aberdeen," I assure her, but I don't even sound convincing to my own ears.

"Yes. I can see that. Please, who are you looking for again?" She's biding time. She's probably paranoid I'm going to hurt someone. "Come to the counter, so we can take the details." Her voice is professional with a practiced, soothing tone but backed by a steel spine. She hands me over to another administrator.

"Good evening, sir," she coos in a syrupy sweet southern drawl. "Can I help you with something?"

"Good evening. Yes, you may help me. I'm looking for Rose Aberdeen." I'm growing frantic as we waste more time. My voice is abrupt. She shifts into action, tapping her keyboard in a staccato rhythm. I'm sure she is used to curt and rude people. This is a hospital, after all.

"What is your relationship with Rose Aberdeen, sir?" She interrogates me.

"She's my fiancée, and she is pregnant with my child," I declare, wanting her to hurry and give me the go ahead. I already know where Rose is. I just need to get past this roadblock. But she simply nods and goes back to peering at her computer while tapping away. Then, after a while, she looks back at me.

"What is your name, sir?"

"Jahi. Jahi Adams." I clear my throat.

After a long pause, she says, "I'm sorry sir, but it does not list your name among her emergency contacts, and you are not her next of kin, so we can't give you any information. You'll have to go now and come back tomorrow afternoon during visiting hours. Then we'll ask her if she wants visitors before we let you into her room."

"What? No! No, it'll be too late by then. I have to see her now. Now!" My voice is growing frantic. "Listen. It is very important for me to see her right now and not tomorrow afternoon. Please," I beg the woman, using all my might to control myself because I'm on the verge of losing it.

"I understand, Mr. Adams, I do, but I can't help you. You'll have to come back tomorrow. I'm sorry." Her voice is resolute, and I collapse my head on her desk, but then I feel a hand on my shoulder. I look up and see Brett winking at me. He shows the woman his badge and asks for her supervisor. She brings back the battle-ax administrator, who looks peeved, but then surprised to see Brett standing beside me.

"Good evening, Alice. Of course you know who I am," Brett says in a friendly tone. "We already know the lady's room number. We just need to see her. Her immediate family requested we see her as soon as possible. Her mom is unwell and can't easily make the trip out here. Ms. Aberdeen is about to make a hasty decision that she'll regret for the rest of her life, and we want to avert that. Listen," he whispers as he looks around furtively. "I know this is against hospital rules, but I'm sure you can make an exception for meeee..." The word "me" rolls out of his lips seductively, and the iron lady, the one who was all rules and regulations a moment ago, blushes and lowers her lashes!

"Brett, I could get into trouble if this goes wrong," she drawls, purring like a kitten.

"In that case, I promise to get you out of trouble. Please, Alice?" His deep voice is velvety, radiating comfort like smooth bourbon beside a warm fire.

"Fine, I'll take your word for it. She's in room 402, but you already know that. Go to the fourth floor, take a right after the emergency exit and then another left. The second room," she finally tells us, nodding at me for my benefit. I nearly kiss Brett. While thanking him profusely, he shrugs me off and motions for me to go.

Rather than taking the elevator, which is slow and carries gurneys like it has all the time in the world, I bound up the stairs, two at a time, thankful I'm in decent shape, adrenaline fueling me like I'm plunging into an emergency fire situation.

I'm racing, running for our lives, Rose—yours, the baby's, Lily's, and mine. Please, don't do this to our little family, Rose. Please, let it not be too late. If I can just see you and tell you I got Susanne to sign the divorce papers, you'll change your mind. Please let the doctor be late.

I feel something warm on my right hand as I'm scanning the halls, searching frantically for Rose's room in the labyrinthine structure of the hospital. What a maze. How come hospitals are always like this? Are they designed by drunk committees after a collective bender? I zoned out when the battle-ax gave directions, but now I'm sorry I didn't listen.

My eyes hone in, like a hawk, on the room numbers, and I count them down. I must have come in from the other direction… 409, 408, 407… and finally I see 402 inscribed on a metal plate attached to the plaster wall beside the door.

My heart is in my throat. I glance down at my shaking hands and am surprised to see blood dotting the sheaf of divorce papers like irregular polka dots. There's a small puncture in the webbing between my index finger and the thumb of my left hand. It must have come from a thorn while I was inspecting the rose hips before I came here. *Susanne wounds me even now, like the sting in the tentacles of a dead jellyfish on the beach. Is this a bad omen? Seeing blood while trying to avoid bloodshed can't mean anything positive, can it? Oh God, I hope things go well. Please let no harm come to Rose and the baby.*

I remove the thorn and suck the blood from my hand before bursting into the room and finding Rose standing in a hospital gown, her back to me. I see her reflection in the glass staring forlornly out the window, mute and trance-like.

Fear grips my body, and my steps falter. She has done it. My eyes lose focus.

I'm too late.

CHAPTER FIVE

ROSE

I gaze out the window, frozen, unable to decide if I'm going through with this, riddled with doubt. When I became pregnant the first time while married to Lee, I was quite excited. I called my mom to tell her the news. My mom felt elated. Enid, too, shared in my joy, already asking me to let her be my child's godmother and I'd agreed.

Everything was on track until the second month when I miscarried. Alone at home that day. I called Lee several times to take me to the hospital, but he didn't answer. I had to call an ambulance.

When I told him about going to the hospital, he blamed me for not being careful and said the miscarriage was my fault. I was so vulnerable at that point that I believed him. I even apologized to him, grieving the loss of my child only in privacy. During my second pregnancy, I wasn't aware I had conceived. One day at work, I bled and fainted. In the hospital, the doctor examined me and announced that I had miscarried.

I took the news well and decided not to let it affect me too much, since I wasn't even aware of it. The third one happened five months later. I got tested, and they confirmed it as positive.

I was careful, extremely so, taking vitamins and all the precautions needed for a healthy pregnancy. Imagine my utter devastation when I went to the hospital one morning after spending the entire night in pain and the doctor said I'm miscarrying again, three months into the pregnancy.

That was the beginning of the end for Lee and me. Depressed and bedridden for days, I constantly cried and wallowed in sorrow. It was Enid who stood by and supported me despite Lee's disapproval. After that, I stopped conceiving. I don't know how or why, but I didn't get pregnant again. Lee asked me for a divorce two years later. Now I wonder if Lee deliberately did something to himself so he couldn't impregnate me. I know he is that vindictive and strategic.

My thoughts drift from my marriage and divorce back to my present situation.

Should I just forget it, forget my dream of having a child? Maybe the timing is wrong and having a baby will destroy my fledgling relationship with Jahi. I'll probably miscarry like all my pregnancies. When did I become so indecisive? Is this what the pregnancy is doing to me? Is it the hormones? Am I a servant of my biology? Or perhaps it's more psychological than physiological. Maybe I'm afraid to be a mother, to be so vulnerable to another living being, their life and wellbeing in my safekeeping. Those three miscarriages devastated me.

How am I going to handle it if something happens to my baby? Or later, when my baby is a child or teenager or even an adult? My grandfather, who we called Papa, once said that children are your greatest joy and deepest sorrow. He lost his twenty-five-year-old son to bone cancer and, of course, he never got over it. Something terrible can happen at any moment. Papa shepherded his son through the illnesses and risks of injuries and accidents of babyhood and childhood and the teen years, only to lose him as a young adult. He was still his baby.

What if my baby dies like Papa's did? What if she suffers terribly dealing with the exigencies of daily life—the disappointments, the injuries, the upheavals, the losses, the heartbreak? Oh, Hattie, I don't know what to do. I need you to send me a sign.

A memory forms in my mind. I remember the day. I came

home from first grade and the living room looked half empty. There were indentations in the carpet where dad's red leather recliner always sat. The house seemed silent except for intermittent gasping.

"Mom," I called out.

No answer.

"Mom, I'm home."

Nothing.

I found Mom lying on her bed with her black leather Mary Jane shoes still on her feet, weeping. Her words made little sense. Nothing made sense for a long time.

Remembering that terrible moment, I look out the window and see a blur of movement. The gray sky is spitting snow, but it's not sticking yet. A woman who looks nine months pregnant appears in my line of vision. She's wearing a long, puffy, pale green coat and holding something in her arms, something wrapped in a blanket. It's a baby, a newborn. She cradles it as if her life depends upon it. My addled mind seeks to see this as a sign, but then I realize this is a common sight at a hospital.

It's now or never.

Goosebumps prickle my arms and chest. *Is this a sign from Hattie? I imagine her voice: "Stand on your own two feet, Rose. Take this chance."*

And then my voice takes over. *Don't give up. This baby is mine. I'm done being haunted by my father's abandonment. I'm having this baby with or without Jahi... regardless of whether he ever gets a divorce.*

I'm riveted by the little family who don't know I'm watching their every move, like an eagle in an aerie from my vantage point, intruding on this pivotal moment of taking their baby home from the hospital.

The nurse clears her throat. "Ms. Aberdeen, you haven't

answered me. Can you hear me?"

"Wait. What?" I question, snapped back into reality from my reverie.

"It's time."

"What?" I'm blinking in the harsh light, uncomprehending.

"I said it's time," the nurse replies, trying to be polite yet firm.

"No," I answer in a soft voice.

"What?"

"No." My voice is firmer.

"What do you mean?"

"I'm not doing it." I set my jaw and my voice is louder than before.

Silence hangs between us.

"Would you… like to speak to the doctor?" she asks slowly.

"No."

Another silence.

"Okay, I'll let the doctor know. I'll get the discharge papers in order. You can get dressed." She's now dropped into a utilitarian voice, her body pivoting and exiting the room with the precision of a soldier. The door clicks shut.

I turn back to the window like I'm returning to a movie unfolding before me, only this is real life. I watch the mother, her back slightly bent forward from the loss of abdominal strength accumulated over ten months, handing her newborn to her husband, who receives the tiny bundle and holds it gingerly. The father places the baby into the red and navy carrier, fumbling with the latches for the first of hundreds, if not thousands, of times to come.

He lifts the carrier into the car and clicks it into position in the center of the back seat. He fastens his baby to safety. This entire sequence of moves of the mother and the father is like choreographed dance steps performed for the first time, and no matter how awkward, it is beautiful. I weep.

I want this, too.

I resent the nurse interrupting my thoughts with her questioning. These fleeting moments I'm witnessing are sacred, a window into something profound and ineffable.

The new mother, her abdomen distended like she could deliver another baby any moment, settles into the rear passenger seat beside the newborn. I see the back of her head and imagine her smitten with her baby, her eyes fixated on its little face. This baby is her world. After a minute, they drive away, never knowing a stranger witnessed their actions. Their family will pass down this heartwarming moment as a story for generations to come, just as my family passed down Hattie Osborn's story and legacy.

This little family does not know that the tenderness they showed to their infant and to each other penetrated the heart of a woman they didn't see and will never know. They changed the trajectory of many lives in a few moments—not only my life, but all the ones I love and have loved, those alive and those long gone and those yet to come. Their tenderness delivered a message radiating in expanding, concentric circles to the outer reaches of time, memory, and possibility. A pebble tossed into a boundless pond. God speaks, always, but we are hard of listening.

Thank you, Hattie. I'm walking out of here gravid into the future.

CHAPTER SIX

JAHI

"Rose. I'm here," I blurt out in anguish. *She's done it. That's why she looks forlorn. I'm too late. If only I had come earlier. Maybe I could have changed her mind. Now, I'll never get to see the baby I made with her. She's not responding. It's all my fault. I've hurt her beyond repair. I've ruined it.*

My fingers flex and the papers slip out of my grip, landing softly on the tiled floor, seven rose hips spilling forth. I barely even notice it. I focus my mind on what would have been if Rose was still pregnant.

I had been looking forward to seeing her in different stages of the pregnancy, accompanying her to her prenatal appointments, caressing her belly and feeling the baby kick, rubbing her feet and massaging her back. Doing my best to make the journey a beautiful one for her.

Would it have been a sweet little boy, with my features or a beautiful little girl just like Rose or Lily? I'm sure Rose will not be with me anymore, because there's nothing tying us together. I feel like hitting my head on the wall or lashing myself with chains until I'm beaten bloody, something, anything, to channel the pain I feel. My heart is breaking.

I wish I could have averted this. "Oh, my little baby," I sob in gasps, my feelings gushing forth, unable to hold it in. I can barely breathe. I feel like I'm having a nervous breakdown. "Rose, I'm here." I whisper to her back, but she doesn't respond.

She turns as if moving in molasses and gazes up at me, her

expression inscrutable. Her complexion pale, like an apparition.

"Rose... Rose," I plead, my voice distraught as a sinking, sickening feeling grows in my stomach. "I'm... I'm so sorry." Guilt wracks me like it did when Dad died.

I hold my breath for an eternity. *Does she hate me?* I'm frozen like a king on a chessboard—facing the opposing queen in a standoff, not knowing what she'll do.

"What are you sorry for?" Rose breaks the silence, her voice steely as she emerges from her trance.

"Bea told me you don't want to continue with the pregnancy, Rose. I didn't know you were having complications. You didn't tell me. If I had known, I'd have come sooner." I cower, sensing her rage, bracing for the level five hurricane of her fury.

She glares at me, but I continue, like a madman defending himself. "You were the one who first started closing up and withdrawing from me. I didn't know what to do, thinking of what to say to you every night or how to help you. You seemed walled off and shut down. I just want you to know how much I love you and the extent of what I'll do to be with you. You mean everything to me, Rose."

"Well, I was dealing with a lot, too. It's hard for me to say things like 'I've developed an acute blood clot in my veins, and had to be placed on blood thinners.'"

"Oh, my God. Acute blood clots? A DVT?!" *Oh my God, there it is, the thing I've feared all along. I can't lose Rose like I lost Dad to a blood clot. I never told Rose that Dad's maternal grandmother died in childbirth in her late thirties.*

"Yes, exactly. A DVT," she affirms.

I exhale shakily, resting my shoulder against the wall for support. "Complications during the delivery could arise, but the doctor can manage them. I've seen cases, and it all worked out. You didn't have to discontinue the pregnancy, Rose."

"Yes, you've not even heard all of it. The doctor diagnosed me with Factor V Leiden, a clotting disorder that places me as a high-risk pregnancy, leaving me with a chance of serious complications like preeclampsia or, God forbid, eclampsia, should I continue with the pregnancy."

It feels like my blood is draining out of me as I crumble to the floor. I'm not ready to lose Rose because of the pregnancy. I'd rather she stay alive than risk her life to bring another life into this world. A normal pregnancy carries plenty of risk on its own, but this is a high-risk one. I look up at her and put out my hand for her to hold. She takes it and kneels in front of me.

"Although I'm not happy you made this decision without telling me, and you've gone ahead with the procedure in my absence, I'd rather have you alive than risk losing your life. I love you, Rose. I want to be with you for better and for worse. If you'll still have me."

Silence.

Oh no. This is bad. Her silence slices through me like a dagger.

"Rose?" I beg with my softest voice, hoping to access the compassionate part of her that can forgive me.

Like the moment an insect breaks through a pond's surface tension, the phase transition when one reality transforms into another, she blurts out defiantly, her eyes hard, "I'm having this baby with or without you, Jahi." She says it confidently, even as tears escape her eyes.

The Earth tilts on its axis. *Am I hearing her right? Did she just say, 'I'm having this baby'?*

Before I can catch my breath, Rose continues, "When Lee left me after I lost my pregnancies, it reminded me of the loss of my father all over again. I thought, not only was I unlucky in love, but worse, I was unlovable. With you, I've felt something I never have before. I can be myself, quirks, and all. And now, with this baby—I almost gave up when the situation seemed impossible because you're still married. The old fears reared up. I almost went along to please you, afraid you'd leave me like all the others."

"But this morning I realized something. I want this baby more than anything, and I'm willing to risk everything for it. When I came to Eureka Springs, I thought my life was pretty much over. I was just going through the motions, thinking it was too late to have a family. I was too old to find anyone, let alone have a baby. But then I met you. I've never met anyone like you. You're one in a billion. And slowly I realized it's never too late to live the life of your dreams. It's never too late to find love."

My heart stops beating for what seems like an eternity, then lurches into a gallop, pumping hot gushes of blood through my veins that roar in my ears. I reach out and cup her stomach tenderly, my hands trembling, my eyes taking her in with awe.

"You're still pregnant?" I whisper, doubting that she can hear me. She nods. "Oh thank God, dear Rose!" My voice breaks as my legs buckle again, and I collapse on the floor near her feet, weeping. "Oh my darling, you'll never have to do this without me. I'm all yours from now till the end."

After a stunned silence, Rose's voice softens, but she still frowns, "I know you want this baby, Jahi, but you're still married."

"Rose. Susanne signed the divorce papers. She's out of our lives," I exclaim.

"What?" she asks, stunned momentarily, but then she folds her arms across her chest. "Please don't joke with me, Jahi. It's been a terribly emotional day, and I can't handle it."

"I'm serious, Rose. She signed. I called and called, trying to tell you this on my way here."

Realizing this is for real, Rose asks, "How in the world did you get her to sign the papers? How did you pull this off?"

"Remember how I told you my attorney, Chad, had the scoop on her, something confidential I couldn't share?"

"Yes."

"I met her at the park with Chad in the car. She threatened me again, but when I confronted her with the sordid facts we discovered about her life, she backed down and signed the papers."

"What is this big secret of hers? Can you tell me now?" Rose's eyes grow bigger.

"I think it's safe to share at this point." I look around just to be sure no one else is in the room. "She had a lover for years, unbeknownst to me. She met him in beauty school."

"What?" Rose stands there, her mouth slack. "You're kidding."

"I'm not kidding. That was a shocker. But that's the least of it. She met up with him at the girls' weekend in Vegas and that's why she didn't come back. She ran off with him to his mansion in Chicago. He's a billionaire."

"Whoa…" Rose draws out the word and her lips remain open in the same position.

"I know. But it gets worse," I say, my voice lowering. "She had a baby girl with him…"

Rose gasps and holds her palms to her face. "Oh, no."

I reel off the rest of the story robotically, feeling numb with every retelling. "She acted strange and her doctor hospitalized her for postpartum depression."

"Oh, that's terrible." Rose is compassionate even though Susanne has inflicted so much suffering on her, Lily, me, and so many others.

"There's more, Rose. She went home and deteriorated. One day, she drove with the baby…"

"Oh, no. Not again." Rose shakes her head. "I think I know where this is going."

"And got pulled over for a DUI." Rose looks at me with sad eyes. "The billionaire dude kicked her to the curb and consulted the best attorneys in Chicago and sued for sole custody of the baby."

"So all the things she accused us of were about her. That's projection, Jahi. It's a defense mechanism," she says in her psychologist's voice.

"I figured you would analyze this in a split second. Yeah, so she's the cheater, not me."

"Exactly."

"And she committed child endangerment, child abandonment again, and two DUIs at least, both involving her children."

"I'm in shock, Jahi."

"I am, too. But you know what this means, don't you?"

"We're free to be together?" Her eyes light up.

"Yes, my love. Finally," I assure her.

"No more hiding?" she asks.

"No. No more hiding." My stance is firm, and Rose exhales loudly as I hold her in my arms. "We're free to be together without apology. This is our time. We'll have our little baby and Lily, and we'll be a happy family."

"What about Susanne? Won't she interfere?" Rose wrinkles her brow.

"She's gone. She disappeared, just like before."

She nods quietly and then notices the blood stained papers on the floor where I dropped them when I collapsed. She notices my bloody hand and examines it. "What happened to your hand?"

"A rose thorn pricked me when I was checking the rose hips this morning before I came here to surprise you. I wasn't in a hurry because I didn't know you were in the hospital. The rose hips in the garden were ready and I was picking them as part of my rose breeding."

"I'll kiss it all better, and you came to the right place for Rose's hips," she soothes, like a mother to a child. "Why were you looking for rose hips in the backyard for breeding when you could come here for Rose's hips and our breeding?" she jokes. Rose presses my hand gently to her lips and kisses it. I swoon. She's going to be the best mother to our baby and to Lily.

"I was so afraid I was too late, Rose."

"Ah… it's okay, Jahi. It all worked out in the end. Something happened to me. Something profound. I dug deep inside myself and came up with my decision. I think I needed that experience without you or Bea or Mom telling me what to do. Something shifted inside me. No more ambivalence, no more fear. I'm ready to be a mother, and I'm ready to have a family, Jahi. Our family."

CHAPTER SEVEN

ROSE

The little family taking their baby home from the hospital was a bluebird, an unforeseen gift changing my life and my baby's. They appeared at the moment of my deepest despair, my dark night of the soul, when all seemed lost.

Years ago, when I was seventeen and in existential angst at the thought of leaving home for college, I turned to literature. I skipped school as often as feasibly possible and read Dad's copy of *The Inferno*. Dante Alighieri's words spoke to me through seven centuries. *In the middle of the road of my life, I awoke in a dark wood, and the true way was wholly lost.*

Being seventeen, I was half Dante's age when he wrote those opening lines, yet they resonated with me. I struggled with a sinking feeling of loss, like I felt when Dad left. Mom and Bea were leaving for Arkansas, and I stayed in California to attend UCLA.

It's hard to be the one left behind, even though it was my decision to stay and even though Mom and Bea tried to talk me into moving to Arkansas and were even angry with me for not coming with them. I grappled with my dark night of the soul, just as Dante wrestled with his. In the story, a guide showed up, the pagan Roman poet Virgil, who lit the way. I've been looking for a guide my whole life and I think I found it. This little family standing outside the hospital, taking their baby home, is my Virgil, and I will never forget them. Sometimes home finds you rather than the other way around.

There were more miracles in store that day in the hospital.

Jahi appearing right after I made my decision to keep our baby. Jahi collapsing with gratitude when he heard I kept the baby will always be one of the most profound moments of my life.

This beautiful, distraught man thought he caused me to give up our baby. It shows me how good he is and how kind, and how much he loves me and wants us to be a little family of four. They say things come in threes, sort of like the Trinity. Sure enough, one more miracle lay in store for me on that auspicious day—the news of Susanne signing the divorce papers.

It's been a week since my fateful decision to keep our baby, and my life is finally falling into place. Mom and Bea wept and yelped with joy when Jahi and I called from the hospital room to inform them of my decision to keep the baby. I'm not sure they heard anything else, even though we told them the good news about the divorce proceedings. To celebrate the baby, my sister and mother insisted on hosting a big dinner for family and friends, marking the watershed moment when everything changed for Jahi and me. Christmas has come early this year.

"Hey, let's invite your mom, Chrissy, and her husband, Lucas," I say. "And of course you'll bring Lily."

"What about Jolene? She's been a great friend to you."

"Yes, she has. Maybe she'll bring some special Korean dish," I joke.

"Since we're inviting best friends, what about Matt and Jane, too, if she wants to come? She's been a fan of our relationship all along."

The feast under the fat moon in Mom's garden greenhouse is a vision I'll never forget. Bea placed two massive wooden picnic tables from the yard end to end, and covered them in fine old tablecloths and festooned them with a dozen tall candles. We set the table with Mom's finest china. Glasses and Italian flatware glimmer amongst the candlelight, moonlight and garden lights strung above, inscribing the perimeter of the space, contributing to the festive atmosphere.

Chrissy and Lucas arrive holding hands, and Chrissy sports a frilly white chiffon French dress, her signature Louboutin pumps, Versace sunglasses perched on her head, and a Hermès handbag slung on her arm. She doesn't need the sunglasses now as it's evening, but I figure she wore them on the drive over or maybe it's a fashionable look I'm not aware of. This must be the look du jour in London or Paris, or maybe it's just Chrissy.

Matt and Jane arrive in Matt's red pickup truck, with Matt looking like the iconic blonde southern California surfer dude standing there with his brunette southern beauty on his arm. Matt spent his youth surfing the waves at Malibu and The Wedge at Newport Beach, that famous site known to have the most powerful beach breaks and surfed by the most advanced surfers. It still shows in his ripped muscles and agile movement. I wonder what it was like for him to exchange West Coast beach life for rural northwest Arkansas.

Jahi, Lily, his mother, and Jolene show up together. Lily bounds out of the car, making a beeline for me and hugging me gently around my belly. I caress her hair and she looks up at me, her eyes sparkling. *She knows. I see it in her eyes. She's happy and relieved. We're going to be a little family and we're going to have a baby.*

Jahi's mom smiles and hugs me tenderly, holding me for a long time. When she releases her arms from my back, she looks up at me with tears in her eyes. "I am so thankful you are part of our family, Rose. This is one of the happiest days of my life," she whispers.

Jolene tilts her head to the side and nods decisively, a sly smile forming on her lips. Her hands are full as she carries in her surprise Korean dish. Wordless, she proceeds to the kitchen to meet Mom and Bea and I hear them welcoming and thanking her for being a genuine friend to me through the predicaments of the past year.

It seems as if everybody is talking at once. There are so many new connections forming, a buzz of excitement in the welter of voices, the realization that this is an evening to be relived and remembered for years to come.

We make our way to the table and the din of overlapping conversations abates, replaced by the clink of glassware and utensils, happy sounds of thanks and contentment, the sacrament of a shared meal, the occasional punctuation of gales of laughter unleashed by recounted stories and jokes.

In the onslaught, a prime rib roast and Jolene's galbi turn into rubble. Even the tomato salad and ginger-garlic Romano beans do not escape the destruction. And then Bea produces a towering six-layer hummingbird cake, and we are all transported into a food coma.

I don't remember the details of the conversations at the table that night, but I remember how alive I felt. Jahi said I looked radiant, otherworldly, like the first time he saw me. Like Botticelli's Venus. I recall how ruggedly handsome he looked, his rough, callused hand holding mine under the table, squeezing it from time to time when someone said something funny or meaningful. I would gaze at him and smile, and he said I was beatific.

I certainly felt at peace, as much as I ever have in my life. The din of talking became a mesmerizing buzzing. At other times, it felt like the entire evening moved in slow motion, one of those forever moments I never want to end. Time is elastic, it's relative, and I want to stretch it, twist it, and squeeze out every drop of its juice.

CHAPTER EIGHT

JAHI

I'm eager to find out where things stand with the divorce, so I call Chad. It's been more than a month since Susanne signed the divorce papers, and she's still nowhere to be found.

"Hey Chad, how's it going with the divorce proceedings?" I hold my breath, hoping for good news.

"It's looking good, Jahi." His voice is jaunty. "You've crossed a threshold. It's been thirty days since Susanne signed the papers. You can't get a divorce completed before that timeframe, but now you can. We consider this an uncontested divorce because she signed the papers willingly."

"What else do we need to do?" I'm eager to get this chapter of my life resolved so I can move forward with Rose.

"Nothing for you to do. We just need the judge to sign off."

"Will he do that?" I hold my breath, praying he says yes.

"Yup. I talked to him today. It's a done deal," he states decisively. I imagine him standing in his kitchen, his chest puffed out. Another win for his client and for his reputation as an attorney.

"What happens now?"

"Now, Jahi, you're free to marry."

"Really?"

"Yes, really," Chad assures me in a fatherly tone.

After I hang up, I call Rose.

"Hello." Oh, how I love her sweet voice.

"Hey babe. I've got a surprise for you."

"What?" Her voice rises expectantly.

"How about I pick you up Saturday morning at ten o'clock and return you to Fayetteville on Sunday evening by seven?"

"What about Lily?"

"She'll stay with Chrissy this weekend. She's looking forward to it."

"Sounds like you've got some news. You still haven't told me what this is about."

"It wouldn't be a surprise if I did, would it?" I tease as I laugh and she laughs, too.

"Oh, just one more thing." I pause for dramatic effect.

"What's that?"

"Wear something romantic."

"Oh, I like the sound of that," she answers playfully. "I will."

The door opens as if by some hidden hand and there stands my green-eyed, strawberry blonde Rose, pregnant with our child. Rose is wearing a diaphanous pale pink gown and looks like a callipygian goddess in a Renaissance masters painting, spectacularly female. She knows the hedonic pleasure I receive from all things old-fashioned and sensed it the moment she saw my old roses. She's a classic beauty. I take her slender hand into mine and walk her down the path to my car.

We drive the northern route to Eureka Springs, a sleeping pastoral landscape unfolding its dormant and tended beauty as we talk and laugh on our way to my house.

When we get home, we settle in. I serve Rose a glass of sweetened tea and prepare a charcuterie board with olives, radishes, edamame, cherry tomatoes, goat and cheddar cheeses, celery, broccolini, cucumber, asparagus, artichoke hearts, cauliflower, carrots, hummus, tahini dip, and a sliced baguette and seeded crackers. Nothing in the stuffed fridge remains untouched.

"Wow, love. This is impressive. You've got everything here one could imagine in a restaurant in San Francisco or LA or Rome," she gushes.

I laugh. "You didn't know I have a talent for creating charcuterie and crudité boards, did you?"

"No, I sure didn't, but I like it. It's sexy for a man to feed a woman." I feel my face flush and Rose notices and jokes, "You're blushing, Jahi."

I smile and we laugh. "Yeah, I can't hide anything from you. I'm an open book," I admit.

"And you know what else? I'd love seeing you mopping the kitchen floor." She looks at me mischievously. Now my neck is growing hot. "There's nothing quite like seeing a man with a mop, especially in his briefs," she jokes. She's on a roll and can't keep from blushing, as if she can't believe she's saying this, revealing her fantasy to me.

After a bit of nervous laughter, I suggest we take a nap. Leading her to my bedroom, I hold her in my arms. I don't want to risk anything in terms of the pregnancy, so I'm cautious and don't make a move on her. I think she understands and silently agrees. She seems content and within a few minutes nods off to sleep, snoring lightly. I watch her for a few minutes before I close my eyes and join her, my sleeping angel.

It's late afternoon, and I tell Rose I have something to show her.

"Remember how I said I have a surprise for you?" I ask softly, anticipating one of the most important moments of my life.

"How could I forget?" she teases, twisting a lock of her luxurious hair flirtatiously, a sure sign she's aroused.

I laugh and my voice sounds shaky, which surprises me because I don't feel nervous. At least, I don't think I am.

"Come with me." I reach out, and she takes my hand in her slender, pale, left hand. She's still in her goddess gown, as beautiful as ever. I move towards the back door, guiding her as she carefully descends the stone steps in her bare feet, holding up the long gown in her right hand.

We walk along the garden path, past rows of rose bushes in their winter sleep, each carefully bred and tended over the years, mulch mounded around their bases, canes bare and sporting clean cuts from expert and loving pruning. She looks at the slumbering rose bushes and says, "I recall hearing stories of my great-grandmother Hattie saying, 'God gave us memories so we can have roses in December'. Right now, I'm remembering this one was a velvety red rose with a heavenly scent of honey. What's its story?"

"That's *Scarlett Leigh*, one of my oldest rose bushes. She's named after my childhood horse."

"Oh, I didn't know you had a horse, but I seem to recall seeing a director's chair stashed away in your garage with the name Scarlett Leigh embroidered on it."

"You're quite observant and astute. Yes, that chair was a gift from Dad when I was twelve and showing Scarlett Leigh in Gymkhana horse shows. There are a lot of things you don't know about me, Rose, and I'm sure there's a lot I don't know about you. But I can't wait to discover all the nuances about you over the years ahead. I know I'll never know you completely. We don't ever fully know another person, but that's part of the magic and beauty of relationships. We're continually exploring the mysteries of each other."

"Wow, Jahi. I love that." Rose looks pensive, then adds, "Hey, you mentioned Scarlett Leigh, the rose, as if it's a female. Do you see roses that way? I mean, that they have gender?"

"That's an interesting question. I didn't realize I did that, but I did, didn't I? I haven't really thought about it, but yeah, in some ways I see some of these roses as female, probably most of them, but a few I see as male. I don't know why, I just do."

"That's cool. It's almost like they're human."

"Yes, exactly." I pause and say something that shocks me. "I think they are."

After a comfortable silence of viewing rose bushes along the path, I turn to Rose and stop holding her hand. I put my hands behind my back after pulling out a silky surprise from my back pocket. "Pick a hand." I tease.

"Oh, I know this game." She gives me a knowing look, throws her head back, and laughs.

"Pick a hand," I repeat playfully.

She picks my left hand and I show her that hand with nothing in it. "Pick a hand," I say again. She picks my right hand, and it comes up with nothing. The game continues for four sets and in the fifth round, there's something in my hand.

"What is it?" she asks quizzically. "It looks like silk."

"It is. It's a silk eye mask, and I'd like you to put it over your eyes."

She takes the mask and asks, "Is this part of the secret?"

"You'll see," I say with a mischievous smile.

Rose places the eye mask over her eyes, and I take her hand. "I'm leading you down the path. We'll walk slowly."

"Okay," Rose whispers, with a smile on her pale pink lips.

I guide her past my collection of old roses, to the special one, the unnamed rose, the one waiting for this moment.

I stop, and she stops, too. "I'm removing your eye mask. Tell me the first thing you see."

I take off her mask and she blinks and squints in the bright afternoon light. Her pupils constrict quickly before focusing on the bare rose bush inches from her face, the one unnamed that she saw before. "I see in my memory the most exquisite rose. I remember this. It's the rose you showed me the first time you took me to your rose garden." Her voice is tender, like a child's. I wonder if she's about to cry.

"I bred this rose," I say, clearing my throat as emotion overtakes my voice. I can't say anything for what seems like minutes. I'm too choked up.

When I'm finally able to speak, I say, "It was waiting." I pause. "*She* was waiting," I insist, correcting myself. "She was waiting for me to name her, but I had nothing. Nothing compelling, nothing worthy, nothing that moved my heart. So I waited. I waited for years to name her, but I couldn't because I felt dead inside, Rose, dead like I felt the day Dad died."

The words spill out of me in a torrent of broken sentences and I go ahead, weeping. "I felt lost. But this rose, this exquisite rose, remained intact and would not perish on me. She waited patiently. I talked to her. She waited for me to name her. I told her of my sorrows and she waited. She listened through a thousand days of my despair, and still she waited. This rose lives in my heart, Rose. She's part of me, part of who I am. The only way to honor my precious old rose with a name worthy of her love and loyalty is through my experience of love, human love. It must be a great love, eternal and true. It's the breaking of a spell cast long ago."

Rose is trembling and speechless, her eyes filled with tears.

"I have found a name for this rose, dear Rose. It's *Botticelli Beauty*." Rose gasps and I pause before continuing, my voice broken from emotion, "It's named after you and memorializes the moment I first laid eyes on you. And like you, in a few months there will be the most lovely flower."

Rose weeps silently and I continue, "My father was a self-educated man. Sure, he went the traditional route of law school, but he had a wide-ranging, unquenchable curiosity. He loved many things and one of his loves was art history. He had a massive library, and I gravitated to his art history books. As a child, I pored through them for hours, stunned by the art, sensing something timeless. It seared one painting in my mind. Sandro Botticelli's *The Birth of Venus*, a masterpiece now living in the Uffizi Gallery in Florence."

"Oh yes, I remember that painting. It's one of my favorites. When I was eight, I had a book on Botticelli, and I copied images from his paintings. I fancied myself as something of an artist and filled pages of sketchbooks with drawings. Later, when I was fourteen, I traveled to Italy with my opera academy group and sang *O Mio Babbino Caro* first on the Ponte Vecchio and later at the Accademia Teatrale di Firenze—the time I told you about where the teacher told me to let my voice out and not be self-conscious. It was then that I saw the painting hanging in the Uffizi."

"It's amazing that as children, we were both mesmerized by that same painting. Do you know about Simonetta Vespucci?" Jahi asks.

"No, who is she?"

"Simonetta was Botticelli's muse, the great beauty of the mid-fifteenth century in Italy, the Helen of Troy of her day. And Vespucci is the same famous family name we heard in elementary school, from Amerigo Vespucci, the Italian explorer whose name became America. She was his cousin-in-law."

"I remember her face from Botticelli's paintings, *Primavera* and *The Birth of Venus.* She's the one I was tracing from the art books when I was a child."

"Yes, that's her in those paintings. Botticelli was smitten and drew hundreds of drawings of her. But she was not long for this world. She died of tuberculosis at twenty-three, and the people of Florence wept as they carried her in an open coffin through the streets. Even in death, they admired her beauty."

"That's sad that she died so young."

"Yes, it is. It was devastating for Botticelli. Ten years after her death, Botticelli painted that famous painting, *The Birth of Venus*. He vowed to be buried at her feet in the Franciscan church, the Chiesa di San Salvatore in Ognissanti, Florence when he died thirty-four years later, and he was."

"That's a beautiful but sad story. I didn't know the backstory of the painting."

"Yeah. It's fascinating when you study art history like my dad and learn the background and the 'why' behind works of art."

"Your dad studied art history?"

"Yeah, on his own. In his free time, when he wasn't practicing law, he studied many subjects, like Archaeology and Anthropology. That's how I got my name, Jahi. He loved Egyptology and my name has Egyptian origins. It means bright, shining and dignified, with understated charm."

"You are all that and more. Does it mean sexy, too?" Rose winks at me adoringly, her eyes moist.

I chuckle, then my mood becomes serious. "You're my Venus, Rose. You're my great love, my Botticelli Beauty. The woman of my dreams. The one I've dreamt of since childhood. Just as Simonetta was Sandro's love. She would have been thirty-two, close to your age, when he finished his masterpiece, but she never lived to see it."

Rose is tearing up, and I am too. This is the moment. This is our time. I bend down on my left knee and look deeply into Rose's emerald eyes with love and tenderness, and I hold her pale, freckled hands in mine.

"Rose Catherine Aberdeen, will you marry me? Will you be my wife?"

Smiling and without a moment's hesitation, Rose answers, "Yes, Jahi Henry Adams. I will."

CHAPTER NINE

ROSE

Jahi holds me and we alternate between uproarious laughter and happy crying. It's happening. I'm marrying my great love, my dream come true.

Mom was right when she told me it's just as easy to find a great man in a small town in Arkansas as it is in the big city of LA, perhaps easier, as in a big place the poseurs and narcissists elbow out the nice guys, making them almost invisible.

My life feels like a dream these last few weeks with the pregnancy and now the proposal. Now I'm hungry again after so much emotional outpouring. It must be my hormones or the need to eat for two.

"Jahi, I'm famished."

"I've got an idea." Jahi's face lights up. "Let's go back to Ermilio's, where we had our first date."

"Oh, that's so sweet and sentimental of you to think of our first date," I gush, and Jahi grins broadly.

I'm flooded with memories of our first date on the drive to the restaurant—the voluptuous landscape, the excitement I felt in Jahi's presence, his handsome face, and how good he smelled and how I wanted that smell all around me from then on.

"Let me get the door for you." Jahi walks around the car and opens my door, taking my hand as I ease out of the seat, feeling unbalanced in my body these days. He opens the restaurant door too, and I inhale the savory aroma of garlic, basil and tomatoes, the Holy Trinity of Italian cooking.

"Yummy," I say, taking in the intimate atmosphere of the small restaurant in the clapboard house on the Upper Historic Loop of Eureka Springs, with its wood floor, angled ceiling, leather seats, ornate chandelier, window sconces and dramatic drapery, old black and white framed photographs, and iconic striped tablecloths.

We're seated at the corner table, which I love, because there's no chance of anyone being behind me. Jahi finds this quirk of mine funny, this preference of having no one behind my back. Where I got this idea, I don't know or remember. Jahi sometimes calls me "The General" because I told him once that if you're a general, you don't allow anyone behind your back. Ever. You don't want to be in a non-defensible position.

We explore the menu, and I order artichoke hearts and Spinach Fettuccine Alfredo. Jahi chooses a Caesar salad and Shrimp Provençal.

"You're a foodie," Jahi teases. "I am too. That's how I notice this about you."

"Yeah, I got that from my dad. Going to the opera at the Dorothy Chandler Pavilion meant indulging in fancy restaurants in LA. We just called it the Pavilion for short. We always snuck in a splendid meal. I don't think it thrilled Mom when Dad spent so much money on opera tickets and eating out. It was ridiculously expensive. It almost seemed like Monopoly money. I also had great food in Venice and Florence and Rome when I toured with the opera troupe."

"You've had an interesting life, Rose. A cultured life. I can't say I've had as much worldly exposure as you, growing up here in the sticks, though Dad taught me a lot from his books on art and archaeology. He was a voracious reader. Europe was always somewhere I'd get to someday. I figured it had been there for thousands of years, so it could wait a few more."

"I bet you miss him. He sounds like he was a lovely man and father," I say softly, knowing I'm treading in tender territory.

Jahi shifts in his seat, tapping the table with his long, rugged fingers. I hope I didn't upset him by mentioning missing his father. "This is an emotional time, Rose. I would give anything for Dad to be here, to meet you, to come to our wedding, to meet our baby and Lily, too. He never got that chance, and that's what hurts the most." Tears fill Jahi's eyes and mine, too. I squeeze his hand and touch his shoulder with my other hand.

It's surreal that Jahi and I have a deep loss in common, losing our fathers. He lost his father, who didn't want to leave. I lost my father, who left by choice. It's an open wound, something time cannot fix no matter what anyone says. You never get over losing your father. Ever.

"Hey," Jahi whispers, his eyes tender. "Listen. Tell me what you hear."

Tilting my head to listen, my mouth ajar, I say, "I hear an aria… it's a Mozart aria." Scanning my mind to pull up the name, a memory comes to me. "We sang it in Venice at the defunct nunnery. It's Mozart's *La ci darem la mano.* It's from the opera *Don Giovanni.* I love the lines, *Come, come, my darling, to restore our pleasure of an innocent love.*"

"Oh, I love that, Rose. That's you and me—restoring innocent love."

"Ah… thank you, Jahi, I believe that's true for us, but in the opera, it wasn't innocent. Don Giovanni is better known as Don Juan, a notorious womanizer. He was fond of Spanish women and in the opera he brags of seducing a thousand and three of them. He was a busy guy! His deeds caught up with him, though, when a stone statue came alive and dragged him down to perdition. But it's still a gorgeous aria, even if used for evil purposes. Like anything truly interesting, it's not all black and white."

"That's what I love about you. I remember when you first told me about your love of opera and everything Puccini created. You knew the aria playing in the background then, too. *O Mio Babbinno Caro*."

"Wow. Impressive. You've got the memory of an elephant. Most people don't care about opera or remember anything about it. They just think it's ridiculous and over-dramatic, not to mention expensive and elitist, but it has lasted centuries for a reason."

"Honestly, I never loved opera until I met you. I remember everything about you, babe. I've made it my mission to study you," he jokes. "You have so many delights and surprises, from psychology, to opera, to literature, to art, to your love of children, and so much more. Plus, you're funny. You keep me on my toes, and I'll never reach the end of knowing you."

"Jahi, I feel the same way. Your love for Lily touches me deeply. You're a wonderful father, and I can't wait to see you with our baby."

"Thank you, sweetheart. I learned from the best—my dad. And I can't wait to meet our baby, too."

"I can see that. Even though I never had the chance to know your dad, I sure wish I did. Besides your tenderness for Lily, I see how you treat me as well as your family and friends. And… your roses. I love what they mean to you and how they connect you to your dad and Big Daddy and Big Momma, too. It speaks volumes about who you are."

"Thanks, Rose. It means the world to hear this."

I hug Jahi and realize I can't get enough of feeling his powerful arms around me. "I'll never forget our first date here. Do you remember what you ordered?"

"Uh, let me guess. Meatballs?"

"Bingo. You ordered Mom's Homemade Meatballs in Red Sauce. It's right here on the menu, and you devoured them. You looked so sexy, with your devilish good looks as you ate those meatballs. I love a man with an appetite and you sure had one that night," I tease, raising my eyebrows seductively for effect and Jahi blushes. "And by the way, I love how you blush when I tease you."

Jahi's eyes light up as he laughs. "Do you remember when we left Ermilio's and strolled in the park?"

"I sure do. How could I forget how you mesmerized me?"

"We made up a game of naming as many plants and flowers as possible," Jahi continues. "I loved it, and we were quite good at it."

"Yes, we were. I love playing our games." I laugh. "There's another thing I'll never forget. I think we were looking at the night sky and talking about constellations and you told me about the Perseids meteor shower. I thought I saw shooting stars to wish on that night, but you taught me they weren't stars, but meteors, some of them no bigger than grains of sand yet able to produce that much light."

"Yeah. I could tell you love to learn new things and that excited me. Plus, it made me look good, knowing about meteors, because you've got to admit, you're so smart it's pretty intimidating." He laughs and then grows pensive. "You know, love, this is only the second time we've been to Ermilio's. The first time was our first date. This time, we're engaged to be married with a baby on the way."

"Whoa. A lot has happened since I arrived."

"Yes, it has. It's been eight months since we first saw each other in the lushness of spring. Now here we are in the depth of winter, but already the days are getting longer, the light stealing a little more of the dark every day. Just like us, turning away from the dark."

"Oh, that's beautiful, Jahi. So much has happened in the past eight months that it's been both fast and slow. Sometimes it's contracted and sometimes it's stretched out. Time is like that. It's elastic."

"I like how you think, Rose. It's been both fast and slow. Lots of drama, some of it good, some of it bad, but it makes for a good story. Because of you showing up in Eureka Springs, this has been the best year of my life."

I'll never forget Bea and Mom squealing and whooping with delight when Jahi and I announced our engagement. Lily danced in celebration and Jahi's mom and Chrissy clasped our hands and Lily's and we formed a circle, laughing and crying simultaneously.

"I knew this would happen," Chrissy exclaimed, her voice an octave higher than usual, and Jahi's mom nodded her approval.

When I told Jolene, she gave me a sly smile. "You two are meant for each other. You're a beautiful couple, and I can't wait to cook you a special Korean meal after you give birth."

Enid gushed over the phone, "Praise God, hallelujah. You deserve this, girl. I've had a good feeling about this man from the beginning. I'm so happy for you, Rose."

When we broke the news to Matt and Jane over dinner, they waxed poetic about what lovebirds we are and how we're going to be the perfect little family.

Remembering these moments of sharing the news of our engagement, I realize time is getting short. "It's time to plan our wedding, Jahi. I'd like it to be small and intimate."

"Me too," he agrees. "I've been thinking about this quite a lot, about where to have the wedding. There's an iconic place I think will be perfect. It's Thorncrown Chapel, a famous glass church designed by an Arkansas architect who taught at the university and later studied under Frank Lloyd Wright. I remember when I first saw it as a kid, it felt like an extension of the forest."

"Wow. Who is the architect?"

"E. Fay Jones. He's no longer living, but he's famous around these parts. This little church in Arkansas gets major press. My dad had books that showed it alongside places like the Sydney Opera House and the Chrysler Building in New York. Can you believe that?"

"That's an enormous accomplishment."

"It sure is. The American Institute of Architects voted Thorncrown Chapel as one of the most important architectural buildings of the 20th century. E. Fay Jones somehow turned a pile of two-by-fours and a truckload of sheet glass into a divine space—soaring, weightless, a hymn full of light. It's always been one of my favorite places."

"Oh, that excites me." I pull up my laptop and search Thorncrown and there it is, a magical masterpiece set in the woods near Eureka Springs. "Oh, listen to this, Jahi. It says his love for the Ozark Mountains inspired his designs."

"Yes, exactly. His works aren't monumental in scale like the Golden Gate Bridge in California, or European cathedrals, or skyscrapers in New York, but they're noted for their intimacy with nature. We love our hollows and springs and stone bluffs towering over rivers. I think this is perfect, Rose. It is perfectly us."

Springtime

I'm stretched out on the backseat of Bea's car, trying to keep my dress from wrinkling. It's a lace tulle A-line wedding gown, with sequined beads, a V-neck, and a court train. I found it at Tesori Bridal in Fayetteville and chose a size eight, so it won't be tight around my slightly bulging waist. Mom is holding my bouquet constructed of seven *Botticelli Beauty* pale pink and white flecked roses from Jahi's garden, a surprise gift from him, the first blooms of the year.

The parking lot looks mostly empty, like a surreal scene out of a Hopper painting, asphalt geometry and green rolling hills beyond, with one silver sedan parked in the far corner. My nerves are raw because I know that no matter how much I plan, someone is likely to act out.

The Trickster always seems to show up at weddings. I've seen this in my life and heard many tales over the years in the psychotherapy consulting room.

Big, pivotal moments like this, as well as births and deaths, seem to bring out the worst in some people. It's almost a law of nature. *Will any of our guests act out and ruin it?* We've only invited nine people: Lily, Jahi's mom, Chrissy, Lucas, Matt, Jane, Jolene, Bea, and Mom. Surely none of them will cause a scene. Will they? Hopefully, no uninvited guests will appear. I think that's my biggest worry.

I tell Bea and Mom about my worries and Mom says, "You can't control birth and you can't control death. And you know what? You can't control a wedding either, because there's always going to be somebody who shows out."

I laugh nervously. "There's a saying in the South…" I start.

"They showed their ass," Bea finishes my sentence before I can. "And that doesn't mean they dropped their pants."

We all laugh uproariously, but my laugh has an edge to it and Mom feels it.

"It's going to be okay, Rose, no matter what. Even if someone shows out, it's okay. It will make for an entertaining story you'll tell your grandchildren, and it will pass down through the generations."

I nod but remain silent.

I think about my first wedding. It differed from this one, fancy, just so, hordes of people I didn't know, even ice sculptures. Somebody once told me that if there are ice sculptures at a wedding, it will fail within a year. If it had, it would have saved me a lot of trouble. I try to push it out of my head, but the harder I try, the more it clings to me like barnacles. *Maybe that's the Trickster? The ghost of a wedding past. Maybe this happens when you've been married before—you're haunted by the last wedding.*

I remember a feeling from my first wedding of being beyond time. It's as if time is elastic and it is stretching and contracting. And here's the interesting thing, it's this almost in-articulable experience, but it happens from time to time at pivotal moments. Like the time my friend defended his doctoral thesis, a dream fifty years in the making, a thesis that exacted ten years from his life. And yet he accomplished it. He never gave up on his dream. That moment was one of those experiences you never forget.

It's like a wedding. It expands and contracts and then maybe you have a reception afterwards like we had the late lunch afterwards with my friend, the PhD candidate, right?

I don't know about having a baby, because I haven't experienced that yet, but I know it's coming. With birth, the reception afterwards is just you, your husband and the baby and it's everything, I'm sure.

But the interesting thing I remember about a wedding is that it's this otherworldly experience even if it's small, and then you have a reception afterwards and there's dancing and *hors d'oeuvres* or dinner. We had both *hors d'oeuvres* and dinner because Lee wanted something lavish. And you dance and cut the cake and listen to speeches and laugh and throw the bouquet and a lucky woman catches it. Everyone throws rice as you depart, and you're surrounded by people laughing and smiling and the camera is flashing and then… and then you run out and get into your car decorated with ribbons, garlands, and balloons, and drive off. You drive away, and it's silent. It's over.

It's like a phase transition, the kind you learn about in chemistry, the subject my dad taught. Like ice to water, connected to disconnected. And then the din. The roar of laughter turns to silence. You're thrown into this other state and it's silent. It's the strangest thing. At first, as you drive away, you're elated, but then you think, *What just happened? You're back to your life, facing yourself. You go from the enormity of this experience, which has a life of its own, back to your life, except your life has changed and you can't go back. It's like you're on the other side of a thick glass partition.*

Bea assists Mom out of the car and wheels her into the chapel. Then she returns to help me carry the train of my gown so it won't get dirty as I make my way into the bridal waiting room.

Bea touches up my makeup and sprays my updo, remarking how well my hair is staying put since the salon session this morning in Eureka Springs. She affixes the floor length veil to the crown of my head.

"Do you hear that?" Bea asks. "What is that song?"

"That's *The Swan* by Saint-Saëns." I fiddle with my veil, securing it on my head. The last thing I need is a wardrobe malfunction.

"You know your music, that's for sure." Bea smiles adoringly and I laugh, grateful she's with me, calming my nerves.

"When we hear the Bach *Cello Suite #1*, we need to walk around the chapel and meet Matt just outside the front door." I explain to Bea because we never had a dress rehearsal.

I take one last look in the mirror to check my hair and makeup while Bea snaps photos with her phone. When I hear the velvety, chocolate sound of the cello, I know it's time to go outside and prepare to be walked down the aisle by Matt. Bea lifts the train, and we make our way to the front of the church. There have been great musical collaborations in history—Gilbert and Sullivan, Lerner and Loewe, Simon and Garfunkel, Mozart and Schikaneder, but it's hard to beat J.S. Bach and God.

Matt stands there grinning, decked out in a tuxedo, around the corner from the front door. We don't want the audience to see us just yet, so we stay hidden.

He reaches out his hand to mine. "Hey Rose, you beautiful bride. Jahi sure is a lucky man."

"Thank you, Matt." I feel myself blushing. "This is my sister, Bea. She'll carry my train as we walk down the aisle, so let's walk slowly," I joke.

Matt and Bea smile and nod silently at one another. As the cello piece ends, I take a deep breath. I curl my right hand around Matt's arm as he stands as a kind of father figure to walk me down the aisle. A wistful feeling comes over me as I hold on to Matt. *Why couldn't Dad be here for my special day? He's missed so much of my life and Bea's and Mom's, too.* I grasp my homemade bouquet of *Botticelli Beauty* roses, a precious gift from Jahi, tightly in my hand, and we turn the corner and wait for the processional music to begin.

The soaring voice of Maria Callas, my opera heroine, fills the sanctuary with *Ave Maria,* the most beautiful and soulful rendition ever sung. Tears well up and my vision blurs, but I see people in the front pews stand and turn to face us. I zero in on Jahi standing near the pastor, handsome as the day I first met him, and gasp. I see a boutonniere of *Botticelli Beauty* old rose buds pinned to his tuxedo lapel and there are bouquets of roses from his garden at the altar.

As I get closer, I see tears in his eyes, too. He smiles, but his chin quivers and he looks choked up. I wonder if either of us will speak our handwritten vows or if we'll fall apart.

Matt leads me to Jahi, who takes my hand. Matt takes his place beside Jahi as his best man, and my sister takes her place beside me as my maid of honor.

The ceremony is a blur until we get to the part when I hear the preacher announce in a booming voice, "It's time for you to say your vows, the ones you've written to each other."

Jahi takes out a piece of paper from his jacket, his hands trembling.

"Dearest Rose, light of my life. You are the sun and the moon and the stars and you changed my life from the moment I first saw you that day at my front door. You showed me and Lily what love is. I vow to spend the rest of my life with you and to treasure you with all my heart." Jahi's voice catches and he's unable to speak. The chapel is deathly silent except for a choked gasp from his mother. I think I know what's coming next. "I wish… I wish Dad could be here today." Jahi's voice is unfamiliar. *Is this how he sounded when he was a little boy?* "He would have loved you, Rose, and he would have been so happy for us. I think he's watching us today."

Jahi's mother is crying softly and Chrissy is, too. Tears are streaming down Jahi's face and mine as well. I'm glad I didn't wear mascara or I would have looked like a zombie in the Eureka Springs ghost tour.

Jahi wipes away his tears. "Dad would have loved how playful we are with each other." Jahi's voice is stronger now. "So I vow to keep our playful spirit alive. I promise to make funny faces, beat you at arm wrestling and chess…" He smiles and the audience laughs, a comic relief to the heaviness of the last few moments. "And I promise to bring you surprises and play our 'pick a hand' game every chance I get," Jahi jokes, and I laugh. "And of course, I promise to grow old roses until the day I die, like Big Daddy and Dad." There's an audible *ahhh* from our guests.

"I love you, dear Rose, my beautiful bride. I can't wait for you to be my wife, and I will love you until the day I die and beyond."

I take a deep breath.

"Dearest Jahi, I love you with all my heart. You are my great love, the one I've dreamt of forever. The best decision of my life was moving to Eureka Springs because it brought me to you and Lily. I can't wait to be your wife and to be a little family with you, Lily, and our baby. I love our playful games, Jahi... but one of these days, I'm going to beat you at chess," I taunt playfully, my eyebrow raised, and the audience roars in laughter. Jahi snorts a laugh and gives me a knowing look. "I want to acknowledge our loved ones, the ones who can't be here today, the ones long gone: your Dad and mine, my great-grandmother Hattie Osborn, Granny and Papa, Mawmaw and Pawpaw, your Big Daddy and Big Momma, your Granny and Popeye, and all the rest of our families who are watching over us today. We are part of them and we will always remember them. And... I believe they are watching over us and that they are happy for us and for our future. So, I love you Jahi. I will always love you, and I can't wait to be your wife."

I hear sighs and sniffling and then the pastor's voice booms in the hallowed hall, "I pronounce you husband and wife. You may kiss the bride."

My heart falls into Jahi's dark chocolate eyes. *I could stay here forever, but the chariot of time calls me forward, ever onward, relentlessly. Can't we stop time, even for a moment?*

Jahi kisses me passionately and before I know it, he has swooped me backwards in a deepening of his dramatic kiss, and the audience oohs and aahs. There is thunderous clapping and yelps of agreement and elation.

The pastor continues, his voice excited, "I present to you Mr.

Jahi Henry Adams and Dr. Rose Catherine Aberdeen Adams."

I look up adoringly at Jahi's beaming face and whisper, "Checkmate."

CHAPTER TEN

JAHI

Two months later

Rose gets the shock of her life one week before our baby's due date. I'm staying with her in Fayetteville and Bea walks into the living room to deliver the news.

"Hi Jahi," Bea nods, then turns towards her sister. "Rose, there's something I need you to know, but I'm almost afraid to tell you in your condition and with only one week before the birth." A furtive look passes over Bea's eyes as if she's afraid to reveal a secret.

Rose, gravid and uncomfortable on the sofa, looks quizzically at Bea. "What is it?"

Bea takes a deep breath. "Dad."

"What about him? Is he alive?" Rose's body stiffens, and a dark look comes over her face.

"He's not just alive… he's here," she states flatly.

"Wait. What?!" Rose is slack jawed, her eyes unblinking. "He's alive?"

"Yes. He's alive."

"Where is he? Does Mom know?"

"In town. He's staying at an inn. And yes, Mom knows. They talked on the phone late last night while you were sleeping. We're all still in shock."

"What? How is Mom doing? How is this affecting her?"

"She's ecstatic."

"What? Really?" Rose asks, incredulous.

"Yes. They talked for two hours, and he's asking to see all of us," Bea says, her voice sounding robotic.

"Does he know I'm having a baby?"

"Yes, he does. He says he can't wait to see you."

Rose looks up at me, tears filling her eyes, then collapses on the sofa, squeezing the pillow and sobbing.

Big Momma always told me that God invented time so everything wouldn't happen all at once, but I'm not sure it's working very well. I'm almost afraid to imagine what else is going to happen next. Is surprise inexhaustible?

CHAPTER ELEVEN

ROSE

I can't believe Dad is back. He's got some explaining to do. A part of me isn't sure I want to see him. The other part, the seven-year-old he left in the driveway that day thirty-one years ago, does.

My dad's sudden reappearance is something I didn't see coming, but we are going to see him today. I'm anxious but try to hide it. Jahi holds my hand as we drive to the inn where Dad is staying on Dickson Street, trying to keep a physical connection with me. And Lily is dozing on and off, strapped into her car seat.

We drive silently, partly because I can't think of anything to say and Jahi is keeping quiet, so he doesn't heighten my anxiety or disturb Lily. When we arrive, Jahi scoops Lily up into his arms and we go in.

Then I see him. Here we are in the same room together after all these years. Mom, Dad, Bea and me… and now my baby, Jahi and Lily, too. I'm still in shock. *Is this really happening?*

Dad's back, although slightly humped and different from my memory, is definitely him. I have his form memorized like a sculptor knows the tilts and angles of the model and expresses them with her hands. It's a kinesthetic memory.

He's standing in front of mom's console table, checking out the picture frames mom displays there. He tucks his left hand into the pocket of his taupe chino trousers as his right hand holds a picture of Beatrice readying me for my senior prom. His checkered blue shirt looks good quality, not too expensive but presentable. His hair is graying at the temples, but it's still as full as I remember.

As if he senses my presence, he turns. We stand there like statues, staring mutely and taking in each other's appearance. He is definitely older, but I would absolutely still recognize him on the street with his professorial look, benevolent and curious, a faint suggestion of a bemused smile. He has a few wrinkles on his forehead and brows. His arms are still hairy and his stance is still domineering. A tentative smile forms on his lips and he opens his arms to me.

"Come, my beautiful Rosebud." And I run into his arms. Once a daddy's girl, always a daddy's girl. He holds me in his embrace as I blubber all over his shoulder. And I cry, for all the times I longed to be held by my daddy's powerful arms but couldn't.

"Shush, it's okay, babydoll. Stop crying, you'll make me cry too, and I've cried an ocean of tears over the years already." I raise my head and see his eyes welling up.

"Where's Mom and Bea?" I ask. Jahi has made himself comfortable on the chair already. And Lily is now awake and I can hear her voice, but she is nowhere in my line of sight.

On cue, my mom, who is not in a wheelchair any more, appears but now she's walking with the aid of a cane in her right hand and Lily's little fingers in her left hand. Beatrice, holding two bottles of wine and some glasses, comes into the living room from the kitchen.

"Grandma Fayvill, wine for me, too," Lily chants as she bounces up and down in place. We're all bemused by this made-up name. It must be because Mom lives in Fayetteville.

"Yes, my darling Lily. Grape juice for you, too," my mom answers, chuckling.

We all sit down. Despite the lightened atmosphere, I still want to know why Dad disappeared and where he's been.

"Dad, I'm thrilled to see you after all these years. But why did you leave?"

"I promised your sister I would tell you all why I left, even though it's not a story I enjoy telling. But I owe it to you all." He pauses and looks at us as we wait in silence for him to continue.

"Back when I ran the chemistry department at UCLA, I had a graduate student, and I supervised her thesis. The first day I saw her, I knew she spelled trouble, but thought I could handle it. One day, after the lecture, I worked on a project. She came in under the guise of needing my help with a paper. Before I knew what hit me, I succumbed to her seduction. Then we started meeting secretly. After that, she threatened to report me to the university board of lecturers for misconduct towards a student."

He pauses again, looking down in shame.

"University rules strictly prohibit lecturers or professors from fraternizing with students, and if I were to engage in such behavior, my position in the department would cause severe disgrace and penalties for me. The first time I fell into her trap, she practically forced herself on me and I wasn't strong enough to resist her. The second time we met, I had no choice because I didn't want to lose my job and tarnish my career. Unfortunately for me, she was married but separated and I wasn't aware because she never mentioned it."

"Her estranged husband found out about our affair when she proudly told him she had moved on from him. She said she was now with me, and we would be married soon. I never promised her I would leave my wife for her or anything, but I guess she had plans to make me marry her. The man became furious, and he waylaid me on my way home one day, threatening my life. He told me, 'I'll disappear you off the bottom of the Santa Monica Pier, if you don't disappear within twenty-four hours. I'll come after your family too, your wife and daughters.' Then he left. You don't normally expect a grad student working diligently on a thesis to get involved with thugs and organized crime, but I suppose there are all kinds of people out there."

"The next day I found a note in my office from him saying the reason his wife left him was because of his involvement in the Mafia. He said he has strong ties everywhere, and that by the time he's done with me and my family, I'd have nothing left. And he attached pictures taken of all of you, Rose and Beatrice, at your school, then your mother at home. He tailed you guys. It terrified me, so I left."

"I drove to my car dealer, sold my car, and told him to change the car color and plate number before selling it to anyone. He agreed and then I fled to Stevensville, Montana, to hide out. As an undergraduate, I hitchhiked there one summer and worked on a ranch for a few weeks. The vision of that place never left me. I had an artist friend there, a sculptor with an old barn. I knew I could hide out at his place and no one would find me. So that's why I went there."

"I lived in fear for decades. It riddled me with regret that I inflicted so much pain on my family, but I couldn't come out into plain sight to explain myself partly due to fear and shame. There were a few times when I thought of tracking you guys down, but I just didn't have the courage. I kept thinking, 'How would I explain it to them?' The longer I thought about this, the longer I stayed away, and the harder it became to face what I had done." He's weeping as he ends his story.

"So why now? Why did you decide to show up now?"

"Well, a man named Chad Murphy contacted me."

"What?!" I gasp, cutting my eyes at Jahi. "Did you know Chad was up to this?"

"No, I didn't. I just told him about you and your dad, and I guess he took matters into his own hands."

"He's a great guy, Jahi. He found me, heaven knows how, because I was almost impossible to find, but I guess he sleuthed it out."

"Yeah, he's quite the relentless investigator," Jahi chuckles.

"What did you do all those thirty years, Dad?" I ask.

"Well, since I lost my position in the department of chemistry..."

"Yeah, you were the chair of the department," Bea blurts out. Dad and Mom nod at the same time. "But go ahead, I didn't mean to interrupt."

"Okay. I decided I better do something with my time besides hiding out."

"So what did you do?" Mom asks.

"I became a western romance author."

After a moment of shocked silence, Bea, Jahi, Mom, and I all chorus, "What?!"

"Yeah. Looking out at the cottonwoods and split-rail fences and fox tracks in the snow with the backdrop of the Bitterroot Mountains, I got lots of ideas. I even learned to ride a horse, but I drew the line at roping cattle. You gotta know when to hold 'em and when to fold 'em. I avoided injury from the Mafia psychopath by moving to Stevensville. After all that drama, I didn't want to get taken out by a cow. Besides, I figure romance is a kind of applied chemistry."

The five of us laugh so uproariously we have tears streaming down our faces and Bea is gasping for breath, saying her stomach hurts. I'm embraced by a warmth and connection to Dad I haven't felt in years. Dad's iconic laughter transports me to moments of childhood, to the time of innocence and possibility and the security of family.

"Guess what?" Dad, ever the trickster, and with an uncanny sense of comedic timing, inquires.

"What? You've got another surprise up your sleeve?"

"I sure do. I've got a pen name, Buck Chisholm," he says, taking a bow legged stance like a gunslinger and tipping an imaginary hat. This throws us further into paroxysms of laughter.

"Buck Chisholm!? Really?" Bea blurts. "I saw that name next to the lurid bodice rippers by the checkout counter at the grocery store. You're famous!"

"More famous than I ever was in chemistry," Dad quips. "When you write a chemistry paper, only ten to fifteen people read it—other chemistry professors and post-docs. If it's really successful, maybe a thousand will read it."

After our guffawing dies down, Dad adds, "When Chad found me, he told me something that changed everything."

"What did he say?" I ask, my mood turning serious as Mom, Bea, and Jahi nod.

"He said the man who threatened my life and my family's lives died a year ago in a suspicious private plane crash in Mexico. His enemies caught up with him. Chad told me I'm free to be with my family, that it's time for me to stop punishing myself for a bad decision I made so many years ago in my late thirties," Dad's eyes dart over to Mom's like he's looking for her approval and she nods without a trace of resentment. "So I decided it is time to forgive myself and reunite with my family."

CHAPTER TWELVE

JAHI

The first time I asked Rose about her dad, she told me he just up and left them when she was a child. I thought about it and said the man is probably dead.

Death is the only thing that can make me stay away from Lily and our unborn child, nothing else. But listening to him this morning, I wonder what I'd have done if faced with his predicament. It's easier to give your verdict when you're not the one in the situation.

I never imagined that Rose's dad would return and at such an auspicious time, let alone reunite with his family, while asking for a chance to make amends. It takes some guts.

It seemed like a lost cause after so many decades of disappearance. He's a brilliant one, like Rose, outwitting the criminal who sought vengeance and making himself unfindable. But boy, he paid for his mistake of betraying his wife and ended up betraying them all, as well as himself. He missed out on his daughters' childhoods, teen years, and young adulthoods. You can't get that time back.

But he redeems himself by returning. Now, he has a second chance through his grandchild, and maybe his wife and daughters. We all do. Every moment is a chance to start over. Even now, Lily has taken to calling him "Grandpa cowboy" and it's that pure love of a child that guides us adults to be more forgiving and see the possibilities we were blind to before.

A week later

I've taken the last week off work and have been staying in Fayetteville with Rose, her mom, and Bea. Rose's dad is still staying at the inn, but he's looking for an apartment in town.

I think back to our wedding. Rose's sparkling presence, a vision like the first time I saw her and how she cracked me up when she whispered, "Checkmate." That's one of those forever moments, one for the books I'll tell our grandchildren.

It's Saturday, the baby is due today, but so far nothing much is happening. We spend the day talking, playing chess, eating snacks, and going for short walks which is hard because Rose's gait is wobbly as her body prepares to give birth and the ligaments of the pubic symphysis loosen to allow the pelvic bones to separate and make room to push the baby out.

I watch my wife waddle up to me in the kitchen, where I'm preparing food to gratify her current cravings. She loves unusual food combinations like scrambled eggs with bananas and strawberries, and she craves peanuts, almond nuts, and rice with no soup to go with it. One day, she craved homemade crispy fried chicken and chocolate chip cookies and bananas. I called my mom, who graciously made some and brought them over for her.

Today she wants a sandwich but with only bananas and avocado spread on the bread. The funniest aspect is when she eats concoctions with so much relish, and then she sighs happily and falls asleep after eating. We must never run out of our banana supply because they are her staple food. Not that I'm complaining. Last week at the hospital when we went to her scheduled last trimester tests, the doctor said she is as healthy as a horse.

We left the hospital happily and my wife was literally bouncing because the doctor didn't tell her to stop those food combinations as I thought she would. I've had to get better at cooking for her sake. I pore over cookbooks for culinary lessons. Matt teases me about it, calling me a lover boy, but I feel it's my responsibility to take care of my wife, and that includes cooking as required. She's forty weeks pregnant to top it off.

Today she says she wants her scrambled eggs brown, almost burnt.

"What will you combine the eggs with this time?" I ask with a raised brow.

"Hmm… maybe I'll mix it with bananas as usual and maybe some nuts." She stands and starts rummaging through the pantry, emerging with a banana and a jar of cashew nuts, raising them up like a trophy. I almost laugh out loud at her waddle. She looks so adorable.

When I finish scrambling the eggs, I serve them to her at the kitchen table and tidy up the place. She wastes no time in wolfing everything down. Afterwards she let fly a rafter-rattling belch followed by a tiny, squeaky "excuse me," and tells me she's going into the room to lie down.

"Alright, I'll be in the study in case you need anything." I follow behind her. I'm leafing through one of her psychology books when I see her coming in.

It's ten o'clock in the evening and time for bed. Rose goes to the bathroom and shrieks.

"What's wrong sweetie?" I ask, alarmed.

"There's blood in the toilet. A big clot." Rose's voice is high-pitched, like she's about to have a panic attack.

I examine the toilet bowl. "Oh, that's the bloody show. Remember how they taught us about that in the labor class? It's when the cervix is thinning and dilating and you see blood-tinged mucus. It's the beginning of labor."

"Oh, thank goodness it's not something ominous. It's the mucus plug in the cervix that dislodges and then there's blood.

It's just so scary, though."

"Yeah, I know," I agree, privately worried, but I don't want to show this to Rose and make her feel worse. "Shall we call Dr. Mason?"

"Yes. Let's call her," Rose agrees without pause.

We call Dr. Mason's exchange and she calls back in five minutes.

"Hey, what's up?" she asks, ever unflappable.

"There's blood in the toilet and I'm pretty sure it's the bloody show. But I'm wondering if I should go to the hospital?" Rose asks with a slight edge to her voice. I'm sure Dr. Mason picks up on it.

"Sure, why not? Labor is beginning. Go get checked out and we'll see where things stand."

Rose hangs up, and I drive her to the hospital. Sure enough, she's in the beginning throes of labor. The baby is in stage zero. The head is engaged in the pelvis, which is good. She tells the nurse she's felt a few minor contractions. They tell us to go home and come back when contractions intensify in strength and frequency. As they grow closer together, every fifteen minutes, is when we need to report to the Labor and Delivery floor.

We drive back to Rose's mom's house to rest and prepare to be admitted when the time comes. I fall asleep but am awakened around five o'clock in the morning by Rose's moaning.

"The contractions increased in the last few hours. I hardly slept."

"How often are they coming?"

"Oh, about every fifteen minutes now."

I'm alarmed. This could go fast and I want to be prepared, so I urge Rose, "We better get to the hospital."

"No," she soothes me. *Why is she soothing me? I should soothe her.* "Make yourself some breakfast. It's going to be a long day."

"Do you want anything?" I ask before realizing that's an inane question.

"Oh no. I have no appetite. Besides, it's not a good idea to eat in case they have to take me in for a Cesarean."

"I don't think you'll need that."

"I don't either, but just in case. It's best if I don't eat. Besides, the idea of eating nauseates me."

I cook scrambled eggs and toast, fortifying myself for a long day, and possibly night, ahead. This will probably be a marathon, not a sprint.

Just before noon, Rose's contractions intensify so much I insist we go to the hospital. She tries talking me out of it, but I'm getting nervous. I want medical supervision, especially given Rose's condition of Factor V Leiden and her risk of clotting and other untold complications I don't want to think about. I think about Dad's pulmonary embolism and shudder. *Surely nothing like that will happen to my dear Rose.*

When we get to the hospital, I jump out to get a wheelchair and Rose resists.

"I can walk. I don't need a wheelchair," Rose states with authority.

"Rose, please. Don't be stubborn. Just this once, get in the wheelchair. Your walking is unstable."

"Okay," she relents.

We get into the elevator and the moment I roll her through the doors and onto the labor and delivery unit, the charge nurse asks, "Has your water broken yet?"

A momentary pause, and we both hear a splash on the floor. Rose is gushing amniotic fluid as if caused by the power of psychological suggestion. I know what this means. This is it. We're in the throes of labor and Rose is getting admitted to the unit.

They take us to room two, which I notice because it's one

of our favorite numbers. A nurse starts an IV and places a fetal monitor belt on Rose's belly.

This is Rose's first delivery, so we may be in for a long ride. At first, the contractions are fifteen minutes apart and bearable. Rose jokes, "If this is as bad as it gets, we'll be okay." We both know it's going to get worse, but no need thinking about that now.

"Jahi, do you know my life started inside my granny?"

"No, sweetheart. Are you sure you're not having a fever dream?" I joke.

"I'm serious, Jahi. Female fetuses develop all the eggs they'll ever have when they're inside their mom. So when Granny was pregnant with Mom, my mother's ovaries had all their eggs and one of them carried me, the potential me."

"Honestly, I didn't know that. So, right now… if you're carrying a daughter, you're also carrying your grandchild, well, half, anyway. You're carrying the future, our future."

"Yes… ahh… it's coming. I feel it coming." Rose groans in pain.

"Breathe…" I instruct her.

A nurse arrives and asks Rose to change out of her white cotton gown, the one she bought specifically for birth.

"It's time to change into a hospital gown," the young nurse instructs Rose.

"No, this is the gown I'm wearing for the birth," Rose insists.

"That will not work. We need you in the hospital gown that opens at the back for easy access when the anesthesiologist gives you an epidural."

"I'm not having an epidural," Rose states.

The nurse suppresses a laugh. She's seen it all. I imagine she's thinking, *That's what they all say. We'll see how that goes when it gets bad.* Instead, she says, "Well, it's hospital protocol. We need you to change your gown."

Rose gives up the argument and complies, though after the nurse leaves, she looks at me and asserts, "I'm not having an epidural, Jahi. I'm not taking any pain meds. I'm doing this naturally."

"I know, love. Don't worry about it. Let's just humor them."

Hours pass. It breaks my heart to watch Rose as she suffers the cataclysmic pain of contractions. It looks torturous. But she insists on no pain medication, no epidural. At some point, things change swiftly, and I'm told to hold Rose's back as she pushes and rests, pushes and rests. Now we're no longer in labor, we're in delivery. There's a rhythm to it and it's intense, but we're getting there, minute by minute, just like life.

CHAPTER THIRTEEN

ROSE

July 7

It's all happening so fast. Jahi says it has been twenty-four hours since the moment the bloody mucous plug appeared in the toilet, but to me, it seems like it's only been one or two hours. I've read that being in labor and delivering a baby is surreal and can be like an out-of-body experience, so I guess this is what they're talking about.

My dream birth plan is a natural birth with no interventions. Having been married to a surgeon once, I remember him saying, "Interventions lead to interventions."

So for me, because I don't want to end up in the surgical suite having to undergo the ultimate intervention, a Cesarean section, I decide to forgo getting an epidural or even receiving pain medications, all of which can slow the delivery and even cause it to stall out. At least that's my understanding, and Dr. Mason confirms this.

I would love to give birth in a squatting position like they do in traditional cultures, but Dr. Mason warns me it's hard for western women to hold that position. The muscle strength is just not there, especially in the late stages of pregnancy. I request she wait before cutting the cord and she agrees and says if it's safe to wait, she will. There's no rush.

Lying on my side like a beached whale while in labor makes me understand why Dr. Mason is right about the squatting issue.

There's no way I can do anything other than lie here, barely able to move. The insistence and building intensity of contractions comes over me like a freight train... it has a life of its own and I just have to get out of the way.

"Your legs are contracting, Rose." Dr. Mason massages my legs. "Let them go. Ride the wave."

Birth has a life of its own. Get out of the way. You aren't driving this train. I breathe into the contractions and try to let my legs go. "Ohm..." I chant. *You just gotta ride those waves. Ride that train in time.* I sing in my head. I've read that it's possible to experience pain without suffering. Suffering is a kind of psychological overlay to pain, and there's no need to suffer. The chanting reminds me to accept the pain, embrace it, and know that I don't have to suffer, and that it will not last forever.

Giving birth is a lot like dying. I don't know how I know this, but I do. I'm sure of it.

The intervals between contractions get shorter and shorter until it practically disappears and I'm feeling out of my mind with near-panic. I barely have a moment to recover before the next wracking spasms arrive. They're layering on top of each other like cascading waves. Suddenly, my body is pushing, but I'm not telling it to.

"Dr. Mason, my body is pushing... it's doing it... I'm not trying to push..." I gasp.

"Let me check. Yeah, there's just a little lip. You're at nine and a half, almost ten centimeters dilation. You're almost there."

This is the dreaded state called transition, when even a woman who has held it together through treacherous contractions without pain medication may finally lose it. It's this moment when everything falls apart, the center does not hold and you may become hysterical with despair. It feels like you're on the border of insanity. You're going out of your mind and can't take one more moment of pain. You can barely catch your breath before the next wave slams into you. It's the transition from labor to delivery.

I swear they move me from the bed on the left side of the room to the bed on the right side of the room. *This must be what my friend, a social worker, told me about. When she was in labor and in transition, she left her body and sat on top of the clock looking down on herself.*

Later, I'll find out it never happened. There was only one bed in that room. This is the strange state of transition, that point when the cervix flattens out, effaces, and dilates to ten centimeters in diameter. The time of transition from the contractions of labor to the pushing of delivery. It's like you're out of your body and in another time dimension.

And to this day, I insist that's what happened. I was in another reality, like a dream, and the din and the roar of it and everything coming to a crescendo, and the celebration, it's all happening right now, in real time, but it's also like slow motion. It's both.

I thought delivery would be the worst, the pushing and the ripping and tearing of delivery, but labor took me to the edge of what is tolerable and what is not and almost broke me. It's harder for me to let go, to get out of the way, which is what labor requires than it is to do something, to be active, to push the baby out. It's a holy trinity—you're here, there, and elsewhere and the "there" is the baby. The "elsewhere" is the out-of-body experience.

"We're almost there. Getting closer... push." Dr. Mason's confident voice assures me my baby is in safe hands.

One last push.

Jahi's eyes light up, a fire I've never seen before—as they travel down my body and over my swollen belly to the miracle emerging from my body and entering our lives.

A soft little cry like a puppy... our baby.

EPILOGUE

ROSE

A year later

Crystalline morning sunlight floods the rose garden as its wide-ranging palette bursts forth in colors, some showy, others subtle—lilac, pink, light yellow, peach, white, salmon, and burgundy.

A woodchip horseshoe shaped path edged by clumps of sweet alyssum circumscribes the lawn. Rose bushes, generously spaced to allow room for admiration and pruning, adorn the path.

I've set out great granny Hattie Osborn's hand pieced quilt for a mid-morning picnic with Daisy and Lily. The aroma of *Botticelli Beauty* saturates the air as I unpack the basket filled with goodies.

"Momma. You… you rose," Daisy points up at *Botticelli Beauty*. "Bah booty," she says, proud of herself.

"Yes, that's the rose Daddy named after me. *Botticelli Beauty*," I gush as Lily claps and Daisy mimics her big sister clapping with her pudgy, dimpled hands.

We eat cheese sandwiches, apple slices, and bits of avocado. I take selfies of our little trio and more photos of the girls as Lily holds Daisy in her lap. After a bit, Daisy squirms out of Lily's arms and stands as she holds onto her sister's shoulder with her left hand. Daisy's hand releases. *I hold my breath as she takes a step. And then another. Everything moves in slow motion.*

Lily's eyes widen. "Daddy, come here quick!"

I join Lily, beseeching, "Jahi, come. Come now."

I grab my phone and film Daisy as she takes three tentative steps.

Jahi appears at the back door. "Oh my goodness, look at our Daisy. Oh Simonetta Daisy, you're walking," Jahi coaxes in his velvety voice, using her first and middle names in that endearing Southern tradition I've come to know and love.

Daisy looks up with her big emerald eyes, her translucent skin framed by strawberry blonde angel hair, smiles at Jahi, and then plops onto the grass in her baby-sized overalls. Jahi scoops her into his arms and tickles her gently. She giggles and Lily and I join in a group hug.

Thinking back on that seminal day when Daisy took her first steps makes me realize every day is a miracle. Who knew my life would turn out this way? I feel complete with Daisy and Lily and Jahi. That bleak day when Lee abandoned me, I never imagined my life becoming something magical. I thought my life was over, and I felt like giving up. Boy, was I wrong. Who knew I'd find the love of my life in Eureka Springs?

Here I am with Jahi on our first wedding anniversary, and we're the little family I always dreamed of. As I look into Jahi's dark chocolate eyes, I remember the moment I first saw him that auspicious day when I marched up his front steps to lecture him on Lily's unkempt hair and unfinished homework. He attracted me with his tall, dark, rugged looks and his stubble, yes, but something far deeper captured me. I loved his sensitivity, quiet dignity, and big heart. I sensed a vulnerability, a bittersweet sadness about him in the early days and of course it turns out we had a kind of twinship around loss, losing our fathers. And we're both helpers and healers, he as a paramedic and firefighter and me as a psychologist.

It takes my breath away to think of how I almost gave up on us, on our baby, on the dream of creating our own little family. It's like the time I drove to the clinic at UCLA and came to a red light at the corner of Westwood and Wilshire Boulevards. An enormous SUV waited in the left turn lane next to me, blocking my view. When the light turned green, I almost drove straight ahead, but some invisible force stopped me. To this day, it feels like a miracle that I didn't go forward. I couldn't see to the left because of the SUV. During that pause, a black Dodge sedan screamed through the intersection at ninety miles an hour. I would have been T-boned and sent to the UCLA emergency room a few blocks away, likely dead on arrival, if I'd simply pressed the gas pedal.

This decision separated life and death. And I was aware of what almost happened. How many decisions of importance happen without our knowledge? Life turns on our decisions. The decision to move to Eureka Springs. The decision to stay still at the intersection. The decision to keep Daisy. The decision to say yes to marrying Jahi.

We've been through so much, Jahi and me, from deaths to births, from illnesses, accidents, abandonments, betrayals, and everything in between, and somehow we found our way to each other.

I'll never forget the little family I watched taking their baby home from my hospital room and how that pivotal moment changed everything. Something changed in *me.* I faced my fears of dying and went ahead, anyway. *Isn't this something I counsel my patients to do?*

I'm fascinated by moments when humans are in a state of flow, like when an Olympic athlete is on a winning streak, accumulating gold medals, and it's almost like it's effortless, a kind of trance state. The athlete can do no wrong. It's like giving birth. There's pain and struggle but also timeless moments, when the clock stands still, and you exist outside of time, like the transition from labor to delivery or the experience of pushing the baby out. It's peak moments like this I'll never forget.

What happens to the athlete after the gold medal is placed around her neck and the anthem stops playing? She cries and looks shocked and I've always wondered what happens when she steps off the podium and returns to her life the next day? She's climbed Mt. Parnassus and now it's over. A denouement. Reality hits. It's a high and then it's done… and she wants it to last forever, or at least longer, but it doesn't. It can't.

Now what? That's the unknown. Giving birth to Simonetta Daisy Adams was the highest high, the most euphoric moment of my life, at least so far. Though I was thirty-eight, I looked like a twenty-five-year-old in the photos Jahi took. Dr. Mason said I looked radiant and that I must have a strong endorphin system. I think so, that's what gave me the high.

And yet as I lay in agony like a beached whale battered by waves taking me nowhere, as I floundered on that bed, I realized the exquisite proximity of birth and death. They're like opposite ends of a loop that come together like the *ouroboros*, the snake eating its tail. Opposites have similarities. Giving birth is like dying. You must let go and then get out of the way because it has a life and force field of its own and will not bend to your will. It's a small part of the Universe endlessly re-inventing itself.

After Daisy's birth, a cloud descended. A mood came over me in a sudden awareness of death and danger. The understanding that I couldn't live if something happened to my little Daisy. It's this massive, overwhelming vulnerability I've never felt before because I was always my mother's child. A momma's girl. Now, I'm a mother.

The realization that this precious baby is in my safekeeping and the world is cruel overtakes the euphoric high of the endorphins. *How will I protect her?* Everything changes. The shift from the euphoria of invincibility that gets a person through the Olympics or childbirth or grad school or a wedding, to the return to regular life which includes loss, pain, boredom, and disappointment, is shocking. The world can be harsh and a mother must protect her baby with everything she's got.

My mother rode home with us from the hospital. After oohing and ahhing over Daisy, she said quietly, "Rose, when I die, I want to be buried at Tomahawk, at the cemetery there on the farm where I grew up."

I was quiet for a moment and then said, "Mom, I can't talk about death. Not now." Mom has always been intuitive, like her grandmother Hattie. Did she sense my mind ruminating about death and vulnerability and how close birth and death are in their very nature?

"Oh, okay. I'm sorry. I shouldn't have mentioned it." Mom switched the subject and gushed over the perfection of her one and only grandchild.

As mothers say, my heart now lives outside my body. It's always out there and ever will be until my last breath. There is no love like this. It's this insane love, and it's everything, and that's the way it's supposed to be.

Papa said: "Our children are our greatest joys and our deepest sorrows."

And so I say yes to this life with its joys and sorrows. I say yes to finding my true love Jahi, of mothering our precious Lily, and of having our miracle baby Daisy.

Gracie Gable grew up in Arkansas, and though she now lives in Santa Cruz, California, she'll always be a Southerner at heart. An author, artist, and psychiatrist, Gracie's writing reflects themes of love, loss, abandonment, and redemption that permeated her decades in the consulting room. *Where The Old Roses Grow* was inspired by the beloved garden of a neurosurgeon and Botticelli's masterpiece *The Birth of Venus*. Away from her writing desk, Gracie enjoys creating abstract art, playing the cello, swimming with her husband, and listening to her daughter's beautiful operatic voice and her stories of adventure.

graciegable.com

@graciegableauthor

@graciegableauthor

AuthorGracieGable

Printed in the USA
CPSIA information can be obtained
at www.ICGtesting.com
JSHW022346060324
58588JS00001B/1